WILD WEST
EXODUS

BASTION

Craig Gallant

Zmok

Zmok Books

To my wife, Karen, without whom none of this would have been possible.

Zmok Books is an imprint of Winged Hussar Publishing, LLC
1525 Hulse Road Unit 1
Point Pleasant, NJ 08742

www.WingedHussarPublishing.com
Twitter: WingHusPubLLC

www.Wildwestexodus.com

Cover by Michael Nigro

ISBN: 978-0-98896926-4-9
LCN: 2014941678

Dedication

Bastion is dedicated to all the good men who I have been blessed to meet throughout my life. The men who made the hard choices and the sacrifices, and took the tougher paths, so that they could meet their obligations and commitments to their countries, their families, and their beliefs. I am blessed to count the LOJOG among them, especially John, who is always looking for a hero. But at the top of the list of truly good men who have influenced me throughout my life will always be my grandfather Leo, who I called Bumpa as a result of a lack of eloquence in my early years, and of course, my father, Gerry, without whom none of this could have happened.

Thanks

As always, I need to thank Vincent, Brandon, and the team at Winged Hussar/Zmok Publishing for what polishing was possible on my original work. Thanks also to Romeo and the good men and women at Outlaw Miniatures for this opportunity and their continued trust, and to the readers who give the books a try, and my listeners over at The D6 Generation, for their continued support. I also need to thank my family, especially my wife Karen, and finally my son Rhys, who bears with fortitude the daily announcement that daddy has to work downstairs for yet another day. Without them, truly, I would not be able to do any of what I do.

Something Wicked is Coming

Blood drenches the sands of the Wild West as the promise of a new age dies, screaming its last breathe into an uncaring night. An ancient evil has arisen in the western territories, calling countless people with a siren song of technology and promises of power and glory the likes of which the world has never known. Forces move into the deserts, some answering the call, others desperate to destroy the evil before it can end all life on Earth.

Legions of reanimated dead rise to serve the greatest scientific minds of the age, while the native tribes of the plains, now united in desperate self-defense, conjure the powers of the Great Spirit to twist their very flesh into ferocious combat forms to match the terrible new technologies. The armies of the victorious Union rumble into these territories heedless of the destruction they may cause in pursuit of their own purposes, while the legendary outlaws of the old west, now armed with stolen weapons and equipment of their own, seek to carve their names into the tortured flesh of the age.Amidst all this conflict, the long-suffering Lawmen, outgunned and undermanned, stand alone, fighting to protect the innocent men and women caught in the middle . . . or so it appears.

Within these pages you will find information on wild skirmishes and desperate battles in this alternative Wild West world, now ravaged with futuristic weapons and technology. Choose the methodical Enlightened, the savage Warrior Nation, the brutal Union, the deceitful Outlaws, or the enigmatic Lawmen, and lead them into the Wild West to earn your glory.

As you struggle across the deserts and mountains, through the forests and cities of the wildest frontier in history, a hidden power will whisper in your ear at every move. Will your spirit be strong enough to prevail, or will the insidious forces of the Dark Council eventually bend you to their will? Be prepared, for truly, something wicked is coming!

Learn more about the world of the Jesse James Chronicles at:

www.wildwestexodus.com

Prologue

The sun peeked over the rim of the amphitheater, caressing the capitals of the high columns with a rosy glow. Shadows clung within the recesses of the ornate carvings as light filled the shallow bowl, warming row after row of carven seats. The smooth, polished marble, the sweeping lines and looming scale, recalled images of the afterlife held dear by countless cultures through the ages. The hands that had shaped this place had clearly followed a tradition whose influence echoed down from the earliest dawn of man.

As the sun reached the polished surface of the raised orchestra, its light fell upon a lone figure in fine white robes. The old man sat calmly upon an armless chair in the center of the clear, open space. His broad face was creased with care and time, but his eyes still held the echoed strength of a crusader. A fringe of fine white hair swept back from ear to ear, cropped short in the manner of warriors of a lost age. Thin, wire-strong fingers grasped the fabric of a ceremonial cap forgotten in his lap.

The man's wizened face tilted up to welcome the rising sun, eyes closed as the light soaked into his tired flesh. His body was relaxed, muscles loose despite the knowledge of what approached. He had fought this battle with his peers countless times before. Until he was called to his final reward, he would always be ready to protect his brothers and his sisters from the folly of their own zeal.

Footsteps announced the approach of another member of the Order. At this place, in this time, it could only be another member of the *Etta*, the ruling council of the Holy Order of Man. No one else would have been allowed past the elder's devoted guards.

Some vague quality to the footsteps provided him with everything he needed to perform one of his favorite tricks. Without opening his eyes, *Sircan* Ignatius, oldest and wisest member of the Holy Order in the Sunset Lands, spoke with a smile that hovered on the edge of a grin.

"Good morning, Nura."

The female *sircan's* shadow passed over him as she settled into a chair to his left without a sound. Her robes murmured softly as she adjusted her position, but she chose not to respond to his childish sally.

His grin widening even more, Ignatius opened his eyes. His head gracefully lowered until he was looking directly at her. She was a strong woman, her face alive with character and a lifetime's experience. There was not a trace of grey within the cascade of her ash-brown hair, and like most of the higher-ranking members of the Order, it was difficult to tell her age with any degree of confidence. She was the youngest of the *sircans*, but she could have been thirty or sixty, or anywhere in between.

Ignatius's grin slipped slightly as he registered the concern plain on his colleague's face. She shook her head, her sweeping hair swaying with the motion and her hands folded elegantly in her lap. "Today is no day for your tricks, Ignatius. They are right behind me, and I promise you, they are in no mood for laughter."

He sighed and nodded. "I know. But you can't fault an old man for trying, my dear." He looked back toward the grand double doors through which Nura had emerged. Nothing moved within the cool shadows of the hall beyond. "Will it be all of them again this year? Or just Abner and yourself?"

Her graceful head inclined a fraction. "Abner was just behind me. I asked the *arcsens* to give us a moment to confer before they joined us. I do not wish to see you embarrassed. I know you don't feel the dignity of your office, but I would rather we not quarrel in front of the junior members."

The grin slid down into a fledgling frown. The *Etta* of the Sunset Lands, as the New World had been referred to by the Order for millennia, followed the structures laid down thousands upon thousands of years ago during the founding of the Holy City, Atlantis itself. Three *sircans*, the highest ranking members, were served and advised by at least three *arcens*, or junior commanders. Although all members within a rank were considered to be equals, a certain reverence and authority was always reserved for the longest-serving. Ignatius had held that position for nearly two decades, and considered himself an excellent judge of his compatriots' tempers. If he had misread the signs, the day was going to be worse than he had anticipated.

"Embarrassed?" Ignatius shrugged, projecting a cool lack of concern. "You feel the inclinations of the *Etta* have shifted so drastically?"

"They have shifted, *Sircan* Ignatius, but you refuse to sense it." The amphitheater echoed with the new voice, and the tall figure of *Sircan* Abner, war leader of the Order, strode through the big, elaborate doors. "No scholar of the prophecies now doubts that the End Times are approaching. You stand alone, wrapped in your naiveté and nostalgia."

Ignatius's grin returned full force as he stood to welcome the last *sircan* with open arms. He forced himself to continue the gesture despite his shock at seeing Abner in full war plate. Members of the Order had not worn full plate within the sacred portions of the Acropolis in nearly a hundred years. He forced a hearty confidence into his tone that he no longer felt and slapped the younger man soundly on the back as Abner deigned to grace him with a perfunctory embrace.

"Abner! Surely there is at least one scholar of the prophecies that disagrees?" He tapped his own chest, his smile warm. "That he is the oldest such scholar should provide some further weight to his arguments, wouldn't you agree?"

Abner sat heavily into the remaining chair, nodding to Nura as he smoothed his chestnut beard with a strong hand. "Age is a source of respect and honor only to the brink of dementia, Ignatius. Beyond that point, it weighs *against* the scholar, not *for* him."

The old man's eyes twinkled as his smile broadened. "So, I'm a dithering old man, then, am I?" He curled one hand into the other and shook as if taken with a palsy. "Perhaps I should just find a comfortable old afghan and curl up with some porridge."

"Abner is not saying—" Nura leaned forward, her composure weakening.

"I understand the rules of the game, Nura, never fear." Ignatius turned to pat the woman on her knee, and then stood spinning in his bright robes to confront them both.

"Shall we begin, before the others arrive and we must tell them what they think?" His smile gleamed in the sun, and both Nura and Abner were forced to squint as they followed his movements, their own expressions far from pleased.

"Ignatius, you must face facts. The other citadels are in agreement. The Dark Council is on the move again, and their gaze will fall upon the Sunset Lands, without doubt." Abner, tired of peering up through the glaring sun, stood with a grunt of exasperation. "Your theatrics and drama aside, the Order must be prepared when they strike."

"There has been a wave of Tainted among the men and women sweeping into the western territories." Nura added her voice to Abner's, rising and joining him as they faced Ignatius. We have had mission teams in the field constantly since before their Civil War began, and the violence has only gotten worse."

"We have seen neither figure of the prophecy manifest yet, however, I believe?" The old man pivoted on his heel and took the small flight of steps down from the level of the orchestra to the front row of benches with a light tread. Speaking over his shoulder, he continued. "No mission teams have reported organized Council activity in over half a century."

"And if we wait until we smell the gangrene, it will be too late." Abner stalked down after the older man as Ignatius moved up the stepped aisle with a swaying gait striding toward the high rim overhead. "Where are you going?"

"I wish to show you something; both of you. But we can talk while we walk." He looked over his shoulder with a gentle smile. "Unless you young ones lack the breath?"

"Ignatius, we must prepare the people for what approaches. We can't do that hiding beneath the mountain." Nura followed after, leaping down off the platform after them. "Denying the inevitable will help no one."

The old man moved briskly up the slope, his voice betraying not the slightest hint of strain. "I don't care for your classification of any of this as inevitable. And I will admit to some alarm after all, my friends. There is a great deal of our history your current position chooses to ignore."

Nura, as the chief scholar of the *Etta*, took special affront at this. Her frustration quickened her pace. "I disagree. Those of us advocating direct action do so based on the past success, and failure, of the Order."

"Applied with full knowledge of the world beyond our walls, Ignatius." Abner tried to keep his tone reasonable, but the brisk stroll through the warm morning air was taking its toll on his patience. "Something we are convinced you are no longer taking into account."

"On the contrary, my son." Ignatius stopped as he came to the top gallery of seats. He rested one elbow against the smooth stone of the amphitheater's outer wall. "I am taking everything into account."

The other two *sircans* stopped one level below the old man, both with their arms folded before them. They shared an exasperated look. Abner began to speak, but was brought up short as Ignatius waved one hand brusquely for him to be quiet. The old man gestured out over the wall, turning around to look out over the vast plains below.

Exchanging another, more measured glance, Nura and Abner joined the older *sircan* at the balustrade. Below them stretched a view of infinite splendor and beauty. Regal mountains stretched away to either side, marching up into the highlands behind. Before them, rolling foothills undulated down into the distant steppes, where much smaller mountains stood like guards against the golden land of the western territories beyond.

The rising sun hung over the entire scene, filling the floating white clouds with vivid colors that brought the sky to life.

Abner and Nura stood silent. It was too easy, with the dire nature of their work, for a member of the *Etta* to forget the natural beauty that lay all around their mountain fastness. This view was something each of them had seen a thousand times, but for the two younger *sircans*, it had been many years. Ignatius looked at them both with a gentle smile, the sun's young rays dancing in his eyes. "I like to think that such views can often bring a certain sense of perspective."

Abner shook off the effect of the view and rounded on his old colleague. "Ignatius, the beauty of the mountains is immaterial. We are discussing the prophecy, and—"

"No, Abner." The touch of sadness in the old man's voice was maddening, but at the same time it stopped the warrior cold. "The beauty of the mountains is everything."

Ignatius leaned back against the cool stone. He looked first at Nura, who remained speechless, and then at Abner, and then out again over the distant plains. "We were placed here to guard this, all of it, from the depredations of the Enemy. That, my friends, is the beginning and the end of our charge: nothing short of the defense of an entire planet from a terrible force that seeks to destroy it entirely, and pluck it, root and branch, from the soil of creation's history."

There was something in his tone that touched the younger *sircans*. "I tell you nothing you do not know. We have dedicated our lives to this pursuit. Countless men and women across the globe breathe their every breath in service to the same goal. Millions have answered the call down the millennia, sacrificing their hopes, their dreams, and their very lives to protect mankind from the forces of darkness."

He turned back to them, his eyes intense. There was no trace of a smile on his lined face. "And yet, how much do we even know about that darkness?"

"There are millions of –"

Ignatius silenced Abner with a single, raised finger. "Of course, we have filled libraries with our observations of the Eternal Enemy, brother. But what do we *know*?" He turned to look back out over the plains. "Our knowledge of our own past is so fragmented and disjointed. We must never lose sight of the fact that we are looking down through countless millennia, through a window frosted with the very breath of our Enemy."

Nura and Abner stood still now, staring at Ignatius's slumped shoulders. The old *sircan* seldom allowed his mind to wander down such dark paths. The bleak reality was terrifying in ways that the current, popular fixation on prophecy within the Order could never be.

"How much did we lose when they burned the Great Library at Alexandria, or in the final sack of Rome?" The old man's voice grew rough. "What truths were lost as our brothers were hunted throughout the Dark Ages, hounded up into the very stone towers of their last redoubts, only to be burned alive with their illuminated manuscripts?"

His eyes were on fire now, and neither Nura nor Abner, despite their own personal strength, could look away. "Everything we know about the world, and our place in it, has been handed down to us by refugees and survivors of one historical failure after another. And even that tale drips with woe and death, hinting at even worse tragedies lost in time." One firm arm rose to point toward a gleaming, red-tinged star that pierced the daytime sky near the horizon. "An entire world was lost to grant us our one advantage in this struggle. We know that. We know that an entire planet's civilization, working in unison to defeat this foe, was unequal to the task."

A gleam of exasperation flickered within Nura's eye. "Oh please, Ignatius. Not more of your nihilistic fatalism. If you truly believe we don't have a prayer, why even try?"

Her words snapped Abner from beneath Ignatius' spell, and he nodded. "Yes, brother. If you wish to lay down your burden, then please, be our guest."

"And see the prophecy raised to gospel truth, and the Order shattered and lost for all time?" The smile had returned, but it shared an edge with the new darkness in the old man's eyes. "Thank you, but no." He turned to Nura. "And what have you learned of our past that leads you to believe we *can* win this eternal struggle?"

"Faith." Her answer was immediate and sharp. She nearly lost her nerve, however, when the old man's face furrowed in sorrow, and he reached out to squeeze her shoulder.

"Bless you, Nura." Ignatius shook his head. "That is the only lesson that makes any sense."

"But the prophecy—" Abner began. He trailed off as the older *sircan* turned to look at him.

"The prophecy is an interesting tool, brother. It is a curiosity upon which we may sharpen our minds and seek a deeper knowledge of the universe around us. But if we can only know so little about the road behind us after thousands of years of toil and suffering, then do you honestly think the Creators would speak so plainly of the path that lies before us?"

Abner shook his head, and finished, "There is nothing clear about the prophecy, Ignatius. It is a warning, a bell tolling in the twilight to warn us of the coming of night."

Ignatius bowed his head for a moment, and then shocked his companions as he reached out and grabbed each of them with one strong hand. "The two of you have been coming to me, at dawn of every All Hallow's Eve, for over a decade with that warning. What is it you would have us do? I am no patriarch, to lead our people without fiat or sanction. We are the three equal pillars of the Order on an entire continent. You may both, or either, work without my leave."

"Too many see you as the spiritual leader of the Order here in the Sunset Lands, Ignatius." The old man smiled sadly as Nura again used the land's ancient name.

"Nonsense." The elder dismissed the argument with a shake of his head. "The entire Order, on this and every other continent, is structured specifically so that no single man or woman can command. The *sircans* watch over the *arcsens*, we of the *Etta* watch over the *spica*, the *mimregs*, and the *altcaps* beneath us. We are, each of us, an essential beam in the construction of our house of faith."

"And yet our preparations would prove much smoother if you would only acknowledge that the prophecy may be real, and that our time of testing may well be upon us." Abner leaned close, sensing a shifting in the argument.

But again Ignatius shook his head. "Abner, what would you have us do? We have mission teams all over the continent. We are seeking allies and initiates from one ocean to another, and from the frozen wastes of the north to the wretched deserts below. We have even requested, and received, support from the other citadels. No other citadel can claim two fragments of the Relic; none but the Acropolis of the Sunset Lands. We train, we build, and we prepare for the coming onslaught, as has been our duty and obligation since before the fall of the First City."

At the mention of Atlantis, the ancient center of human civilization on Earth, the younger *sircans* bowed their heads for a moment. But Ignatius did not lose the thread of his story.

"We do everything in our power to prepare for the next foul resurgence of the Dark Council, according to Holy

Writ as we understand it, and as it has been passed down through the countless generations who have come before us." He squeezed their hands more firmly. "Please, my brother and my sister, have faith in the old ways, in the tried and true ways. Give our people moving in the shadows time to build the structures we will need to survive our emergence into the light, before you would throw us upon the mercy of a society that has already been torn by war and exhausted by bloodshed."

Abner stared for a moment, and when his head began to shake slightly back and forth, it was almost as if it were moving of its own volition. The sadness this caused in the old man's eyes almost stopped him from speaking, but he felt, just as strongly as Ignatius did, that his path was the only one that promised even a chance of survival for the human race.

"We will not put the issue before the *Etta* today." Nura's voice was sharp, cutting into the silence before Abner could speak his mind. "The factions demanding action will not be silenced for much longer, Ignatius, but I think we can give you one more year."

She looked at Abner, her eyes burning with a silent plea. He stared at her, his lip curled in frustration. Then he looked away. "One year. But you should know, Ignatius, our numbers are growing." He burnished one silvered vambrace. "We will wear our armor, even in the most holy sanctums, as a sign of our dedication and acknowledgement of the dire plight we know ourselves to be in."

The old man nodded, and then looked to Nura's lack of armor with a raised eyebrow. She shrugged. "It's being repaired from my last mission. I'm sure it will be ready shortly." Ignatius sighed, nodded with waning energy, and then turned to move back down the sloped array of benches toward the stage and the grand doors beyond. "I will take your offered year," he tossed over his shoulder as he moved away through the bowl, now emptied of shadows. "And you may wear whatever you wish. I only ask you to remember that there are more who serve the Holy Order of Man than those of us who show our fealty through our fashion choices."

The two younger *sircans* watched him disappear into the darkness of their mountain stronghold, separated from each other by the silence that descended.

Chapter 1

The broad, hard-looking man held a cup of wine in both hands, staring into its ruby depths. A faint smile tugged at the corner of his mouth as the reflected gleam of the oil lamps rippled and flowed within the liquid. His eyes rose, scanning the small, noontime crowd scattered across the common room and at the bar against one wall. He shook his head, looking back down into his cup. Many of his brothers within the Order felt uncomfortable among the uninitiated, but it was moments like this that reminded him of what he had left behind, and what he had dedicated his life to defend.

The door to the taproom banged open and a figure tumbled in, pushed by a gust of cold wind. A bundled wool cloak muffled the man's face, while a heavy felt bowler shadowed darting, nervous eyes. The man with the wine noted the green-covered book gripped in one gloved hand as the newcomer turned to heave the door closed. He nodded his head gentlywhen he saw the man's roving eyes settle on the isolated corner table. Another tilt of his head indicated the empty chair opposite him.

The nervous man unwrapped himself from his cloak as he wove through the empty tables, raising a single thumb to the barman. The cloak was thrown over an empty chair and he sank down across from the seated man, his shoulders hunched and his eyes moving about like tiny bait fish caught within a closing net. The man with the wine leaned back, his chair giving off a gentle creak, and took a sip from his glass. It always paid to let a mark settle down a moment before taking up the business at hand. With a nod, he gave the man what a lifetime's experience had taught him was a most-convincing, comforting smile.

The man's mouth twitched in automatic response, but his eyes did not settle and his shoulders did not relax. The barman came by, deposited a heavy lead mug with a solid thud, and swept the man's coins up before moving back toward his station. The nervous man downed half the drink in a single swallow. He was gasping for breath as he put down the mug.

"You're Uri." It sounded like an accusation, but the waiting man maintained his smile and merely nodded in response. The nervous man looked around again, and then leaned closer. "They said you'd have money."

The broad man, Uri, nodded again, taking a small leather bag from within his cloak and placing it on the table. "I have the coin you were promised, Mr. . . ." He paused for a moment, waiting for the man to provide his name. When none was forthcoming, Uri shrugged and settled back. "There must be some small modicum of trust here or we may as well finish our drinks and go our separate ways, Mr. Rathbone." He ignored the man's shocked look and gestured toward the book. "What do you have for me?"

Rathbone looked around again, clutching the small book with fat, white-knuckled hands. The man looked like a rodent, with hair lashing out from beneath the bowler and dripping down the sides of his face in bedraggled muttonchops setting off a sharp nose and small, stained teeth. "I want to see the money."

Uri sighed. It was always difficult dealing with this sort of man. It came with the territory, he knew. Upright, honorable citizens were seldom moved to provide clandestine information to unknown parties for money. Still, as much as he loved moving freely among the people when his duties allowed, he often wished he could move among a better *class* of people.

The pouch was dumped onto the dark wood of the table, gold and silver coins tinkling dully as they slid into the light. "Fifty dollars, just as you were promised." Uri motioned again toward the book. "Now, could I please see what it is my money is buying, Mr. Rathbone?"

The other man jerked slightly, looked around again, and then slid the book across the table. "It's a draft. It might change again before he delivers it, but he'll stick to the gist."

Uri opened the book and a small slip of paper fell out. It was written in a strong hand, each of the letters tilting gracefully to the right. He felt a slight tick of surprise at the length; something this momentous should surely be longer. A quick scan revealed that the words written on this paper would take less than five minutes to read.

Uri looked up again, leaning forward. "Still to be delivered where you thought?"

Rathbone nodded. "They're heading out to the battlefield tomorrow. The ceremony is set for Thursday."

Uri eased back in his chair and took the paper up in one gentle hand. "This is going to ruffle a lot of feathers." His eyes rose to pin the fidgeting man in place. "There can't be unanimous support for this in the White House."

Rathbone shrugged. "There isn't, but there's rarely been unanimous support up there for anything he does. He's his own man. That," the man gestured toward the slip of paper. "That is going to change the whole war. There's many that think he's taking too much upon himself, throwing away our best chance at peace." A bitter undertone slipped into the man's voice. "He's basically putting the whole Republic on the table, and making this as much about the blacks as it is about the damned Secesh breakers."

Uri nodded, looking back down at the paper. "So, he's committed." His eyes rose again and he tapped the paper. "To both preserving the Union and for standing by the Africans?"
Rathbone nodded darkly. "He is. There won't be much room to stand between the two sides, once he's said his words there." He looked suspiciously at Uri, eyes flicking from the big man's face, to the spilled coins, and back. "This will all be public knowledge in a matter of days. In less than a week, the whole world will know what he says on that field. I'm going to take your money, sir, but I'd love to know what makes that slip of paper worth fifty dollars."

Uri smiled, shuffled the coins back into their bag, and slid the bag across the table. "It's all in the timing, Mr. Rathbone. Have no fear. No harm will come to the president or his cause from what you've done here today. As you have been told, we are all working toward the same goals."

Rathbone snatched the bag and clutched it in one greedy hand, weighing it as if, despite the evidence of his own eyes, he doubted that the full amount was inside. "Well, you better be. The General's coming back east, and when he gets here, anyone on the wrong side of the president is going to have a hot time of it!"

Uri's smile wavered slightly. "The General?" The weight of the title was clear in Rathbone's tone, and he was not sure he liked the flavor behind the words.

Rathbone nodded. "Grant's being recalled. There's many think he's to be censured for the violence back west, but that ain't so." The little man leaned over the table, his eyes gleaming while his voice dropped to a conspiratorial whisper. "Might be, for a bit more coin, we've got more to discuss?"

The tall man settled back in his chair and considered his hunched companion. Without a word, one strong hand dipped within the cloak and returned holding a pair of gold coins.

"Will ten dollar suffice to loosen your tongue further?" The disks gleamed, Lady Liberty's enigmatic smile shining up at them.

Rathbone looked down at the money and Uri could see the flare of greed behind his eyes. Then the bowler twitched from side to side, the thin hand snapped out, and the coins disappeared.

"The president's giving Grant the army; the *whole* army.And the mandate to crush the rebellion once and for all. The lines are solidifying down by Petersburg, but these eastern rebs ain't seen what Grant and his group from out west are capable of. The whole thing'll be over in a matter of months now."

Uri's eyes drifted toward the low ceiling as he processed this new information. General Ulysses S. Grant was known to be a cold, analytical commander. He had come into conflict with his own commanders and subordinates on more than one occasion. If the president was recalling him, with the intention of giving him full command of the forces of the Republic, it could well mean a new course for the war. That, coupled with this speech the president intended to deliver, might turn things around more quickly than Uri's superiors had anticipated.

The tall man nodded to himself. The board was taking shape, and time was nipping at their heels. His eyes shifted back to the rat-faced man twitching across from him.

"Thank you for your consideration and your help, Mr. Rathbone. You have been a great boon to me in my work. If you should find yourself in possession of further information you think might interest me, please do not hesitate to leave word here, and one of my associates will contact you."

Rathbone's head jerked down once in a spasmodic nod, his eyes once again snapping from side to side. He moved to rise, but froze when Uri gently placed one hand upon his own.

"I believe it will look moderately suspicious of we leave together, Mr. Rathbone." The tall man's voice was reasonable and calm. "Please, allow me to depart. Have another drink, on me. Make it leisurely. When you are finished, I will be long gone, and none will be the wiser. Yes?"

Rathbone nodded again, eyes fixed on a crumpled note that floated to the table. That one note would pay for considerably more than a single drink.

Uri nodded once more to the nervous little man, his pleasant smile still firmly affixed. He pulled his leather-trimmed hood up over his hair and moved toward the door with a calm, graceful gait. The cloak, a gray-green that blended into shadows equally well in forest or city, was pulled tightly about him as he pushed out into the cold Washington streets.

Behind Uri, the man called Rathbone stared at the closed door, his nervous eyes darting to the darker corners of the common room.

*****

There was little foot traffic on the streets of Washington D.C. A fierce cold had swept in from the plains, settling over the city with a vengeance. Unless one had pressing business, people were staying in, huddled around their fires, and waiting for the weather to regain its senses. The cobbles of the street radiated a numbing chill through the thin soles of Uri's boots.

Casual glances established that he was alone on the street. His footgear, thinner than the weather would seem to warrant, was nevertheless completely silent on the stones. With little effort, he adapted his steps to the weary movements of a man heading home after a long day of work. The streets were narrow, with dark alleys coming up and passing by on either side. Even a trained observer could have missed how well he scrutinized each shadow as he passed; not a single line of his body betraying anything beyond idle curiosity.

His silent footsteps took him out onto a wider street, buildings now interspersed with small fields and stable yards. A man in a cloak of similar cut to Uri's stepped out of a shadow and fell into step beside him. The new man's cloak was different enough in color and design that they avoided the appearance of a uniform, while at the same time providing similar camouflage and protection.

Uri glanced aside at the new man, one eyebrow quirked up in question. The man's gaze did not waver from its casual survey of the street, but he shook his head briefly.

"No one followed." The man's head gave a quick, nearly imperceptible jerk backward. "The rat declined your offer of another drink, but he waited long enough."

Uri shook his head, a slight smile appearing behind puffs of frigid breath. "Arja, you must learn to take a lighter hand with our charges. It's not their fault they live in ignorance."

The younger man snorted, a plume of steam erupting from within his hood. "Their ignorance may not be of their own choosing, but their souls are black enough without needing to take that into account. The man sold out his own ruler. And for what?" One gloved hand snapped out dismissively. "A handful of metal. I cannot wait until we can return to the Acropolis and leave this cesspit behind us."

They walked on in silence for several paces, neither man relaxing in their vigilance. But when Uri spoke again, his words carried a heavy weight. "Arja, it is our task in this life to protect them from themselves. The Creators have placed us between humanity and the darkness. We cannot perform that task if we hold them in nothing but contempt."

Arja shrugged beneath his heavy cloak. "My apologies, *Mimreg*." The ancient title of rank, the Holy Order equivalent of a sergeant, was a gentle reminder of Uri's own responsibilities. "I but live to serve."

Uri snaked one arm out from beneath his mantle to pat the younger man on the shoulder. "We each have our burdens to bear, Arja. If the president is truly the man the *Etta* believe him to be, we may well be returning home soon."

Arja grunted. "The *Etta* is torn, as you well know. All of the signs point to the coming of the End Times, and all they do is twist and twirl in their eternal dance."

Uri stopped in the street and grabbed at the younger man's shoulder. Arja's arms swung outto maintain balance, his cloak swirling as he stepped into a combat stance, glaring at his superior with flashing eyes. The older man did not release Arja's shoulder, his free hand clamping down and dragging him close.

"*Spica*, you will show respect when you speak of our leaders in the *Etta*." The older man used the title of Arja's lower rank, that of a foot soldier with no command authority, as a rebuke. "The *sircans* and *arcsens* have led us for countless millennia. The shadow war has cost the lives of uncountable millions through the ages, and would have claimed every last man, woman, and child on the planet if it were not for the selfless men and women of the *Etta*. Do not allow your personal tedium to mark you as a fool, Arja, lest you allow the Enemy into your heart and render all our work for naught."

Arja's eyes flared for a moment, anger and resentment burning within their depths, but then he looked away, shame dousing the fires of rage. "My apologies, *Mimreg*."

Uri cast one last look into the young man's eyes to assure himself the fires were quenched, and then gently clapped him on the shoulder before releasing him. "It is difficult, I know. These people lack the focus, the commitment, and the discipline of mind we grow accustomed to within the Acropolis. The chaos of their thoughts is their true weakness. It is a disease that can claim any member or our Order who does not maintain constant vigilance." He stepped back and gestured at the streets around them, soft lights beginning to glow from curtained windows. "But it is a great strength, as well. If we can find a way to guide them, if amongst them we can find worthy allies, our position, in the end, will be all the stronger."

Arja's eyes scanned the streets and he shrugged. "From your lips to the Creators' ears, *Mimreg*."

Uri nodded again and gestured for Arja to continue down the street. "We should keep moving. Solas will be worried. You take the high road, I will go down toward the docks. We will check each other's back trails as we approach the house."

Arja nodded in response, taking a deep breath of the cold air and striding off to the left, his boots silent on the cobbles.

Uri watched him go. The set of the younger man's shoulders was still rigid. Uri knew both of his *spicas* tended to suffer from nervous frustration when forced to move among the general population alone. He tried not to hold it against them. He shrugged as he turned down toward the right. Even among the higher ranking members of the Order, he was often seen as strange for his affection for the people under their care.

It was considered a virtue to hold the greater part of mankind in esteem in a general, distanced sense. Very few of the Order held any real affection for them on a more personal level, however. A familiar smile curved his lips as he walked. It was an old argument, one that had held little heat for the last several centuries. The current *Etta* believed that as long as a member of the Order was pure, and pursued his duties with the utmost vigilance and integrity, then his personal feelings for his charges were immaterial.

Uri shook his head. Immaterial those emotions may be, but he could never understand where warriors like Arja, who felt such contempt for the average run of Man, could find the strength and focus to maintain their commitments to the Order. When the ancient Enemy tested them, how would such men hold the line?

*****

Tucked in among the tumbled down, decrepit buildings of the less-than-desirable neighborhood of Bloodfield, a small, nondescript house was differentiated by its neighbors simply by how often the police were NOT called in to settle violent disputes. As was often the case in such turbulent boroughs, the local peace officers were more than happy to leave the three quiet, solitary men who called the place home to their own devices.

For their part, the lawless denizens of Bloodfield had learned early on to leave the mysterious gentlemen in their strange cloaks and leather-pointed hoods alone. Word spread quickly, once the newcomers had bloodied the most infamous toughs of the neighborhood a time or two without apparent effort.

Uri had selected the location of their current safe house primarily *because* of the lawless nature of the neighborhood. In and among the many brothels, bars, and taverns that took up so much of the local real estate, the comings and goings of his three-man mission team would easily be lost in the general tumult and confusion. Local boys, occasionally granted a shiny penny or two, made excellent watchers as well, should anything change within the community.

Uri made his way down the waterfront, the Potomac River rolling along cold and black on his right. The biting wind and thin, failing sunlight, filtered through a layer of high white clouds, was enough to keep the streets of Bloodfield relatively clear. He nodded confidently to the occasional traveler, his face a mask of pleasant neutrality. As he turned up the point of the river, following the Eastern Branch around, he bowed his head and kept his face hidden, however. Where Bloodfield bordered the Navy Yard, with its local and federal guards, eye contact was far more likely to cause problems than to dissuade them.

A movement caught out of the corner of his eye proved to be *Spica* Arja coming down the steeply-sloped street connecting Bloodfield withthe Fifth Ward. Arja nodded silently to him, casting his eyes casually along Uri's own back trail while the *mimreg* glanced back up the street toward the distant Fifth Ward. There was no movement behind the young warrior.

Uri nodded to Arja and tilted his head toward the safe house. The younger man cut across the street, taking the rickety porch stairs two at a time. He rapped a quick sequence against the peeled paint of the door and waited, head bowed within his hood, until it opened. In the blink of an eye, the small porch was empty again. Uri continued walking, taking an additional turn around the block, avoiding the streets running along the Navy Yard, and then hopped up onto the porch himself. He was hardly finished with his first knock before the door swung open and the smiling face of *Spica* Solas, the third member of his mission team, appeared, gesturing his superior through the doorway with a grand sweep of his arm.

The *mimreg* smiled and slid by into the darkened interior. He noted as he passed that Solas was wearing full armor beneath his cloak. Uri smiled wider as the door closed behind.

"Expecting an invasion, *Spica*?" The *mimreg* moved to the fireplace and pulled his gloves off, rubbing cold hands against each other in the warmth. "Whatever would the landlady think?"

Solas' armor was made of leather and banded steel that would have been more familiar to a citizen of ancient Rome than the denizens of Bloodfield just outside their door. Most of the armor was usually hidden within wrappings and layers of more mundane clothing, further obscured by their cloaks. Within the confines of the small foyer, however, there was no mistaking the suit for what it was.

Dimples appeared beneath the dark shadows of Solas' unshaven cheeks. "As long as the coins keep flowing, that old woman wouldn't care if I answered the door in my altogether."

Uri shook his head and shifted his chin toward a doorway behind Arja, unwrapping his own cloak to hang upon the wall. "Any word from the Acropolis?"

Solas' eyes darkened and he nodded. "They've been waiting to hear from you. I think the members of the *Etta* are getting restless."

Uri stood quickly and moved toward the back room. "Best not to keep them waiting, then."

The small chamber at the rear of the house would have been outlandish to any inhabitant of Bloodfield, or any other part of Washington D.C. for that matter. A strange stone shrine sat on a low table at one end, while along another wall a rack contained an array of items that bore only a passing resemblance to weapons that would be familiar to their neighbors. Each item was unique, a core of dull metal mechanisms wrapped in artistic silvered sheaths etched with flowing runes.

Beneath the guns hung blades that were, at best, distant cousins to the more common small swords and cavalry sabers wielded in modern battle. Again, these were of a dull metal with bright sheathing and beautiful scrollwork. Beneath these swords and daggers, set upon a low table, were various articles of gear and armor that would have been more difficult to disguise; thick, metal-framed goggles, face shields, and variously-shaped containers glowing a soft, gentle blue.

The shrine on the far table was built around a large stone disk, roughly the size of a serving plate, set upright in an elaborate framework of dull metal and silvered casing. Several small wheels embraced the bottom of the disk, capable of spinning it within the setting. Around the outer edge of the disk a chain of small metal plates had been fixed to the smooth stone. An ornate frame at the top of the structure revealed a single plate at a time, separating it from its brothers. Two handles projected from the base of the shrine, and several small windows spaced across the object glowed a steady, shining blue.

Uri stepped up to the small table and took the only chair in the room. He pulled a softly-glowing pendant from beneath his leather tunic. The glowing windows within the machine brightened with an answering cobalt spark, pulsing with the beat of a slow human heart. The *mimreg* reached out and grasped the shrine's handles.

As soon as the *mimreg*'s hands touched the stone, the disk began to spin. Uri's eyes locked on the upper window and then phased slowly out of focus. The spinning of the ring hesitated repeatedly, showing a different glyph for the merest fraction of a second before it spun off to the next.

Uri's eyes flickered as he received the message.

MIMREG URI, THE *ETTA* OF THE ACROPOLIS OF THE SUNSET LANDS AWAITS YOUR REPORT.

Uri bowed his head and his voice took on a soft, steady rhythm as if he were chanting in a church or temple. "This isMimreg Uri of the Holy Order of Man and leader of the Washington mission team. All reverence to the Creators and to the *Etta*." As he spoke the stilted, ritual words, the ring spun and clicked. He knew a similar ring in the Communing Chamber of the Acropolis, far to the west, moved in sympathy. "I have received word from our contact within the administration. The president will deliver the speech as anticipated. He will take a public stand beside the cause of equality and justice on the fields of Gettysburg."

His eyes drifted back up to watch the ring. The metal gleamed in the candlelight as the machine quivered for a moment, and then began to spin once again.

IS IT POSSIBLE TO CONVEY THE TEXT OF THE MESSAGE?

Uri released one handle and fished within a pocket to pull out the crumpled paper. He smoothed it down on the table before the machine, grasped the handle again, and read the speech in the same slow tones. He had been right: it took less than four minutes to read, even at the steady, chanting pace.

Again, the machine quivered with potential energy before the *Etta* responded.

EXCELLENT. WE WILL BE IN TERRIBLE NEED OF SUCH ALLIES SHOULD THE PROPHECY COME TO PASS.

Uri bowed his head again. The last thing he wanted to suffer through right now was one of the interminable squabbles among the *Etta* over the nature and timing of the prophecy. Before he could respond, however, the ring began to spin again.

YOU MUST APPROACH THE PRESIDENT WITH THE TRUTH.

The *mimreg*'s head snapped up. "The full truth?"

Initiates into the Holy Order of Man were tested most rigorously, for months on end, before they were entrusted with even the vaguest shadow of the full truth of Man's place in the universe.

WE HAVE NO TIME LEFT. THIS WAR IS TEARING THE NATION APART. THE DARK COUNCIL WILL SEIZE THE OPPORTUNITY, AND MANKIND WILL BLEED. WITHOUTLINCOLN'S ASSISTANCE WE WILL FAIL AND THIS CONTINENT WILL BE LOST.

Uri shook his head. "But what if I'm wrong? What if he's Tainted? What if he has been turned?"

The wheel spun with the same smooth grace, and the glyphs flickered past with the same implacable speed, but something in the choice of words told Uri that another member of the *Etta* was now speaking.

THE SUNSET IS UPON US, *MIMREG* URI. TRUST IS OUR ONLY HOPE NOW. IF WE CANNOT TRUST ONE OF OUR OWN, WHAT HOPE DO WE HAVE? WE TRUST YOU. YOU MUST BE OUR VOICE TO PRESIDENT LINCOLN. HE MUST KNOW OF US, OF THE TRUE STRUGGLE, AND THAT WE STAND WITH HIM.

Uri nodded, his head bowed beneath the weight of this new responsibility. The plan had been for a member of the *Etta* to travel to Washington and begin these proceedings. Things were moving much too quickly. Either the prophecy was moving faster than he knew, or other events in the world were overtaking them here. Each continent contained its own Citadel of the Order, and any of them could be under siege even now. "I will approach the president as soon as can be arranged."

YOU MUST MOVE IMMEDIATELY. HE IS BEING POISONED AGAINST THE TRIBES OF WESTERN LANDS. IF THE DARK COUNCIL CAN TURN HIM AGAINST THEM, IT WILL BE A GRIEVOUS BLOW.THE NATIONS, THE UNITED STATES, AND THE HOLY ORDER MAY BE ABLE TO ANSWER THE COUNCIL'S EFFORTS IN THE NEW WORLD. IF ANY ONE OF THOSE COMPONENTS FALTERS, WE WILL ALL BE LOST.

Uri nodded again. "I understand." He knew the president had been receiving tainted reports regarding the tribal nations of the west. He should have seen the danger that might pose to the plans of the *Etta*.

Thoughts of the west brought something else to mind. "May I inquire about another possible avenue of alliance?"

OF COURSE.

Uri looked through the ring at the wall on the far side. "General Grant is being recalled to Washington. My contact seems to think he will be given command of the entire Union Army. I was thinking—"

The ring stuttered away from its smooth iteration of his words, stopped for a moment, and then was overridden by the *Etta*, thousands of miles away.

NEGATIVE. GENERAL GRANT HAS BEEN BRANDED A FRANGIBLE SOUL. ANY TRUST IN HIM WILL BE MISPLACED. HE HAS BEEN IDENTIFIED AS A POSSIBLE TARGET FOR REMOVAL, AS WELL. DO NOT APPROACH THE GENERAL UNDER ANY CIRCUMSTANCES.

Uri's eyebrows rose at this. The *Etta* rarely reacted so intensely. They must have had very strong indications that his soul would fracture under the pressure of the Dark Council to contemplate his removal.

The *mimreg* bowed his head again. "As you will, of course. Are there further instructions?"

NO, *MIMREG* URI. GO WITH THE GOOD GRACE OF THE CREATORS, AND MAY THEY SMILE UPON YOUR MISSION.

"May They smile upon us all." The wheel spun into stillness and the lights faded away.

Uri sat back, rubbed at his eyes with the palms of his hands, and blew a prodigious breath between pursed lips. He reached into a pocket in his tunic and pulled out a brass pocket watch. If he moved quickly, he could clean himself up in time for the president's regular afternoon levy, when he would see anyone willing to wait in line. Whether one believed in the imminence of the prophecy or not, once the *Etta* used the term 'immediately', there truly was no time to lose.

Uri moved back into the front room of the little house. Arja and Solas sat at the small kitchen table, heads bent over a scattering of mechanical components, many of which gleamed with a pure blue glow. The two *spica* looked up as Uri came back into the room.

"How do we stand, *Mimreg*?" Solas' hands blurred on the table as he reassembled a small weapon that looked more like a piece of art than a pistol.

"Were they satisfied? Or do we need to deal further with that rat-faced little weasel?" Arja did not look up from where he worked on his own weapon.

Uri sighed as he moved to take the remaining seat around the table. "I'm going to need those fancy clothes you found for me, Solas. I've just come up in the world. I'm going to meet the president!" He knew his smile was more forced than he would have liked.

Arja shook his head. "Why is the president going to listen to you, *Mimreg*? No matter how fancy your clothes are?"

Uri shrugged. "I'm going to have to make him listen." He took his medallion up in one rough hand and raised it before his eye. As he focused upon the little gem, it began to glow blue. "At the very least, this parlor trick ought to buy me a few minutes, anyway."

Solas pushed his chair away from the table and holstered his small pistol. He moved toward a bureau in the corner, cursing floorboards that creaked with each step. This little rat hole was the farthest he had ever been from the grandeur of the Acropolis.

The older *spica* bent over the bureau to gather up the formalwear they had collected in case the *mimreg* was forced to take a more official role in proceedings. A loud pop sounded from outside in the street, and the window beside the battered piece of furniture shattered with a thin, fragile sound. Solas was thrown across the room as if he had been kicked by a mule.

Chapter 2

Rolling fields flashed past beyond the rippled glass. Browns, tans, and reds intermixed with the pale greens of desert grass and scrub trees in a blur of muted color. Far off to the north, moving at a more sedate pace, the angular shapes of distant mountains and plateaus marched past. The buff lines and edges looked more like the buildings of Upper Manhattan than anything he had expected to see once he left civilization behind. Even so, they possessed a strangeness as well, to a man who had never made it much past Paradise Park in his first two decades of life.

Civilization. The thought came with a grunt of discomfort; as if the Five Points had been any more civilized than the bleak views dominating the landscape since the train had passed through Kansas City the day before.

With the word 'civilization' echoing in his head, his large hands tightened in his lap. He looked down, imagining he could still see the traces of blood that had driven him away from the only home he had ever known. Peeking out from the cuff of his shirtsleeve was an inky black image, a sinuous curve with a subtle scale pattern dusted into its darkness. With a self-conscious glance around the car, he pulled the cuff lower, covering the design.

He rested his forehead once more against the warm glass of the window and let his eyes drift over the alien landscape. He could not imagine being farther away from New York than he was, and yet, there was no sense of relief or escape. He closed his eyes and gave a brief shake of his head. He had known this from the moment he boarded the B&O back in Ellicott City and probably before. He was fooling himself to think he was running from the riots, the death, and the violence of the Five Points. He was running from himself. And as the nuns had always been quick to tell him back in Bishop Hughes' school, you can never run from yourself.

The rocking of the passenger car had nearly lulled him back into a depressed slumber despite the hard, rough wood of his bench, when a shadow moved over his closed eyes. He pushed himself upright, glaring at the older man sliding into the seat opposite him. The sun shining through the window gleamed off the man's broad, bald pate and his thick, wire-rimmed spectacles. His forearms, crossed against a thick chest, were knotted with muscle. A thick, grizzled beard framed a smile that didlittle to warm the green eyes peering from behind the glass.

The newcomer nodded once, shifted his weight on the bench, and then turned to look out at the Arizona desert rumbling along outside. The silence stretched into uncomfortable territory, and the big kid glanced pointedly around, noting that the car was nearly empty. After several moments, he sat up straighter, rested his arms on the knees of his trousers, and shrugged.

"Okay. I'll bite, old man." He tried to keep his voice steady despite the rocking of the train. "Anything in particular I can do for you?"

The man lazily brought his gaze back around to look into the boy's eyes, the grin widening by a fraction. "You got some sand, kid. Most men, they'da spoke up 'r moved quite a few harrumphs ago."

The younger man leaned back, not trying to hide his annoyance. "Sir, I don't know you, and I don't care to. If you don't mind, I'd just as soon go back to—"

"Brooding, son?" The older man's forehead wrinkled as if he was trying to puzzle out some annoying little trick. "You'd rather go back to staring out at the desert and wishin' you'd never left home?"

The young man stared at the intruder without expression for a moment, then, blinking slowly, said, "I think we're done here."

He moved to push himself off the bench, when the other man reached out with one calloused hand and tapped him on the knee. The older man made a vaguely placating gesture and his smile warmed up just a bit.

"Easy on there, son. I'm just testin' the waters." He sat back, hands on knees. "Name's Tuck.Tucker Soza." One hand reached across the space between them, hanging in the air.

The younger man's eyes tightened, still not sure if he cared to continue the conversation, but he had no idea how much longer it would take for the train to reach the railhead. As annoying as the stranger had been, he had been right about one thing: he had spent too much time brooding already.

"Varro." He left the man's hand hanging in the air. After a moment, Tuck shrugged and lowered it back to his knee with a snort of amusement.

"Varro." The man pronounced the name as if he were testing it. "Just Varro?"

The kid nodded once. "At the moment."

Tuck Soza smiled again, and this time his green eyes warmed with the expression. "Well, Varro, I guess that'll have to do for now. So, what brings you out to the great desert of the western territories?"

Varro shrugged. "I wanted a change of scenery."

Tuck nodded, throwing one elbow over the back of his bench. "So, judging from your accent, I'd say you've been riding the rails for quite a ways, Varro. All the way back east, I'd say?"

Varro tried to hide his surprise, but judging from the look of satisfaction that bloomed across Tuck's weathered face, he knew he had failed. He shrugged again and nodded. Tuck sucked at his teeth for a moment and then looked out the window. "Interesting that you're headed west, and not south. No interest in dyin' in Lincoln's war?"

The young man shook his head. "I don't have a dog in that fight."

The older man nodded, his eyes narrowing. "And yet you're no stranger to fighting, if I can make a guess? You've got the shoulders for it, the hands." He scratched at his bearded chin with blunt fingers. "Just gang fighting? Or were you roped into those draft riots?"

At the words 'draft riots', he felt himself twitch and looked quickly away.

"Ah, the riots." Tuck nodded slowly. "And if I don't miss my mark, we're not talking those tame little demonstrations farther north. The big riots? New York?"

Varro sat up, his fists in tight balls in his lap. "Sir, if you've got a point, you better come around to it pretty quick."

Soza pursed his lips and continued talking with a nod, as if the boy had not spoken. "New York. And that'll mean Five Points, then. And that'll mean you really have seen your share of fighting." He leaned closer. "More winning, or more losing?"

The boy felt his face writhe with frustration, guilt, and a growing anger that scared him, given what he had learned about himself in those dark nights of fighting. "Did anyone win?"

The older man leaned back, shaking his head slightly. "Well, those that died might think so. And those that got shipped to the front, they might think a kid on a train bound for the western territories, he might have won. But I see your point."

As he said the word 'died', Varro felt his shoulders tense, and looked back out the window, not wanting to give anything more away. He should have known better at this point.

"And you lost someone too, eh?" Tuck shook his head and took his own turn looking out the window. "I read about it. It was rough, they say – fires, looting, rape. They say no one was safe."

Varro cleared his throat, marshaled his calm, and turned back to look through the glinting lenses on the older man's battered face. "I'd rather not talk about it, if you don't mind. And if there wasn't anything else . . . ?"

Tuck sighed, slapped his hands down on his thighs, and rocked forward. "Well, kid, to be honest, I thought we might be able to help each other out. See, I'm foreman for one of the railhead crews. The railroad hit a rough patch, and we've been stalled out here for a couple weeks. I went back east to recruit new blood for the teams, just my luck. Seems I followed in the footsteps of the latest draft announcement everywhere I went. Came up all but empty." He pointed at Varro with two scarred fingers. "And then there's you, son. I'm guessing, if you're still on this train after KC, you're either looking for a new start as far as you can travel, or you're running out of money, or maybe both?"

Varro thought about the pathetic fold of worn bills in his pocket; all that remained of the stash he had pulled from his family's burning apartment his last night in the city. All that tied him to the life he had lost that night. He shook his head, not meeting Soza's eyes.

The older man leaned forward. "Son, you are about to land in a world of hurt. I don't know what you thought you'd find out this way, but you didn't outrun anything you might be hiding from. The war's just as much out in the territories as it is anywhere else. And a kid without money or friends? Well, the desert outside that window, it ain't none too friendly to folks like that."

The barren landscape rolled past, the greens slowly giving way to dry, dusty sand. Why *had* he come out here? He looked down at his hands. He could still see the blood that was not there.

"Might be, like I said, we could help each other?" Soza repeated.

Varro looked back up at the man who was offering him exactly what he had come out here to find. Maybe working with his hands, working an honest job, to build something bigger than himself; maybe that would help wash that blood away. He had followed a vague memory of Father Stevens' sermons on penance and forgiveness all the way out into the western territories. Helping to build the rail line as far as the continent would allow might be the best way to cleanse himself of that night once and for all.

Soza raised his hand again, and this time Varro reached out and clasped it. The older man grinned and reached out to slap his shoulder. "Damn straight, kid! Don't worry. It's hard work, but it's honest, and there's money to be made by those who aren't afraid of a little sweat."

Soza rose, thrusting his hands into his pockets, and surveyed the passenger car. "Well, we ain't too far from the railhead, if I don't miss my guess. I gotta gather up the rest of the boys. The foremen's shack should be where I left it, just a bit beyond the last tracks we laid down. Why don't you gather up whatever baggage you've got and meet me there?"

The young man nodded, and the foreman nodded back, sunlight gleaming off the glasses. He smiled again and walked back through the car and out the far door with a rolling gait.

Varro settled back against his seat and turned to the window. Working the railhead might not fill the emptiness that had built up inside him after years of bad choices, but it was a damn sight better than having no plan at all. He had known the Atlantic and Pacific Line was going to come to an end soon. He had avoided giving any thought to what happened when it did. There was a certain poetry to his joining the crew that would continue that line.

Maybe, if he stayed with the A&P, he would never have to stop running. And maybe, if he never stopped running, he'd never have to face what had driven him away from his home in the first place.

*****

Varro stood by the dusty tent, his shoulders slumped in disbelief. Having lacked a coherent plan for so long, it felt like the height of cruelty to have this opportunity yanked from beneath him so abruptly. He had known, as the train had pulled up to the tangled chaos of the tent city growing up around the railhead, that something was not quite right. Everything he had read about these endeavors spoke about the speed with which the men in charge drove their charges, spearing the rail lines as fast as flesh and blood could support, to complete their circuits before competition working to the north or south could beat them.

But in the nameless settlement that had grown up around the A&P railhead driving toward California, there was no sense of noble urgency. In fact, there was no sense of urgency at all. From what he had seen through the rippled window glass of his passenger car, and then climbing down onto the dirt embankment from the iron steps of the train, the chaotic mess growing up in the middle of the desert could have given the Five Points a run for its money.

Varro moved up behind the small knot of men standing near the tent. Soza's bald head, sweat glistening amidst the stubble, was shaking back and forth, his hands up in a warding gesture.

"Listen, boys, I'm sorry, but that's the situation! A&P got sent the wrong bridge to span the canyon. Until the new parts arrive, I ain't got nothing to pay you with, and nothing to pay you for."

"You bastard!" One of the men in the group, older than the others by several years, was near tears. "You brought me all the way out here to—"

Soza held up a hand. "A&P'll send you all back to Kansas City, free of charge. But that's the best I got for you. I'm sorry, boys, but believe me, this'll be the last place you want to wait out the time before those bastards get around to sending us more steel."

The men were clearly still angry, but they turned away from the foremen's tent, grumbling to themselves and shaking their heads, as they moved deeper into the warren of tents and stockpiles. After a moment, only Varro was left, a worn leather messenger bag slung over one slumped shoulder. Soza sighed and slapped at the dust on his pants before registering that he was not alone. His mouth twisted in distaste when he recognized Varro.

"Son, there's not much I can do for you, either." He wiped the sweat from his brow and cast a look around the chaos of the camp. "It didn't take long for the whores and shysters to set up shop, that's for sure. I even saw a couple wooden shacks going up by the lip of the canyon. Won't be long before this is the last place a kid like you's going to want to be hanging his hat."

Varro looked around again. Even in the burning heat of midday, there seemed to be a lot of men wandering about aimlessly. Women were lounging in the gaping doorways of tents, luring the men in with blatant offers of what bounty nature had bestowed upon them. Although there were piles of ties, stock iron, and construction tools and materials, there seemed to be precious little actual work being done, aside from the oldest profession of all, of course.

"How long do you think this will last?" Varro's voice was flat. He was numb to the despair that had gripped the other men. Hope had been a very new feeling for him, and there had been no time for it to take root.

The foreman shrugged and then gestured for Varro to follow him with a tilt of his head. "There's really no telling. The original bridge was supposed to take six months, but the war has been wreaking havoc with supply and labor. It came in a couple months late, but like I said . . . it was the wrong bridge."

They moved through the tents, leaving the gurgling, hissing train in their wake. Soon, they were standing upon the lip of a steep canyon. The opposite edge seemed to loom impossibly far away. Soza pointed at the crumbling lip, hazy with heat in the distance. "The bridge comes in sections, to be assembled on-sight. Like any difficult task, the secret is in the pace." He smiled grimly. "Except, of course, when you don't have enough bridge left to span the space."

They turned their backs on the canyon and stood there, taking in the swirling variety and violence of the scene. "So, we'll have to wait for the new bridge to arrive. But the way these railhead tent cities can get out of hand with even the slightest delay?" Soza shrugged. "I wouldn't be surprised if these jackals didn't destroy the entire railhead long before we get the new bridge. If they stall here for more than another six months? I'd imagine this particular line will never get finished. Diablo Canyon will be well named. At least, as far as the A&P stockholders are concerned."

"I can stay, for a little while." Varro's stomach churned as the words emerged, unbidden, from his lips. He owed this man nothing. And yet, with no other options, and the last bank notes crumbling in his pocket . . .

Soza shook his head. "Kid, I *am* sorry. I have nothing to offer you. Hell, if they don't give me something to do, I'll be heading back east myself. God alone knows how long this war's going to drag on. I've got too much time invested with the Atlantic and Pacific to start over with any of the other rail lines, but until the war's over, I'm not sure anyone's going to be laying much more track."

Varro felt the gulf of space behind him, and cinched the strap of the messenger bag high up on his shoulder. He nodded sharply. This was what came of hope. He should have known. He did know, but he should have remembered. No matter what Father Stevens had said, there had never been any sign that God took even a passing interest in the Varros or their trials and tribulations. And this was just another example.

He was up there, Varro had no doubt. But that did not mean He cared in the slightest.

"Kid, the least I can do is get you back to KC on the A&P's coin." The older man clapped him on the back. "She'll be heading back east before dark, and I don't doubt she'll be full. It'll only be the desperate and the twisted that want to wait things out at the end of the line. But I can get you back on her, at least."

Varro nodded without looking over. "Thanks. I think I'll take a walk." His pride warred with the reality of his situation, and he knew, unless a miracle descended upon him in the next couple of hours, he really could not afford to turn down the man's charitable offer. "I'll swing back around this way in a little bit?"

Soza tried an encouraging smile, and seeing the effort made Varro feel worse. "Yeah. I shouldn't be too far away. And she'll give out a whistle or three before she leaves. You won't be able to miss it." He took off his glasses and made a brave attempt to buff the grit off of them with his shirt. "Kid, you mind if I ask you a question?"

Despite the heat of the afternoon, Varro felt a sudden chill. He turned back to Soza and jerked his chin in a rough nod.

The older man grinned awkwardly, then tapped Varro's sleeve; the sleeve that hid the swirling blackness. "That's pretty high quality ink."

The chill sank into Varro's heart, and his head sank to his chest. He pulled the cuff of his right sleeve up to reveal an ornate serpent tattoo, its flanks rippling with the muscles of his arm.

Soza bent down to look more closely, whistling in appreciation. "I thought so." He straightened, looking at Varro with a respect that twisted like a knife in his gut. "Swamp Angels, am I right?"

Varro pulled the sleeve down over the tattoo, shrugging. "Not anymore."

The older man's smile faltered, sensing that he had caused offense. "I didn't mean nothing by it, kid. It's nice work, is all. Anyone from back east knows anything, they'll give you a wide berth, you flash that ink around."

Varro took a deep breath and turned to give the older man a tight smile of his own, reaching out with his free hand. Soza took it with a grin and a nod. "Don't worry, kid. It'll all work out. My mother always said everything works out for the best."

The kid faltered at that, but then he nodded, smiling through the shadows in his eyes, and turned back toward the rumbling community growing up around the lip of DiabloCanyon.

"I'll see you in a bit."

He moved off, making his way through the jostling, riotous crowd before Soza could say another word.

*****

There were no real streets in the settlement around the cliff edge, although they would most likely develop if given enough time. The entire little town, clustered around the railhead and the massive steam train that had brought them all, was a mess of tents, lean-tos, and shacks. Two or three more-permanent buildings were being constructed, their frames rising into the sky, bustling with what little honest work Varro could see. The natural haze and grit of the desert battled with the lingering taste of cooking fires, road dust, and the sewer stench of rudimentary latrines. He began to walk, following an almost animal need to escape the smells if nothing else.

Throughout his time in the Five Points, both with his family and later with the Swamp Angels, Varro had never wanted for companionship of any kind. He had never had to pay for the friendship of a lady, and did not intend to start now. He walked past the brothel tents, paying no attention to the women who brayed from them, neither their compliments as he approached nor their curses as he walked on by. He did drop a little of his dwindling wealth on the plank and barrel bar of an open air saloon, but his light wallet was enough to convince him that a single whisky to fortify himself against the day's disappointments would be plenty of indulgence for the time being.

Aside from the establishments offering companionship of any stripe and spirits of the less-refined variety, Varro saw many folks trying to sell their own survey, construction, and clearing equipment. There was never a lack of opportunists willing to pay bottom dollar to men and women desperate for a berth aboard the train back east. And those who had nothing left to sell made no bones about their willingness to liberate the price of a train ticket from another man's purse. More than one fight broke out in the winding alleys as a pickpocket, less gifted than he might have wished, was caught slashing into the pants of a more prosperous-seeming target.

As he walked through the chaos, Varro was more and more convinced he could not wait out the delivery of the new bridge. The burgeoning town growing here had nothing to offer a young man trying his damnedest to cultivate his better nature and deny the devil riding his left shoulder its due. He was going to have to take Soza up on his offer, head on back to Kansas City, and see what he might be able to pick up for work at that end. Even with the war churning along back east, things seemed to be settling down out in the territories. He should be able to find scut work enough to keep body and soul together until the bridge came through. Then he would head back this way and see if Soza still had work.

Varro's work boots meandered along the dusty paths between tents and shacks of their own accord while his mind ground through infinite possibilities, each of them less pleasant than the last. Something nagged at him as he rounded one of the construction sites. A manner or cadence of speech caught his mind, steering his feet without his conscious direction. He found himself outside one of the last tents marking the outskirts of the bustling encampment.

The tent was large, clearly the work of professionals, and nothing like the haphazard collection of canvas, ropes, and poles that made up the majority of the place's structures. A fabric sign hanging above the main entrance spelled out 'Fellowship' in vivid red tones, while a small, tattered white flag flew from an extension of the central tent pole, a cross splashed across it in the same shade.

From within, Varro heard the familiar tones of a preacher in high fervor, exhorting his flock to some great deed of faith or conviction. He cast a quick look up and down the narrow alley and out to the wider cluster of structures nearby. It seemed like a strange place to find a preacher, but then, perhaps not. The darker the time, the more people seemed to need to believe in something better. The more he thought about it, the more sense it made. The harsh, buzzing tones of the preacher's voice held little in common with the lilting flow of words from Father Stevens, but with nothing more pressing demanding his time, there seemed little harm in hearing the man out.

Varro looked around at the nearby tents one last time before ducking his head and moving inside.

*****

No matter the lawless chaos all around, it seemed this preacher had collected more than his fair share of sheep within the stifling confines of the heavy canvas. The air was thick with the heat and breath of nearly a hundred men and women. Most were standing, as there were only a scattering of chairs and benches. There was a constant low murmur of agreement. At the front of the congregation stood the preacher, a gaunt man in a long dark great coat and wide-brimmed hat. Long, lank hair hung down on either side of his grim face, but his eyes blazed with the fire of his belief.

"And this is only the beginning, my brothers and sisters!" His voice had a thin, reedy quality that nagged at the ears, and lacked the depth of the priests and pastors back home. Varro moved deeper into the tent, trying to see more clearly, moving through the swaying crowd as if driven by some unknown compulsion.

Someone in the crowd shouted their support for the preacher's testimony.

"This war is only the first step in our trial and our judgment!"

Someone else shouted, "Amen!"

"We stand now upon the threshold of a new era, my children, and only those worthy in the eyes of the Lord will march forward. The wayward and the lost will fall behind and be destroyed!" The voice seemed to dig into Varro's ear. He opened his mouth, working his lower jaw back and forth to address an itch growing in the back of his throat.

"And woe betide those who forget that we are all unworthy in the eyes of the Lord!" The preacher's thin face contorted with contempt for mankind and all his works. "No single life adds value or holds significance in this world without bearing testimony to that power and majesty greater than itself!"

"Amen!" several voices cried.

"Testify to the Lord!" another shouted from the rear.

Varro continued to push through the crowd. They allowed themselves to be moved, seemingly oblivious. Something drove him forward, but he could never have explained what it might have been. It was not the words of the sermon, for they scratched at his ears like the claws of rabid vermin. It was not the fires blazing from the preacher's eyes, for they seemed to burn with a cold, lifeless heat. It was something within himself, some sick fascination that he was powerless to deny, that pressed him through the crowd.

"For the lawless and the wretched will drown in rivers of blood," the preacher's clenched fist quivered as he held it before his snarling mouth. "Liquid fire will rise up from the earth and consume all those who would deny the truth!"

"Tell us the truth!" a woman's voice, crying from the middle of the crowd, begged.

"Tell us!" Several other voices took up the call.

"My brothers and my sisters," the preacher's voice fell to a still whisper, and suddenly everyone in the crowded, steaming tent fell silent, the better to hear the preacher's words.

"My brothers and my sisters, the truth will set you free. And the truth is this: We are not alone upon the Lord's chosen world. No. We share the Earth with all manner of fallen souls: the savages, the unbelievers, the deniers." The rough, buzzing voice grew in strength, louder and louder, recapturing its former command.

"We are enjoined by our Lord and Savior, my brothers and sisters, to fall down upon these pariahs, to fall upon them with the fiery sword of the Lord Himself, and smite them down in His name!"

The crowd surged forward, many brandishing knives, cudgels, and even revolvers and rifles. Cries of wordless agreement and ecstasy added their weight to the heavy air. Varro, jostled now from all sides as the congregation pushed forward, continued to move with the press, paying no attention to the people around him as his eyes focused solely on the shadows beneath the preacher's wide-brimmed hat. The man's lank hair swung about as if it had a life of its own. The kid who had spent his last dollars traveling across a continent to stand in that fetid tent could not turn his eyes away.

"And when the Lord's fiery rain falls to consume the land, only those who have served His greater cause, only those who have submitted their souls fully to his purpose, will find shelter from the storm!"

Varro stopped dead in his tracks. As if he had broken past some sort of invisible barrier, he felt as if he were seeing the preacher clearly for the first time. The man's skin was an unhealthy, pallid white. It had an unnatural sheen to it, as if it were soaked in oil or corpse sweat. His eyes were hollow, lacking any sense of humanity. Despite the fusty heat of the tent, a chill swept down the young man's spine; he took an involuntary step backward, away from the preacher and his empty eyes.

Those eyes flicked sideways, pinning him in place.

The words of the sermon did not falter. The momentum of the crowd, now whipped up into a frenzy, did not waver. Varro knew, without a shadow of a doubt, that the full weight of the preacher's attention was now on him alone. He felt the pressure of the hatred that boiled within the tent surging around him. It was unlike anything he had experienced in any of the churches he had visited as a child. It was unlike even the boisterous rallies the gangs back home indulged in before meeting their enemies in open battle. It was blind, raw, and animal.

He knew, with a surety like a blade at his throat, that it could be directed against him without a moment's hesitation.

Varro did not try to break eye contact with the preacher, but rather continued his retreat, focusing all of his energy and discipline into keeping his legs steady, his steps firm. The dark figure continued to spout his vile poison. The crowd continued to eat it up, throwing back choice tidbits of parroted anger. But the preacher's eyes never wavered.

As Varro felt the heavy canvas of the tent's wall brush against his shoulder, he reached out, through the edges of the crowd, and grasped the tent flap, feeling air that was somehow cooler, despite the desert heat, and somehow more pure, despite the smoke, dust, and latrine stink. He stood in the doorway for a long moment, trying to process what he had seen. When the preacher gave him a sudden, hungry smile, Varro spun on one heel and was gone into the crowd outside, leaving the fluttering, blood-red cross floating behind him.

Chapter 3

"Attack!" Arja shouted, knocking the table over and pushing it up against the front door. Uri dove for the floor, landing near Solas' writhing form. The rest of the windows along the front of the house exploded inward, showering the room with sparkling shards of glass. The younger *spica* crouched behind the table, looking to his *mimreg* for guidance, but Uri was too busy checking Solas.

"I'm alright!" Solas grunted, twisting around to lie on his stomach, shaking glass out of his short hair. "My armor, I'm alright. Go." He gestured toward the windows as he spat a gob of blood onto the floor.

Uri nodded and then shuffled toward the door. The gunshots had petered out from the street, leaving a ragged line of holes punched through the thin clapboard walls of the house. Faltering sunlight filtered through the holes, falling in heavy bars in the dust-laden air.

"There's got to be ten of them, *Mimreg*; regular weapons." They faced mundane, black-powder firearms, then. The attackers would be ready to shoot again in about—

Another rolling crash slammed into the house, more ragged this time, accounting for the various reloading speeds of their attackers. The balls shattered the front of the house, flying right through and blasting into the walls behind them. There was shouting in the street now, voices harsh and guttural as they worked themselves into a frenzy suitable for the close-in violence of clearing the house.

Arja reached for his small pistol, a silent plea furrowing his brow.

Uri looked down at the sleek little weapon, to the shattered wall before him, and to Solas, who had pushed himself into a corner behind the bureau. He looked back to the young *spica* and shook his head. "Standard defense at this point. No reliquary weapons unless the Enemy shows itself."

A shattering boom sounded from the street as the entire house shook around them. The door imploded, scattering splinters of smoking wood across the front room amidst the rattling steel rain of grapeshot.

Uri slapped Arja's shoulder to get his attention, and then signaled with a series of rapid hand movements. *Lay low. Wait for the enemy to approach*. He looked around and grabbed one of the knives that had been scattered across the floor. He held it out to Arja, gesturing toward the fractured door with a nod.

Arja's dark eyes were hard as he accepted the knife and pushed himself to the wall beside the doorframe, splintered wood and shattered glass crunching beneath his feet.

Uri tapped Solas' leg, and then nodded when the man smiled grimly at him. The older of his two *spicas* was already clutching a swept-hilt knife in one tight fist.

Uri pushed his way toward the back of the small building and glanced out a side window as he passed. The space between buildings in Bloodfield was sparse, alleyways that could barely fit a walking man. There was no movement in the confined space, and Uri pushed deeper, making for a small side door that led out into the alley behind the building.

Uri stopped at a table beside the door and grabbed a well-maintained Colt Army Model 1860 revolver wrapped in a worn holster. He thought grimly of the weapons kept in the mission's armory, but knew his order to Arja had been the correct one.

With a single movement, Uri kicked the small door off its hinges and threw himself into the courtyard outside, rolling into cover in the far corner against a neighboring building. He scanned the shadows with the unwavering threat of the eight inch barrel. Sporadic firing still echoed from the front of the house; no one would have heard the single sharp report of the lock giving way out back.

The alley was empty. This attack did not have the feel of a well-crafted, professional operation, but rather the kind of amateur strike quickly becoming famous out in the western territories. There was no telling who might be behind it, although Uri was afraid he knew where the trail would ultimately lead. Whatever might come at them next, the men currently assaulting the safe house were not top caliber trigger men by anyone's calculations.

Crouching low and taking every advantage he could from the hazy shadows, Uri moved down a side alley. He could emerge into the street several houses down and take the attacking enemy in their exposed flank.

*****

Arja clenched the mundane knife to his chest and struggled to keep his snarl from erupting into a full-throated war cry. Being assigned to this hellhole had been the worst burden ever visited upon him. Surrounded by the ignorant peasants of a fallen world, he hated being so far from the western mountains and the important work being done there. Now, cornered by this mongrel horde, threatened with such feeble weapons and unable to respond with the relic's true fire? It was beyond endurance.

The young *spica* had only received his illuminated name a year earlier. His years of training, indoctrination, and education had all come to this. The crude handle of the knife bit into his calloused palm as his anger drove his fist tighter. They would be rushing the house soon; he would not have to lie still much longer. Until then, the best he could do was to brew in his own rage, feeling the heat of his loathing burning away his trained, hard-won restraint.

Across the blasted room, Solas made a patting gesture with his knife hand, sensing Arja's growing anger. The younger man shook his head. He was no fool, to throw away his life against such ill-equipped sheep. Nothing they had seen from the crowd of dogs in the street posed any serious threat to them. He was not going to hand the mongrels an advantage they clearly had not brought to the battle on their own. However, he would be taking several captives in the next few moments, and not even the control of *Mimreg* Uri would keep him from cutting what they needed to know from the flesh of the Tainted scum that fell into his hands.

The growling and shouting out in the street rose to a fevered pitch, and Arja tensed, knowing what had to come next. Across the small room, Solas readied himself as well. Timing would be critical facing such a great disadvantage in numbers. Too soon, and the men in the street would be warned, pulling back and gunning them down at their leisure. Too late, and the first men into the house would have had time to make a telling strike of their own.

But each of the *spicas* crouching within the battered shed was the product of the harshest training practiced on seven continents for thousands of years. They were masters of the hunt, and feeling the right moment was second nature.

The tattered remains of the door crashed inward as a bulky man came barreling through, howling in a harsh voice. Two more men pushed past the first, each clutching a repeating rifle to their chests as their heads swiveled wildly, searching for targets.

Moments after the door succumbed, the windows to either side exploded as men leapt through them, rolling on the floor, heavy pistols and knives flashing in their hands. Arja could hear the growling bustle of a crowd of men on the front porch quite clearly from where he crouched, and he felt the moment arrive as if a bell had been struck. From the corner of his eye he saw Solas float up onto his feet as well.

Arja let his knife hand drift low as he stood up behind the first line of men coming through the door. He struck the nearest a terrific blow with his open palm, knocking the stunned man into a companion, and they both fell back to the floor. The *spica* then spun on one heel, the knife coming up and around, sliding through the exposed throat of the man who had come through the window. The blade slipped through flesh and slammed into the second man through the window, cracking into the side of his head. As the man fell back through the window, Arja fell down to one knee, the knife flashing out to end both of the men still squirming on the floor.

Beyond him, Arja saw Solas stab one of their attackers three times in the chest before reaching past him, pushing his face into the ruined floor with his free hand, and lashing out, first right and then left, to gut the two men coming in from the window on his side. Both *spicas* rolled to the side, grabbing heavy revolvers abandoned by their dead assailants as the crowd outside unleashed their rifles and carbines again on the luckless room.

The seven bodies of the first wave of attackers jerked spasmodically as their erstwhile companions filled the room with lead. Gun smoke washed across them with its acrid tang, nearly blotting out the smell of blood and death. Beneath the ear-shattering blasts of gunfire they could hear fierce, terrified howls of frustrated rage.

Arja spared a moment's grin for Solas, who shook his head ruefully. Each man held a revolver in a steady grip, knife blades glistening with hot blood.

Neither was so much as winded.

Solas crouched down near the smoking bodies, now still as their former brethren paused in their firing, stalking closer through the swirls of gun smoke. He peered down at the fallen men, looking for any of the tell-tale signs of Taint or corruption, but there was nothing to be seen. These were mere pawns in the eternal game.

He looked up and shook his head at Arja, his face grim. There was certainly worse to come.

*****

Uri emerged onto the street just as the attackers announced the failure of their first assault with a renewed eruption of firepower. The *mimreg* kept to the side of the street, his eyes in constant motion, building an image of the current situation in his mind. There was a small knot of men on the porch of the safe house, and his mind stuttered for a moment at the sight of the devastation their initial attacks had wrought upon the inoffensive little building. A small field piece sat abandoned in the middle of the road, a curl of smoke rising up from its snout. He saw no sign of a commander in the enemy ranks as he moved toward the chattering gunfire reducing the safe house to wreckage.

The *mimreg* had the Colt drawn and low in his right hand. He spared a moment to wish he had thought to grab his cloak, for its armored plates as much for its camouflage. Then again, if he was wishing for things, there were several potent weapons that would have reduced the entire mob to cinders in moments. Why not wish for one of those?

Uri paced down the center of the street until he was even with the safe house. The attackers were so crazed, engaged with the *spicas* within, that they had spared not a moment's thought on securing themselves from a counter attack. Whoever these men were, it was almost an insult to have set them against a Holy Order mission team.

The chill wind tugged at Uri's tunic as he stopped to survey the chaotic nature of the attack. There were two men at each window, three crouched around the door, each trying to find an angle on the two defenders. Two bodies lay on their backs, blank eyes staring up at the sagging porch roof overhead. Clearly, Arja and Solas were taking their time with the rest.

Time was not something any of them had to spare now that they had been attacked openly. These men needed to be stopped, the mission team needed to secure another base of operations, and he needed to get to the White House as soon as he could. Things were happening too quickly now for them to lose even a single day. Such a delay might be measured in hundreds of thousands of lives.

Uri took a casual bead on the rearmost target and placed a single bullet through the back of the man's head. The body fell heavily against his partners before slumping to the floor. Even as they turned in disbelief to watch the faceless man slide to the boards, two more cracks from the revolver sent another two down to meet their masters. By the time the survivors on the porch realized they were facing a threat from behind, Arja and Solas erupted from behind the battered windows with a disciplined roar of fire. The remaining thugs spun to the saturated floorboards, joining their own blood to the viscous mix already soaking into the ancient wood.

Uri moved calmly up the rickety stairs of the porch, his smoking Colt gliding across the still forms of the attackers, looking for any signs of life. Aside from the dancing smoke and the heavy dripping of blood, there was no movement at all.

Arja stood up in the closest window, reloading an enemy revolver from shells he must have claimed from one of the bodies inside. He scanned the street behind Uri before his angry eyes settled on his *mimreg*. "This can't have been all." His voice was bleak. "There was no reason to attack us like this. It has to be the work of the Council, and that means this can't have been all they scraped up against us."

"There's no sign of Taint here, Uri. These men bear none of the marks." Solas pushed one body over with a heavy boot. The man's eyes were staring blankly up into nothingness. "They were a distraction, nothing more."

The *mimreg* nodded and turned around to look up and down the street. Aside from some furtive movement behind shuttered and curtained windows, there was no sign of life anywhere. Given the black reputation of Bloodfield, it would be some time before the constabulary came by to investigate. He turned back to the house, moving toward the door.

"You're right, but we can't wait for more. We have to move out now. Gather the reliquary items and the weapons. We'll need to find a place to regroup and work out a better idea of what happened later. Our first priority has to be reaching the president. Solas, see what you can salvage from the finery. I'm going to do a sweep of the neighborhood and make sure—"

Solas and Arja were turning back into the house, nodding their understanding and bending to their tasks, when a bolt of coherent ruby light punched through Uri's back and erupted from the center of his chest.

The *mimreg* staggered forward, a look of vague confusion twisting his features as he took a clumsy step forward, trying to turn around to face his new attackers. He could hear his men shouting, but he could make no sense of their words. Heavy bars of red-tinged light slashed out of the alleys across the street, lashing the dry wood of the safe house with heat and flame. Amidst the swirling fires Uri staggered down the stairs, the Colt spinning loosely from his limp trigger finger. One leg gave way and he fell heavily to his knees. He tried with all his strength to bring his head up, to scan for his killers, to help his brothers, but his body would not respond.

He felt the cold stones of the street against his fevered cheek with no memory of having fallen. Blood and pain pumped from the wounds in his chest and back, his hands and feet twitched weakly, and the world around him began to lose its bright definition. Overhead, answering bolts of searing cerulean force crashed from the collapsing house at shadowy targets that skulked out of the shadows.

A last twitch of the *mimreg*'s face left his mouth twisted in a slight, hopeless smile.

*****

Solas knew that the Council had found them as he watched the scarlet beam explode from his *mimreg*'s chest. As he stood there, lost in disbelief, Arja dove back into the building, shouting for him to take cover, running for the armory and the reliquary weapons.

"No, Arja! We have to *destroy* the reliquary bonds! We can't risk them falling into the hands of the Council!" Solas grabbed for the younger *spica* as he lunged past, but he missed. "Arja! Remember your duty!"

The younger man disappeared into the armory and then dashed back out again, a sleek pistol in either hand. "I shall remember our duty to our *mimreg*, Solas. You remember our duty to the *Etta*."

Without another word, the younger man dashed back to the front of the building and laid down a flickering, rapid stream of blue fire that pounded across the street and blasted the houses there. Solas watched him for a moment, and then ducked back into the back room himself.

The items of the mission team's reliquary were all glowing with blue-white intensity, and Solas knew, if he had needed further proof, that his end was near. The blessed items of the reliquary only gleamed so intensely when in the presence of the Council or those they had Tainted thoroughly and completely. The *spica* sat heavily before the communing stones and grasped the artfully turned handles, his head bowed low. He began to chant in a sonorous voice, and the small windows flared to furious life, then each snapped into utter darkness with bursts of incandescent discharge that grounded into the walls around him. As the last light flared and died, Solas grabbed the first of the weapons off the wall behind him and performed the same ritual. Again, the glowing components burst and died. Tears of frustration and anger burned down his cheeks as he destroyed artifacts more ancient than the fallen pillars of Rome.

Out in the street, sensing the destruction of the relic-bound artifacts, a dark presence howled in thwarted anger.

The ferocity of the assault redoubled as the powers of Hell itself lashed at the shattered, splintered wood. Solas extinguished the last of the relic-fires, his shoulders slumped with relief and pain in equal parts. The high-pitched flare of reliquary pistols firing from the front of the house, however, sent a shiver down his spine: Arja's weapons.

Solas moved through the ruins of the collapsing house, following the blasting sounds of his brother's pistols. He found Arja slumped against the window sill, one arm hanging limply at his side, the other braced against the cracked wood. Shapes moved within the swirling smoke filling the street, but Arja sent them scurrying with a heat-lightning blast each time they moved closer.

Tears flowed once again down the senior *spica's* begrimed face. He wanted nothing more than to take up his brother's fallen weapon and burn down their enemies, fighting side by side until the infernal powers claimed them. But even in his hopeless desperation, Solas knew that they could leave behind no link to the Acropolis for the Dark Council to exploit. Their first duty was to the security of the brothers and sisters they were leaving behind to continue the war.

Solas reached out and grasped the fallen pistol, bowing over the smoking weapon and chanting the words of unbinding. With a flaring snap, the weapon's energy died. Arja's eyes, wild with pain and hatred, wheeled toward him, then fluttered upward as his heart quivered heavily within his chest. Solas reached around his brother's heaving shoulder, rested one hand lightly on the last pistol, and began the final chant. Arja rested his own shaking hand upon his brother's before the ritual was done, and they both felt the Relic's force surge upward and away, into the west.

As the pistol's energy fled, the tiny windows along its barrel sheath darkening, Arja sank to the floor, his final breath spent.

Solas crouched beside the body of his brother, breath heaving in a fury that could no longer be contained. With the reliquary items destroyed, he had completed his last duty to the *Etta*. His only remaining obligation now was to the brothers that had fallen before him.

Solas picked up a pair of heavy Colt revolvers from where they lay discarded amidst the wreckage. A snarl of hatred twisted his lips and he launched himself through the sagging doorframe. Each of his hands acted independently, years of training and experience guiding every step, motion, and breath. Each time one of the crude weapons barked out its wrath, a target spun onto the grimy cobbles, thrown down into death.

Even as he stepped past the slumped figure of his dead *mimreg*, Solas did not hesitate in his vengeful hunt. The smoke of burning tenements swirling around him, the *spica* moved gracefully through the destruction like a figure out of legend. Anyone he sensed coming out of the shadows, he ended.

He saw it then: what he had feared all along. The men attacking now bore the slick, sickening aura of the truly corrupted, their flesh glowing with corpse-sweat that only the chosen of the Order could perceive. And behind their eyes crouched an empty, howling nothingness. These were the truly damned; the enemies of the Order and traitors to their own kind. And Solas, *spica*, trained machinist, and gifted scholar, dashed them down into Hell with wild abandon.

When first one hammer and then the other slapped into spent, empty cartridges, he only smiled. The solid clang of the pistols hitting the stones of the road shrouded the lethal hiss of two fighting knives sliding from sheathes strapped along his forearms. The last gleaming of the sun, all but swallowed by the dust and smoke, glittered off the blades as *Spica* Solas of the Holy Order of Man settled into a fighter's crouch, welcoming a warrior's death in battle.

*****

Men shrouded in dark, nondescript cloaks moved toward the blasted frame of the house. Each held a heavy cast-iron rifle in an easy, confident grip. The weapons were crudely formed compared to the reliquary weapons of the mission team, but they were still generations removed from the mundane black powder weapons of the day.

Smoke poured from the tiny garret windows in the second story of the shattered house. The structure would probably not last through the night. There was no uniformity of equipment or attire in the men forming a circle around the grisly scene, but they were all strong and clean, moving with the sure steps of practiced killers.

Lesser men were piled up in the street and on the porch, men who had been less-trusted and less trustworthy than this last wave of soulless mercenaries. A path was pushed through the wreckage and the bodies. Two men, bearing no weapons at all, were escorted to what remained of the front door. A tall man with the air of an officer nodded a greeting.

"We lost over fifty men, sir, but the house, for what it's worth, is yours." He made a gesture with one arm indicating that they should enter. The shorter of the two unarmed men sneered at the mercenary, pushing past him into the smoke-filled house. The taller figure followed silently. The mercenary officer trailed after them both.

The small man made his faltering, clumsy way through the front room, catching one heel on the leg of *Spica* Arja and almost stumbling to his knees into the ankle-deep wreckage. Muttering curses under his breath, he pushed into the back room, peering into the smoke-wreathed gloom at the twisted wreckage that was all that remained of the mission team's reliquary arsenal.

"They destroyed it all." The man spoke in flat tones.

"Of course they did." The taller man's voice was coarse and raspy: the sound of snake scales slithering over hot stone.

The smaller man turned, his bowler hat nearly toppling into the wreckage. "If you knew they were going to destroy it all, why didn't we come at them sooner? Why didn't we start with your most powerful weapons?"

The tall figure stared at the wreckage of the communing engine, its lips twisted in a vicious smile as the guttering flames reflected redly in its dark, fathomless eyes. "The Acropolis has lost one of its most important, trusted mission teams. They are gone without a trace. All of their efforts regarding the president, whatever they might have been, have come to naught."

"It could have ended very differently, you know." The smaller, Mr. Rathbone blustered. "If they had found someone else in the administration, someone not yet privy to your plans and intentions, things could have gone very differently indeed."

The flickering eyes twitched from the ruined equipment to the small man, the flesh at their corners wrinkled in amusement. "How fortunate for us all, then." The eyes flicked to the silent mercenary commander standing in the doorway. The tall figure gave a single, sharp nod.

The men outside did not flinch at the sound of a sudden, startled gasp, nor at the heavy thud of a body falling to the wreckage-strewn floor. When the tall figure emerged, their commander silent alonebehind him, they formed up around the pair and disappeared into the descending gloom.

When the constabulary finally arrived over an hour later, the house was a charred shell, the bodies stripped of anything of value or identification.

There were no witnesses, of course. It was Bloodfield, after all.

Chapter 4

Deep within a tall mountainin the very heart of the Rocky Mountains, lay the enormous fortress known to the Holy Order of Man as the Acropolis. The ruling body of the Order in the Sunset Lands sat around a massive stone table in a chamber that had been known as the Sanctum for longer than the divided tribes had wandered the surrounding plains. In elaborately-carved marble thrones sat the three highest ranking members of the *Etta*: *Sircan* Abner, the war leader of the Order, *Sircan* Nura, keeper of knowledge and temporal mistress of the citadel, and *Sircan* Ignatius, the spiritual leader of the Order and by far the oldest man in the chamber.

Across the oval table from the senior members sat their three lieutenants: the *arcsens* of the *Etta*. Their faces were solemn, their eyes downcast. Both Nura and Abner wore their ornate battle vestments and plate armor in support of those within the Order who believed the end was near. On the other side of the granite table, however, only *Arcsen* Siraj, Champion of the Order and Abner's lieutenant, was arrayed for war, his broad helmet on the table by his gauntleted hand. *Arcsen* Noor, seneschal of the citadel and Nura's lieutenant, and *Arcsen* Ivar, chaplain of the faith and right hand of *Sircan* Ignatius, wore only their ceremonial robes of gray and gold.

The three *arcsens* were younger than their masters, although each was a proven warrior and leader in his own right. Only Ivar shared the pale complexions of the three *sircans*. Siraj's dark skin and flowing black hair had always been a challenge on mission teams working beyond the walls of the Acropolis; not nearly so much so, however, as the African complexion of *Arcsen* Noor.

"I don't understand how they could have been so thoroughly compromised." Siraj's angry voice echoed back from the dark, vaulted ceilings of the great chamber. "There was no hint of danger before this?"

Abner frowned at his lieutenant and raised a single armored finger in disapproval. "Siraj, you were in the

Communing Chamber with the rest of us. You know what we know. The mission team in Washington believed themselves safe. They were making great progress toward vetting President Lincoln as a potential ally."

"*Mimreg* Uri had established contact within the highest levels of the administration. Someone there must have given him away." Noor smoothed the long ends of his mustache with one thoughtful hand. "No *mimreg* would be spotted so easily in the daily attendance of his duties."

"Do not judge so quickly, Noor." Ignatius's face was worn. He had been the last to commune with the mission team before contact was lost. When the links between the mission team's equipment and the Communing Chamber had been severed, the implications had been obvious. Ignatius had taken the loss the hardest. "*Mimreg* Uri was a gifted envoy and a keen warrior. He would not have been easily fooled, even by the Enemy."

"The administration must be rife with Taint, *Sircan*." *Arcsen* Ivar spoke softly into his folded hands. "It was one of the reasons you were so hesitant to consider an alliance in the first place."

"That is true, Ignatius, we have spotted no less than five men and women very close to the president who were thoroughly corrupted." Abner's armored fingers drummed a subdued tattoo on the stone table. "Our desperation to find an ally within the American government may well have blinded us all to a greater danger there."

Ignatius waved that away. "That may be true, but matters little now. Our need remains. We cannot conduct the operations we must without at least tacit collaboration within the ruling powers. Their congress is flush with division and spite, more so since the war began than ever before. There is no hope for us beneath this new dome they raise upon their Capitol Hill." He cast a steely glare at each of the others. "If Abraham Lincoln cannot be trusted, then I do not know what hope we have remaining."

Noor nodded slowly. "We need the support of the Union. With these last battles, there is no realistic hope of the rebellion emerging victorious. Are there other mission teams that can be re-tasked to Washington? There is no more urgent work being done outside our walls."

Ivar grinned at the African commander. "You're just eager for this war to be over. It will be much easier for you to move about when the stain of slavery is behind us."

The big, dark skinned man shrugged. "It is never pleasant to be forced to don chains, even if only in a charade."

"At least there is some hope for you, Noor." Siraj's eyes flashed in his dark face. "I will be forced to resort to kitchens and rail crews for cover for the rest of my life, unless I sorely miss my guess."

Abner and Nura both frowned at their young warriors, but Ignatius smiled. He splayed his hands out before him on the cold stone and returned to the discussion at hand. "I believe Lincoln is our best hope. There is a sense of destiny, of greatness, about him. It would be a shame if we were to allow that potential to be lost; or even worse, to be turned to the purposes of the Enemy."

"What about General Grant?" Ivar's voice was low, his eyes on the table. "A man of singular vision, you have said: a great leader. Grant has shown himself, on several occasions, to be all of that and more."

"No." Nura leaned back in her throne, her face rigid and her tone as hard as stone. "General Grant possesses a fragile soul. If struck, it will fracture, and he will become a monster the likes of which this continent has not seen in over a thousand years. Putting any of our knowledge in that man's hands, we will risk losing half the world."

Noor's eyebrows dropped with incredulity. "Surely you're not suggesting he could—"

"You know the shadow scriptures, *Arcsen*." Ignatius's voice snapped out. "The Dark Council has imposed their evil will upon humanity more than once, using the lever of a single soul as their instrument. Many believe that the loss of Atlantis itself can be traced back to the weaknesses of one magi of the high conclave."

Nura nodded, her hair brushing the burnished ivory of her armored shoulders. "Many would say, and I among them, that working through the deep flaws of a single, well-placed pawn is their favorite technique by far."

"We are agreed, then. We must continue cultivating President Lincoln." Ignatius held each member of the *Etta*'s eyes until they nodded in turn.

Abner's, however, were hard as flint as he nodded his head, and then added, "Lest we forget the massive shadow in the room that you refuse to address, however, *Sircan* Ignatius. The prophecy could well be at work with the destruction of Uri and his men."

The sadness returned to Ignatius's eyes at mention of the *mimreg*. "The tragedy of their passing, and the horrible timing of their deaths, is calamity enough for the Order, Abner, without peering into the dark and dusty shadows of prophecy for further danger."

Nura's eyes were hard as well. "Not this time, Ignatius. These are dark times for all our Order, and as the prophecy says, 'in just such a time will the harbingers arise, and bring with them the howlings of the damned, and the trumps of the End Times.' Across the Earth, we are hard pressed. More and more of our brothers and sisters within the Acropolis don their armor in solidarity with our conviction. We are living under the shadow of the end, and we must be ready to confront the Enemy when they come charging out of the darkness."

"What of the troubling words from Eastern Europe recently?" Siraj folded his armored forearms over his broad chest. "If even half the stories are true, only one who has been touched by the Council could be at the root of them."

"The European citadel is bending all of its efforts to finding the truth of the rumors." Abner assured the rest of the *Etta*. "All the signs they have read, however, still indicate that the fulcrum of the coming events will be here, in the Sunset Lands. Their mission teams have not yet managed to track the tales down to their source, or pin them to a single man. But when they do, he will be taken in and put to the question."

"None of which invalidates our concern over the prophecy here, Ignatius." Nura turned her burning gaze on the old man. "The time for direct action is upon us. We must mobilize our full power and establish order among the people."

Ignatius nodded, slowly, his shoulders slumped. Nura and Abner exchanged a glance, not believing that the old man could finally be giving in. When the old *sircan* looked up again, his eyes were shadowed. "And where, pray tell, do we strike, *Sircan* Nura?"

Nura paused, her smile dying on her lips. "What?"

Ignatius gestured toward the rest of the room with wide, open hands. "You believe we should mobilize our full strength, strike out from the Acropolis and establish order." He shrugged. "Where should we strike?"

The woman's brows came down at a dangerous angle, her nostrils flaring with growing frustration. Before she could speak, however, the old *sircan* continued.

"Do you know who destroyed Uri and his team tonight? Perhaps we should start with them."

"Well, of course not, but—"

"Or maybe we should strike out at the men twisting the president's impressions of the tribes. Do we know who they are?"

"Ignatius, you are—"

"Abner, are your mission teams dispatched regularly to eliminate any of the Tainted that are discovered?" The old man's eyes were pinned, burning with intensity, on Nura's face.

"Of course, Ignatius. But—" A raised hand silenced his hedging tone.

"And has any expense been spared, in treasure, blood, or time, in finding the Tainted, wherever they may hide, that we might eliminate them as soon as is practicable, and safe for the innocent nearby?"

"*Sircan*, you know this to be true." *Arcsen* Siraj's dark eyes were hard as well.

Ignatius turned to look at each of them again in turn, his face open. "Then what, my brothers and sisters, would you have us do beyond these things? Do you wish for us to transport our armories and our forces into the field, where they can be seen, counted by the Enemy, and then defeated in detail? Our best defense now, has it always been, and will always be, is the shadows."

A cold, uncomfortable silence filled the large room. The lights, dim blue gems glowing with a steady, constant gleam, cast hard shadows across the ornate walls and the faces of the *Etta*. Slowly, Abner, Nura, and Siraj lowered their eyes. Noor and Ivar exchanged an uncomfortable look. Ignatius looked at them all, and then nodded sadly.

"Whether we believe in the prophecy or not, we are doing all that we can *now*. We are ready within the strength of our walls. Our *true* strength, however, lies in the hearts of the men and women who will stand with us. We need to reach out to them, secure their support, and see to their instruction before the darkness can turn them from the Creators' light."

Nura and Abner nodded without looking up. "I trust we may send another mission team to Washington? The president is still our best chance at securing the assistance we need." Nura's voice was subdued.

Abner looked up. "And we must continue the drive to fill our ranks. The Enemy is coming, and we will need the numbers to meet it." There was a stubborn edge to his voice, but Ignatius only nodded.

"Absolutely. We will send another team to Washington, and we will have all mission teams maintain the highest level of vigilance while outside the Acropolis, to watch for suitable candidates for the Order."

"Are we done here, then?" Siraj rose, sweeping his crested helm up into the crook of his arm. "We begin another training cycle tomorrow."

Ignatius looked first to Nura and then to Abner, both of whom bowed their heads. He nodded, then, to the three *arcsens*. "The work of the *Etta* this day is concluded. Go about your day's tasks in the light of the Creators."

Each stood to stiff attention and then relaxed as if an invisible pressure had left the room. Noor and Siraj moved toward the main doors out of the Sanctum, while Nura and Abner settled back in their thrones, looking at each other with enigmatic faces. Ignatius rose with a slight grunt and then moved to follow the *arcsens* out into the hall. Ivar moved quickly to help him maneuver out from behind the table.

The old man nodded his thanks, nodded a quiet salute to the remaining *sircans*, and then moved toward the door.

"There is no staving off the darkness, Ignatius." Abner's voice echoed with a hollow ring in the vast room. "Your belief or denial of the prophecies cannot change that. I pray to the Creators that we are ready when it comes."

Ignatius paused, nodded to himself, and then looked over one rounded shoulder. "I know, Abner. Believe me, I know. I have prayed for the self-same thing every night of my life."

Ivar walked proudly beside the *sircan* as they left the room.

Moving down the dim corridor, the blue lights softly glowing to either side, the old man looked up into the troubled face of his *arcsen*. Ivar's face bore a thousand tiny scars from a childhood pox that had nearly taken his life, but beneath that rugged surface, his bones were strong and his eyes steady. Lately, however, there seemed to be doubt there that no amount of discussion or debate could touch.

"What is it that troubles you, my son?" Ignatius patted the young warrior on the arm. "I would help you with this burden, if I could."

Ivar shook his head and gave a thin smile. "It's nothing, *sircan*, honestly; just the darkness of the days."

Ignatius nodded, his lips pursed with this thought. "They are dark, Ivar. But without the darkness, the coming of the dawn would have no meaning, yes?"

Ivar nodded in turn, his eyes thoughtful. But there was still a tautness there as the two men moved deeper into the Acropolis.

*****

The young man let his feet select his path, moving slowly and without direction down tight, winding alleys between the tents and shacks of the railhead settlement. He did not register the crowds that surrounded him, or the merchants and peddlers hawking their wares and services from every side. His mind was still trapped in the shadowy tent. The oily sheen of the preacher's skin, the hollow darkness behind his eyes . . . it was the stuff of nightmares. And not least because he had seen such things before.

Varro remembered the dark days before the final riots back home. The rising tension had been marked, or maybe even caused by, a sweeping change in the leadership of many of the oldest gangs. The men and women who had risen to power, usually over the bodies of their former leaders, had almost all been poorly-regarded before their elevation. They had taken over their gangs in a flood of blood and violence, and then the Five Points had gone straight to Hell.

He had thought little of it then, but they had all shared that same corpse-sweat sheen. Every one of them had looked out at the burning world through dark and shadowed eyes.

Varro had no idea what it meant. He had, on more than one occasion, been accused of having an over-active imagination while growing up. There was every chance he was misremembering these details now. That had been a violent, turbulent time in the Points, and he knew his mind was not working at its best now, with his life tossed to the wind again, and no clear path forward.

He was trying to shake off the shadows and the chill, when he came to the sudden awareness that his feet had stopped their forward progress. A mean-looking kid stood in his path, hands hitched behind worn holsters. A snide grin stretched across a pale, gaunt face shadowed by a broad-brimmed hat. Sparse, dark stubble clung to the man's chin and jawline.

Varro came up short, nearly striking the younger man, and looked to the side, stepping away with an apologetic nod. The gunslinger, his grin broadening, mirrored the move, keeping himself directly in Varro's path.

"You plannin' on takin' up the whole street, shave tail?" The voice was higher than Varro had expected, and he realized that the kid was even younger than he had first believed; not too far out of his mid-teens, in fact: a couple years younger than Varro himself.

He cleared his throat, looking again from side to side, and then shrugged. "No. Sorry." He tried to slide sideways again, and again the kid intercepted him.

"Boy, you got this whole shoddy burg to traipse through, you gotta keep bumpin' into me?" He had a home-rolled cigarette hanging from one corner of his mouth. He switched it to the other side, his grin never wavering.

Varro saw then that the kid was not alone, two older men standing just behind him. One seemed amused by the exchange, leaning off to the side to spit a stream of tobacco juice against the side of a nearby tent. The other man, the oldest of the three although still hardly out of his twenties, looked frustrated and bored. Varro noticed that the clothing of all three incorporated the remnants of tattered, old uniforms. He may have fled the Union draft, but he recognized the color of the uniforms before him, despite the bleaching of the sun and a layer of trail dust.

"Look, I'm not after any trouble, I—" He raised both his hands in what he hoped was a universal gesture of good will and nonaggression. The kid in the Confederate uniform followed him.

"You might not a' been lookin' for it, Billy Yank, but it's done come an' found you, an' no mistake." The kid's hands moved slightly, fingers coming around to grasp the grips of his pistols.

Varro stared into the kid's eyes, trying to find some way out of this confrontation without violence. He had faced down armed men before, and he knew he could do it again. He just was not sure he wanted to pay the price. But there was something different about this kid; something about his eyes. They weren't as shadowed as the preacher's, but they looked like they were well on their way.

"Please," Varro began again, keeping his hands steady despite the fear that had started to churn below his heart. Not fear of this kid with his tattered uniform and swaggering ways, but fear of himself, of what he was capable of, and what he had been only a short while ago. "Please," he repeated. "I just want to go my own way."

The kid moved in quickly, one of his hands rising from its weapon to point a finger into Varro's face. The moment seemed to freeze in time, and Varro saw every detail with rigid clarity. The tanned skin of the kid's hands, the dirt beneath the nail thrust toward his left eye, the dark glitter of the kid's stare. "You ain't got no idea where you are, Yank." The kid was snarling now. "Ain't no blue-bellies around hereabouts to save your sorry hide. And ain't no law here now neither, not on the edge of DiabloCanyon. I end you here and now, ain't nobody gonna care."

The older man jerked on the kid's shoulder. "Jesse, enough playin' around. We gotta get back to the cap'n, 'r he's gonna be riled up but good."

The other man standing behind the kid spit again, and then grinned his own, brown-stained smile. "Don't look like this mudsill's worth the powder anyways, Jesse."

The young kid gave Varro a slow up and down, then shook his head, his grin returning. "Frank, you ain't never up for no fun." He took his cigarette between one tanned thumb and index finger, and spit a fleck of tobacco into the dust. He grinned again. "Keep to your own side of the trail, shave tail. I see so much as your shadow cross my path again, my brother ain't gonna save you."

Before Varro could respond, the trio swept past him. The kid chuckled an evil little laugh, the younger of his companions joining in. The older man only gave him a blank stare as he walked by.

The gang fighter from New York stood still, jostled as the traffic around him resumed its normal, hurried pace. When he finally twisted to look behind him, the three men had been swallowed by the crowd. Varro shook his head. Soza had been right: he could not stay in Diablo Canyon.

Varro continued walking. The train would not be leaving for another couple of hours. He ducked beneath a placard declaring the dusty tent beyond it a saloon, and had another drink, trying to settle his nerves and kill a bit of time. His roll of cash was feeling lighter and lighter, and if he was going to need to set himself up in Kansas City for a while, he was going to need every dime.

The whisky he ordered turned out to be three fingers of tepid cat piss, which made nursing it all the easier. Even sipping at the glacial pace dictated by the vile potion, he was at the bottom of the glass much sooner than he would have liked. Neither his stomach, his tongue, nor his wallet would allow for a second, so under the baleful eye of the man tending the makeshift bar, he pushed out of the tent and back into the late afternoon shadows, looking both ways before jumping back into the flow of traffic.

Again, Varro allowed his feet to do the navigating as his mind brooded on his current situation, his lack of options, and the shadows of his past. Had things really been that bad back in the Points? After the riots had settled down, there would have been plenty of opportunities to start his own gang, with most of the old ones ground into the mud or conscripted. But even the thought twisted his stomach. Like a sharp spike into the back of his head, he remembered all the blood, the killing, and the hopelessness that had driven him from his childhood home. His gut churned at the memory of seeing the family's tenement on fire.

He was never going back to New York. They said anyone could make himself over out here in the territories. And with the draft on, it was the best place for a man running from his own violent past, with no interest in opening up that part of his soul again.

Around Varro, the shadows lengthened and the buff canvas of the tents began to glow like giant lamps as candles and lanterns were lit within. The shouts and laughter got even louder, as if rising to defy the darkness.

One particularly piercing laugh snapped him out of his dark thoughts. He stopped, looking from side to side, trying to decide where his wandering mind had led him. To one side was a broad, low wall made of bleached and faded wood; either a fence or the back wall of shack. A series of tents made a solid wall to the other side, each dark and quiet even as the camp came to life around him. Ahead of him, stretching across the narrow street, was another tent, closing off the path and forming a dead end. A wagon sat against this last one, its tongue resting in the dust. One iron-rimmed tire leaned drunkenly against the wagon bed while a rain barrel held its place. A large hammer stood on its rusting iron head nearby.

Varro stood still. The little blind alley seemed completely cut off from the rest of the rowdy settlement. The voices of revelers were loud but distant. The sudden shriek of the train's whistle echoed through the labyrinth of tents and hovels, and with a chill, Varro realized he could not tell where it had come from. He knew what the whistle meant, though; the train was preparing to leave.

He spun about, taking several steps back the way he had come, when he pulled up short. A tall, gaunt figure stood in the mouth of the dead end, its long coat blowing in the fitful breeze that plucked at the surrounding tents and pulled at the figure's pale, lank hair. A strange smile tugged at the tight flesh of the figure's cheeks but came nowhere near touching its cold, dark eyes.

The preacher had found him.

"Fancy runnin' into you again, son." The voice was still thin, scratching within Varro's ears.

Looking quickly to either side, he confirmed what he already knew: there was no way out except past the tall figure in the dark coat.

"You look worried, son." The preacher took a step toward him, gloved hands held out, palms down, in a calming gesture. "Nothin' to worry about. I was just out perambulatin'. But perhaps this happy little bit o' serendipity might be brought to both our mutual advancements, do you think?"

The cadence of the words was numbing, a low rumbling deep in the pit of his stomach. Or was that the engine of the locomotive, building up steam for its return to Kansas City?

"Look, sir, I don't mean any disrespect." Varro moved to the side of the alley, his shoulder brushing against the desiccated wood of the shanty wall. "I've got a train to catch, though. I hope you don't mind me running—"

"Son, don't mistake my kindness for foolishness." The preacher moved forward again, his mouth straightening into a stark, thin line. "We're goin' to have some words now, before you head on out of town."

Varro could feel the old impulses rising. They had been stirred by the young tough in the street earlier, but now the quickening of the blood, the rising hairs on the back of his neck, all felt much more real. This man was a threat; the kind of threat Varro had learned to deal with back in New York many years ago.

"Sir," he forced his voice into a steady calmness. "I think there may have been a misunderstanding, and if I've given offense, I apologize." He began to inch along the wall, his hands up in a warding pose. "But I'll be leaving this alley now, and I'd rather it be without any trouble."

The word seemed to give the preacher pause, and he lowered his hands, his head rearing back, tilting off-center as if trying to puzzle something out.

"Son, we just need to have a quick chat is all. No need for *trouble*." But the smile that returned to the lean face was predatory, and the cold, empty eyes seemed to draw the fading light into their limitless depths.

Varro paused, his eyes flicking around the alley. They were alone. He was only a single man, no matter how intimidating his manner. There was nothing here for the gang fighter to fear. He was sad to think how well he knew that to be true. This man was no match for him. He nodded, reluctantly, for the preacher to continue.

"Alrighty then." The smile lost a little of its edge, although the eyes were still burning with black fire. "See, son, I saw something in you back in that tent. Something I think you know is there. Something I think could see you to a very nice position out here on the edge of nothing."

As he spoke, the reverend relaxed, easing his shoulder up against the weathered boards. "You see, I happen to be acquainted with a very special man who can make excellent use of a person with your . . . well, shall we say, your natural proclivities?"

"I don't know what you're talking about." Varro straightened, his face turning hard at the old man's words.

"Oh, I think you do. But we'll leave that for later." The preacher waved the objection away. "You see, my friend happens to be building something very special out here on the edge of civilization. We've laid the groundwork for a new settlement just up the Little Colorado aways. It's goin' to be a beacon in the night when we finish; usher in a whole new age of prosperity an' civilization out past the territories."

"I'm heading back east, I'm not—"

"Enough with the nonsense, boy." Varro's head jerked back as if he had been slapped. "You and me both know you ain't returnin' home. We both know you ain't got no home to return to." One clawed hand pointed at Varro's arm, where the tail end of his tattoo was just visible. "The Swamp Angels are no more, son. You've got nowhere to go but west."

Varro took a step back. There was no way some strange tent revivalist in the territories could have known about a two-bit New York gang like the Swamp Angels. Even so . . .

The train's whistle sounded again, this time a long, plaintive wail.

"Look, mister, I don't know who you are, but I have to go. I can't stay here—"

The preacher's arm shot out like a spring-loaded trap and his palm slapped into the splintery boards of the wall. "You deaf, son?" The voice, still thin and troubling, was now hollow, like the wind blowing through an abandoned cemetery. "Maybe you don't quite understand what's happenin' here."

Varro's back straightened, his face twisting at the man's tone. Back in the Points, folks had known not to lecture Giovanni Varro. He took a step forward, his fists curling into hammers of calloused flesh: all the weapons he'd ever needed against a lone man in his life. Then his burning gaze met the cold, dark eyes of the preacher, and he froze.

The figure in the mouth of the alley smiled, and this time it was an expression of victory. "You see something in my eyes, don't you son." It was a statement, not a question. "Well, I see something in yours as well." The dark eyes tightened. "You only leave this alley one of two ways." He stood taller and seemed to draw strength from the lengthening shadows. "You either walk out of here beside me, or they come drag you out in the morning."

Varro could feel his knuckles popping as the muscles of his fists spasmed with anger. He took another step toward the tall figure, and then stopped. Four men entered the alley behind the preacher, brandishing stout cudgels and canes. He paused for a moment, watching the newcomers warily, when he caught a blur of motion out of the corner of his eye. The preacher's arm caught him on the right cheek in a vicious backhand that had far more force behind it than it should have. He went spinning through the air to crash heavily into the wagon. The vehicle was pushed sideways against the nearby tent, tottering on its makeshift support, and Varro fell to his knees, his head ringing and his cheek on fire.

Through the roaring in his ears, he could just make out the preacher's next words. "It's a shame, son. Tolchico could have used a killer like you."

It was the word *killer* that did it, of course. A red flood of rage burst behind Varro's eyes, and he launched himself out of his crouch and toward the alley's mouth. Everything he had struggled to control was unleashed; nothing of the reserved young man who had journeyed so far remained.

The preacher stepped back as his four thugs moved toward what they had thought was helpless prey. At the incoherent roar, they all stopped. The preacher tilted his head again, this time in amused vindication.

Varro ducked the first clumsy swing, moving inside the closest man's reach, and began to drive him backward with a series of terrible uppercuts to the gut that carried all the power of his heavy body behind them. Each blow raised the attacker onto the balls of his feet, breath hissing past clenched teeth. One last solid shot to the jaw sent the man tumbling backward into the dust. As his foe fell, Varro grabbed the gnarled stick he had been wielding and swung around to face the remaining three.

Two sticks were sailing in from opposite sides, and with two quick motions Varro blocked them both. Before the third man could adjust, the berserk gang fighter was upon him, raining blows down at his head and shoulders. The cudgel snapped in from either side, so fast the thug could barely follow. His own cane, much thinner and more elegant, stopped the first strikes before snapping with a sound that echoed off the soft tent walls like a pistol shot. The man's eyes widened in fearful disbelief moments before the cudgel came crashing down onto his forehead. Another sharp sound snapped through the darkness, and the man sank into the dust, his crossed eyes filling with blood.

Varro's forearms were straight, his shoulder hunched, as he followed through on that last blow. The two remaining attackers did not hesitate, but brought their own weapons down sharply on the New York boy's back. Varro barely grunted as he looked back at the tough on his left while his right arm, seemingly of its own accord, spun his weapon out and to the right. With a startled cry, the man there flinched away, his cane falling to the ground as his hand was crushed by the blurring stick.

Varro smiled into the eyes of the last man standing. The man's own eyes began to waver as certainty collapsed, giving way to a very mortal doubt. These were not empty, shadowed eyes like the preacher's, but Varro hardly cared. He spun his cudgel up into a guard position, drops of blood arching off into the shadows. His smile was an untamed, feral thing that fed hungrily on the man's fear.

The attacker jabbed at Varro's face, trying to draw the stick away from its shielding position. His movements were hesitant and unsure, but they gained a sudden burst of energy as something flickered in his eyes. That flicker gave Varro a moment's warning, but it was not enough. Behind him, the man who had lost his cane had retrieved it, not as injured as Varro believed. He came leaping back into the fight, bringing the cane down savagely across both of the New Yorker's forearms with a vicious crack. At the same time, abandoning subtlety, the man before him bulled directly into his chest, thrusting him deeper into the alley with his knotted stick.

Varro's weapon fell away. His arms windmilled wildly as he hurtled backward, again fetching up against the wagon. This time he fell to the dirt, his back to the detached wheel, which canted awkwardly behind him. One hand groped out blindly, stiff with pain, and his fingers closed around the haft of the heavy sledge.

The preacher's two remaining brutes closed in, both thirsty for payback and eager for blood. Neither of them saw the hammer that Varro held behind his leg as he uncurled back up to his full, impressive height.

"You hayseeds just about done playing around?" The voice was hardly recognizable as his own and his smile widened, his mouth salty with his own blood.

The thug Varro had disarmed lunged in first, perhaps feeling he had something to prove. All he ended up proving was his own mortality, as the heavy hammer came sweeping up and then down onto the crown of his head. The weight sank into his skull with a meaty crunch and the man's limp body dropped to the dirt.

The remaining tough, a man who had yet to feel Varro's wrath, halted his advance, eyeing the hammer nervously. Blood and bits of hair stuck to the broad face of the tool, glistening in the last gleams of sunset. An answering gleam sparked in Varro's savage eyes.

In the end, the man decided whatever recompense the preacher was offering was not enough. He dropped his weapon, put up his hands, and began to inch back toward the alley mouth, muttering apologetic noises as he moved away.

Varro's smile widened, and he stalked forward, the hammer held across his body in a two-handed grip.

"Dance ain't over, highbinder." The man stumbled, falling to one knee and raising his arms over his head, his voice rising to a plaintive whine.

A whine that cut off abruptly with a wet crunch.

Varro stood in the suddenly silent alley, his breath coming in heaving gasps, and the heavy hammer fell from nerveless fingers. He spun in place, his dull eyes taking in the three bodies sprawled at his feet. The first man he had attacked was gone. That was a small blessing.

From the mouth of the alley behind Varro, the preacher's shrill, empty tone reached out with cold amusement. "What a waste."

Varro stopped. Was the preacher referring to his own hatchet men? His shoulder blades crawled as his animal instincts screamed out a warning. He began to turn back toward the man. Too late.

A heavy pistol barked thunder, and Varro felt as if his own hammer had struck him high in the back, shoving him forward into the bloody dirt.

Varro's breath rushed in his ears, a harsh, broken wheezing that rattled, unfelt, in his throat. The crunch of a boot coming down into the dirt by his ear sounded like an avalanche dropping down to bury him. The preacher's voice, fading in and out as if heard over a high wind, reached down into the dark place that threatened to engulf him.

"What a complete waste of good material." He heard the distinctive snap of the hammer being drawn back on a heavy revolver and tried to close his eyes. They would not respond.

A calm acceptance swept over him as he lay anticipating the killing blow. It was nothing less than he deserved after everything he had done. These three men were only the latest, and hardly a drop in the bucket. A cold, lonely death was exactly what he had earned. He knew it with more certainty than he had known anything in many, many years.

His vision was fading, and the sounds of the alley were farther and farther away. When an explosion of bright white light lit up the alley, he knew it was the shot that would kill him. Except that his thoughts continued, the pain spreading its cold fingers through his body, and there was no sensation of impact as there had been with the first shot. There was only the eye-searing intensity of cold white light.

Another bolt slapped through the air over his head, blue-white lightning that snapped down the alley, tendrils of energy arcing off to ground into tent poles, the wagon's iron-rimmed wheels, and bits of metal on the bodies around him.

"Damn you chiselin' gospel sharps!" Even to Varro's fading sensibilities, the preacher's voice sounded more shrill. "Not now!"

The heavy concussions of the preacher's pistol hammered above Varro, but they seemed to be crashing over him, not down into his helpless body. Three more cerulean bolts snapped through the alley, their cracking passage dull over the maddened cries of the preacher.

The last bolt ended with a sickening smack that also ended the preacher's cries. Something heavy hit the dirt beside Varro, and the sickly-sweet stink of charred flesh wafted over him.

Careful footsteps moved toward him as he hovered between the last lingering lights of sunset and a far more profound darkness. A hooded shape crouched over him, but he could not turn his head to look.

"That was some fancy work, no?" The voice was soft and close.

"Better than many. Not good enough, though." The response came from farther away. "Come on. We have to get clear."

"Why? There's no law hereabouts. Not yet. Besides, don't you think we owe him something?"

Although he could make out the words, Varro was having a harder and harder time holding onto their meaning.

"What, do you think we should bring him with us?" The more distant voice sounded skeptical.

"Well, that was pretty impressive—"

"And the preacher was interested in him. It doesn't necessarily follow that we should be, too. Might be the old goat did us a kindness before you took him down."

Far, far away, something whistled like a lost, wailing soul.

"I don't know." The close voice sounded hollow now, drifting in and out of clarity. "Something about him . . ."

An unreasoning fear gripped Varro. He deserved to die. He wanted to die. They had to let him die . . .

Then there was only darkness.

Chapter 5

Pain speared directly into his numb brain and he coughed with animal anguish, trying to turn away from the burning heat. His throat felt raw, his lips loose and rubbery as he tried to cry out, and a cough became a spasm of painful grunts as his lungs seized up. A blazing light erupted between his gummy eyelids. All of his other pains faded to nothingness as an explosion of agony tore through his back when he tried to turn away from the light. His entire body shook with the force of the agony.

The pain, burning in his eyes, seizing up his lungs, and searing down his back, drove his cringing mind back into the darkness. Cold, shadow-filled emptiness rose up to swallow him, drawing him downward into a chaotic swirl of images and impressions that barely registered against the numb, raw backdrop of pain.

The darkness was cool. It promised relief from the physical torment, at least; and so he surrendered to it, floating down into the shadows, and lost the light.

As everything faded into darkness he thought he could hear a calm, earnest voice calling out to him. For reasons he did not remember, he fled faster from that voice than he had fled from the pain.

*****

Varro came slowly to himself, a series of labored, shallow breaths pushing him back into his pain-wracked body and the shadows around him.

With agonizing slowness, the darkness resolved itself into a neat, tidy room. Slatted walls, their colors lost in the shadows, rose up around him. He was lying on his chest on a soft bed, elbows tucked in at his sides. Out of the corner of his eye he could just make out a small table holding a pitcher, a pan, and a small pile of cloths. He tried to take a deeper breath and began coughing in a convulsive, clenching series of hacks that rattled wetly in his tight chest. His back blossomed with agony, and amidst the shuddering coughs, he was horrified to hear a pathetic whimper escape his parched lips.

Behind him, out of his line of view, a door opened and footsteps approached. He could barely here them over his pain. He was shaking, caught between the animal urge to curl up around the pain in his lungs and a compulsion to straighten his spine to relieve the burning pain in his back. He tried to hold his gasping breaths to shallow sips of air, but his whole body was tight with anticipation of the next convulsive outburst.

"Sorry! I'm sorry!" The voice seemed young, probably a little younger than Varro himself, but deep. A shadow in the gloom moved quickly up to the bed and dipped one of the cloths in the bowl, wringing out excess water and wiping sweat from his brow. "I fell asleep. I was sure you wouldn't be waking up so soon. Not after . . ."

Varro groped for meaning among the apologetic words. Where was he? How had he gotten here? Who was this apologetic kid wiping his forehead as if they were brothers? He could remember nothing. Was this one of the mercy clinics outside of the Points? The riots . . . He remembered the riots. He remembered the Swamp Angels emerging from the sewers on the docks, moving back toward the Points, meeting up with the Bowery Boys and the White Hand Gang in open battle . . . he remembered the slanted tenement, the burning . . . the bodies.

He heard a banshee wail, as if a scream or a whistle from far off. The boy hovering over him did not react, and he slowly forced himself to the conclusion that the sound had been in his head.

He tried again to ask his questions. Taking a shallow breath, he grimaced with anticipation. His throat burned as he tried to push himself up, and he immediately collapsed to the bed as the coughs wracked his body.

"Easy, easy!" The young man soothed. "You've been down for a good long while. You can't just be jumping out of bed." He reached over, wet the cloth again, and draped it over Varro's back. The young bruiser from New York turned to look at his strange benefactor, but in the dark he could make out nothing more than a silhouette against some dim light coming through a door behind him.

"Oh, you probably want to see!" The voice sounded surprised and disappointed in itself at the same time. He pushed off the bed and moved out through the door, bringing a small hooded lantern back in and setting it on the table.

Varro cringed a bit from the stabbing pain even this soft light caused. How long had he been down? He felt like he had not opened his eyes in a year. His joints felt stiff and brittle. He took a moment to survey the room in the light. The clapboard walls were painted a neutral white. The room lacked any serious decoration, but the craftsmanship of its construction was excellent, with small flourishes that were adornments in and of themselves.

In addition to the bed and the small table, there was a tall dresser against one wall and a chair sitting in the corner. The chair had some clothes draped over it; his pants, he could see; and his dark leather coat. Except that the back of the coat looked darkerthan the rest, for some reason. There was a lighter patch in the center of the stain, and his mind cringed away from the sight. He also noticed that his shirt was missing. He looked up at his caretaker next. He had been right. The boy was roughly his own age, perhaps a little younger. His skin looked dark, darker than anyone from the Five Points, anyway. His face looked soft, but contained within it the proud lines of the few natives he had seen since he arrived in the territories. Natives? Again, Varro struggled to spin around and sit up, his entire body flaring with agony as he fell back to the sweat-drenched sheets with a grunt. He looked up again and muttered through gritted teeth. "Where am I?"

The boy smiled at him, his eyes crinkling innocently at the corners. "You're safe! You were found at the railhead down by DiabloCanyon." The eyes turned serious. "You were wounded. Shot in the back." He gestured to the pile of cloths, and Varro could see that many of them were dark with blood. "Do you remember any of that?"

Varro shook his head once, feeling the muscles twinge with the movement.

The boy nodded. "Well, that makes sense, actually. You were almost gone when they brought you in. Most thought you were headed down the river for sure. But you hung in there. You don't remember at all how you got to the railhead?"

Varro shook his head again, this time more gently, and eased himself back toward the thin pillow. The railhead sounded familiar, now that the boy had mentioned it, but the more he fixed his mind upon the concept, the more slippery it became.

He gritted his teeth again, braced himself, and growled out, "How long?"

The boy looked a little nervous. His eyes shifted back to the door, down at his lap, and then toward Varro again. He shrugged, his mouth quirking to one side, and then muttered. "It's been a while."

The vague answer sent another chill down Varro's back, although he could not say why.

"How long have I been here?" He found it hard to project intimidation while lying on his stomach in a strange room, but he felt the frustration driving the pain away, and knew that in a moment he would be on his feet and damn the consequences.

The other man shrugged, failing to meet his eyes. "It's been a while. You were hurt really badly. The gunshot had penetrated your lung, you had broken bones in your cheek and one of your arms, and you had lost a lot of blood. You've been out of it for some time."

Varro's teeth ground together. "Why can't you tell me how long I've been here?"

The boy shook his head. "It's late. Everyone else is asleep. I'm sure you'll learn more in the morning. Do you need some water? I can get you some water."

Varro settled his sore cheek on the cool cotton of the pillow. The strength and anger were draining out of him even as he tried to grasp at them in frustration. He felt his eyelids growing heavy. But his throat throbbed as if in response to the boy's words, and he nodded weakly, his eyes sinking shut.

"Water . . ."

He heard a clinking of stoneware that made his throat ache even more. After negotiating the awkward process of getting water into his parched mouth, Varro sank back to the pillow. He tried to hold onto his desperation even as it slid away. There were things he needed to know. Something he knew he needed to do. He tried to claw at these things, but against the cool softness of the pillow they began to drift away despite his silent cries.

It all faded into the soft blackness around him.

*****

Varro awoke to the soothing feeling of a soft breeze blowing across his back. The small, bright room was warm with sunlight flooding in through an open window. The breeze kept the curtains floating back and forth into the light, throwing shifting shadows across his face.

He struggled to raise himself up on his elbows, working through the twinges of pain shooting through his arching back. He kept his breathing slow and steady, managing to keep the coughing down to a few short, soft barks. It was enough, however, to alert his benefactor, and a door behind him creaked open, footsteps approaching the bed.

"Awake again?" It was the same young-but-deep voice, and Varro craned his head to the side to look up at the tall young man standing beside the bed. He was wearing a loose black shirt and tan canvas pants. His black hair was cropped short, but gathered into a tail at the back of his neck. His round face smiled openly, and again Varro thought of native faces he could not even remember seeing.

"So, you're awake?" The boy asked again.

"Hmm?" Varro shook his head. "Ah, yeah. I figure."

A lingering sense of anger and resentment caught in his throat. There were things he wanted to know; questions he had asked that wanted for answers. But the emotions were vague, as if they belonged to another person, or another time in his life. He came back to his senses as the boy dragged the room's sole chair across the wooden floor to set it beside the bed.

"So, I know you have questions," his smile was open and happy, with an eagerness that seemed somehow out of place.

Varro looked at him from the corner of his eye, and then nodded warily. He tried to shift himself up onto his side, and the boy jumped up to help, moving the pillow around to prop him up and protect his back. When his patient was situated, the boy nodded and returned to his chair.

"Firstly, you've been here for just over a week." The boy's eyes were serious, but he held them steady even as Varro's own widened in disbelief.

"Over a week?" He twisted his back from side to side, testing the wound. It still flared sorely, but the pain was dull and distant.

The boy nodded again. "Nine days, actually. And they said it took them over two days to get you here from the railhead, after they did their best to patch you up where they found you. So it's been about eleven days since you took that bullet." There was an enthusiasm in his tone that Varro found just a little offensive, but he decided to let it go for now.

"You said 'they'. Who brought me here—" Before he finished that question another, perhaps more important, rose to mind. "Where am I?"

The boy took a deep breath, looked out the window for a moment, then turned back to Varro. "You're in a town called Sacred Lake. It's a ways south of the railhead where you were shot. You were brought here by a small group of folks who had ventured down to see what all the fuss was about." The words were clear and matter-of-fact, and the boy's eyes never wavered as he spoke. Yet, for some reason Varro was sure he was not hearing everything.

"Sacred Lake." He said the words slowly, tasting them. He shrugged carefully. "Never heard of it."

"It's a small settlement. We're nothing fancy. Just some farmers, a blacksmith, a cooper and the like, trying to keep out of the troubles and mind our own business." This time his eyes flicked away from Varro's. The feeling that there was more here than it seemed came back even stronger.

"Minding your own business by sending men up to the railhead to check it out?" Knowing as little as he did, only a vague skepticism scratched at the back of his mind each time the other boy spoke.

"Well, if you had new neighbors moving in, and they seemed like maybe they were the rowdy sort, you'd want to check in on them, no?" The boy sat up straighter in the chair.

"We're not looking for trouble, and we want to keep to ourselves, but we're not about to let anyone cause undue commotion around here, either."

Varro nodded, his lips turned down in a sour frown. "So, your men went up to check the railhead, and just happened to . . . find me . . . there?" The specifics of the events that ended with him lying in an alley bleeding into the dust were still hazy, floating farther into the back of his mind each time he tried to grasp them. He looked back up at the boy. Something in his chest shifted and he gave in to the fear whispering at the back of his mind.

"What happened to me?" His voice was soft.

The boy frowned. When he spoke, his words were quick and pointed. "You don't remember what happened?"

Varro eased himself down onto one elbow. His back was sore, the pain sharpening, and he could feel his mind starting to wander again. His eyelids were growing more and more heavy.

Seeing his patient fade back into the sheets, the boy jumped up and helped Varro down. "Don't worry. I'm sure it'll come back to you." He held a cup of water for Varro to sip and then stepped back from the bed. "You should really get more rest. I'll come back up around supper time, maybe you'll be hungry?"

Varro's stomach grumbled at the mention of food, and he wondered how they had sustained him if he had truly been unconscious for so long. The answers all seemed less urgent, however, and the cotton was cool and soft against his cheeks. He was asleep before the door closed behind him.

*****

Varro sat up in the bed, several pillows piled behind him to protect his back from the hard wood of the headboard, and wolfed down a heel of bread soaked in chicken gravy. He felt like he had not eaten in forever . . . which was closer to the truth than it had ever likely been before.

His benefactor sat beside the bed, his smile open and honest again. He handed Varro the cup of cool water, and the gang fighter took a quick sip before diving back into the bread and chicken.

"Looks like your appetite's come back." The boy said with a smile. "Which is good. Not sure how much longer I was going to able to stand dribbling sugar water onto your cracked lips."

Varro looked darkly at him, but then shook his head. "Sounds awful." His words were muffled by a mouthful of chicken.

The boy shrugged with a grin. "It could have been worse." At a questioning look from Varro, his grin grew wider. "Since you showed up, I haven't had to muck out the stalls once!"

Varro mopped up the last of the gravy with the remnant of his bread and tossed it back. Nothing, he was sure, had ever tasted that good before.

"Thank you . . ." He stopped, suddenly realizing that he did not even know the other man's name.

His hesitation was met with a wide smile and a nod. "It was bound to happen sooner or later. I'm Jomei."

The strange name hung in the air for a moment, then Varro nodded, wiped his hand on the blanket that covered his thigh, and held it out. "My name's Giovanni Varro."

Jomei's handshake was firm, the fingers hard and calloused. Varro knew his own hand was tough as well. He also knew he had probably come by that toughness through a far less honest path than this earnest kid. He looked down at his hand, curled in his lap. He was wearing a plain, light blue shirt that hung loose over his frame. It had been a long time since he had worn clothing too big for him. The strange sensation was almost enough to distract him from his dark thoughts.

He looked again around the bare room. He had many questions, and he cleared his throat, tried to look nonchalant, and asked, without looking up at Jomei, "So, where's everyone else?" He looked up with what he hoped was an open smile, one hand raised in a conciliatory gesture. "Not that you're not a swell companion, and all. But, isn't there anyone else around here that might have wanted to pop in and check out the new arrival?"

Jomei looked mildly offended. "I reached my majority over a year ago, and was initiated—"

The response shut off abruptly, and again something niggled at the back of Varro's mind. He waved his hand from side to side, looking quickly away. "I didn't mean any offense. Honest. I meant, aren't there older folks around here? Why's it just been you and me?"

Jomei frowned, but responded quickly enough. "The elders have looked in on you from time to time. Old Fosh, the closet thing we have to a doctor, has been in regularly to check on you. But I was assigned to keep watch, and make sure you recovered enough to head back when you're ready."

The prospect of returning to the railhead was hardly comforting. Everything that had happened there was still vague, still elusive. It was no place from which he could derive any sort of comfort. But then, with his returned memories of the Five Points and what had happened to his family, comfort would be in short supply anywhere he went.

"Are you?" Jomei looked slightly uncomfortable asking, and Varro was too lost in his thoughts to understand the question. When he looked apologetically blank, the other young man expanded the question. "Are you ready to move on?"

Varro looked up at his benefactor for a moment, and then out the window in front of the bed. He twisted his shoulders to one side, then the other. The range of motion was limited by tight jabs of pain both times. He looked sideways at Jomei. "I figure I can make my way, if I've overstayed my welcome . . ."

Jomei looked relieved, his shoulders slumping. "No! There's no need for you to head out yet. You can stay as long as you like. In fact, Fosh says you should probably stay for another week at least."

Varro looked back out the window. All he could see was sky, which led him to believe he was in an upper floor, or on a tall hill. "Another week in this bed?In this room?"

And again, Jomei's face closed down. "Well, of course not. When you're feeling a little better . . ."

Varro nodded. There were things that Jomei could not, or would not, talk about. And that meant there were things that Varro wanted, or more likely needed, to know.

"Tomorrow." The word was sharp, and dropped into the awkward silence like a gunshot.

"Tomorrow?" Jomei's response was slow, his open smile fading.

"Tomorrow, after breakfast, I want to see if I can get up. Maybe see a little bit of your town." His smile had an edge to it. "I'm feeling better already."

"Alright . . ." Jomei hesitated. "If you think you'll be up to it."

*****

There was not much light. Walls rose up on either side as he moved down the narrow way. Earth crunched under the heavy soles of his boots. The air was hot and dry. The sun, beating down from somewhere overhead, was hidden by the looming shapes leaning in around him. There was no one nearby. He walked softly. He could not have explained why, but he knew that he did not want to attract attention.

As the path opened up into a wider street ahead of him, he saw the way blocked by a tall, gaunt figure facing away from him. The still figure wore a loose dark coat that hung limp and stiff in the dead air. A wide-brimmed hat hid the man's head from view, streamers of lank hair hanging down from underneath.

Something about the figure caught at the back of his mind. A familiarity, or a fear, settled there but refused to come into the light. He knew the figure. He could not say how, or from where, but he knew him. He continued moving forward, slowing his gait and looking around for anything that could be used as a weapon. Somehow, he knew he would need a weapon.

His eyes alit upon a long, heavy hammer set against one wall. There were dark stains on the broad metal head, with clumps of matter giving the hammer's face a rough, textured appearance. As he reached for it, something in his mind screamed at him to leave it alone. He stood, frozen in a half crouch, his hand outstretched for the tool, when the figure turned around.

Its face was pale, its features skeletal. From within the shadow of the hat's brim, the eyes burned with a dark fire that mocked him. The flesh around those eyes glistened wetly, as if the man was sweating in the heat. The thin lips stretched into a pleased, hungry smile.

"What a waste . . ."

*****

Varro's body tried to shoot upright, but was thrown back down against the bed by the pain in his back. He grunted, landing on his side against the sweat-damp sheets. He curled tightly, recent experience driving him to focus all of his efforts on his breathing, despite the pain. After only a few moments, and a single cough, he opened his eyes. It was dim, the first glimmers of a red dawn streaming in through the window. But his mind was far from this mysterious little room.

He remembered.

He remembered the railhead, he remembered Diablo Canyon and the Confederate bullyboys. He remembered fighting in the alleyway, blood and death in the dust.

He remembered the preacher.

With a shaking hand, Varro reached out to the side table and grasped the cool stoneware cup. The water within was tepid, but it felt like it had flowed straight from Heaven as he craned his neck back and poured it past parched lips. Replacing the cup, he turned himself gingerly around so that he was sitting up, and pushed back until he rested against the headboard.

It was early, but he had no way of telling how early. Jomei could come in any moment, or it could be more than an hour.

With a careful shrug, Varro swung his legs off the side of the bed. His first few attempts to stand met with embarrassing failure, and he was glad he had decided to try before anyone could witness his weakness. Eventually, he levered himself upright and took a couple of tottering steps toward the window. He felt himself moving like an old man, and forced his stiff back to straighten against the pain.

He made it to the foot of the bed before he surrendered and sank back onto the mattress with a soft hiss of breath.

He gave himself a few minutes to recover some of his strength, and then pushed himself up again. This time he moved carefully across the floor, his eyes fixed on the fluttering curtains glowing in the new sunlight. His mind fixed upon that fluttering light as he pushed through the pain and the weakness, and after what felt like an eternity, his hands gripped the wood of the window's sill as if he were hanging desperately out the other side. His head bowed as he caught his breath, then he leaned a little further down and glanced out the window.

The sun was rising up behind him, and deep shadows darkened the well-maintained dirt road that passed in front of the building. A neat, split-rail fence separated a small lawn below from the road, with hitching posts sunk into the verge on the far side. The buildings he saw across the street were well-built homes, widely placed to allow space for a variety of gardens and outbuildings. A tall barn rose over the homes off to his right, farther up the road, and in the distance he could see rolling fields that swept upward to a dark line of pine trees in the distance.

The soft lowing of cows could be heard from the direction of the barn, and hints of movement in the shadow showed where they were being driven out toward the pastures. Lights could be seen behind several of the windows in the houses opposite him, but as yet no one was out and about. He rested against the sill for a few more minutes, but nothing more exciting presented itself.

Varro straightened and twisted to look back at the bed. He wanted nothing so much as to crawl back beneath the sheet and give in to the bone-deep exhaustion left by the short walk to the window. But he had no idea where he was. He knew nothing about these people except that they had dragged him here, nursed him back to health, and yet expected him to leave as soon as he could. He was not a thankless man, but if they wanted him gone, he wanted to go.

After taking a moment to steel himself against the pain, he began to pace the small confines of the room. He forced himself to move back and forth, from one clean white wall to the other. He worked out the tightness and the pain as best he could, and then moved back to the bed, settled down, and pushed himself up against the headboard to wait for Jomei.

Varro snapped awake as the door eased open. His attendant poked his head into the room, an expectant smile on his honest face. When he saw his guest sitting up, he brightened even further and straightened, moving into the room.

"You're awake! Excellent!" He checked the pitcher of water by the bedside and poured more into the cup, offering it.

"I was actually thinking, if this is an inn, we might have breakfast down in the common room, or tavern, or whatever you have?" Varro kept his voice relaxed and casual, but watched Jomei for any reaction. He saw the smile flicker, the brow furrow, and the smile return, all within a heartbeat. Jomei's response, then, caught him off guard.

"Absolutely." Putting the pitcher down, he moved to help Varro stand. He looked impressed when he was waved aside, and the patient rose, with only slight hesitation, under his own power.

"Gio, that is amazing!" The smile faltered slightly. "Do you mind if I call you Gio?"

Varro thought for a moment, and then shrugged. No one had called him Gio but his mother, and those memories were still jagged. But Varro, the name most of the people of the Five Points had used, carried more than its fair share of memories as well.

"That's fine, Jomei. So, what's for breakfast?"

Chapter 6

Jomei took the narrow stairs backward, arms braced as if to steady Varro with good intentions alone. For his part, Varro moved slowly, one hand white-knuckled around the thin bannister. He stood straight, however; his back rigid and his legsstiff, he tookone steady step at a time. Aside from his tight grip, only his thin lips and glistening brow betrayed the effort each step required.

The common room below was small, a series of mismatched tables and chairs filling the space completely. A large fireplace took up most of the far wall, and Varro's eyes were drawn to a large sword hanging over the mantle. It was a graceful ripple of silvered steel with an ornate, divided grip clearly meant for two hands.

A man stood silently by one of the tables, a cleaning rag in one hand. He was several years older than Jomei, his dark blonde hair cut in a similar fashion, but without Jomei's tail. Cold blue eyes followed the pair as they came down the stairs. They flickered toward Jomei, then back to Varro. An uncomfortable silence settled over the room.

Jomei looked back and forth between Varro and the blonde man, his smile faltering. Then he coughed, moved deeper into the room, and gestured for his charge to have a seat at one of the tables.

"Gio," his voice was loud, overcompensating for his sudden discomfort. "This is Gol—"

"Elijah." The man snapped, glaring a warning at Jomei that Varro, easing himself into the hard-backed chair, just caught.

"Elijah . . . right." Jomei sat down beside Varro, shaking his head slightly. Somehow, Varro knew that he was berating himself, not the other man. "Elijah is the landlord here at Sacred Lake Lodge."

"Pleasure to meet you." Varro put no more sincerity into the empty platitude than necessary.

"Likewise." The other man, Elijah, nodded slightly, his face blank.

"Well . . . I think Giovanni and I would like some breakfast . . . Elijah?" The strange, deferential way he said it unsettled Varro further.

Elijah nodded once, looked again at the newcomer, then moved gracefully through the tables and chairs and out through a door by the stairs.

"Doesn't talk much." Varro shifted in his chair. His back was still stiff and sore, and the trip down the stairs had taken more energy than he would admit.

Jomei shrugged, glancing back at the doorway. "I think you'll find most of the folks here in Sacred Lake don't talk much, to be honest." He turned back to smile at the wounded man. "We mostly keep to ourselves."

Varro nodded vaguely and looked around the room. It could have held maybe twenty or thirty people, at most. The fact that it was empty now, when any travelers staying overnight should be getting up and ready to move out, struck him as odd.

"Not a lot of lodgers, at the moment?"

Jomei slid sideways in his chair, throwing one elbow up over the back. "Well, no. We've got some folks still sleeping, but to be honest, Sacred Lake's a ways off the beaten path. We have the Mary Lake Trail, heading down into the Coconino Forest and the western territories, but most folks keep pretty much to the south these days." He paused, his head tilting in thought. "If that railhead up by the canyon don't move on soon, I guess there'll be a bigger trail forming eventually, but that'll probably be further east of here, heading back toward Kansas City and the like."

Mention of the canyon and Kansas City brought his night's dreams back into focus, and a shiver passed through Varro that he was too weak to suppress. He flicked a glance at Jomei, hoping his reaction had not noticed, but the man was staring at him, concern clear on his face.

"Are you cold, Gio? If you're catching a chill, Fosh won't forgive me. I can fetch a blanket from your room, if you want?" He was so sincere that Varro had a hard time focusing on his own apprehensions.

"No, I'm fine." He waved the other man's worry away and looked around the room again. There was little decoration, other than the sword over the mantle. It was a plain, serviceable room meant to host folks with little interest in comfort or knickknacks, on their way from one distant place to another.

Something about the whole situation still struck Varro as strange; Jomei was not being entirely candid with him. Something inside him whispered that he should keep some secrets of his own, but he was just too exhausted. His body, mind, and soul were beat. His suspicions aside, he could not doubt Jomei's honest concern. He took a deep breath, looking down at his broad, hard hands.

"A lot of what happened at the railhead shanty town came back to me last night."

Jomei straightened in his chair, his dark eyes tightening. He reined in his eagerness, but his voice was still buzzing as he eased back. "Yeah?"

His reaction struck yet another odd note, but Varro focused on his hands and nodded. "Some damn preacher, had it out for me for some reason."

Jomei leaned in closer, forgetting to hide the intensity of his interest. "A preacher? Do you remember anything about him? Do you have any idea why he was singling you out?"
Varro shook his head. "No. He said something about a job." The big hands flexed and clenched on the table. "That he knew of a place for men like . . . like me."

Slight tremors began to build in Varro's chest. The fear and anger of those moments in the alley were coming back to him. So many bad choices had led him there, so many times where he had taken the wrong path, or done the wrong thing. And at the end of that trail, a strange preacher man had stood with cryptic words and a loaded gun. The shaking got worse.

"A place for men like you." Jomei's words were quiet, but flat. "Do you know what he meant?"

Varro shrugged. The decision came and went before he knew it was his to make. There were some secrets he meant to keep after all. "I don't know. But it didn't sound like a compliment."

Jomei nodded, his attempts to hide his eagerness a total failure. "Do you remember anything else about this . . . preacher?"

Varro's eyes came back up, his brow wrinkling. It suddenly irked him to be this open with a man who was clearly hiding things of his own. "What's your stake in this?"

Jomei jumped, then eased himself back in his chair with an obvious attempt to appear relaxed. "Just curious, is all." The last memories of the alley emerged from the shadows of his mind. With them, a new suspicion arose as well.

"You said I was found by your men." Visions of blue-white lightning flickered in his mind. "Did they find the preacher as well? Or his men?"

Jomei froze, his eyes wide. He moved as if to speak, but made no sound. Then his mouth closed with an audible snap, and his lips twisted to the side.

Before Varro could pursue these reactions, heavy, creaking footsteps sounded on the stairs, and both young men turned to watch.

Three men descended, each dressed in nondescript leathers over light-colored shirts. Each wore a pair of elaborate, over-sized holsters. They wore dark, battered hats with leather edged brims and short leather cloaks trimmed in a darker rawhide, with attached hoods hanging down their backs. Their coats were high-collared, and kerchiefs hung loosely down their chests. There was a strange glint of gridded metal within the folds of the kerchiefs that Varro, with his limited exposure to the fashions of the territories, could not quite puzzle out.

The men nodded to Jomei, looking blankly at Varro without a gesture or a word, and took a table in the far corner, talking quietly amongst themselves.

Varro looked for a moment more at the trio, and then turned back to Jomei. "Well, looks like they're talking; just not to me."

Jomei's eyes lingered on the three men for a moment. When he looked back at Varro he looked genuinely at a loss for words. He shrugged apologetically, and then settled back in his chair with a shrug.

Varro glanced back at the men, looking more closely at the hood hanging down the closest man's back. There was something familiar about that hood.

He snapped back to look at the young man sitting across from him, his brows lowering over his eyes. "You were going to tell me what your men found in the alley with me?"

Jomei shook his head slowly, then he looked down as if surrendering a point. "It was the preacher that shot you, we figure. Our men put him down before he could finish the job, but we didn't know why he was gunning for you."

The wound in his back throbbed at the statement, even as phantom lightning pulsed behind his eyes. "Put him down how, exactly?"

Those last moments were vague and nightmarish, and he knew his memory had to be wrong. He had been shot, he had lost a lot of blood, and his mind had been swimming with the pain and confusion. And yet those bolts of bright blue were the clearest thing he remembered.

Jomei shrugged again, this time with more force, and when he spoke it was with matter-of-fact conviction. "Guns, I would imagine."

Elijah came back in at that moment, dropping two plates on their table and two mugs of steaming coffee without a word or a glance. He moved quickly to the other table and leaned into the conversation.

"You don't remember anything else about the preacher?" Jomei pressed after a moment.

Varro looked back at him, then back down at his hands. "I don't know. Seemed pretty standard to me. Fire and brimstone and the like, even if there was a darkness to him. And his eyes . . ."

Jomei leaned in closer. "What about his eyes?"

Varro shrugged, looking up at the other man with a quirked eyebrow. "I don't know. Probably nothing."

"Probably nothing, but maybe . . . ?" Jomei's eyes flickered to the table where the other men sat talking quietly.

They showed no signs of listening. "Gio, did you notice something strange about the man's eyes?"

Varro shrugged again, looking down at his plate of eggs and bread. "I guess I did. They looked dark, empty. Almost like a dead man's, but with the weight of Hell behind them."

Jomei sat back, his own eyes wide, his food forgotten. He nodded slightly, his eyes moving quickly to the other table again, and then stabbing back at Varro. "Was there anything else strange about him?"

Varro looked suspiciously at Jomei for a moment, then looked down and picked up a spoon. "He sweat a lot."

Jomei's chair scraped the floor as he straightened at this. His elbows hit the table and he stared at Varro with a sharp, clear gaze. "He sweat a lot? What do you mean? Did his skin look shiny, glossy?"

Varro looked up, his mouth full of egg. He nodded, muttering around his food. "Yeah, I guess so."

Jomei's body quivered with sudden tension. His face was a strange mixture of nerves, excitement, and anticipation. However, he asked no more questions, settling back, with an occasional glance at the other table, and only made a half-hearted show of pushing the food around his plate.

The men in the corner left with bundles of food from the kitchen after a few minutes, each nodding to Jomei but ignoring Varro again. After they went, Elijah came to collect their plates, Varro's completely empty, his companion's almost untouched.

They had spoken very little after Jomei had dropped his questioning about the preacher. Varro looked toward the front door of the lodge with a little trepidation. His legs still ached from the stairs, and now that he had eaten, he was starting to feel tired again. His wounds were a dull, constant ache, and he felt slightly dizzy.

"Tell you what, kid." Jomei was too preoccupied to take offense. "I'm starting to think maybe this was enough exercise for one day. Maybe you help me back upstairs, and we try to get a little farther tomorrow?"

The other man's preoccupied look was quickly shaken off, his grin returning for the first time since they sat down. "Yeah, that sounds good."

Jomei braced Varro's elbow as he stood, and then helped him back up to the room, seeing him gently back into the bed. With a smile, he declared that he would check in and see if maybe coming down for dinner was in the cards.

Varro nodded his keeper out the door, and then collapsed back against the pillows, closing his eyes with sheer relief.

Going down to the common room had not been the distraction he had hoped for, and the reception from the other men had troubled him more than he wanted to admit. He felt more isolated and alone than he had never been in his life. He was used to being at the center of the action, in the thick of the fighting or the planning. Even fleeing out here to the back end of the Earth, he had been on trains full of other people willing to speak to him, like Tucker Soza, if he had wanted to talk.

Here, he was beginning to feel like a leper.

And who were these people anyway? All five of the men he had seen so far had the same strange haircut, and wore similar clothes. The sword downstairs was another dissonant note. He was no expert, but he had not recognized the style or the workmanship from anything he had ever seen. Everything about Sacred Lake seemed as normal to him as could be, and yet everything, from the architecture and the craftsmanship of the buildings to the people and their clothing, seemed strange at the same time, as if it all came from different, distant times or places. And was it at all strange that he had seen no women? He knew that the hardship and danger of the territories meant there were far more men than ladies, but still. Not a one?

And of course none of that addressed the major issue that still haunted his mind: how had he come to be here? What did these people want from him?

He was still puzzling over the hundred mysteries, large and small, that Sacred Lake presented, when he drifted off back to sleep.

*****

The next few days were more of the same, with Jomei and Varro starting each one with a hearty, if plain, breakfast in the common room. Elijah always presided over the meal, but had not spoken a word to Varro since giving his name that first day. The common room was almost always empty, although occasionally other groups of men would take their meals there. Always in teams of two or three, and always similarly dressed, yet Varro never saw the same men, other than Jomei and Elijah, in the common room.

Once he felt strong enough to venture out beyond the lodge, they began to meet more of the people who called Sacred Lake home. Still there were only men, and Varro began to suspect that maybe the villagers were keeping their womenfolk away from him. He found that a little amusing. Did he look that dangerous? Once again, his questions were deflected, though. Jomei always maneuvered their conversations away from women and into any of a number of less-interesting topics.

The men they met on their walks were no more talkative than Elijah or the men in the common room. Often they would approach a group talking in the street, and as they neared, the conversation would stop. The men would nod to Jomei, who would nod back, and then the men would either separate, moving off in different directions, or they would remain silent until the two had moved past, only then continuing their conversation.

It did nothing to make Varro feel more welcomed. He began to feel uncomfortable and unwanted, and started to think about where he might want to go next.

Jomei's conversations always came back around to the railhead and the preacher. He asked more and more detailed questions, trying to tease out every last detail about the attack, the revivalist tent, and Varro's conversation with the man in the alleyway. Varro stopped trying to be cagey after the first day, and answered the strange, detailed questions as clearly and honestly as he could. He was still frustrated, however, as that openness was never returned by Jomei or any of the other men of Sacred Lake.

As the days wore on and his frustration mounted, Varro began to make his plans for returning to the railhead and catching the train back to Kansas City. If Soza was gone and he had to pay for his passage, so be it. He had a little money left, and if it was not enough, he would figure something out when he came to it. He always did.

Sacred Lake, he decided, was not a place he wanted to stay for much longer.

*****

"He's going to leave if we don't come clean soon." Jomei's words were anxious, his eyes pleading. He looked across the table to the two men who sat there, staring back at him with hard expressions.

Mimreg Fosh was an old warrior, his hair, neatly-trimmed beard, and mustache white as sand from the high desert. He had served the Order for his entire life, all over the world. He had settled down at the Acropolis of the Sunset Lands in his winter years, following the prophecy. He was the *Etta*'s eyes and ears at the staging area disguised as a harmless little town called Sacred Lake.

Altcap Golah, Elijah, to outsiders, was the commander of the camp. He used the Sacred Lake Lodge as his quarters and command post. Most mission teams stayed at the Lodge as they prepared for their journeys into the western territories, or as they returned back to the Acropolis in the distant mountains to the north.

It was also Golah who interacted with those rare strangers who stumbled upon Sacred Lake, which explained why the Lodge was designed as a typical inn or hostel similar to those found in any similar town. Much larger than it should have been, of course, to serve the needs of the many teams moving throughout the chaotic territories, but the occasional chance visitor never seemed to notice the incongruity.

"We're still not sure we don't want him to leave, *Spica* Jomei." The hard lines of Golah's face were impassive. "We have no idea what the Tainted preacher saw in Giovanni Varro, or why they came to blows in that alley. The team that silenced the creature brought Varro back on a whim, aware of the edicts for recruitment from the *Etta*."

"Edicts that young Jomei does well to remember, *Altcap*." Fosh's voice was deep and gravelly, with the tones and inflections of a far off land. Most who served at the Acropolis were born in the New World, either in America or in the provinces to the north. There were many still, however, who had been born in distant lands, following the calling of their faith to the Sunset Lands of legend. There was even a lesser member of the *Etta*, *Arcsen* Siraj, who had emigrated from distant India. For reasons even the *Etta* could not fathom, many of the American-born members of the Order tended to hold their foreign counterparts in very high esteem.

"I understand, Fosh. And I know that we are heading into desperate times, where we will need every sword. " Golah nodded respectfully, but his voice remained firm. "And yet, this man was being courted by a servant of the Enemy. Does that not sound alarms in your mind?"

"Garnering the interest of the Enemy could be as strong a recommendation as it is a condemnation. You know the Enemy is always trying to pierce the veil around the Order, to steal from us the tools needed to combat them." The old man gestured with gnarled hands. "Could it be that this man's value to us is exactly the quality that attracted the creature's attention?"

"He perceived the aura of evil." Jomei's eager voice followed without a break. "He sensed it on his own, before the preacher tracked him to the alley."
Golah shook his head. "He saw a man sweating, nothing more."

Jomei's face folded into an angry frown. "No! You know as well as I do that many of the Order perceive the aura as a glossy sheen. My own vision manifests in much the same way, when confronted with a servant of the Enemy."

"And Varro perceived the Tainted state of this preacher's soul through his eyes as well, *Altcap*. How many candidates have you ever heard of that had such finely-tuned perceptions before training? There is no doubt in my mind that this creature had been touched by the Dark Council."

"There were others as well," Jomei added. "He remembers men and women with similar signs rising to power among the clans and gangs of his home, before the draft riots."

Golah still looked skeptical. "Are you telling me that every petty spat throughout the northeast is the work of the Enemy, now? There is a danger to being over-vigilant as well, Jomei."

Fosh raised one hand. "Wait. What better way to prolong the death and violence of the war than to ensure that the Union cannot muster enough troops to complete it? And that speaks nothing to the possibility that the Enemy has something even more momentous planned, and is only laying the groundwork for darker days to come."

The old man's voice was low and ominous, his eyes drifting down to the table top. He had never made any secret of his dedication to the prophecy. *Mimreg* Fosh believed that the End Times were near, and that they would begin somewhere in America, in the near future.

"And there's the tattoo . . ." Jomei was hesitant to speak, but on the heels of Fosh's last words, it seemed appropriate. He did not try to hide his relief when the old man nodded, pointing at the *altcap*.

"And there are his tribal markings: the rearing serpent. Surely even a skeptic such as you must wonder at that."

Altcap Golah looked down at his folded hands. He put no faith in the prophecy himself, but even without taking the markings on the young stranger's arm into account, there was much to recommend him as a candidate.

And yet the Tainted preacher's interest still made him leery.

After a moment's further reflection, Golah looked up across the table with a slow, reluctant nod. "Alright. I am not completely convinced, but I think this warrants a conference with the *Etta*. I will contact them tonight. I want an amulet to be brought into your new friend's presence, Jomei. See how it reacts. They will want to know."

"Shall I sound him out? As I say, he grows suspicious."

Fosh nodded, looking to the commander with stern eyes. "We cannot risk losing a possible candidate of such sensitivity, *Altcap*."

Golah nodded again, with even more reluctance. "You may not reveal any of the mysteries to him. But reveal a little of the Order's mission, and sound him out as to his own future plans and desires."

Jomei nodded with a smile, but the commander halted his rising with a single flat palm. "We know very little of this man, Jomei. If he is to join us, that choice must be of his own free will. One cannot be coerced into entering the Holy Order of Man, either through direct compulsion or through the pressures of circumstance."

The young man nodded, his face assuming a serious expression. "Of course, *Altcap*."

"Have Fosh provide you with an amulet. Tomorrow, when you take your walk with Giovanni, note its reaction. I will have news for you from the *Etta* before you join him for breakfast in the morning."

Jomei nodded and left the small room in Fosh's little hut. The two older men sat in companionable silence for a moment, before Fosh smiled at his commander. "I think the new soul is going to be an important addition to the Order, *Altcap*. You have made a wise decision this day."

Golah leaned back over the table with a sigh, his fingers interlaced. "I hope you're right, Fosh. I hope and pray that you're right."

*****

The 'lake' was a flat, dry mud plain off to their right. It ebbed and flowed with the seasons, or so Jomei had told him. And here, at the tail end of autumn, it had been dry for months now. Several lonely, rickety old docks stood like strange constructs, almost unrecognizable out of their natural context. The two young men had walked along the rough borders of the missing lake several times in the past few days, wandering farther and farther from the small town.

This morning Varro had sensed a change in his young steward. Jomei walked with more energy than he had since they started wandering from the lodge. His bright, honest smile was back, and Varro had the strong impression that something important, and overwhelmingly positive, had happened the night before. He also noticed the other man was wearing a strange medallion around his neck that had not been there before. The stone in the center of the pendant seemed to almost glow with its own, strange, sapphire light.

"I know you're planning on leaving soon." The statement was accompanied by an odd smile.

Jomei's words struck him as strange, given how inhospitable the rest of the village had been, and Varro had no interest in denying that impression.

"I don't see any reason for me to stay, Jomei. The world's moving on out there somewhere. I can't stay here, being ignored by everyone but you, eating food and sleeping under a roof I can't pay for, for the rest of my life."

Jomei was not looking at him, but rather squinting off into the middle distance, toward the mountains that rose over the horizon far to the north. "No, that makes sense. Sacred Lake doesn't have much to offer, that's for certain." The smile was there again.

Varro's frown deepened. "I was thinking of leaving tomorrow, or the day after, actually. The train might—"

The other man looked sideways at him, and then shook his head. "The railhead? No. The train hasn't been back since it left the night you were found. Best we can figure, it won't be back until it brings the parts they need to bridge the canyon. The settlement around there is even more dangerous than your last visit, though. If you're leaving, you might want to strike southwest, try to get to Kansas City directly, if that's where you're thinking of heading."

Varro's brow wrinkled even as he nodded. "Well, I can't think of anywhere else I could go."

Jomei stopped for a moment, staring out at the mountains, and then raised a hand to point at them. "What about up there?"

Varro's cocked his head in confused annoyance. "The mountains? What's up there, other than savages and wild animals, and a few gold mining camps? You thinking of becoming a prospector, Jomei?"

The other man smiled and then turned to look right at him. "No. I think your destiny might just be up in those mountains, Gio."

The direct look was more than Varro had been granted in days, and coupled with the strange statement, he stopped, unsure how to respond. "Your sense of humor seems a bit off, old son."

Jomei shook his head. "No, Gio. No joking. I've been given permission to speak with you about something very important. Just this morning, in fact, I was ordered to."

Varro cocked his head. "Ordered? By who? About what?" The frustration and the suspicions that had been niggling at the back of his mind since he first woke up in Sacred Lake came boiling back. "You haven't been exactly straight with me since I got here, Jomei. You telling me now, out here, in the middle of nowhere, you're going to open up?"

Jomei nodded, his smile warm and honest. "Exactly."

Varro stared at the other man for a long minute, then shook his head in resignation, eased himself down to the grass, and made a grand gesture. "Sure, kid. Let's hear it. What have you got?"

Jomei looked down at Varro for a moment, and then lowered himself beside him on one knee, like a savage scout. His face shifted from open and friendly to the earnest features of a true believer, and Varro found himself leaning back from the intensity.

"You know there's more to Sacred Lake than it seems. I know you've noticed, and you have been too polite to mention it."

"Or too sure you wouldn't have told me the truth anyway." Varro did not try to disguise the sour note in his voice, and Jomei cringed slightly in apology.

"Well, no, you're probably right. You see, we all belong to a larger group. A group that works toward making the territories safer for everyone." Varro could see Jomei struggling to find the right words, and had a sudden suspicion that even now he was not being told the whole story.

"Look, if you're not going to be completely straight with me, I'm not sure why I'd even listen at this point. I'll buy a horse from someone in town, or hell, steal one if nobody will talk to me, and I can be on my way today. Not going to be worrying about any damn destiny or anything like that."

Jomei shook his head. "No, sorry." He sat down, his hands jerking as if trying to catch the right words. "There are things I can't tell you yet. Things you have to be told by other people, higher than me, and things you need to earn the right to know. But honestly, I only want to tell you the truth at this point. I think it might be very important."

Varro cocked his head again. "Important? Important to who?"

Again, Jomei groped with a hand. "Important to everyone, I think."

Varro shook his head. "Okay. You go ahead, and tell me this dime store novel story about destiny and justice for the little people, and then I'll go see about that horse."

Jomei nodded, clearly trying to marshal his words. "Anyway, as I said, we of Sacred Lake are a part of something much, much larger. We work hard to keep the territories safe for the good men and women who come here looking to better their lives. And the people in charge of this group, the people who rule over Sacred Lake and far beyond, they think you would be a good candidate to become one of us." The smile on his face was radiant, and Varro could tell he believed he was delivering truly good news.

But Varro was not so sure. "So, you and your boys, and those teams I've seen coming in and out of town all week, you're sort of like sheriffs, or marshals?" His past had not left him with a warm inclination toward such men.

Jomei nodded.

"And you all think I'd make a good policeman?" He could not keep the offended tone from his voice.

"Not a policeman, really, but—"

Varro silenced him with a raised hand. "You know nothing about me, Jomei. You have no idea what kind of man I am." He felt the old guilt and sadness rising in his chest. "I'm not a person who protects the innocent. I'm a person you protect the innocent *from*."

Jomei stopped, looking confused for a moment, then shook his head with iron certainty. "No, that's not true. Whatever you've done in your past, that's not who you are. I know that." He fingered the medallion and repeated, "I know that."

Varro shook his head again. "Well, whatever you think you know, I've lived it." He looked out over the dusty plain and lapsed into silence.

He jerked back when Jomei's hand landed on his shoulder, but the other man's solemn face held him in place. "Your past does not define your future, Gio. This may just be the opportunity you're looking for, to put that past behind you."

Varro looked back out over the baked mud. What he had seen of Sacred Lake had impressed him: a society of men working together to build something out of the nothingness of the borderlands. Despite the isolation and the silence, he had come to appreciate them as hardworking and dedicated. He had sensed in them a goodness that he had not seen in a very long time. Even the armed teams coming and going, policing the frontier if Jomei was telling the truth, had been solid, honest-looking men. The violence that they must apply to their work, the violence that they must have used against the preacher at the railhead shanty town, was not who they were, but rather a necessary part of what they saw as their duty.

He looked back over to Jomei. "I don't want to fight anymore."

The other man brightened at even this thawing of resolve. "Well, not everyone in our organization fights, that's true. But we all do what we are best-suited to doing, to further the work."

"The men back at Sacred Lake don't fight." Varro's voice was stiff and stubborn, but he faltered when Jomei shook his head.

"They don't now, but every one of them is a trained warrior, and will fight when . . . if . . . the time comes."

A tone in the other man's words struck something deep inside the broken parts of Varro's being. For the first time, he began to think about the possibility that there could be a way to cleanse himself of the darkness that he had let inside; that he could somehow face his past instead of running from it, and make of himself a better man. Another thought stopped him.

"Who are you people?"

Jomei blinked at him, and then shook his head. "That is not my secret to tell, I'm afraid. There is a certain amount of faith you must carry with you into this new adventure, if you choose to accept our offer."

Varro stood, still with the stiffness of his wound slowing him a little, and stretched, looking up toward the mountains. "Up there?"

Jomei nodded. "Yes. It will not be an easy journey, and the challenges of the trail will be just the beginning."

Varro stared at the distant Rockies. Something had been missing in his life for longer than he cared to contemplate. He had known power and influence within the structure of the gangs of the Five Points. He had been feared and admired throughout those unfortunate neighborhoods, and known security and position as high as anyone else in that culture could know it. But he had not known peace of mind or strength of conviction. There had been no faith in his life, in himself, in God, or in anything else. He could only see that lack now, looking at things from the other end.

Jomei had it. He had a quiet confidence and a faith in something larger than himself, and it showed in his open smile and his steady eyes. Even Elijah had it, watching Varro from a distance, never saying a word. The men he had seen, both the teams at the lodge and the men he had assumed were farmers throughout the village, had it. A calm strength, a mental or spiritual power that seemed as much a part of them as the brash swagger and brutal suspicion had been a part of the gangs.

Varro wanted that assurance and confidence. He wanted that faith.

His shoulders slumped a little as his brain continued on down a path grown dark with the shadows of his past. What else did he have to return to? There was nowhere for him to go. No one awaited his arrival, no one expected his assistance. He was literally at the end of the known world, with almost nothing.

He shook his head, the excitement and expectations of a moment before crumbling a little as the old feelings of helplessness and hopelessness gave way. "I'll go with you."

Rather than a victorious light, Jomei's eyes grew hooded with suspicion. "You cannot choose this path through anything other than your own free will," he warned. "I have been instructed to tell you that I can see you delivered anywhere you wish. If you wish to go to Kansas City, I can get you there. If you wish to return to New York City, that can be done as well. But you cannot join us merely because you believe there are no other options open to you."

Varro looked at his companion in honest confusion. "I thought you were offering . . ."

Jomei shook his head. "I believe this is what is right. I believe that this is what is meant to be. But *you* must believe that, or this path is not for you."

Varro looked back out at the mountains. What had happened to the boy he had grown to think of almost as a friend? Jomei's confidence and calm demeanor were almost unsettling; they were so different from the diffident, eager-to-please attendant he had grown accustomed to. It appeared that hiding these truths had been taking their toll, and only now, with the truth even partially revealed, was his real personality coming through: the open and honest young man, but with the conviction and the certitude of a seasoned veteran.

Varro knew he was seeing the real Jomei for the first time.

And for the first time in a long time, he felt sure of something himself. He wanted that confidence more than he had ever wanted anything in his life.

He jerked his chin back up toward the distant mountains. "When do we leave?"

There was no suspicion or doubt now behind Jomei's returning smile.

Chapter 7

The Little Colorado River was starting to flow in earnest again. The fall rains, as little as there had been of them, had given the river just enough of a kick to get it rolling over the rocks of the thirsty badlands. It was a seasonal river, and for several months of the year it registered as barely a strip of damp mud running between the tumbled boulders of the high desert. For most of the year, though, it flowed enough to keep river rafts moving up and down, making it a decent location for an outpost on the edge of civilization.

A small community arose around a particularly important ford of the river more than twenty years before the A&P Railroad Company came to grief at DiabloCanyon many miles to the north and east. A trading post was first placed near the ford, serving trappers and miners coming down off the mountains or trying to establish themselves in the inhospitable region, following claims of gold and silver, orjust looking to get away.

The trading post, a small, single story red stone building, now squatted amongst a collection of wooden structures and tents. There was an order and a discipline to the streets, though. There was a sense that a man would be safe hanging his hat in Tolchico, and that big things were in the works. There may be a war tearing the rest of the continent apart, but in this little town on the edge of the Arizona Territory, things were looking nothing but up.

At least, that's what Tucker Soza had been told by one of the locals the night he wandered in off the desert. He was not sure how much of that to believe, and he did not really care. He looked down through dust-coated spectacles into the cloudy elixir that passed for whiskey here, and hoped that the future of the town was happier than their choice of popskull. The bitter fluid leaving a greasy sheen along the sides of his glass was just the latest in a long line of indignities life had heaped upon him since DiabloCanyon.

The Atlantic and Pacific Railroad, not knowing who to blame for the debacle that cost them the race to the west coast, had all but closed down after the last engine had returned to Kansas City. He had stayed behind, along with hundreds of others, assuming that the train would return. The little shanty town around the railhead had degenerated into a hell hole in a matter of days. Limited supplies of food, the uncertainty of the situation, and no law had all added up to the kind of violent free for all that he had read about in the penny dreadfuls but had never seen before in real life. Had someone asked him, he would have said there was no place on Earth that bad.

He knew better now.

Soza's faith in the human race had taken a severe beating in recent days. He had led a small group of his recruited boys away from the canyon when it became clear the railroad would not be returning anytime soon. He had rounded up every lad he had enticed to make the journey who had not left with the locomotive. He had even tried to find the big kid from New York, but without success. In the end, he began the long walk south with twelve men.

The unforgiving sun had beaten down on his bald head all that first day, and he had severe doubts they were going to survive. The plan, such as it was, had been to reach Camp McDowell and beg assistance from the Union troops and workers there. This far west, there was not much in the way of cities and towns. Some of the boys had recommended they follow the rail line back toward KC, but after being let go by the railroad, for some reason Soza did not want to return to the city. He wanted to strike out further into the territory and see what there was to see of the opportunities that had driven so many others out ahead of him.

But the trek through the desert had been hard. Water was scarce, and none of the boys had any more experience than him. It was a close run thing, and in their exhaustion and confusion, they had gotten turned around, began heading west without realizing it, and found themselves quickly in the shaded pines of the Coconino Forest. He knew there was talk about some strange religious settlement in the area, but he did not even know where to begin looking, so decided not to mention it to the boys. They moved through the forest, enjoying the shade and the water from the small streams. The red mesas peering up just over the horizon in almost every direction were a constant reminder that death loomed just outside the dusty forest.

Soza pushed onward, continuing to move west. By the time they reached the edge of the forest, there were only three boys left. Most had decided to stay in the forest, or turned back east to take their chances at the canyon railhead. One unfortunate kid had disappeared into one of the larger streams when the clay canyon wall he had been standing on collapsed beneath him. The boy had struck his head on a rock and never emerged again.

Soza and his remaining boys had finally stood on the edge of the forest, looking out once again over the western desert. They had had no real expectation of finding salvation out there, and had stayed an entire day, trying to fortify themselves for the trek into the unknown. On the few occasions when he was being honest with himself afterward, Soza knew he could not say whether or not he would have pushed on if a hunting party out from Tolchico had not found them.

The small group was mounted on healthy horses, happy to help the railway man and his boys. They had some frightening stories to push the lads along, as well. Bodies had turned up in the Coconino, their flesh torn and their eyes wide in pain and terror. Someone, or something, was moving through the forest, and the wounds had not been made by claw or tooth.

And so, Soza and his boys had accompanied the hunters, each bearing a heavy burden of deer and countless smaller animals. The men had been in good spirits, knowing that between the meat and furs in their haul, they would not be wanting for food, lodging, or company when they got to Tolchico. Their banter was less than comforting to Soza, however. It served to remind him that he and his boys would have precious little to offer a rugged frontier town when they finally arrived.

But he had been wrong. As they had rounded a tall red mesa and moved down toward the sluggish brown river, he had seen that Tolchico was a bustling town still in the process of construction. The townsfolk had welcomed the newcomers with open arms, and soon all four of them had been employed as laborers working on a large stone building that would serve as trading post and administrative center. There were also darker mutterings that such a stronghold could withstand anything the cursed frontier threw at them, but Soza had not given those whispers any credence. At least, not for the first couple of days.

He swirled the oily whiskey around in his glass again and sighed. What a difference a couple of days had made. The atmosphere around the saloons and the small dance hall had gotten more and more somber with each night. Hunting parties, traders, and workers enticed in from across the area seemed to bring with them stories of death and torture from all around. One group of desperately thirsty and starved creatures had crawled into town just this morning talking of an entire farming settlement up north that had disappeared overnight. The houses were all left intact; no sign of savages or animals; no indications of a struggle, not so much as a drop of blood or an overturned chair. But every living person was gone without a trace, leaving their wagons, their livestock, and all their worldly possessions behind.

It had been enough to drive this latest lot to abandon their homes and make for Tolchico.

That had been the moment that Soza had finally realized the truth of his new situation. Something terrible was happening out in the deserts and plains surrounding them, but somehow he had managed to stumble into the safest place in the region. He had brought his boys to someplace safe. And for that, he was truly grateful.

Soza checked his cheap, tin pocket watch. He knew the thing was always running about a half hour slow, but even allowing for that, he figured it was getting on toward the time when the mayor was supposed to address all the newcomers about the rumors and the tales that had arisen surrounding the recent reports.

The mayor, Truman Maddox, was usually in his offices in the smaller stone trading post. He had been the driving force behind that first construction, and the development that had occurred ever since. No one knew what he did in those offices all day, but Soza had only ever caught glimpses of the man, and even then only from a distance. One of the main reasons he had decided to attend the speech was to see the mayor close up for himself. There had to be something special about a man who could rally the efforts that had raised Tolchico out of the desert sands so far from civilization. Soza wanted to see what that kind of special looked like.

With a wince, the railroad man tossed the last of the rotgut down his throat, gave one hoarse bark at the heat, and then spun off his chair to move through the saloon and toward the half-completed trading post and town hall. Whatever happened, he knew it was going to be more interesting than listening to another round of ghost stories.

*****

The trading post and town hall was going to be truly impressive. The red stone walls rose high into the sky behind the nearly completed facade of the building with its stone pillars, wide windows, and double doors. It had a porch that wrapped completely around the front, and squat stone bases built into it to support the columns that would brace the wooden porch roof when they got around to the finish work.

The uncompleted sections were mostly around back. The building was situated on an uneven rise, so the back was actually even taller than the front. It would eventually look even more impressive, but it was proving much harder to complete. Soza knew that two men had been severely injured in the hurried construction, and that had just beenin the time he had worked here. One man, falling from a ladder around back, had crushed his back and died not long before they first arrived.

There was already a crowd forming around the base of the porch, and a few of the mayor's big, tough enforcers stood around the bottom of the red stone stairs, keeping folks at a safe distance. Soza had had a hard time figuring these guys out. They were clearly gun hands, all of them carrying heavy rigs slung around their waists. They never spoke much, and were never seen in the saloons, brothels, or the dance hall.

Things had been getting worse out beyond town, and he figured these hardened men were the mayor's answer to the growing town's safety.

But they looked a lot meaner than the old railway man thought lawmen ought to look.

Soza scanned the crowd, but none of his boys seemed to be in attendance. The three of them had continued working with him on the trading post, but they had taken to spending their off time alone, or with new friends closer to their own age. He could not fault that, but it did serve to make him feel a little more isolated than he would have liked. He knew Floyd Brant, an innocent kid from back east fleeing into the territories from a broken heart, blamed him for their current situation. He was a good kid, but completely unprepared for life outside of his home town half a world away. Another of the boys had been spending more and more time within the trading post than building it. He figured that one would be one of the mayor's assistants in good time.

There were over a hundred folks huddled in the lamplight around the towering red building now, but there was no sense of celebration or festivity. These were all frightened people, growing worse by the day. Each hoped to hear words of comfort from a man they all admired but few knew anything about. The menfolk muttered quietly to each other, many holding onto cups of tin, stoneware, or glass. He knew from the smell that most of those cups contained excellent examples of the worst liquid courage the town had to offer.

The women were more subdued than the men. Soza found this particularly unsettling, given the types of ladies that found themselves this far out on the fringes of civilization. These ladies were tough and rambunctious. Many would smile in the face of the devil himself and ask if he wanted a dance. There was not a smile to be seen among the gowns and lace that night. In fact, most of the ladies were huddled together, casting suspicious looks all around. He noticed that they were not just watching the shadows around the town's impromptu square warily, they were watching the men of the town as well. And there was fear in their eyes.

Soza figured it made sense. Abuse of women, all forms of horrific abuse, had figured prominently in the stories building over the last few days. Even the tough grass widows that washed up on a shore as remote as Tolchico would think twice before brazening it out in the face of the whispered tales of rape, torture, and horrible desecration that had been arriving from the surrounding countryside.

Soza had been a railway man all his adult life. He had worked some of the roughest railheads in the country as one line or another was pushed into the wilds of the expanding frontier. He had seen shanty towns wracked with fear over imminent savage attack. He had seen camps explode into violence as an argument about the distant war got out of hand. He had even once found himself working a railhead that had fallen victim to the kind of sick, demented murderer that generally only featured in the worst kinds of dime store pamphlet stories.

But he had never seen a group as scared as the crowd that surged around the new trading post that night.

A harsh round of muttering brought him back to the moment. The crowd jostled around him, orienting themselves toward the porch, where one of the big double doors, doors Soza himself had set just that day, swung ponderously open. He knew how big those doors were. He had figured they were designed to impress and intimidate folks heading into the trading post on official business. They were somewhere north of seven feet tall, each of them, and over four feet wide; made of thick, solid pine dragged back over the desert from the Coconino. It was this familiarity with the doors that probably shook Soza up even more than the men and women around him; because the man who emerged through them came very close to bumping his head on the top of the doorframe.

The crowd craned their necks up to watch as the man appeared from the shadows and stood at the very top of the sweeping red staircase. He wore a faded pair of dark blue pants with a gold stripe down the outside seam and an old tunic with a high collar. The clothes bore no insignia, but had an unmistakably military aura about them. They did nothing to conceal the impressive physique of the man, standing there with his arms slightly bent as if was contemplating rushing the crowd. His light hair was closely cropped, his scalp showing plainly through bristles that glowed with red highlights in the porch lamps' glow. A neatly-trimmed goatee and mustache framed a hard, thin mouth, and his eyes were a cold, ice blue as he scanned the crowd.

"Euans." Soza heard someone behind him whisper.

"Bruce Euans." Several other people muttered, confirming their suspicions.

Soza had never heard the man's name before, but he figured, as there was not a dissenting voice in the crowd, that he was looking up at the impressive bulk of a man named Bruce Euans.

The thought had barely formed in his head when the man on the porch, his thumbs hooked behind two massive pistol holsters, cleared his throat and began to speak in a low and gravelly voice that matched his appearance perfectly.

"You folks listen up. The mayor's going to be coming out presently, but I don't want you to be askin' no questions or pushin' on my men down there." He pointed loosely at the bottom of the stairs where the mayor's men had produced long, heavy-looking rifles held casually across their bodies. "The mayor'll get to all your questions, but he ain't gonna be holdin' any hands." The man's face was cold and cruel, and he clearly had very little regard for the worries and cares of the people below. "I know a lot of stories are bein' told down at the sinks and the cathouses, an' the mayor'll lay that all out for ya. But he's gonna be a few more minutes, an' he don't want no one gettin' uppity. You're all goin' to have to be patient, and I'm sure everythin'll be made clear shortly."

He gave one last warning glare, scanning the entire crowd, and then turned to duck back into the building.

Soza looked around. The crowd was over two hundred strong now. Almost everyone he knew could be seen staring dumbly up at the tall, distant porch. The people around him had started to mutter again before Euans had shut the door, so he crossed his arms and settled back to listen to the conversations.

It appeared that Euans had arrived earlier that day while Soza had been working on the front doors, and had entered from around back, through the unfinished section. Most folks knew nothing about him, but there were some mutterings about him being some sort of Union trooper from one of the western states. Most of the whispers agreed he had come out of Ohio.

Things got more confusing, however, when others began to contradict that view, saying that the man was a lawman, come out to the territories to set things right. Soza was a man of the world, he had travelled up and down the nation, both before and during its current crisis. He knew that a man could easily be a soldier and a lawman, but he was not too sure that the big, hulking brute he had just seen growling at the frightened townsfolk from the porch would be a stellar example of either.

Something about the big figure worried Soza, but he was not sure what it might be. While he was still trying to puzzle his vague fears out into the light, the door swung open again. The crowd hushed around him, all looking back up at the porch expectantly.

The man who came through now was not nearly as tall as Euans, although he was probably closer to six feet than most men got. He wore matching dark pants and coat, as clean as if he had just walked out of a big city clothier. His shirt was crisp and white beneath a tight vest, with a neck cloth that matched his coat draped down the front. He looked relatively slight beside Euans, who came out behind him, but he seemed plenty imposing on his own.

The man kept his iron gray hair short, although not as short as Euans. His heavy brows shadowed eyes that flashed green in the lamplight. His face was lined, but looked more worn from care and weather than age. He had not shaved in a couple days, and the stubble marking his cheeks was much darker than the grizzled hair on his head. He looked out over the waiting crowd with a neutral face without much comfort in its gaze.

"Ladies and gentlemen," the mayor raised his hands as if trying to get everyone's attention, despite the fact that everyone was already silent, staring at up at him in hope and fear. His voice was soft, but Soza thought he caught a hint of steel behind it that fit with what he had seen around town since his arrival.

"Ladies and gentlemen," he repeated. "Most of you know me." He begrudged them a little smile at that point, and Soza could feel a small bit of the tension ease from the crowd. "For those of you who have come in over the last couple of days, let me introduce myself. My name is Truman Maddox, and as you may have gathered, I'm the mayor of our little burg." The smile creaked a bit wider this time, and the tension dropped some more.

"I came to Tolchico when it was just an old way station at the ford, and I built it into something special. With these hands," he held up his broad, thin-fingered hands. "I helped to build the first trading post. And then folks started to come. Many of you, I see out there in the night, have been with me since the very beginning. You remember the first building that went up? Down by the river? Old man Andy's place, with that pretty little French wife of his?" Several soft laughs and mutters of agreement marked a further relaxing in the crowd. "Yeah. You remember when Pascha went up, boys?" The men in the crowd gave a good chuckle, elbowing each other and grinning wildly. The Pascha was the first cathouse that had gone up in Tolchico, and it was still considered one of the best. Soza looked around him and marveled at how well Maddox was playing the crowd. Only moments before, they had been terrified. Now, they were jostling each other and grinning like tomcats. But looking closer, he could still see the fear in the eyes of most of the women. There were men who looked unconvinced as well.

"We've built something special here, people!" The mayor continued, pitching his voice to carry over the self-congratulatory comments drifting up from his last sally. "More and more folks come here every day, and we're establishing a regular trail, heading through the Coconino and down through the Tonto, into the rest of the territory! Folks are coming here to realize the dreams the rest of the country has left behind in the bloody midst of this endless war!"

More of the folks in the crowd cheered. Many of these men had fled the war for one reason or another, and the mayor's words gave legitimacy to their flight, casting it in a far more heroic light. Soza had always been fairly comfortable with his relationship with the war. He was a pretty staunch supporter of the Union cause, but the railroad had seen him as an asset worthy of protection, and so the drafts had never been a danger. Judging from many of the reactions of the men around him, they had not shared his immunity.

"That's right." The mayor continued. "We have, all of us, worked our fingers to the bone to build Tolchico. We've got our own mining interests in the hills, we've helped all the other miners moving up into the mountains, and we've tied the farming collectives and the cattlemen moving out west together in a way that no other town was in a position to do. Tolchico is a certifiable gem in the crown of the western territories!"

The men around Soza gave a cheer, and even the women seemed to be coming alive throughout the crowd. Fear still hung thick over everyone, but the momentum the mayor had built with his first words continued to roll them in his direction.

Maddox's face grew more somber, like a stern father with serious news to deliver. "Now, we've seen some dark times of late, and no mistake." The grins faded somewhat, as the current crisis that had brought them all together was dragged back into the light. "There are some savage monsters roaming the dark, and there have been done some deeds of dreadful note in the night."

The words sounded vaguely familiar to Soza, but he shrugged it off, just happy that the mayor had come to the point.

The man's eyes were shadowed again, ominous in the darkness. "There is an evil wandering the deserts and the forests and the mountains here abouts, and it's appeared that no one is safe." He pointed to a huddled group of newcomers that had taken no part in the lighter moments of the evening, their faces haggard, pale, and lost. "Word has come to us of entire villages wiped off the map, every man, woman, and child gone without a trace to God knows where, and for God knows what evil purpose."

The mayor's voice was harsh now, full of jagged tones and burrs that hinted at danger and threat behind every rock and cactus. "Something has crawled out of the very pits of Hell to challenge our mastery of this new land, and I, for one, will not let it win!"

The people were growling in support of the mayor's bluster, their fear transformed into anger and energy. Soza could feel the subtle shift from paralysis to a frantic willingness to act. In his experience, such a sudden, drastic swing was almost never a good thing.

"Together, we will beat back the darkness! We will find these monsters, whoever or whatever they might be, and we will crush them!" Maddox put his hands on his hips, nodding to the roaring crowd. The gesture pushed the fabric of his coat aside to reveal a massive pistol resting in an elaborate holster. Soza peered closer, as something about the shape and size of the weapon, very reminiscent of the guns Euans was wearing, caught his attention. There appeared to be gems or something similar affixed to various points of the gun. These little baubles were glowing a dull red as if they were small windows into the sullen fires of a well-stoked furnace. He had never seen anything like them before, and his eyes flicked over to the guns on the tall enforcer's hips. There, too, he could see strange, glittering crimson motes.

The crowd around the railway man surged forward, cheering through angry, gritted teeth. The mayor had taken their fear and had masterfully turned it into anger. But no . . . As Soza looked into the eyes of the men and women around him, he could still see the fear there. The anger was a thin veneer layered atop the dread. There was an edge of terror behind even the most fervent voice shouting for revenge and justice.

Soza thought for a moment that the mayor had failed in his efforts, as the fear was still very much alive in the men and women of Tolchico. As he looked up to the nodding, savage grin on the mayor's face and at the green glint in the man's eyes, something clicked in the back of the old man's mind. The mayor looked like a man who had just succeeded in doing exactly what he had set out to do.

Soza began to think that maybe it was time to put Tolchico far behind him.

Chapter 8

Varro felt another spasm shoot up through his legs and back, and he grimaced as it shook down into his arms. His horse sensed the hesitation and threw a disdainful glance over its shoulder. It was all he could do not to jab his heels into the animal's sides. From the moment they had left Sacred Lake, his relationship with the beast had been combative. If the journey up into the mountains was as long as Jomei had said, only one of them would be surviving the passage.

As they moved toward the distant mountains, difficulties with his horse aside, Varro felt a growing conviction that he had made the right choice. Jomei was more open with every swaying step they took over the parched grass, and every revelation he gave pushed heavily upon a lifetime of Varro's assumptions. Whoever they were, these people his new friend worked for were serious folks.

"So, there are others out there, like that preacher?" That the strange man had been more than he had appeared unnerved Varro, but it also vindicated his own gut reaction. Something had struck him as wrong about the man in the dark coat from his first moment in that revivalist tent, but he had lacked any framework upon which to hang his misgivings.

"Many." Jomei's brow furrowed as he spoke, sitting easily in his own saddle. His mount rolled beneath him, and Varro felt another surge of jealousy. He had never learned how to ride a horse in the twisted streets of the Five Points, of course. Still, he thought the silent men at the stables of Sacred Lake could have given him a mount more like Jomei's and less like the bully they had cursed him with.

"And they're more than just run of the mill hard cases?" Varro felt there was a scope to what he had fallen into that still escaped him. It made him uneasy to imagine a shadow legion of men like the preacher wandering the land, spreading poison and discord. If true, it raised a host of other uneasy questions.

"Well," Jomei considered for a moment, his head cocked, his eyes cast vaguely up toward the looming mountains. "You said you think the people who had risen to lead the gangs of your neighborhood similar to the preacher, right?"

Varro grunted assent as he pulled on the reins, trying to drag the horse's head away from a rocky-looking patch of trail.

"It makes perfect sense, from what you've told me, that those men and women were touched by the same evil that had claimed the preacher. Those are things that our Enemy would love to see happen: sowing violence in the streets, causing death and destruction. On a wider scale, those riots disrupted the attempts of the government in Washington to raise the troops they needed to finish the war, forcing it to drag on, killing countless more than the riots alone." He stopped speaking and shot Varro an apologetic look. "I'm sorry. I didn't mean to say—"

Varro had told Jomei a lot about himself during their trek, including the deaths of his parents in the riots. He shook his head. "Don't worry. I know what you meant." He rolled along for a few paces, and then said, "But I still don't understand. Who is this Enemy?" Varro had sensed the capitalization of the word the very first time Jomei had used it. He knew the wider implications were still beyond him, but a suspicion had been forming in the back of his mind for the last few days. "You're not talking about Old Scratch, are you? Are you saying the Devil touched those folks and turned them bad?"

Jomei rode on for a few moments before he responded. "It's a lot more complicated than that."

Varro reared back in his saddle, stunned at the lack of an immediate denial. Sensing another shift in balance, the horse surged and almost threw him into the dusty trail. He sawed at the reins, bringing the beast to an awkward, painful halt, and put his hand up in the air.

"You're not telling me you and all those folks up there believe you're fighting Mephistopheles himself?" A look of skeptical disgust drew down his features. "Are we heading up toward some camp of damned Bible sharps up in the mountains?"

Jomei's head fell to his chest, moving back and forth in minute degrees. When he looked up, there was nothing but pity in his eyes. "Gio, your view of the world, from 'Gospelsharps' to 'Old Scratch', is painfully narrowed by your upbringing and your education. It is a wider world than you could ever possibly imagine, and everything you need to know in order to understand it awaits you up in the mountains." His eyes lost a touch of their pity and grew just a bit harder. "And no, it's not a Bible camp."

Varro shook his head. "No. You've been talking a lot about this big mob running around finding bad folks and taking them down, and that sounds great to me; better than you can know. But if this whole thing is going to come down to chasing God through the meadows and fields, then count me out."

Jomei nudged his horse around in a tight circle to come face to face with Varro. "You have given your word to continue this journey to its end. You have promised that you would not turn back until we had reached our destination. If you are thinking of turning back now, then you are not the man I thought you were, and you should, indeed, turn around here."

Varro jerked his head back as if the other man had slapped him. "I'm just saying . . ."

"You are just saying you doubt our sincerity and, if I'm following your train of thought, our sanity as well. If you cannot conceive of evil in a manifest form, despite what you saw in that tent and what hunted you into that alley, then you are not suited to the tasks ahead. If you recoil at the thought of serving a higher power than yourself, then I do not understand why you mounted that horse in the first place. I have never hidden from you the nature of our Order, or the mission it serves."

Varro stared into those hard, dark eyes. He had never seen Jomei angry before, but the strength and conviction he saw now, he realized, was only a sharper-edged side of the qualities that had convinced him to agree to this journey in the first place. Until now, they had spoken of this 'Order' of Jomei's in only the vaguest of terms, and there had been no real discussion of higher powers or infernal forces.

Their eyes locked, and Jomei's did not waver. It was the young man from the Five Points who eventually looked away.

"I'll be continuing upward. If you return, please see that the horse makes it back to Sacred Lake safe. They will see that you go wherever you wish to go, and you can be done with us." Without waiting for a reply, Jomei turned his mount around and urged it back into a steady pace up the slope.

Varro heard his friend leaving. Pride very nearly caused him to turn back, but in the end, again, he knew there was nothing for him down there.

With a soft sigh, he sawed the reins and kicked his horse back onto the trail, following upward in Jomei's wake.

*****

The fire turned the trees all around them into stark lines of shifting light and shadow, casting a deeper darkness up into the higher branches overhead. The horses whickered softly to each other, standing side by side in the cool moonlight of an adjacent clearing. Jomei sat with his legs folded beneath him, elbows resting on his knees, medallion held loosely in his hands. Varro sat with his back against a tree, staring into the fire from across their little camp.

They had not spoken since their argument the day before.

Varro knew he owed his friend an apology for the judgmental tone he had used, if nothing else. If he were being honest with himself, however, there was probably plenty else. Despite what Jomei had told him about this choice being of his own free will, he knew that his desperation and sense of defeat were more responsible for driving him into the mountains than any conviction or commitment to his friend's strange, vague tales.

There was no denying the strength of Jomei's conviction, or the resolve and peace of the men of Sacred Lake. And there was certainly no doubting the evil of the preacher who had tried to kill him in that alley.

He shifted slightly against the rough bark of the tree; pine needles hissing beneath him. Thoughts of the preacher caused his back to twinge, as they always did.

Off in the distance insects buzzed and hummed. Varro felt his eyes sliding closed as he struggled to stay focused on the fire. Even now, he found that he tired easily. They had maintained a slow and steady pace throughout their journey, but even given all that, each night found him dull with fatigue.

There was so much he wanted to know; so much he did not understand. He had run from his old life and he had been foundering ever since. He was no stranger to violence or crime. He had seen death in half a hundred forms. But to think that it might all be orchestrated by some sinister group? That did not fit with the chaos and the confusion he had experienced in his life, especially the brutal anarchy of the Five Points.

The preacher still haunted his dreams. The empty, shadowed eyes and the glistening corpse sweat followed him down into sleep no matter how exhausted he was. He knew, despite his skepticism, that there was more in that glare than he could understand. It was becoming clear that no matter how ridiculous it seemed, Jomei had the answers to his questions.

And Jomei had not spoken to him since the confrontation on the trail yesterday. Varro was certain there was only one way to get the other man talking again, and his pride was not going to enjoy the process.

"I'm sorry." He blurted the words out, knowing that the more he thought about it, the more difficult it was going to be to say. "I didn't mean to make fun of your faith, or of the Order."

Jomei's shoulders moved with a long slow breath. When he looked up, there was a rueful smile on his face, and he shrugged a sheepish motion. "No sorrier than I am that I lost my temper."

Varro did not return the grin. He shook his head instead, and his eyes were serious. "No, Jomei. I'm lost. From the moment I looked into that . . . that man's eyes in that tent . . . I entered another world. You were right. And the men and women who tore apart the Points *did* have the same look in their eyes. There's too much that I don't know. And I have no reason to doubt that you and your . . . organization, may well have those answers."

Jomei nodded, looking back into the fire. "Please, I understand: I remember what it was like to hear about these things for the first time." He looked up again. "Nothing about the real world is easy to understand, at first glance."

The tree seemed to dig into Varro's wound, and he shifted around again. His horse snorted at the sudden movement, but settled right down. "Please, tell me more about your Order, and what it is, exactly, that they do."

The figure across the fire smiled, this time grimly, and looked back down at the medallion in his hands. "Well, that is a long story. Most of it, sadly, I cannot tell you myself. But suffice it to say, there *are* evil forces at work on Earth, and they *are* working behind the scenes to twist the world into a more brutal, bloody shape. They find men and women like that preacher, and they touch their souls with darkness." His voice sank into a more ominous tone, and his hand floated up to touch the center of his own chest. "Those men go forth and they bring nothing but death and destruction with them." He looked back up. "If there were no one to stand against them, everything would have been lost a long time ago."

Varro looked confused. "Everything . . . as in America?Looks like we're not that far from lost as it is."

Jomei shook his head sharply. "I mean everything, Gio. If it were not for the Order, mankind would have been destroyed long ago."

Varro held up a doubtful hand. "Just how long are you saying your'Order's'been around?"

The fire crackled between them, sending a snap of sparks up into the boughs overhead. Jomei's eyes were solemn as he looked through the burning motes. "Longer than you can understand right now. A lot will be made clear when we arrive at our destination."

Varro nodded and then looked back into the fire. "I've stumbled into something pretty deep, haven't I." It was not a question, but a dull, heavy statement. His eyes flicked up again without warning. "Who is it you work for, Jomei? Who do you serve?"

The other man's head tilted quickly, his lips pursed. "You mean, do we serve God?"

Varro was completely still, but his head jerked a single, shallow nod.

Jomei bowed down over the medallion for a moment, heaving a great, silent sigh. When he looked up again his look was wary. "Gio, there is so much that has been forgotten. And I am woefully unprepared to teach you. All of this will be revealed when we reach—"

"The mountains. I know." Varro picked up a stick nearby and tossed it toward the fire. "I'm beginning to feel like my life is trapped in ice."

"I will tell you that we *do* serve a greater power than mankind, Gio. Is that enough for now?" His look was pleading.

Varro stared at his friend for a moment and then nodded. "It'll have to be, won't it?"

"I'm afraid it will."

The smile that cracked Varro's dour expression was only half-hearted, but it felt better than anything he had worn since the fight. "Well, then, I guess it is."

He went back to looking into the flames, trying to find a comfortable position for his back. The skepticism and loose, vague faith of the Five Points would not serve him well in the mountains, he realized. And to a young man who had lost what little faith he had, that was a nervous thought indeed.

*****

"Does it pay well?" Varro's mouth quirked in a smile as he asked, once again struggling with his mount as the trail narrowed, dropping into a small valley, tall pines rising up on either side.

"Does what pay well?" His companion did not rise to the question, keeping his eyes on the trail, his mouth expressionless.

"Serving a greater power. How's the pay?" His smile grew wider. Things had settled down between them over the last couple of days, and they had found a more comfortable, friendly balance after their talk around the fire.

Jomei shrugged. "We don't really use money." He raised a hand to hold off Varro's scoffing response. "We have money when we need it. We just don't use it amongst ourselves. And we don't spend much time away from the Order unless we're working with a mission team."

Varro shook his head. "It's a lot to get your head around. Sometimes you make it sound like you're an army, and then other times you make it seem like you're a bunch of monks."

"We've already talked about this, Gio." Jomei nudged his horse across a small stream at the center of the canyon, speaking over his shoulder. "Members of the Order serve because they are called. Doing the right thing carries rewards of its own. There is a certain satisfaction in serving something greater than yourself."

"So you keep telling me." He was troubled.

"There is a great evil in the world, Gio. If we do not stand against it, who will? The Union? They serve a grand purpose, but they have more than their fair share of blood on their hands. The Confederacy, steeped in the blood of slaves and freedmen alike?"

"There are lawmen . . ." Varro's tone said even he did not think that was the answer. He had seen more crooked gendarmes in New York than he liked to think, listening to Jomei's words of a coming tide of evil.

"Your lack of faith in the lawmen is telling, Gio." His friend nodded in sympathy. "The Army cannot stop what is coming. The laws of man cannot stop what is coming." His smile faded. "In truth, there is no guarantee that even *we* will be able to stop what is coming." His eyes turned back to Varro with an eerie mixture of conviction and pleading. "And in the face of that, those who know what is coming *must* do everything they can to try, right?"

Varro stared back at him. The fear he saw there was new, and it chilled him, given everything else Jomei had said with such confidence over the last few weeks. He gave a hesitant nod. "I'd say you have to do something."

Jomei nodded, and then turned back in his saddle. They began to rise up out of the valley, their horses pushing hard up the rocky slope. Varro was swearing at his own mount, lashing at its flanks with his slack reins, when he almost drove the animal right into his companion's stationary mount.

"What the—" He was about to give a sharp observation on his guide's horsemanship when he saw what had stopped Jomei.

Sitting their horses with calm majesty, a small party of men was observing them from an outcropping above. Varro instantly recognized the leather, the feathers, and the intricate beadwork from those few, sad half-breeds he had seen since coming west.

They were all men, their long black hair pulled back in braided tails. Each held a short bow, an arrow nocked against the string, held in place with the same hand that held the bow. They watched impassively with glittering black eyes as the two young men gaped up at them.

Varro looked to Jomei's belt where the only weapon they had brought with them rode in a worn old holster. One revolver was not going to make enough of a difference against five tested warriors. He eased his hand down toward his belt knife. If this was his day, he would go down fighting. He was drawing the blade when Jomei's head whipped around, glaring at him.

"Are you an idiot? Sheath your blade before you get us both killed!" The man's eyes were hot with anger, but Varro could only stare at the medallion around his friend's neck. It glowed as brightly as a tiny blue-white sun.

Jomei turned back to the scouting party on the cliff, putting a single empty hand out in a show of peaceful intent.

The tallest of the warriors watched for a moment, then gave a single, solemn nod. The entire group backed their horses out of sight with easy grace. They seemed to disappear into the earth as Varro watched.

When they were gone, Jomei spun on him again. "You were going to take the entire scouting party on with just that damned pocket knife? Even *if* they were inclined to fight, do you think that would have helped at all?"

Varro was still staring up at the cliff where the natives had sat their horses with such easy poise. "I don't understand. They're just going to let us go?" He looked back at Jomei with puzzled eyes.

"Of course they let us go. The Order and the free tribes are fellow travelers in many ways." Jomei seemed somewhat mollified by Varro's continued concern. Clearly he had forgotten what sorts of preconceived notions a man from the Old States might bring with him into the frontier. "If not allies, they are nonetheless on excellent terms with the Order."

Varro shook his head. "You're telling me, you people are friendly with the savages?" His tone went up a notch as fear warred with disbelief. He looked again through the hot, hazy air to where the natives had been. "You're on the same side as the savages?" He could hear a slight note of hysteria in his own voice, and he did not like it. But still, his fear would not loosen its grip.

"Gio, you *must* release what you think you know. The tribes are as diverse as any other peoples of the world, but a great many of them are our friends, yes. They ultimately serve the same masters as we: the natural order of the Earth, as intended by the Creators, over the corruption and desecration of the Enemy."

Varro was not so far gone that his mind did not skip a beat as he registered the word 'Creators'. It became just another piece of information swirling through his head that had no obvious place to land, however. These orphan thoughts were like a flock of confused birds spinning above a storm-wracked beach. "This is their land, isn't it?"

Jomei shook his head. "They do not recognize ownership of the land as you do. They would say, rather, that they are the stewards of the land through which we now pass. Much as my people are the stewards of the high mountain. But to answer the more mundane element of your question, yes, this is their land."

"And they are going to let us pass through it? We're not going to be killed in our sleep?" The fear was ebbing, but a lifetime of preconceptions was not going to wash away in the face of a single encounter.

"They are, and we are not." His companion sat his horse patiently, arms crossed at the wrists over the pummel of his saddle.

Varro knew, had known all his life, that it was death to wander into the territories of the savages. He had heard the stories, seen the images. The barbarian tribes killed without hesitation or compunction when their territory was violated, and often enough, even when it was not. Taking another step into the upper mountains, knowing that there were savages present, was suicide.

And yet the confidence beneath Jomei's words touched those fears. Somehow, he knew they would be safe as they moved further up into the mountains. Something within him, reacting directly to the other man's words or tone, was letting him know they would be alright.

As they pushed their horses back into motion, a more frightening thought occurred to him. He could not have said why, but he suddenly knew he was safer up here, with this strange young man and those silent savages, than he would have been if he had stayed back east.

*****

"I just don't know what to make of all the violence lately." The old man shook his head sadly as he closed the door behind his guest. "That nasty business down in Bloodfield just this past autumn was only the most egregious example." He shook his head again as he moved through the clutter of his office and around the massive oak desk, waving at a hard backed chair for his guest. "Dark times, my friend. Dark times."

The old man's guest nodded in sympathy. Without comment, he lifted a small stack of books from the chair and placed them on a corner of the desk before taking a seat. He pushed his hood back over a head nearly bald, what hair there was cropped so close as to be nearly nonexistent.

"I know, Reverend Stiles, I know." He muttered. "These truly are cursed times."

The reverend peered over the landscape of books, papers, and inkwells between them. His guest was younger than he had expected, but then, everyone looked young to him these days. "So, you were a friend of Uri's, you were saying? Another tragic death.Too many of our good boys taken too soon.Whether it's away on distant battlefields, or here in our own streets." The wispy hair hovering around his glowing pink scalp waved as he shook his head again.

"Thank you, reverend. That means a lot, coming from a man such as yourself. But yes, Uri was a very good friend. He told me, should anything ever happen to him, that you would be able to help me?"

The old man nodded, settling against the cushioned back of his chair. "Yes, yes. Uri was a careful man. A cautious man. I never knew quite what work he did for the church, but he was always busy."

The guest nodded again, his patience slipping. "He was, sir. Did he leave anything behind? A packet, perhaps, for anyone who might be sent to follow him?"

Reverend Stiles tilted his ancient head up to glare aimlessly at the ceiling, one long finger tapping on his pointed chin. "Did he leave . . . oh, my, yes! He did!" The old man lurched out of his chair, stumbled over to a large wardrobe, and began to dredge through drifts of packets and folders stacked haphazardly within. "He left a legal packet. His affairs and whatnot, I believe. Ah, here it is."

The old man held out a thick sheaf of papers, tied together with a crimson leather cord. The guest leaned forward in the rickety old chair to accept it.

The reverend made his slow way back to his own chair and settled in. "I just don't know what to make of it all. All this violence and lack of faith. Some of my more dramatic congregants believe the rapture may soon be upon us, my friend. Do you believe that nonsense?"

The guest nodded, his face somber. "These are dark times, reverend." He repeated the words, feeling the weight and the truth of them as he knew the old man never could. "Well, thank you very much, sir. I do appreciate you holding these for us. It will make completing Brother Uri's mission here much easier."

The old man rose with a smile. "It was my pleasure, my son. The allied churches must help one another whenever we can. Especially when in the pursuit of God's work."

His guest nodded again, bowing slightly over the heavy packet, and backed toward the door. "Please, reverend, allow me to see myself out. Don't trouble yourself."

The old man eased himself back into his chair. "Bless you, my son. And go with God in all your works."

"Indeed reverend. I shall." The door closed with a click, and the reverend's guest pulled his hood back up over his short hair, pushing out the heavy front door of the church and into the winter chill.

*****

The chill that had settled over Washington D.C. in November had been the vanguard of a vicious winter. Frigid air crouched over the capital like a beast settling upon prey. Violent crime was rampant in the poorer quarters as the fear of further war ground down the patience and the nerves of even the most persevering of men. It was, indeed, dark times in the capital.

The hooded man pushed through the frozen, near-empty streets until he came to a small corner tavern, a wooden sign swinging wildly in the wind proclaimed it the 'Pewter Tankard'. A burst of warm, moist air thrust through the opening door to engulf him, and he slammed the door behind him with an almost spiteful burst of strength.

The man scanned the crowded room. It was late afternoon on a bitterly cold day in a dark time for the Republic. Of course, even this shack of a taproom was going to be crowded. He spotted his party wedged into a corner table, and pushed his way through the throng until he could collapse into the hard chair, grabbing a tankard and tossing the contents down without seeking permission.

The men who had been waiting for him watched with dark amusement. The shorter of the two was a dark-skinned man, his close-cropped hair thick, with a fine mustache and a pointed chin beard enhancing the image of a Spanish don suggested by his coloration. The other was a bigger man, the hair on the back of his head tumbling down over his folded hood in a blond wave, his face shaved smooth, looked down as his now-empty mug crashed into the table, and then looked up with one eyebrow quirking upward ominously.

"I expect the next round will be on you, *Mimreg* Antum, or I shall be filing a complaint with the *Etta*." The words were delivered with deadpan sincerity.

"Can we assume things did not go according to plan?" The darker man smiled, throwing an unkind look at his companion as he curled one hand around his own drink.

The *mimreg*, his hood once again pushed back from his gleaming head, looked at the second man as he tossed the thick packet of papers onto the table. "No, I've got everything we need. It's just that I had to go to five different churches before I found the one Uri ended up using."

"Uri was always a canny one." The dark man raised his mug in salute and downed the contents in a single swallow. "But thank the Creators we won't have to stay another night in that blasted inn. It's going to take weeks getting rid of the little friends I picked up there." He gave a vigorous scratch to the side of his head.

"Is there provisions for a new safe house?" The blonde man asked. He waved one hand in the direction of the bar, three thick, calloused fingers raised in silent command.

"I'm sure there is. As you say, Uri was thorough. I don't doubt everything we'll need is in there somewhere. How did the two of you fare in *your* day's activities?"

The three men fell silent as the barkeep navigated through the crowd and dropped three tankards onto the table. He hovered, annoyed, until the bald newcomer slapped coins into his fist.

"There are far more Tainted here than Uri's reports indicated." The darker man leaned close as he talked. "I spent the day walking Independence and Constitution. Work has progressed nicely on their monument to their own inefficiency. They've completed everything but the dome. Rumor has it that construction on that has been suspended, though, with the end of the war so close." He shook his head, looking into the warm amber of his drink. "But as I said. The Tainted seemed to be everywhere."

Antum turned to look at the broad blonde, who nodded in agreement. "I spent most of my day in the taprooms and alehouses between First and Second Streets, behind the Capitol, raising glasses with the true masters of the universe: the bureaucrats." He looked uncomfortable, shooting a glance first toward the darker man, then toward the bald man. "Most of the talk seemed to revolve around the tribes. Someone is stoking up the locals' fear and resentment." He shrugged. "If I didn't know better, I'd say it seems like someone is trying to open a second front in the war, and the free peoples are the target."

The bald man nodded slowly, taking a more measured sip of his new drink. "Good work, both of you. I know it cannot have been easy, given the nature of the men we hunt." He turned to the darker man. "Luys, was there any sign of Uri's contacts? Anything left at any of the usual spots?"

The Spaniard shook his head. "No, none at all. It was eerie, actually. It felt as if the entire city had been scoured of their presence. Fener said he felt the same."

The blonde man nodded. "I tried to reach contacts Uri and his team had made in Congress. No one was to be found. Rathbone, his man inside the White House?Has not been seen since the riots in Bloodfield. Not even a rumor of what might have happened to him. And he was close to the president himself!"

Antum looked back into his drink. "Fener, if you had to gauge how serious the threat to our friends in the west is right now, what would you say?"

The big blonde shrugged, his blunt, honest face troubled. "It's heavy on the ground, *Mimreg*. There is a lot of pressure behind the scenes, and I have to assume it's coming from the Enemy. If you force me to guess, I would say, given the right conditions, the Union will be turning any forces it can spare westward as soon as they finish off the Confederate forces down around Petersburg."

Luys nodded, his own dark eyes shadowed. "None of Uri's contacts within the White House remain, but rumor is that Grant has been back for some time now, preparing for the final push into the Confederacy. They will most likely strike as soon as the weather clears. That will leave them plenty of time to push west before next winter."

Antum leaned back in his chair, the fingers of one hand tapping absently on the table. "The good General's wife is actually a parishioner at one of Uri's allied churches. I spoke with the reverend who presides over the congregation. It is possible, although not entirely likely, that we may be able to influence the General, at least subtly, toward a more moderate pace, if nothing else."

The three men sat quietly, each nursing his tankard and lost in his own thoughts. In the end, Antum looked up again, sparing a glance for each of his men, and placed both hands splayed on the table before him. "Our first priority will have to be a new safe house. But as soon as we are established, we need to get back into the White House. And we will need more than a suborned underling." He looked directly at Fener. "One of us is going to have to gain access to the president."

Fener grinned. "Well, you brought me all the way out here for my easy way with the people, didn't you, *Mimreg*?"

The *mimreg* gave him a sour look and downed the rest of his ale.

Chapter 9

Below them, the plains of the western territories stretched toward the distant horizon. Around them, the vanguard of the towering mountains gathered like Titans preparing to storm the lowlands. Before them, loomed the true peaks of the Rocky Mountains, giving the lie to the intimidating lower peaks. These monsters challenged the very definition of the word 'mountain' Varro had carried with him out of the west.

They had left the dragging heat of the desert far behind. Each morning greeted them with the biting chill of the mountains, and did not grow much warmer afterward. The sun seemed distant and remote in the high, thin air. Thick pine forests lapped out of the low, folded valleys like enormous green ocean waves frozen in time. It was a landscape alien to a child of the twisted alleys and byways of the Five Points.

"I'm curious as to what you people could have built up here." Varro jerked his chin toward the towering peaks above. "This far from civilization, even a camp would have to be tough."

Jomei looked over to him, pushing the cork back into a fur-lined canteen. "Oh, I think you'll be impressed. And when the citadel was built, civilization was even further away."

Varro shook his head. "Another piece that doesn't fit the puzzle. Where does your Order come from? How long have they been up here? Have you always been friendly with the savages?"

Jomei gave him a sharp look as he reined his horse around and back toward the highlands. "You're going to have to learn to curb your language around them, first. They prefer being called the free people, or just the people. Sometimes we call them the tribes, as well. And yes, we have always been friendly with them. In fact, our ancestors were here in the mountains before their ancestors first came up out of the south. Most of them think of us as spirit people, or ghost people. We are usually seen as servants of the land, and thus, of course, the Great Spirit."

Varro kicked his own mount into action, catching up after a few awkward leaps on the uneven ground. "The Great Spirit." His voice was doubtful. "And *do* you? Serve the Great Spirit, I mean?"

Jomei shrugged. "It all depends, of course. The concept of the Great Spirit is fluid, often shifting drastically between tribes and bloodlines. We like to think that the Great Spirit is akin to our own objects of faith."

Varro rode in silence for a while, trying to fathom the scope of time his friend was so casually referencing. There was no doubting the faith behind Jomei's words. And as that faith was central to what Varro had decided he himself needed, he tried to open his mind to the possibilities. Even with that conscious decision, however, it was not something that came easily.

They were moving up through another cleft in the tumbled granite, pines rising up on either side, when Varro spoke again. "So, this Order must be pretty big, all over the world and all. Where do you fit into it, Jomei? If you don't mind my asking."

Jomei smiled. "At the bottom, of course. How else would I have ended up escorting your sorry carcass up into the high peaks, eh?"

Varro nodded. "Of course. And someone like Elijah, or Fosh, they're probably pretty high up?"

Jomei shook his head, looking at him from the corner of his eye. "Perhaps. Elijah and Fosh are field commanders. Fosh is a *mimreg*; they usually lead small teams, or, as Fosh, perform a support function within a larger command. Elijah, on the other hand, is an *altcap*, a frontline commander, responsible for a larger team of men, often over a hundred warriors at once. Both command respect and obedience, although of different degrees. Both titles derive from a language older than history itself."

"*Mimregs* . . . *Altcaps* . . ." Varro rolled the names around in his mouth. They fit poorly, not touching upon even the hint of a familiar word or sound in his mind. A smile escaped his thoughtful demeanor. "And what are you, then? A *nimrod*?"

Jomei shot him a look. "I serve as a *spica* to the cause."

Varro's accent, and his experiences in the Five Points, caused immediate confusion. "Speaker? Your bosses are called *mumrahs*, or *murogs* . . . and you're a *speaker*?"

"*Spica*. S – P – I – C – A. It means servant, or one who serves, in the ancient tongue."

"The ancient tongue of what? Rome?" Varro sawed the reins to the side, driving his mount around a fallen boulder.

"More ancient than that." Jomei waited on the other side of the tumbled stone, then whickered at his own horse, gently nudging it back into motion. "And infinitely farther away."

Another blank stare, and then Varro shook his head, deciding to move on before he was lost completely within the labyrinth of his companion's seemingly senseless commentaries. "Okay. *Spic-Ah*.And the *mumrugs*, or whatever.If they are the lower level commanders, who's next? How high up does it go?"

Jomei shaded his eyes and looked up at the gleaming peak hovering overhead. "Well, above the *mimreg*s and the *altcap*s stand the *arcsens*. They are the strategic commanders of the Order, dictating the greater movements and missions of the warriors and mission teams."

Varro nodded. "Okay, that makes sense to me, I guess. And above the . . . *artisans*?"

His companion bowed his head, one hand running through the bristles of his hair. "*Arcsens*. And above the *arcsens* are the *sircans*. They are the leaders of the Order. There are very few, and they serve as the rulers and advisors of the entire Order. Each continent is ruled over by a body known as an *Etta*, named for the brightest star in the night sky. Each *Etta* is comprised of the three *sircans* of that continent and their *arcsen* companions, who work as advisors and foils."

The strange names and concepts swirled through Varro's mind, and a sharp pain began to form behind his left eye. He pinched the bridge of his nose, shaking it back and forth as if trying to dislodge some clinging nuisance. "I think that's about enough for now, Jomei. I'm sure there will be plenty of time to learn more once we get wherever we're going. Anyway—"

Varro's breath left his lungs in a painful wash as the mountain itself struck him in the chest and swept him from his horse's back.

*****

The world devolved into a swirling kaleidoscope of sky, rock, and tree as he tumbled down a jagged slope. An enormous, furious beast was latched to his chest, snarling and growling with primal fury, claws scrabbling at him as they fell. His hand fumbled for the knife at his belt, but he fetched up against a sharp boulder and again his breath exploded from his body. In the pain and the stunned confusion it felt as if the beast that clung to him was larger than his horse. He had never seen a mountain lion before, and in the swirling chaos he could not think clearly, but a steady drumbeat of disbelief at the thing's size throbbed within his head as he tumbled down the slope.

Somewhere high overhead he could hear Jomei screaming somethinghe could not understand. The guttural snarling in his ear drowned out the sense of his words. Hot, wet breath gusted into his face, and again, with the strength of desperation, he clawed for the knife at his belt. He had no idea what was happening, but he felt every bruise and scratch from his fall, and the claws of the creature hovering over him pressed him against cold, jagged rock. His back twisted with agony as his wound was ground into the stone.

With the frenetic power of fear and frustration, Varro twisted himself out of the beast's grasp, rolling to his feet and drawing the short blade. He scrambled backward, glancing behind him to make sure he did not throw himself off another cliff. When he was sure of his footing, he swung back around, the knife weaving before him in a practiced fighter's grip . . . and froze in place, his mouth falling open.

The thing standing before him was no mountain lion; it was like nothing he had ever seen before. Standing on its hind legs like a man, its form was twisted and blurred, with muscles that strained beneath the sleek, shadow gray pelt of a big cat. Arms like those of a man hung loosely at the thing's sides, clawed hands splayed. Emerging from the bunched, gnarled strength of obscenely brawny shoulders, the thing's head was transformed and misshapen, an obscene fusion of human and feline features currently twisted into an expression that was unmistakably enraged.

Varro looked wildly around for some means of escape, but his fall had taken him down to a small plateau; there was nothing but open air or sheer cliff face looming on every side. The few pines clinging to the thin soil offered no protection, and with a sinking feeling that was barely discernible beneath the churning fear and disbelief in his gut, he realized that he was about to be killed by a creature that could not possibly exist.

Far above, Jomei continued to shout, his voice hoarse and frantic. Other voices, lower but no less urgent, bellowed as well, throwing back berating tones in words he did not understand. Varro had eyes only for the warped beast that slavered before him. Details that had escaped him on his first, panicked glance stood out to him as he struggled to bring his breath back under control.

The beast wore what looked like native jewelry, plates of a glossy, blue-green material chased with gleaming silver details hung with feathers and bits of fur to form primitive talismans with an undeniable beauty and power all their own. Despite Varro's own imposing height, the creature towered over him, even in its fighter's crouch. Its black, rubbery lips pulled back from cruel fangs. The monster leapt at him with a snarl like the massive blade of a sawmill biting into ancient pine.

Varro leaned to his right, his knife hand coming up across his body, guarding against a punch or slash. Instinct locked into place despite the mind-numbing denial rushing through his blood. He had responded to the charge of larger opponents with exactly this move countless times before back in the Points. Invariably, they had been clumsy, relying on their bulk and momentum. They always left themselves open to a low slash or punch, which would either put them out of the fight for good or leave them with a wound that would weaken them as the combat raged on, rendering the end a foregone conclusion.

A furry arm snaked out from the thing's storming charge and grabbed him by the shoulder, rolling him into a crushing bear hug that pinned his arms to his sides and forced what breath he had recovered from his mouth as his ribs creaked alarmingly. A burning rush of new pain flashed through the dull ache of his healing injuries. It happened so fast that he had no time to bring the knife up. The weapon was pinned by his thigh, useless. The monster shook him twice, slamming his feet into the ground, and the knife fell, clattering among the rocks and pine needles.

The beast's mouth was by his left ear as it crushed him to its chest, both of its cable-like arms tightening around him. Its breath was hot on his cheek as he struggled to escape. His mind, starved for breath, trapped within the nightmare grip of a horrific beast, suffered another terrible blow as he realized, with growing horror, that the snarling, snapping sounds were resolving into words.

"You defile the sacred ground with your footsteps, wretch." The breath burned on his skin. "You die here, and the Earth will be well-rid of you."

Varro was lashing back and forth now, his mind incapable of any thought beyond escape. Everything else faded to a vague, unimportant background noise. The creature, its words, his injuries, even the shouting from the cliffs above meant nothing to him as he struggled for breath. His strength had always been equal to any task. The utter helplessness and despair rising up to choke him now was completely alien. A blackness leeched into his vision, closing the bright world into a distant tunnel growing more and more remote with each failed attempt to draw in air.

"Irontooth!" The word was gibberish. He was too concerned with his imminent death to concern himself with nonsense sounds. More voices took up the call, repeating the sound over and over, but they were muffled and distant, barely audible over the roaring in his ears.

"Irontooth, *stop*! He is chosen of the Spirit People!" The words, spoken in a thick accent, again meant nothing to him, but they meant something to the beast. The arms around him loosened their grip, just enough that Varro's lungs, of their own accord, heaved in a breath of cold mountain air. Several more followed, and his mind and vision began to clear.

"You must release him, for the sake of the ancient bonds!"

The snarling voice in his ear spoke again. "Spirit People." The beast snuffled as if checking his scent. "Not likely, with the blood I smell upon him."

Next, he heard Jomei's voice, shouting down from above. "He is an Initiate of the Holy Order of Man, my lord Irontooth. He is protected by the rights and laws of the free people!"

Varro craned his face up toward the light and saw that Jomei was holding out his medallion, its gem glowing a fierce blue-white.

The creature released him with a violent jerk, spinning him to the rocky ground where he landed on all fours, his burning lungs heaving. The beast snarled something under its breath in its strange language, and then turned away from him dismissively, climbing up the sheer face of the cliff without seeming effort.

Varro, falling onto his side, glanced up to watch the creature. He stared at it, its muscles shifting smoothly as it rose above him. He bowed his head to the cool dirt, his mind shivering at the repeated shocks of recent memory.

It took Jomei several minutes to bring Varro back up to the top of the cliff, even when several of the native warriors dropped down to help. Eventually, he was huddled by his friend's side, a canteen clutched in one shaking hand, staring at the towering beast that continued to glare at him through dark, inscrutable eyes. He knew that if the creature had its way, he would be dead.

It spat into the churned needles at his feet, muttering something. One of the warriors nodded and turned back to where Varro sat, propped against a rocky outcropping, the canteen curled to his chest. Jomei stood nearby, his arms folded. He looked annoyed, rather than angry. Varro noticed, with returning anger, that his friend had never even drawn a weapon.

"Chief Irontooth would have you understand that this newcomer enters the lands of the Great Spirit stinking of blood. If you would have him enjoy the protection of the ancient pacts, you must keep him closer to you, and wear your talisman more openly." The man gestured with an ornate staff at the medallion glowing on Jomei's chest. "There are rumblings of war coming out of the east, and his kind," the man indicated the bent and bowed figure at his feet with a jerk of his chin. "His kind are howling for blood in voices that will not be long denied. There will be war, and even the Great Spirit does not yet know how the free people will respond."

Jomei nodded, and Varro was reminded that the young man was at least part native himself. "We understand." He turned to the hulking feline figure. "Please accept my apologies, Chief Irontooth. I will keep my charge closer and be certain he does not wander from my gaze. The reliquary medallion shall be clearer from this moment forward."

The beast, Irontooth apparently, grunted. It spat another comment, looking over its massive, hunched shoulder to glare at the *spica*.

The warrior cleared his throat. "Chief Irontooth wishes you to tell your elders about this incident. There will come a time when a choice must be made. Chief Irontooth says that this time is near at hand, and soon the land will burn from sea to sea, and the mountains will be no refuge for the Spirit People."

Varro looked up at Jomei, and was startled to see shock and concern on his friend's face.

Jomei nodded again. "I will make sure the *Etta* hear the words of the great Chief Irontooth. Come the flames or no, the Order will always stand with the free tribes."

The monster's enormous head nodded once, the big black eyes flicked between the two men, then blinked, and he was gone, striding purposefully into the darkening pines.

Varro grunted as he pushed himself gently to his feet. He stood, with only a slight stoop in favor of the burning pains along his back and the flaring discomfort radiating out from his gunshot wound, as the scouting party began to follow their enormous chieftain. Each warrior nodded solemnly to Jomei as they passed. Back in the woods, watching through the spiky branches of the surrounding trees, glittering eyes twinkled in the shadows. Several young tribesman stood watching their elders take their leave. The young men clutched weapons in uncertain hands, several turning to follow the others away.

Soon, only one figure remained to watch the last of the warriors depart.

The boy was young, not yet ten years at the oldest, despite a body that rippled with muscle. His skin was as dark as midnight, his broad features speaking of the distant plains half a world away, or the slave plantations tragically nearer at hand. Varro's brows came down as he peered closer. The boy saw him and clutched at his own weapon more tightly. It was an enormous tomahawk: a hammer whose massive stone head would have been a challenge for Varro himself to wield with any grace. The boy nodded, probably mimicking the warriors, and Varro found himself nodding back, wincing slightly at the pain the motion drove up his back and neck.

The large dark-skinned boy backed into the shadows until the pine forest swallowed him, as it had the rest of his party. As soon as they were alone, Varro collapsed back onto his rocky seat with a pained gust of breath. His mind was still cold from his brush with death, his arms tingling with the memory of the creature's grip crushing the life from him. It was too much, and his body started to shake in delayed reaction.

Jomei stood for a moment, watching the forest, before he realized that his friend had collapsed yet again. He hurried to Varro's side, and then moved to his own mount, pulling a thick blanket from one of his saddlebags.

"Here," the *spica* tossed the blanket over his companion's shoulders. "You're suffering from shock. You need to keep warm until we can make a camp and get a fire going." He stood, surveying the narrow trail for a moment. "There's a stand of lodgepole pines a little way ahead. It should keep the wind off our backs while I make a fire."

Varro was still shaking despite the blanket, his battered body shiveringwith dull denial. He looked up at Jomei with hollow eyes, his brows pleading for some return to normalcy.

His friend nodded, helping him to his feet and easing him toward his horse. The animal was skittish with the lingering smell of fear and blood. With Jomei's help, the beast stayed still long enough for Varro to mount, his hand clutching the reins like a man clinging to a lifeline. For once, the mount did not challenge the rider's uneasy seat, and even in his shocked state, he smiled in tired thanks. His mind was fixed upon far more troubling issues.

"I know you have a lot of questions." Jomei pulled himself up into his own saddle, looking sideways at his friend. "I promise, we will take care of your wounds, get you all cleaned up, and I will answer any questions you may have, as soon as we get a bit further up the mountain."

Varro nodded again, concentrating on getting his horse moving in the right direction, and Jomei smiled at him.

"I told you there were more things happening here than you could understand."

*****

"And they can change into animals . . ." Varro's voice was flat. His reins were loose in his hands, his battered body, swathed in bandages, swayed absently with his horse's every step. His eyes were dull with shock.

"Not all of them." Jomei watched his friend warily. Varro had been repeating similar listless questions for more than a day. He had never meant for the big man to face such drastic truths so quickly on the heels of his encounter with the Tainted preacher at the railhead. But events in the tribal lands, and whatever was going on out east, had taken that decision out of his hands.

"Not all of them can change into animals . . ." It was clear Varro saw this as scant comfort.

Jomei shrugged. "No. We do not know the full extent of their powers, how they work, or what their limitations are. But we know that only the most powerful are able to transform themselves as Irontooth did yesterday."

Varro continued moving steadily forward, his eyes staring into the trail ahead of him without seeing. "Only the most powerful."

Jomei felt frustration building in his chest, but knew he had to contain it. His friend had just had his eyes torn painfully open to some of the deeper realities of the world. Things Jomei himself had taken for granted for over a decade, Varro was trying to process now, on the trail, mere weeks after suffering a grievous, life-threatening wound at the hands of the evil minions of the great Enemy itself. If anyone deserved some patience at this point, it was Gio.

"I told you, Gio, the powers of the Earth are greater than you could ever believe. With the Order, should you complete your training and choose to join, you will learn this for yourself. The free peoples of the tribal lands manipulate the powers of the Earth in their own way, channeling the powers of the sky into their weapons, manipulating the powers of the ghost world in battle, and the most powerful warriors calling forth the might of their spirit guides to change the very flesh of their bodies." He gestured vaguely into the surrounding pine forests. "They have always been careful to conceal their powers from even their own, uninitiated people." A slight tremor vibrated beneath his voice. "It is very rare to see one of their great war leaders in the fullness of his power."

Varro's head rose, his haunted eyes finding his friend's earnest face. "And you are allied to these creatures."

"Alliance is too strong a term, it is more of—"

"And yet they attacked us, and very nearly killed me." Even these words lacked the heat they seemed to deserve.

Jomei felt a bubble of guilt rising in his throat. "I don't understand that. Something bad must be happening back east if they are so concerned with defending their territory, they would attack travelers on this trail. Only those of the Order could have made it this far."

Varro nodded. His eyes still dull as he turned back up the slope. "This trail. And how far are we from the end of this trail?"

There was something troubling buzzing just beneath his voice, and Jomei tried to infuse his words with as much energy and enthusiasm as he could. "No more than two days, Gio. And I promise you: when we arrive, your heart will truly be filled with awe, and your spirits raised anew."

Varro nodded again, but his shoulders were still slumped, his face was still slack, and he gave no further response as he allowed his mount to pick its own way up the trail.

*****

A ragged escarpment rose up before them in the chill dawn light. The trail, more clearly defined than it had been for many days, wound around the rocky ledge and disappeared from view. Jomei had pulled his horse up as soon as they were clear of a last, thick stand of fir and spruce trees erupting from the rocky soil of the high valley.

"Just around this rise lies the next step in your life, Gio, if you still feel strongly enough to take it." Jomei's voice was solemn, and Varro felt as if they carried some deep, ritual meaning.

Varro had had a rough time of it in the days immediately following Irontooth's attack, but at last a shadow of his old spirit was starting to come through. He nodded, his eyes drawn to where the trail disappeared behind the rocks.

Jomei maneuvered his horse around to search Varro's face. "Everything changes as soon as we ride around this corner, Gio. Everything. Nothing in your life will ever be the same."

Varro's lack of deeper conviction, the hole in his heart that had secretly driven him up into this high place, ate at him now. He knew that his choice to come here, despite the deep draw that he felt, was motivated more by a lack of faith in himself and in the future, than in any work Jomei and his brothers had done, even in saving his life.

He nodded his head sharply. "I understand." He wanted to jab his heels into his horse's barrel and drive it around the corner, forcing the issue and leaving the old world behind.

Jomei peered into his eyes, not satisfied until Varro met his gaze. "Your training will be hard, Gio. It will be the hardest thing you have ever done. It will test your mind, your body, and your soul, and the truth of it will take place within the silence of your heart." He leaned into the space between them, repeating with gritted teeth, "within the *silence* of your heart, Gio."

"I understand." Varro did not understand. But he knew that if he thought about things any longer, his guilt would get the better of him and he would drag the damned horse's head around and head back down to the plains. "Let's go."

Jomei sat back in his saddle, watching Varro's shifting gaze, then nodded again. He looked at the rocky spine for a moment, and then flicked his reins with a soft snick. "Alright then. Let us see what we shall see."

Together their horses began to walk forward, toward the featureless gray cliff and whatever lay beyond.

*****

Varro braced himself as they rode toward the rampart of broken stone. After everything he had heard and seen on his journey, and before at Sacred Lake and the railhead, his concept of reality had been so shaken that his mind was nearly blank as he stared straight ahead. The sense of expectation was vague, tinged with an edge of nervous fear. Over a week ago he had left the hot, dry plains with a vague sense that there were no other choices left open to him. His faith in the concrete world of the everyday, however, had been firmly in place. Now? He had no idea what to expect.

Jomei rode a length or two ahead, casting expectant looks over his shoulder. His friend's anticipation was palpable, and Varro began to resent the attention. He wished, for a moment, that he was alone, so that he could experience whatever awaited him on the other side of the ridge without the weight of the other's expectations on his mind.

All of those thoughts, and indeed thought all together, abandoned him as he pulled his horse around the corner, brushing against the tall pines at the foot of the cliff, and beheld what the fold of the mountain had hidden from view. Rising above him, impossibly large and yet ponderous in its concrete reality, was a vision that looked as if it had been dropped directly from some Oriental's opium dream and into the forbidding mountains of the western territories.

Carved from the living stone of the mountain face was the intricate facade of some ancient temple or palace. Pillars, fluted and engraved with elaborate detailing, rose from imposing foundations at the foot of the wall to dizzying heights high overhead. Windows and balconies, formed from the very rock of the mountain itself, pierced the imposing vastness with an aesthetic that seemed both alien and pleasing at the same time. Towers and turrets rose seamlessly from natural folds and ramparts in the mountain itself, guarded the citadel. The views from their lofty heights must have been incredible, reaching all the way down to the plains far below.

Fortress-like details and features sprouted from as far up the mountain face as Varro could see, hinting at the cyclopean scope of the structure and the extent of the excavations within. The mountain before him had been transformed into the largest structure he had ever seen or even heard of. It dwarfed any of the buildings around the Five Points, and the rest of New York City. He sat on his horse, his eyes wide and his mouth gaping, craning his neck at the ornate details of the amazing facade obscured by the clouds above.

He could identify no single style or characteristic that he could recognize. All he knew of art and architecture he had glimpsed, vaguely, from the dirty streets of New York, but even so, he noticed the confusion of styles and shapes. The pillars looked as if they could be Roman or Greek, and yet there was a flair to them that denied any such mundane heritage. The high, sweeping style of the walls, towers, and buttresses reminded him of pictures he had once seen of European palaces, and yet, again, something about them seemed to disdain being pinned down to any particular time or place. He recognized it for the fortress and castle that it was, and yet it was alien and strange at the same time, with an impact all its own.

Slowly, he came to realize that they were no longer alone. The leveled floor of the valley, forming an expansive field reaching off into the distance to either side, was full of men and women in a variety of clothes, performing a dizzying array of activities. He recognized several different training exercises, including a large group of people in armor-like padding going through an elaborate dance of attack and defense, each following the graceful flow of an instructor who stood before them. In other places, warriors on horseback, their gear and tack strange and sweeping, performed complex maneuvers recreating the ebb and flow of cavalry attacks with a classical flair.Other than an occasional shouted order, the scene unfolded before him in perfect silence.

Varro swung his head mutely toward Jomei, who watched him with a broad, expectant smile. "I told you that you would be impressed." His voice was light, but there was a proud fire in his eyes. "Giovanni Varro of the Five Points, I give you The Acropolis, Citadel of the Holy Order of Man in the Sunset Lands."

The title seemed grandiose, and yet at the same time it seemed to fit this colossal edifice perfectly. The militant activities sweeping across the fields before them, as archaic and remote as they appeared, fit the moment and the scene, perfectly.

"It's . . . amazing . . ." Varro's voice caught in his throat. He could never remember having felt such crushing awe before. The faith and commitment that had crafted such a fantastical stronghold in such a bleak, remote location must surely be miraculous. He struggled to drag his eyes from the scene. "The Sunset Lands?"

Jomei, his smile still firmly in place, shrugged. "It's an ancient name. Spreading out across the world, mankind often named remote regions of the world in relation to its current position. The Orient is to the east, but to the east of what? The exotic empire of Nipon is called the Land of the Rising Sun, and yet, from the west coast of the Americas, the sun *sets*over that distant island. It was much the same for the New World, for those who were aware it existed at all. From ancient Europe, the west was always seen as a magical destination. Many cultures believed that the land of the dead was located beyond the horizon that swallowed the sun each evening. Many of them took to calling any land found to the west the Sunset Lands because of it." He shrugged again. "Like I said, it's an old name."

Varro went back to watching the activities coursing across the marshaling fields around them. A man detached himself from a group wearing plain, pale shirts and pants despite the chill air. The man wore armor that made him look as if he had walked out of some tale of knights and princesses, although his face, peering from the shadows of his elaborate helm, had nothing of the fairytale about it. Blonde hair, long and ratty, hung down the sides of his head within the helmet, while a full beard and mustache of the same yellow gold surrounded a firm, disapproving mouth.

Jomei cleared his throat and leaned toward his friend, whispering, "Remember: your training takes place in the silence of your heart."

The young gang fighter from the Five Points looked a question at his companion, but the armored man was upon him, standing only a few strides away, his gauntleted hands balled on his hips in an attitude of easy disdain.

"*Spica* Jomei." The voice was harsh, as if it had been ravaged to a hoarse phantom of its former strength, and yet there was still great power within it. "A recruit?"

"Yes, *Mimreg* Zain. Giovanni Varro, of New York City."

The man called Zain looked up at Varro as if he were staring at a broken piece of machinery. "Indicators?"

Jomei looked down. "He has the sight, *Mimreg*. Also, a reliquary medallion of Sacred Lake acknowledges him. Both *Altcap* Golah and *Mimreg* Fosh assented to his recruitment."

The armored man nodded. Not once had he addressed Varro, and he was beginning to feel the old familiar burn in his gut. He had never appreciated being ignored.

Mimreg Zain spoke again, once more addressing Jomei and not Varro. "The *Etta* was apprised of your arrival, and it was anticipated you would arrive in time for your recruit to be included in my current wave. Have him join the others in the far field, and you may go."

The man turned and walked away without waiting for a reply.

Jomei nudged his horse closer to Varro's. "Remember, Gio. The silence of your heart."

Varro looked at him sideways. He looked down at his horse and his gear, and then back again to his friend. "Alright. But—"

"*Spica*, is there an issue?" Zain had stopped ten paces away, twisting to look back at them.

"No, *Mimreg*. He will be along presently." Jomei called out, and then reached out to take Varro's reins. "You've wanted to get rid of this horse for days anyway. Go. It's probably easier this way." He gestured with an abrupt hand. "Go."

Varro stared at Jomei for a moment, and then slid off his horse. He took a few steps toward the training group, but then turned to look at his friend and his horse. Jomei waved him away, pulling the riderless horse around and heading toward the enormous main gates, concealed behind soaring pillars.

Mimreg Zain was surging across the field with purposeful strides when Varro finally caught up with him, nearly sprinting the last few steps. "I'm sorry, um . . . *Mimreg*. I thought—"

Zain spun around, the back of his open hand cracking across Varro's cheek and throwing him to the ground.

The seasoned gang fighter shook his head, the ringing in his ears subsiding only after he shuffled himself upright, glaring at the armored man. His cheek throbbed. Every cut and bruise he had earned on the trail ached from the wrenching impact.

"Why—"

This time he saw the other man wind up to strike. He even raised his hands in a familiar guarding attitude that had saved him from countless blows throughout his short life. Somehow, the *mimreg*'s open hand wove through the defensive block contemptuously, slapping him across the opposite cheek with an open hand. The strike burned, anger rose in his eyes, but beneath it there was a vague sense of betrayal. In the face of all the wonder and beauty that had just been revealed to him, the only bright moment in the last few weeks of strangeness, threat, and pain, this man was slapping him like a wayward child?

The warrior stood relaxed in his archaic armor, his face calm if somewhat sneering, his eyes cold and steady. The bustling activity all around them had ceased and every pair of eyes stared at Varro with inscrutable indifference.

Fueled by both the pain and the embarrassment, Varro's hand dropped from his burning cheek. "You bas—"

This time the *mimreg*'s gauntleted fist, closed into a battering ram of steel-sheathed leather and muscle, slid through his hastily raised arms to strike him on the point of his jaw. Varro felt his feet leave the ground. He felt the entire world lurch out from underneath him as he knew a moment of weightless, disorienting flight. Then he crashed to the earth, landing on his torn, bruised, and scarred back with a sharp cry. This time the pain was a roaring, discordant symphony. A rushing in his ears drowned out all other sound, his entire face pulsing with thought-shattering agony. He tried to blink away flashes of bright light that washed out any other sight. He tried to push himself up into a sitting position, his head reeling, the world unsteady beneath him. *Mimreg* Zain towered above him, the beautiful outer walls of the Acropolis glowing dully behind him. The man held up a single, warning finger.

Their eyes remained locked as the big New Yorker pushed himself upright, first to one knee, then rising unsteadily to his feet. From the corner of his eye he could see Jomei sitting his horse, staring at them with an unreadable expression.

And in the swirl of Varro's mind, with a world of possible responses churning through his head, almost all of them probably guaranteed to end with his death, his friend's words came back to him. Silence. His training would occur within the *silence* of his heart.

Even with the realization, part of Varro wanted to scream at the man standing before him, or even shout out to his friend. Why the secrecy? Why the charade?

But where else did he have to go?

Slowly and painfully, Varro dipped his head to Zain, and then gestured for him to continue on toward the training group. The trainer stared at him for a moment, the corners of his eyes tightening, then nodded in turn and spun away, his armor glinting.

Silent against the blue sky, the Acropolis was carved out of a mountain that loomed above them like the palace of an Olympian god.

Chapter 10

High up on the forward wall of the Acropolis, notionally supported by the immense pillars carved into the stone of the mountain, was a large chamber known only as the Balcony. Intended as a vantage point for the commanders of the citadel's defenders should they ever come under direct attack, the room was wide and airy. Long, high, open windows stretched across its front. In the absence of discovery or imminent attack, it was often a location for higher-ranking members of the Order to meet, often to watch the training and exercises of the forces below, or to reflect upon the strength of the Order in the open air of the Creators' beauty.

Sircans Ignatius and Nura met upon the Balcony now, accompanied by their arcsens, Siraj and Ivar. Nura and Siraj stood by the windows while Ignatius and his lieutenant sat at a long, heavy table that could have hosted half a hundred revelers should the Order decide a fete was in order.

No member of the Order had been in the mood for celebration for many months now.

"Well, he arrived just in time." *Arcsen* Siraj, still wearing his ornate armor, folded his encased arms over the stone sill of the railing. "You know there would have been no forcing Zain to take him had he missed this wave's commencement."

"I'm not concerned with which *mimreg* trains the boy." *Sircan* Ignatius sat at the table, his chair canted toward the windows and one of his elbows resting on the glossy surface, hand loosely grasping the stem of a goblet. "He will be trained, and he will succeed or fail as his own abilities and spirit dictate. There is no higher power steering his path."

"He is an . . . impressive specimen." *Sircan* Nura, now wearing her own armor, rested her delicate chin on the palm of one hand, the other hanging out into open air through the window. "If ever there was a man who looked touched by prophecy, it is this one."

"There are many warriors on the field below." *Arcsen* Ivar, in a loose tunic and pants, sat across from Ignatius, his elbows on his knees and his head bowed down, staring at a medallion he held in both hands. "This easterner is no special case in that regard."

"Have you seen the markings on his arm?" Siraj turned, one elbow hitched onto the sill. "The man is marked as if he had walked out of the prophecy itself. Surely you don't intend to ignore that?"

"In my experience, young Siraj, the Creators are never so literal as to stamp a label on one of their chosen instruments." Ignatius's mild rebuke was accompanied with a gentle smile.

"Reports out of Washington do nothing to assuage fears of an approaching battle, though, Ignatius." Nura tilted her head to speak into the room, but her eyes were still wandering the field below. "If the Enemy succeeds in convincing Grant to move west against the free tribes, all of the pieces will be in place. Even you will not be able to deny the tide of history then." Her voice was reasonable, but there was a new hardness beneath it.

Tensions within the Acropolis had been steadily rising since *Mimreg* Uri's mission team had been destroyed in Washington. Those members of the Order who held that they were living in the era of the ancient prophecy's fulfillment were growing in number, while the voices of reasoned restraint, though respected, were becoming fewer and less convincing.

"I would not hang my hopes on this boy from the old states, regardless." Ivar looked up from the gleaming reliquary pendent. "I have observed him on the trail into the mountains, and in the face of Chief Irontooth's indiscretion. The boy lacks discipline and strength of will. He may be a scrapper from some hellish street, but he is no spiritual warrior."

"And that is why we conduct our training as we do." *Arcsen* Siraj turned back to look at the men and women moving about on the field far below. "None of us were stalwart warriors of the faith when we were brought here, Ivar. There is growth required of all before we can meet the challenges the Creators put in our paths. That young man is a fighter, as you say. And Fosh and Golah both saw something in him. He has met all the necessary criteria for training. If nothing else, he will hold a sword in the line on the day of judgment."

"And because of the ink on his arm, you believe that the world will twist and turn to put the boy in the right place at the right time, to bring about your precious prophecy, and stave off disaster for yet another generation." *Arcsen* Ivar bent back to the medallion, his lips twisted in a bitter snarl, his voice dripping scorn.

The other members of the *Etta* in attendance shared a concerned look. Ignatius, the most familiar with Ivar's moods and dispositions, leaned closer to his subordinate. "I know you feel the divide within the Order bitterly, Ivar. But you seem to hold a special resentment for this boy. Do you sense something in him as you watch? Is there a danger here, to the Order or our work, that you feel you should share?"

Ivar shook his head. "No, *Sircan*." He looked up, a faint, harsh smile floating around the edges of his mouth. "I just find it distasteful, taking such ephemeral things into account as we strive to keep the Enemy and all his works at bay." He stood abruptly. "This boy is nothing but a mortal man, like the rest of us. He is no avatar of a forgotten prophecy to save us from the Enemy, ourselves, or anyone else."

Without waiting for a reply, Ivar nodded a terse farewell to Ignatius and strode from the hall, his heavy boots echoing off the carved walls.

Nura and Siraj both turned back to look down upon the fields far below. The training group was following *Mimreg* Zain out into the surrounding forests. The infamous trainer ran as if he were not wearing battle plate. The trainees all wore loose, pale clothes. All except for the newcomer, this Giovanni Varro. The poor man wore heavy pants and a button-down shirt with a vest. Not clothing that lent itself well to a terrain run into the wilds.

"We will watch Varro as we would watch any other recruit that came to us with an open heart." Ignatius spoke, not moving from the table. "Thoughts on the prophecy cannot twist our observations or expectations, lest the Enemy breach our defenses through our blind hubris. It has happened before. You all know this."

"Faith is only referred to as hubris by those who do not believe, *Sircan* Ignatius." Nura's voice carried a warning edge. "And the blade of excessive pride cuts both ways." She turned slightly at the hips to look back at him. "Perhaps you, too, should be careful, lest you fall into the sin yourself."

With a smile, Ignatius raised a hand, acknowledging the point with a nod. He sipped the last of his wine, placed the glass gently on the table before him, and pushed himself to his feet. "I believe I will take to an inner sanctum and meditate upon what we have all said here." He waved over his shoulder as he moved toward the door. "Watch the boy. There is something there, for certain. Whether he is the serpent of your prophecy, I do not know. But there is something there."

After the eldest *sircan* had left, Nura and Siraj exchanged a silent look laden with meaning, and then turned back to the fields. Zain's training group had already disappeared into the forest.

*****

Varro gasped for breath. He had always been a large man, physically strong and intimidating. Yet, the concept of training or exercise had been alien to the culture of the Five Points. Here, among the silent initiates of the Order, it was his stark, everyday reality.

They were never allowed to speak, to their trainer, to the other members of the Order, or to each other. Any attempts at communication were met with physical violence that made Zain's initial lessons appear restrained by comparison. In fact, the entire Acropolis seemed, to Varro, as silent and solemn as a tomb. He found himself harboring serious doubts about the rash-seeming decisions that had led him to this remote, alien fortress.

Most of the men and women wandering free within the Acropolis wore robes or cloaks, leather-fringed hoods pulled low over shadowed faces. Full members of the Order, usually seen at a distance, could be seen speaking with each other, heads bowed together with a conspiratorial air. Invariably, these conversations would fall into silence as the trainees were marched passed. Varro and his compatriots never heard anything more than formless, meaningless mutterings as their days within the confines of the fortress stretched into weeks.

The members of his training wave slept on hard pallets in a communal dormitory with nothing but thin blankets to keep out the chill of the mountain's frozen heart. The clothing they wore was crude, undyed cotton that seemed to grow larger with each day. He knew, with quiet alarm, that this was an illusion created as his body, near starved and pushed to the breaking point, wasted away. He preferred not to think about that. The food they were fed, when they were fed, was plain, and there was never enough of it. They took their meals in large common rooms as silent as the rest of the crypt that surrounded them.

Denied the release of speech or idle time, Varro spent those moments not lost to pain or exhaustion observing those around him. The trainers, foremost among them *Mimreg* Zain, were not excessively cruel. There was no shouting or snarling. Rather, they seemed to view the trainees as raw materials that did not entirely meet their expectations, but would have to do. They spoke sparingly, giving directions in quick bursts of speech, and they never repeated themselves. Most of the time they wore clothing similar to their charges, although of a higher quality and more durable construction. He developed a fascination with them, as they seemed utterly immune to any human weakness. They never suffered for lack of food, or sleep, or rest; unlike the trainees, who did nothing but suffer.

The first thing Varro had noticed about the men and women he shared every waking moment with was the radical range of their ages. Most of them were several years younger than himself. Just into their early teens, they were the most focused and disciplined of the group. These young warriors never slipped in training, never spoke, and their steady eyes never wavered no matter the brutal extremes that were visited upon them. Varro often envied these younger initiates. They seemed to share the confidence and calm peace of Jomei and the teams he had seen at Sacred Lake. He wondered if perhaps they had been raised within the Order, and were thus more comfortable with their surroundings.

Although several of the trainees appeared to be roughly Varro's age, by far the strangest group was the three men who were clearly much older. Two of them had to be in their forties, while the last, a white haired candidate, looked like an ancient caricature in the company of younger would-be warriors. These three had a desperate air, tackling every exercise with a vicious will that spoke more to their desire and less to their ability. Varro spent a great deal of his time, during runs or in the moments between collapse and sleep, wondering about the story behind these oldsters and their presence in the training wave.

But those moments of casual reflection were few and far between. For the most part, the trainees moved from one torturous, soul-crushing exercise to the next, running all the way. If they had been given more time to think, there was no doubt in Varro's mind that more of them would have abandoned the effort. The thought hovered in the back of his mind, he knew, every moment of every day.

*****

The rough-woven cord bit painfully into his hands. Varro watched as the carved stone weight high overhead wavered, threatening to drop to the polished floor with what he knew would be a deafening crash. His clenched jaw clicked as his teeth ground together, and he twisted his hands inward, raising the weight by an inch or so and setting himself against the brutal, tireless power of gravity.

There is absolutely no reason that giant block of stone needs to be up there. The thought came into his head without warning. He knew it was true. He knew there was no point in his suffering to see that the stone stayed in the air, swinging slightly on its frayed rope, but he had been told to hoist it up toward the ceiling, to hold it inches below the pulley system, and to keep it there until given further instructions. It was far from the first time a test of strength and endurance had seen him performing some foolish, pointless task. But for some reason, the silent voice, scratching with odd familiarity at the back of his mind, seemed strangely insistent.

They're just trying to prove that I will do whatever they tell me to do, no matter how much it hurts, and no matter how ridiculous it might be. His entire body was shaking with pain and concentration as his arms burned, screaming with the tension. But beneath the shaking, he felt his head nodding in agreement with the sentiments that echoed in his mind.

Dropping the stone would send a message none of them could miss. It would prove that I am my own person, and they might appreciate the independence and confidence it would show. They want strong, powerful individuals, not mindless drones to follow orders without thought. He remembered the quiet men in the Sacred Lake Lodge. They were not blind followers, but rather confident warriors capable of standing on their own initiative. He felt his fingers, trembling with the strain, begin to loosen their grip on the rough cable.

The stone high overhead began to sway alarmingly, and in his mind's eye he saw it fall, shattering on the smooth floor and filling the air with crashing echoes and billowing dust. Something in his chest recoiled at the vision, and his fingers, almost on their own, tightened once more about the rope. The silent voice in his mind retreated before the certainty that he wanted nothing in life so much as to keep that stone in the air.

Varro felt a burning on his face, as if the sun had emerged from a bank of dark cloud. Across the room, standing with his arms crossed over his broad chest, *Mimreg* Zain was staring at him with an intensity that scared him more than he would admit. The man looked into his eyes and something passed between them that the trainee did not understand. Whatever the commander saw there, he nodded slightly, almost grudgingly, and then turned his head a small degree to watch the other trainees struggling with their own cables.

He had no idea what had happened, but for some reason, Varro felt like something very important had passed between Zain and himself. The strange, scratching thoughts in his head were silent, but he could feel them, crouching amidst his doubts and fears, watching from behind his dark eyes.

*****

Varro's lungs were burning in his chest. His arms pumped at his sides as he concentrated on the feet of the initiate in front of him. The wave was taking a terrain run, loping through the pine forests surrounding the Acropolis. They leapt from boulder to boulder, splashing through frozen streams. Snow had been falling nearly every day for over a week, and their light pants and shirts did nothing to insulate the candidates from the oppressive cold. As usual, he was at the tail end of the formation. Although his endurance had expanded impressively with the constant training, he was one of the slowest runners in the group.

Between the fatigue of the run, the exhaustion of the constant focus required to speed across such irregular ground, and the grinding, biting cold, these runs had taken their toll on the group. The original wave had consisted of nearly twenty initiates. They were down to fourteen after only a few weeks of training. These grueling runs had claimed both of the most recent losses. One of the older men had just stopped running one day, turned up toward the mountain peaks high overhead, and disappeared into the forest. He had not been seen since. The latest loss was harder to bear. One of the youngest members, a pale blonde girl who had been one of the most tenacious scrabblers in the group, had slipped on an icy rock and tumbled into a deep gorge. Her body had been swept under the surface of a rushing river before the rest had come even with the lip. Zain had muttered something that sounded like a curse under his breath, and then snapped at the rest of them to continue the run.

It was the first time Varro had seen the *mimreg* show any emotion at all, and it gave him some small hope that his fate was not in the hands of a completely heartless butcher. Still, Zain had never shown any such concern for him.

Varro was one of the strongest in the training wave, and his physical prowess, always formidable, had grown under the punishing stress of their drilling. Although the runs were torture given his larger size and the imposing weight of his muscles, there were few exercises in which he had not excelled when he applied himself. Yet, no matter how well he did, Zain and the other trainers did not spare him a second glance. There were no chances to speak with the other initiates, either to share in their triumphs or to pass along advice or encouragement. Each of them was succeeding or failing the regimen alone . . . in the silence of their hearts, as Jomei had said.

The candidate in front of Varro skip-stepped across a small stone and then leapt into the air like a gazelle, sailing across a wide gap and landing lightly amid a jumble of tumbled rock on the other side. His pace immediately picked up again, breath puffing out behind him like the steam from a railroad engine. He disappeared around a tight copse of lodgepole pines.

Varro staggered. He had let his mind wander instead of watching the trail ahead, and his feet, clumsy with cold and fatigue, staggered upon the stones as he attempted to set himself up for a successful leap. He missed his timing, coming down hard, and felt his ankle twist beneath his weight. He tried to compensate as his other foot came down, but canted to one side and slammed into the rough bark of a lodgepole. The impact sent him spinning around and down into the rocks with a grunt of pain. Even that sound made him start with a guilty pang, and he surged back to his feet, teeth grinding as he pushed the pain aside, leaping back onto the trail after the other initiates.

Running was his least favorite part of the training regimen. In his experience, whether predator or prey, running was of only limited value in a fight. One burst of speed and you had either lost your pursuer, or you were upon your prey. *What does it matter if I can run for hours on end through the freezing cold?* The thought scratched at his mind. He had foundhimself struggling with such thoughts more and more often.

He shook his head as he ran. He knew there were things he just needed to do in order to pass this phase of training. There may seem to be no rhyme or reason to it, but he needed to get it done, if for no other reason than to be able to look back and say to himself, in the silence of his heart, that he had not backed down from any challenge.

He put his head down and forced a burst of speed from his already wrung-out body, ignoring the sickening twinge each time his injured ankle took the strain. The concussive slam of each foot landing on the uneven ground, crunching through snow or frozen pine needle loam, shook his whole body. The raging heat that surged from his core met the freezing goose flesh of his frigid skin with an exquisite, boiling pain all its own; but that very pain drove all but the most basic, primitive thoughts from his mind. He could see the next initiate flashing through the trees ahead. Pulling from reserves of energy he hardly knew he had, he dug even deeper and closed the gap.

He was so focused on the chase, he never noticed *Arcsen* Ivar staring at him from the shadows of another stand of lodgepole pines as he tore past.

*****

When the polished hardwood cracked into his ribs, he grunted; his teeth gritted against the hated sound, but he did not flinch. Tumbling cylinders of obsidian spun around him on all sides. The room was deep within the Acropolis, lit only by the unwavering blue-white glow of dim reliquary gems in gold settings low along the walls. His hands tightened around the sweat-slick grips of the two wooden practice knives, each held in reversed defensive fighter's holds, their blades hanging down to guard his forearms. Dressed only in his baggy training pants, his bare torso shining with sweat, he twisted and turned, dancing among the spinning cylinders. Each had long, dark staves emerging from their smooth sides at random points, and these swept around out of the darkness to strike him if he was less than vigilant.

He bent his back as one staff whistled at his head, the breeze of its passage cold on his sweat-slick forehead. It had been a long time since he had last felt the twinge from his gunshot wound. His body had forgotten the injury, if his mind had not. He moved smoothly from that awkward bend into a crouch that saw another staff sail over his head from the other direction as he stepped passed its pillar. Two more staves came at him from either direction as he completed his turn, and he took each blow on one of his practice blades, the hard wood sending echoing cracksinto the murk.

He had lost track of time long ago. It felt like it had been months since they had been outdoors to train, but it could have been days or weeks. Without the rising and setting sun to gauge the passage of time, it could have been almost anything. Even after they had retreated into the bowels of the Acropolis, their training had been entirely focused on strength, balance, and endurance. Only recently had he been tossed into this chamber, without direction, of course, for long stretches of time each day. There had been several options for practice weapons in a rack to one side, and as soon as he stepped close enough to the black stone pillars for their wooden appendages to reach him, they would quickly spin up to speed and he would be off.

It had taken several painful sessions before his body, drained from the continued physical training, had begun to negotiate the gauntlet of spinning, whirring staves with anything close to the skill and dexterity he felt he should expect. Once he had become familiar with the heft and weight of the smaller knives, he had started looking forward to his sessions in the gauntlet more than he had anticipated anything in a very long time.

He leapt into the air as a heavy staff swept beneath him, then tucked into a roll to avoid a series of three that swept in high from either side. There was a savage sense of satisfaction as he deflected first one, then another, then a rapid series of blows with the dagger-length wood blades in his hands. His breath came in silent, heaving gasps, and yet he could feel a savage smile stretching across his face. *This is what I was made for*, he thought. *This kind of close-in fighting.* He remembered the feel of blades sinking into flesh, of an opponent's well-aimed blows glancing off a raised knife or slashing through thin air as he dodged aside.

The sudden memory caused his grin to falter. He had never taken any joy in those moments. There was always a sense of satisfaction in walking away from a fight that had claimed another's life, but there was no glee in the bloodshed itself. He had never felt a surge of enjoyment such as the false memory that had just sparked through his mind. His brow furrowed with concern and he misplaced a foot in his intricate dance.

A staff cracked against the back of his head, forcing his whole body to arc forward. Another staff struck him in the arm, numbing the limb and sending his practice blade spinning into the shadows. Another slapped into his back, then his ribs, then the side of his head. He was reeling through the pillars now, his hands up in a futile mockery of defense as he staggered toward what he hoped was the edge of the array. As he passed between the last two pillars on the outskirts of the gauntlet, one final staff swung around and crashed into his forehead. His legs continued to move forward as his upper body was thrown backward into the smooth floor. The cold stone soared up to slap into his back, and his head cracked painfully off the unforgiving surface.

Behind him, Varro could hear the whine of the spinning pillars drop lower as they slowed. With an audible click somewhere beneath him, they stopped. He was barely aware. His head was full of roaring light and screeching noise, and he rocked from side to side in a mindless attempt to ease the pain.

He slowly came to the awareness of footsteps approaching. He looked up to find *Mimreg* Zain standing over him. The man's face was blank behind the unruly blonde beard. A single quirked eyebrow was as close to an inquiry of well-being as Zain had ever deigned to show one of his trainees. Varro nodded.

The trainer stood waiting for the younger man to climb to his feet. Varro used every last ounce of self-control to stifle the moan that rose up in his throat. When he was standing, albeit still wavering despite a wide stance, Zain gestured for him to follow.

With faltering footsteps he moved after the *mimreg* and into the darkened corridor outside.

*****

He had never seen the room before. It was plain; a marked contrast to the elaborately decorative style common to the Acropolis in general. A single stone table sat in the middle, a black metal chair on either side. A lone reliquary gem glowed in the center of the ceiling, illuminating the stark scene in a soft wash of light.

Varro moved with an unsteady gait at odds with his usual confidence and strength. Pain flared dully from every bruise the spinning pillars of the gauntlet room had left him. His head still rang with distant music, and a ghostly tickle down the back of his neck made him think that he was bleeding from at least one of the blows to his head, as well.

Mimreg Zain gestured to the near chair as he stalked around the table. He did not sit in the other, but stood behind it, his broad hands falling absently on its back. Varro slid into the indicated seat without a word. He had not been alone with a member of the Order since Jomei had abandoned him on the field before the fortress. Being alone with any of the training cadre would have been a strange experience at this point, but being alone with *Mimreg* Zain, the very man he had been left with on that day, felt downright unnatural.

The *mimreg* stared at him for several moments. He was in his training pants and tunic, his armor left behind for the day. His beard hung down his chest, and the loose, long sidelocks of his hair were gathered up in a tail that draped over one shoulder. His facial expression offered no hint as to why they were in the dark, isolated room alone, although his eyes seemed to hold just a hint of speculation as they shifted from Varro's own eyes, to his chest and arms, then back up again.

The trainee sat unmoving in the chair. Even a few short months ago he would have been fidgeting after the first minute. He took a moment's pride in this proof of his evolution, but realized that the thought was unworthy of him. He kept his face immobile and matched the *mimreg*'s blank stare.

He could not shake the feeling that Zain wanted to ask him something. The man's eyes kept flicking down to Varro's right arm, where the image of a striking serpent glistened beneath a coat of drying sweat. He had no idea why, but the tattoo seemed to hold an intense fascination for many members of the Order.

Zain reached inside his tunic and brought out a small piece of folded parchment. He looked at it with a frown for a moment, looked up at Varro, then reached out to place it on the table. With a single finger he pushed the packet across the smooth stone and left it lying in front of the trainee, watching him as if he were a particularly intriguing animal who may or may not perform an impressive trick.

Varro looked down at the piece of paper. After months of near-total isolation and silence, there was something vaguely threatening about the folded slip. He looked back up at the trainer, who raised a single eyebrow with a tilt of his head; singularly unhelpful.

He reached out and picked the fold of parchment up with one hand. He plucked at it with fingers still numb from fatigue and pain, opening it out to the dim light. Smooth dark markings resolved themselves into a terse message as he held it up.

Trust in the silence of your heart. Do not heed thoughts that are not your own.

Varro stared at the words. The pain of his countless bruises faded as a frozen chill rose up from his chest, along the back of his neck, and wrapped around his head to nestle behind his eyes. The voices in his mind; the voices that scratched at the back of his thoughts; the trainers knew. Zain knew.

He looked up, and it seemed to him as if the trainer was trying to stare a hole through the center of his forehead. Zain's eyes tightened a twitch more, then he nodded. Somehow, Varro knew the nod was a request for confirmation and not a mark of approval.

He looked back down at the paper, up at the trainer's blank stare, and then nodded.

Zain reached across the table and plucked the piece of paper out of his hands. The man walked out without further comment or communication, leaving Varro to limp after him. Soon they were back in familiar halls, moving toward the dormitory.

He had no idea what might be next, but he did not want to spend another moment in that tiny room alone.

Chapter 11

The light spilling through the grimy windows was brighter than it had been in days, and Antum was hopeful that winter had finally turned. Spring might well be just around the corner, but biting cold still haunted the streets of the capital. He had been briefed to expect Washington to be on the mild side, but this had reminded him of nothing so much as the winters that raged outside the Acropolis each year. His lip curled in frustration. It had been a difficult mission from the start. He had been hoping, at least, that his shanks would have been given a chance to thaw.

On the faded tabletop before the *mimreg* were the scattered pieces of a reliquary pistol. The chased silver enhancements stood out from the darker metal of the weapon's body, wrapped around several smooth-faced gems that glowed with a reassuring, aquamarine light. They had not used the weapons for all the months they had spent rebuilding the Order's network within the capital, but they knew that the Enemy was all around them. The disappearance of Uri and his mission team was more than enough proof that the danger was very real.

The front door creaked and rattled as someone struggled with the ancient lock. The house was one of dozens of decrepit specimens clinging to the hill overlooking the Eastern Branch of the Potomac River from the nearly abandoned Pipetown region. It was always safer to keep these houses in districts where a culture of neighbors leaving each other alone was more well-established than in the more polite areas. Still, Antum reflected, it would be nice if, for once, they were able to stay in a safe house that did not reek of urine.

On the porch, Luys cursed under his breath as the lock finally opened. A cold wind pushed past him, sending a chill up Antum's back before the door was slammed shut once again. The *spica's* teeth were chattering as he threw an apologetic look at the *mimreg* with a slight shake of his head.

Antum stood up and poured a quick drop of tea into a chipped cup, handing it over to the dark-skinned *spica*, who grinned and nodded his thanks. The *mimreg* refreshed his own cup while Luys gathered his thoughts and tried to stamp the ice from his feet.

"It's no good." Luys's voice was still tight with cold as he sat at the table, hands wrapped around the old cup. "Not a single one of Uri's contacts remains. It's almost as if someone were clearing the area around the president, getting rid of anyone that might possibly be of any use."

"That's exactly what is happening, Luys." Antum's voice was bitter; he could not help it. For months they had been trying to track down anyone who might grant them access to President Lincoln. Anyone who had developed even half a reputation for such things had been removed long before the latest mission team had arrived.

"It's even happening within his cabinet." Luys' voice had steadied, but his elegant eyebrows were lowered in worry. "He had the same men beside him, for the most part, throughout his first term. Now, people are muttering that he has a whole new group of advisors, and there's no continuity with the old guard at all."

"It's a fairly standard tactic, Luys. They're clearing the decks for something big." Antum stood up and walked to one of the front windows. There were ratty curtains hanging before each one to make casual observation as difficult as possible. "Is there any sense that the president is complicit in this shuffling?"

Luys shook his head. "None from the people I've spoken to. Everyone's concerned for the old man's health. He spends so much time down at the War Office, or closeted with 'specialists' concerning the western territories. It appears that he is so wrapped up with everything that's happening, from these Civil Rights pushes to the casualty counts, that he's too busy to notice what's going on in his own cabinet."

"They are masters at their craft, Luys." Antum looked back at him, a warning look in his eyes. "They've done it many times before."

"Yes," Luys muttered. "But not when it was our job to stop them."

That brought a smile to Antum's face. "Feeling less than up to the task, *Spica*?"

The younger man snorted. "Not bloody likely, commander. But I would very much rather something break our way before we have to report another wasted week back to the *Etta*."

Antum leaned down, lifting a curtain with one hand and looking out into the brightening street. "Well, maybe Fener has had better luck. He's always been better at making friends."

"I wish him well of it." There was little hope in Luys' voice. "The president used to hold public levees every afternoon; he would see anyone willing to wait in line right there in the White House. That tradition has grown far less regular, I'm afraid. If Fener can use it to his advantage, however, then more power to him. The sooner we can get out of this frozen hellhole, the happier I will be."

"I would not hold such hopes too tightly, Luys." Antum made his way back to the table, easing behind the scarred surface, and putting his hands gently on the smooth flanks of the pistol. It was reassembled, the jewels glowing with a contained, subtle power. "I don't see us getting out of this city anytime soon, no matter how Fener fares."

*****

A small, disconsolate group huddled around a side door on the northern portico of the White House. Fener stomped his feet, trying to rouse circulation that had grown sluggish with the cold. His leather cloak was wrapped about him as tightly as he could manage, but it did little against the brutal, relentless chill of the late winter afternoon.

The men he stood with were each lost in their own miserable thoughts. Each one harbored a grievance or a concern serious enough to drive them into the cold, standing along the muddy track for hours, staring at the blank faces of the strange men who now guarded the president day and night. Fener watched the guardians out of the corner of his eye. They were dressed in business suits that looked more expensive than anything your average hired gun might aspire to. There were no smiles or open expressions. They watched the group of petitioners with hard, suspicious faces, as if seeing a potential assassin behind every mustache and under every bowler.

Fener knew that *Mimreg* Antum would be losing his patience. This was one of their last legitimate opportunities to speak with the president and gauge the feasibility of the *Etta*'s dictate that they try to form an alliance with the man. If this did not work, he did not know what their next course of action was going to be. Luys had mentioned kidnapping with a half-hearted chuckle, and Antum had not been quick enough, in Fener's estimation, in denying that as a possible option.

A particularly cutting gust of wind pushed at the *spica*, forcing him to shift his footing against the thrust. Several of the men around him staggered as they lost their balance or slipped on the icy strips of wheel tracks in the frozen mud. One man went down hard, and Fener sank to one knee beside him, putting an arm behind the old man to help him back onto his feet.

"Thank you, son." The man's smile was wan, his eyes vague.

Fener shook his head and looked back over to the door, warm light glowing through the windows, dapper guards standing to either side. "Hey, you swells have any idea when we're going to be able to go inside? Some of these gents could use a break from the wind!"

One of the guards turned to look at the other. His blank expression would have done *Mimreg* Zain justice. The man's head swiveled back in the direction of the cluster of supplicants, his eyes blank and his mouth a thin, flat line.

"You've been told. There's no guarantee the president will be available today." The man's tone was as flat as his expression.
"President Lincoln's been available to the common man since he took office!" Fener put just the right note of plaintive whining in his voice to get under any functionary's skin, but the man's face remained impassive.

"Times change, friend." The guard's head turned slightly to look off toward the fields in the distance. "If your case is urgent, and you feel it's worth your time to wait, then it's your time to waste."

Several of the other men had begun shouting as well, but Fener knew what he needed to know. These guards would not be letting anyone in to see the president. He had feared as much. He had told Antum this would be a dead end, but they decided to try this last, legitimate approach before taking more drastic measures.

"Oh, throw this over for a game of soldiers!" Fener put as much frustrated rage into his voice as he thought appropriate, then waved dismissively at the two guards and stormed back around the corner as if heading for Pennsylvania Avenue. The guards made no note of his departure.

There were more guards in the same fancy-dress out front at the south entrance, but along the sides of the building there were often no sentries at all. Two small wings thrust out from either side of the building, their roofs kept clear of snow and debris. Guards would sometimes venture out onto these platforms for a quick look at the lawns in both directions, before returning to the warmth of the building proper. These occasional forays aside, however, the sides of the big building would be his best bet.

Fener reached the corner, ducking down beside the wall. He looked out over the open fields to the west. The harsh weather was keeping most people inside, and there was no one visible. He inched along the wall, keeping his eyes moving from the corner to the platform ahead and back again in a practiced, flowing pattern. He passed a row of darkened windows, ignoring the crawling feeling such daytime skulking always sent down his spine.

Uri had procured detailed plans of the White House early in his assignment, and copies of them had been readily available at the Acropolis. Fener knew exactly where he was trying to go and how to get there. These ground floor windows, although inviting and easy to infiltrate, would require far more bothersome work once he was inside.

Taking one more look around, Fener drew a slim, hinged hook from underneath his cloak, fine silken cord already fastened to it, and with a graceful flip of his arm, sent it sailing upward to wrap around the corner balustrade above. He scrambled up the rope with long, smooth motions, pulling a small reliquary blade from its sheath on his leg.

With a moment's concentration, Fener activated the blade. A series of small blue-white lights gleamed to life and the handle vibrated in his hand. A thin wisp of smoke rose from it as he lifted it up to the thick, distorting glass of a second story window and gently pressed it into its own reflection. The knife sank into the glass as if it were cheesecloth, and he quickly cut a man-sized hole from the pane, holding to the thick frame with one gloved hand and easing the severed section down to the carpeted floor within.

Once he was inside the White House, Fener leaned the irregular oval of glass back in place neatly enough to bare cursory inspection. He pulled the heavy drapes closed to hide the damage, and then cast about him to establish his bearings. After only a moment, he moved toward the darkened room's main door.

He was like a ghost within the huge mansion, sliding through empty hallways with easy practice. Whenever anyone approached, he disappeared into a side room, behind a plinth or statue, or even into the shadows of a simple wall niche.

He reached a large intersection guarded by more men in tailored suits. An elaborately arranged distraction constructed from a tea cart, a lantern, and some twine he always had with him, saw the guards abandon their post and run down the hall, leaving the way open for him to ease into the president's hallway.

He was a shadow, sliding forward on the balls of his feet, his ears picking up every sound around him, his eyes not missing a single detail of his surroundings. He came to a heavy door and his hand settled on the ornate knob. Before he could turn it, however, several muffled voices rumbled within. He could not make out words, but he was certain that one of the voices was the high-pitched orator's voice of President Lincoln.

But who could be in there with him at this time of day? His plan was to brace the president in his den during his accustomed afternoon rest, and hope that the tales of his curiosity and forbearance were not exaggerated. But if he were closeted with the Enemy, or a Tainted human . . .

Fener pulled a reliquary medallion from around his neck. Normally, he would have had to invoke the talisman before ascertaining anything of importance in a situation like this one, but as soon as the medallion was free of his shirt, it began to glow a deep, dangerous blue.

The Enemy.

Fener quickly looked to either side. If the Enemy was within, it might sense him at any moment. There was no way he could approach the president now. They would have to resort to one of the more drastic plans they had laughed about only a week or two before.

But first, Fener needed to get out of the White House.

*****

Tensions ran high in theSanctum as the *Etta* digested the latest report from *Mimreg* Antum and his mission team. They had known for some time that the Enemy was maneuvering behind the scenes, removing key players around the president and replacing them with Tainted individuals more to their liking, as well as directly corrupting any members of the president's cabinet and staff they could subvert. But knowing that one of the Enemy had been directly with the president had been a blow to all their hopes.

"We can't know if the man is aware of the true nature of the Enemy." *Sircan* Ignatiusleaned into the words, hands folded on the table before him. His face was earnest as he looked across at Nura and Abner. "Nothing we have ever seen in the past should lead us to believe that he is susceptible to their blandishments."

"Purer men have fallen farther, Ignatius." Nura's expression was dark, her shoulders straight. "There may be no proof that he has fallen, but likewise, there is no proof that he stands untouched either."

"No man in such close proximity to the Enemy remains untouched." Abner's tone was dark and heavy. Behind him, *Arcsen* Siraj nodded, his dark topknot swaying.

"Faith is the very touchstone of our existence." Ignatius spread his hands as a benevolent smile touched the corners of his mouth. "Without faith, we are nothing. Can we not spare some faith for this beset man who has spent so long fighting on the side of righteousness?"

"Has he?" *Arcsen* Ivar, still refusing to don the field armor of his position, stood with his back against one ornate wall, his heavy arms crossed over his chest. "Hundreds of thousands have died, *Sircan*. And millions more stand on the brink of disaster. There are many who do not view this man in the hallowed light into which you have cast him."

Ignatius cast a sour look over his shoulder at his lieutenant, and then looked back at the other *sircans*. His face was somber now, the smile gone. "We cannot stand against the Enemy alone. We must have allies. If not President Lincoln, then who?"

The others avoided his gaze, looking away into the room's shadows. *Arcsen* Noor, speaking from where he rested his shoulder against a massive window sill, looking out at a swirling blanket of snow, cleared his throat and muttered into the silence, "Do we need to abandon this man now? Are there not options to be considered before we cut him loose?"

Ivar straightened, a snarl emerging across his face. "You allow your race to dictate to your sense, Noor, and it does not become you. There are plenty of Africans still wearing chains that have nothing to thank this man for."

Noor stood away from the window, turning toward the other *arcsen*. "Your words betray a mind decided, brother. We cannot afford to deny ourselves any possibility now." He sneered down his nose at the other commander. "As for your charge, I will ascribe it to high nerves, and forgive you the slight."

Ivar took two steps across the Sanctum, his heels ringing on the polished stone, when Ignatius's hand came down with a sharp slap upon the table's surface. All three *arcsens* turned to stare at him. Seldom did the senior *sircan* of the *Etta* show any outward sign of frustration or annoyance.

"Ivar, please go attend to that concern we discussed earlier. I would like to have all the information before I make any sort of lasting judgment." The old man's voice was steady, his eyes fixed on the storm through the window.

The large *arcsen* stood still for a moment longer, then nodded once, glanced at Noor and Siraj, and whirled on his heel, stalking from the room.

An uncomfortable silence settled upon the Sanctum. Aside from flickering eyes, there was no movement.

"You have a concern?" Nura's voice was carefully neutral, with barely enough inflection to carry a questioning tone.

Ignatius shrugged. "I wish him to speak with *Mimreg* Zain regarding your young serpent-marked savior. His training wave fast approaches the initiation phase. I believe a moment's extra care will serve us well before we decide if he should move on from there or be held back."

"Is there reason to believe he has been lost?" Nura's tone was cold. She had kept a close watch on Giovanni Varro's progress, and knew his status better than any other within the *Etta*.

"Of course not. No more than the usual difficulties initiates meet, as their minds are honed and the accumulated detritus of a lifetime of misunderstanding is cleared away." Abner gestured dismissively. "The Enemy scrabbles at the door to every initiate's mind during the training. The boy proceeds exactly as one would expect. Better, in fact, as far as his physical training is concerned."

"He moves himself through the forms of the gauntlet room with a hunger I have not seen in years." Siraj nodded. "He has mastered almost every weapon the room provides. He has moved on now to the great sword." He shook his head ruefully. "Even Ivar only braves that clumsy cudgel when forced."

Noor shook his head. "His spiritual training, however, shows alarming gaps in development. Problem solving and initiative he mastered long before he came to us. But he is still nearly incapable of sustained focus, or channeling any source of inner peace into his meditations."

Siraj's lips twisted into a slight sneer. "I seriously doubt there is any inner peace there to channel."

Ignatius smiled and eased back in his chair. "I wonder if ever there was an initiate so closely studied by the entire

Etta. But as you say, Siraj, the boy's spiritual strength is still in question. I only wish to be sure he is worthy, lest institutional wishful thinking within the Order place a flawed shaft into our quiver on the eve of battle. It only seems prudent, no?"

The young *arcsen* reared back with sudden indignation. "You have no right to make such a decision on your own, *Sircan*." Siraj stepped forward. "That is, by rights, a decision for the *Etta* in full session to deliberate together."

The old man raised one frail-seeming hand, patting at the air gently. "And we shall, *Arcsen*, we shall. Never fear. But do you not think we should consult the man's mentor before we pass judgment upon his fate?"

"I sense a masterful transition approaching." Abner's voice carried a slight undertone of amusement, although his face had turned sour.

Ignatius nodded with a smile. "As *Arcsen* Noor has said, there is no need to abandon President Lincoln at this time. We can continue Antum's mission, allow them to escalate their activities, and see if, perhaps, we cannot remove the scales from the president's eyes and save for ourselves an excellent ally."

"There's still General Grant, as well." Noor spoke up. "Antum's efforts to influence Mrs. Grant toward temperance and restraint through our allied congregations have been bearing fruit. He believes that the general could actually be an asset as well. With the end of the current war, having two such allies would be priceless. Lest we forget, there are the growing efforts of the Enemy to turn the full might of the Union against the free people next. There is almost no way that could succeed, were we to have both President Lincoln and the General of the Army on our side."

"Grant is a conscienceless machine." Nura muttered, her shaking head sending her elaborately piled hair swaying from side to side. "There is no soul there for us to ally with."

"And yet still," Ignatius said, drumming on the table with the pads of his fingers. "Even if Antum's efforts serve only to take Grant from the board, they will be immensely helpful in our work."

"You continue to muddle the issue, old man." Abner's expression had soured further. "I move that we abandon our efforts to recruit President Lincoln to our cause. Maintain the mission team in place to collect information and prepare any necessary actions should time begin to outstrip us, but look elsewhere for those who will stand by our side in the final battle."

"Where, Abner?" Ignatius did not rise to the other *sircan*'s bait. "Where else, but with the righteous of the Union, can we find the strength to face what you believe approaches? It is not blind faith that sees me clinging to my hope; it is nothing short of a complete lack of options. If we cannot find allies within the Union, there *is* nowhere else for us to turn."

"You are quick to discount the free tribes." Abner snapped back. "They rediscover their ancient power with each new day. There is a movement among the elders to open the mysteries to their younger warriors. If they truly unleash their full potential and reawaken their bond with the Earth, they will be allies worthy of the name."

Ignatius pursed his lips, a deeper crease falling into the many wrinkles of his forehead. "This is true. A fully reawakened nation of the free tribes would be formidable indeed." His eyes were alight. "And how much more powerful could we be, should we combine their might to the power of the Union?"

It was Abner's turn to slap the table. "Damn it, Ignatius! The man was closeted with the Enemy! He was seated at a table with one of the most foul creatures ever spawned in creation! We cannot take that chance!"

Everyone in the room reared back slightly as Ignatius rose from his seat. "We cannot take the chance not to!" He leaned over the table, his old hands splayed. "If there is so much as a jot of a possibility that President Lincoln can be saved and his influence used to further our cause, then there is no choice but to seize that jot and not let go!"

Nura looked back and forth between her two colleagues, and then her head bowed forward over her folded hands. Abner saw the movement and looked down at her with disbelief.

"You would do this? You would expose the Order to this kind of risk?" His voice was soft.

The youngest *sircan* nodded without raising her regal face to the light. "He is right, Abner. Our position is never so strong as to allow us the luxury of foregoing any possible ally. I move that we allow *Mimreg* Antum to continue his efforts. Approach the president, and attempt to win him to our cause."

Abner threw his hands in the air in disgust. "And if we lose another mission team? What if Antum and his men are destroyed as well?" He whipped his head around to look at the two remaining *arcsens* in the room. With two *sircans* against one, the only way for Abner's opinion to carry the day would be for all three of the lower-ranking members of the *Etta* to side with him. But as his eyes met Noor's, he knew that he had lost.

The *Sircan* of Battle bowed his head. "History balances on the blade of a knife. I only pray you have not all toppled us off of it today."

*****

Varro clung to the slick wood with all his strength. It was easy to lose track of his progress in the utter darkness of the deep chamber. He hugged the log to his numb chest, his legs bowed painfully beneath him. His feet pressed against the rough cordage wrapped around the log, keeping him from sliding down into the shadows. He knew that somewhere beneath him, the room was flooded with dark, frigid water. There was no sound but his own labored breathing.

His legs shook with fatigue and cold. His feet were raw, nearly all the flesh rubbed off them as he had made his slow, inevitable descent down the pole, despite his best efforts. His arms burned with a fire that did nothing to dispel the cold, as the skin on his biceps and forearms was slowly abraded away as well. He snarled and grunted with each inch lost, trying to wrench his mind into a calm, still place that eluded him no matter how hard he tried.

He knew that the primary purpose of this exercise was to force him to confront the nervous agitation of his own mind. His lack of equanimity in the face of endurance challenges had surfaced as a primary weakness throughout his training. It was a weakness that could not be forgiven despite the advances he had made in almost every other aspect of his work. And so, as was the nature of training, the more he failed at this one aspect, the more it came to dominate his life.

He lost his grip and slid, his feet screaming their agony as his arms skidded down the rough surface and even his chest seemed to have lost some skin. Focus. Serenity.Silence. These were things he must master, he knew, but he also knew that the longer he spent in this dark and soundless chamber, the more likely it would be that the thoughts that were not his own would slink out from the back of his mind to scratch at his resolve.

His vigilance against the alien voice had been nearly constant since Zain had given him the strange, terse note. Whenever he caught his mind wandering, no matter what the exercise or how painful living within his body had become, he would wrench his awareness back to the moment and not let go. He still heard echoes of the voice, but he had gotten better at ignoring them, at least, if not banishing them completely.

The voice had taken on a more menacing cast as the battle had continued across the landscapes of his tortured mind. Its otherness had become more obvious, and the fact that some foreign . . . thing . . . had been inside his head, gave everything that had happened to him since the alleyway in the railhead a stark, concrete reality that even the blood, sweat, and tears of his training had failed to instill.

He felt himself shifting; his tormented muscles, pushed far beyond mortal limitations, were threatening to fail him, dropping him into the icy water below. One of his legs slipped again, the raw flesh of his sole slapping down into the pool. Drawing his leg back up and bringing his foot against the ropes cost him a pain he could never have comprehended in his darkest moments back in the Five Points. He pressed his cheek against the pole, cinched his arms tighter despite the howling agony of his torn flesh and the vibrating tension of his drained muscles, and settled in for long, quiet session in the silence of his own heart.

Chapter 12

Soza pulled a handkerchief from his front pocket and tried to clear the grit from his spectacles. He surveyed his crew's work and was surprised to see how far along the new stretch of palisade had come. While he had been helping with a length of parapet, the wall had moved down another twenty feet or more. Soon, Tolchico would be completely surrounded, and as safe as they could make it. Mayor Maddox would be pleased.

It had been a relatively easy winter for the growing town of Tolchico. They had had plenty of food, the weather on the desert plains had been mild, and between the mayor's guards, the frontiersmen with their own weaponry, and the vigilance of the mayor himself, the town had thrived. Sadly, that could not be said for many other settlements in the region.

Refugees from the surrounding area had been trickling in since the late fall, and each sorry figure had stumbled in with tales of unbelievable horror and sorrow. Families had mourned menfolk who had sacrificed themselves in an attempt to see their loved ones safely away. Children had come in led by older siblings, their parents no longer among the living. Soza felt worstfor the adults who staggered numbly into town, dead and empty eyes speaking, without words, of a loss he could never understand. Something out there was killing anyone it could get its claws into, and it was not shy of taking children.

There *had* been men among the refugees as well. Sheepish, timid things, they would meekly do what they were told, met no one's eyes, and would not speak of the trail that had led them to Tolchico. Soza suspected that more than a few of them had abandoned families out there in the dust and the sand, victims of a fear that had robbed them of any sense of manhood.

As Tolchico's resources began to feel the strain, Mayor Maddox had sent armed parties out farther and farther afield. They tried to help fortify those few settlements left standing, but they also looted abandoned towns of any viable foodstuffs their terrified inhabitants had lacked the forethought, or the strength, to bring away.

These parties were not all the Mayor's personal guardsmen. Each party always contained several civilians to help with the searching and the carrying. Soza had so far avoided making the journey himself, but he knew that kind of luck could not last forever.

As the town continued to expand, his experience as a crew boss proved invaluable. He had started with small construction teams, but soon the mayor would consult with him concerning any major project. The entire palisade was his, and he was mighty proud of it.

The work also kept him from having to head out into the desert, which suited him just fine.

The men coming back from these trips always rode back into town with haunted looks. They usually went straight to one of the saloons, or the dance hall. The barkeeps and drink girls kept their glasses filled until, eyes still hollowed by whatever they had seen, they were helped back to their rooms. The next day they would invariably go about their business as if they had never left, avoiding the subject of the world outside of town.

No one talked much to Maddox's boys, so there was no learning what lay beyond the far horizon from them.

In fact, no one talked much at all. Yet, stories constantly circulated about desecrated bodies, men and women tortured to death; their dry, sightless eyes unnaturally wide with a speechless horror. There were stories of entire towns covered in buzzing, gem-like flies; of piles of bones, small and fine, piled neatly along trails, tooth and claw marks giving mute testimony to an unholy feast.

Even as life continued in Tolchico at a frenzied, almost spasmodic rate, there was a growing sense that they were a besieged outpost on the edge of nowhere. The surrounding land was no longer burgeoning with opportunity. It was now a silent menace, a creature that threatened to reach out and destroy them without provocation. It seemed more and more like they were living at the sufferance of some crouching, evil beast, and reveling in the light and the drink and the noise each night was their only way to deny that beast its power.

It never really worked. There was always an edge of fear in town. But damn, they tried hard every night.

*****

Soza had just dipped his bandana into a water bucket and was sluicing away as much of the sweat as he could manage, when a shadow eclipsed the sun. Twisting slightly and looking over his shoulder, he saw the unmistakable bulk of Bruce Euans standing over him, huge hands resting easily behind enormous, fancy guns.

"The Mayor wants a word, Soza." The gravelly voice, full with the flat tones of Ohio, always struck the railway man as false, somehow. It felt as if the man were not living his own life, but rather playing a dancehall roll. He was also clearly annoyed at being used as anyone's errand boy, and he sneered down at the crew boss.

Soza grabbed his shirt from where he had hung it over the rung of a ladder and threw it over his head. It was a chore, as the sweat pulled at the fabric, but he was not about to meet the mayor in a grimy, sweat-drenched undershirt. At the same time, he did not want to make Euans cool his heels any longer than necessary, either.

"Let's not keep 'im waiting, then, shall we?" He grinned at the hulking brute, but Bruce Euans' face was not one God had made for smiling, and Soza shrugged, following after with a conscious decision not to take offense.

The new trading post, finished months ago, was now the bustling center of Tolchico. Its red stone bricks rose up like an imposing manner house amidst the lesser structures. All of the newest streets radiated out from that central point. At least two of Mayor Maddox's guards, each armed with heavy-looking long rifles, were always standing on the broad, shadowy porch.

Soza avoided the trading post whenever he could. He respected the mayor and what he had done for the people of Tolchico; but there was something cold and distant about the man. Until he could manage to get back to the railhead on the other side of the forest and head back east toward more civilized lands, he had promised himself he would keep his head down and stay out of trouble.

Euans led him up the broad stairs to the sheltered porch. The men posted there glanced at him briefly, nodded, and then went back to scanning the town. The big doors were still smooth on their hinges, Soza noticed with a small burst of pride. He crossed into the blessedly cool interior after the lieutenant, who then stalked off on his own business without a second glance, waving him deeper into the post.

A few people moved around the trading post, manning narrow tables of pelts, foodstuff, and tools or walking aimlessly, picking among the bits and pieces that the hard winter had left behind. He walked past, nodding here or there to folks he knew, and pushed through an inner door on the far side. Another guard stood by the door, watching over the mayor's inner sanctum, but waved him in without a second glance.

Beyond, halls branched off in several directions. It was dark inside, as the trading post had very few windows. Strange, red-tinged lamps hung from hooks every few yards, casting the hallways into dim, somber tunnels of ruddy light. He followed the main hall back to the mayor's office, where he knocked quietly, his hands folded over his belt, his head down.

"C'mon in." Mayor Maddox's voice sounded distracted.

Soza turned the delicate knob and eased the door open. The office was much brighter than the rest of the building, and he had to squint until the painful, flashing sparks faded. Maddox was sitting behind a heavy wood desk whose presence always mystified the railway man. Folks were serving drinks on wood planks cast over rain barrels in town, but somehow the mayor had managed to secure this enormous antique for his personal use.

As his vision cleared, Soza realized he was not alone with the mayor. A small group of men and women, one clutching a scared-looking little girl to her skirts, stood in one corner of the big room. The women looked frightened but determined, for the most part. The men were doing a better job of hiding their fear, but it was there for those who knew to look for it. One woman, though, the one with the little girl, looked directly into his eyes with no fear at all. Her mouth was set in a firm, thin line. Her face would have been pretty with a softer expression.

"Tucker, thank you for coming." The mayor's customary smile was strained. He gestured toward the tight knot of townsfolk in the corner. "I thought maybe you could help me out with a little problem."

Soza looked again at the group of settlers. He recognized some of them from around town, but he was not especially friendly with any of them. He had tried to keep to himself, knowing that he would be leaving at the first opportunity. He nodded to the men and women he recognized, and was about to turn back to the mayor for further explanation, when one of the faces jumped out at him. Floyd Brant . . . one of the boys that had made the deadly trek out here with him; one of his boys.

He nodded. "Brant . . . how're things?" He kept his voice neutral. The kid had always blamed him for their situation, and the last he had heard, Floyd had been getting close to the mayor, trying to secure himself a position with the guards. It would have seemed like an odd choice to anyone who had not made the journey across desert and forest with him. With his curly, dark blonde hair and his big, blue eyes, he looked more like a city swell than a frontiersman. However, the kid had been tenacious, and he had completed that passage when many other, more imposing men had not.

"Tucker." The kid's voice was flat. Everything about him declared that he was expecting a fight of some kind.

"You can't make him stay here!" The woman with the little girl spat. Her voice was harsh, her face gaunt but filled with anger. "Floyd wants to go, and so do we!"

Tucker's head tilted in confusion. He glanced back up to Brant, who managed to look provoked and sheepish at the same.

"Might be I can clear up some of the confusion." The mayor's voice was reasonable again, his smile more relaxed. But there was an edge to his eyes that Soza found unnerving. It usually meant that things were not going exactly as he had planned. "We had another bunch come in last night," he dismissed the event with a shrug. "Same stories about ghosts, savages, and whatnot." He bowed his head and flicked a pointing finger toward the group. "Turns out to've been the last straw for Miss Reba Preston, here."

"The trails are open." Her chin lifted defiantly, sending sparks of sunlight off her red-gold hair. "There's no reason anyone should stay here any longer. There's something out in the desert, and it ain't gonna stop till it kills everyone here."

"Well, there *is* something out there; I think we can all agree on that." Maddox's smile had an edge to it. "That seems to strike me, however, as all the more reason to stay here, where we've created a safe, comfortable refuge from the violence and fear beyond the rising walls."

His words seemed entirely reasonable, but the woman shook her head, her long neck twisting from side to side. "It's gotten worse all winter long, Mayor Maddox. Something is hunting the people out here, and it's only a matter of time. I won't see my little sister. . . killed . . . or worse." She clutched the little girl even closer to her skirts. "No one is going to hurt Ellie." Ellie, eyes wide with confused fear, said nothing. "Back east there are soldiers, lawmen, bigger towns. It's safer out that way, and I think you know it."

The mayor looked at her sideways. "You think the Union's got soldiers to spare, they can pull your burning bacon out of the fire this far west? They're finishin' up the Confederacy, miss. They got bigger fish to fry. And as for the lawmen . . . Which ones, exactly? There's nothing close to a unified group of defenders of truth and justice anywhere within five hundred miles. The bigger and brighter the badge, the more you better believe the man behind it is going to take his piece of the action before he lifts a finger to help."

She stared at him for a moment, and then shook her head dully. "I don't choose to believe things are that bleak out beyond the forest, Mr. Mayor. This is still the United States of America, and the rule of law still prevails, even in the territories. And that's not so very far from here."

Maddox nodded again. He rose from behind his desk and the people in the corner shied away as if he were about to charge them. It made Soza wonder what had happened before he had been called in. The mayor came around the desk and perched casually on one corner.

"My people and I have worked very hard to make Tolchico a safe place no matter what menace wanders the desert outside." His voice was even, but there was no mistaking the condescending undertone. "You can't deny that there is no safer place west of the Coconino." He shrugged, his smile elaborating on the undertone of his little speech. "I just don't think I understand where it is you think you might be better off."

Reba Preston's chin ratcheted up a little higher. "We'd be safer back in Kansas City, sir; or any of the towns east of the forest."

Maddox shook his head in a show of tired frustration. He looked back up at Soza with a plea in his eye. "Tucker, I was hoping, since you and young Brant here came out together, maybe you could talk some sense into him? This little group seems to think the lad can lead them back east."

Soza turned to look at Brant. The kid's blue eyes were dancing between pleading and defiance. It was clear that even he did not know which way he was going to jump. "Floyd . . . ?" He tried to keep his tone level. There was no need to antagonize these folks further. "You leading this little group back out into the desert?"

Floyd Brant nodded sharply. He had decided to jump toward defiance. "There's nothin' keepin' us here, Tucker. We make a run for it, with some good horses and decent supplies, we'll be back at the railhead, or one of the other towns east of the forest, before anyone much knows we're gone."

The Preston girl nodded, edging closer to him. God bless the kid, Soza thought. If a girl like that had been willing to look *his* way, he would like to think it would have brought out the hero in *him* as well. As much of one as there was, anyway.

He forced himself to nod. There was not much meat on the bones of that plan. He thought he knew where it came from. He turned back to the woman. "Miss Preston . . . I assume you agree with Floyd's proposal?"

She nodded sharply as one corner of her thin mouth turned up in a sneer. "There's nothing any of you can do to stop us. It's suicide to stay here. If you had any brains, you'd be planning on coming with us instead of brazening it out here."

Soza looked back at the mayor with a helpless shrug. The man looked sour, but nodded. "Well, if you're bound and determined, I won't see you head into the desert unprepared. I hope you can hold off your departure until tomorrow? That would give us enough time to gather the supplies and equipment you'll need to give yourselves the best chance you'll have."

All of the people in the clustered group looked surprised at that. The most surprised looks were on the faces of Floyd Brant and Reba Preston.

"You're just going to let us go?" The woman's voice was suspicious, although Brant's face was flushed with relief.

Maddox shrugged again. "As you say, I can't force you to stay. It's still a free country, no matter how far we are from civilization. I think you're making a big mistake, but I won't let pride keep you from your best chance of surviving it."

He spun off the desk and slid back into the comfortable, leather-bound chair. "Tucker, if you would be so kind as to see that Mr. Brant and Miss Preston are well-supplied for their journey? Draw credit with the merchants from the town account." He pulled a small sheaf of papers toward himself, his mind obviously already on other matters. His voice was fading into a disinterested mumble. "Make sure they have everything they need."

Soza nodded, but the mayor was paying him no mind. He looked over at the stunned group of travelers, and then moved toward the door. He ushered them out, returning their nods of thanks, but not sure what he had done for them. He cast one last look at the mayor, toiling away at his desk, before closing the door behind himself, shaking his own head in confusion.

*****

Soza was standing by the frame that would hold the main gate into Tolchico, watching his boys finish up the palisades on either side, when the mayor found him. The man's face was grim as he walked up to the work crew, and Euans, behind him, looked even darker.

"Okay, boys, you keep those posts even, and make sure there's enough support at the bottom to hold up the crossbars. I'll be right back." He stepped away from the men, already craning their heads curiously to see what might have brought the mayor out of the trading post this early in the day.

Maddox walked right up to Soza and only stopped when they were inches apart. "Can your boys finish this up on their own, Tucker? I think you need to come with me."

Soza looked back up at the men, all of whom were very busy not listening. He barked out some quick instructions, waited for the nods in reply, and then turned back to the mayor. "Of course, sir. What can I do?"

Maddox put a hand around Soza's shoulders and steered him away from the gate and back toward the trading post on its distant hill. "You're a good man, Tucker. The people respect you. Even though we couldn't dissuade your boy Brant and his bed warmer to stay where it was safe, the people respect you, and they know you for a straight shooter."

He did not know anything of the sort. He had kept to himself as much as he could through the winter. He was on good terms with most of the merchants and the shop owners, but he would never have said he had made any lasting friendships in the fear-shrouded township.

The mayor was moving too fast to argue, though, and now did not seem the time to disagree, with Euans striding along behind them. Soza was surprised when they turned away from the front door of the trading post and down the alley with the building's stables and storehouses in back.

"We're heading out into the wastes." Maddox clapped him on the back and then pushed a side door open into the stables. A large group of men were readying horses. They barely looked up as the three newcomers entered.

Soza looked at the horses with a leery eye. There was a reason he had made his life on the railroad. A quick count showed him that there was an animal prepared for him.

"Sir, I'm not sure exactly what it is that you think I can do for you out there that these boys can't?" He watched, feeling helpless, as the mayor pulled himself up onto one horse's back.

"Just come along, Tucker. Let me worry about the whys and the wherefores." He looked down and jerked his head toward the last free horse. "We need to get a move on, though, if we're goin' to be able to get out to where we're goin' and back again before the daylight fails."

Soza gave one last glance at the serious men all looking down at him. Each was armed with those heavy pistols, and there were larger weapons in boots fixed to saddles. If there was something dangerous out there in the desert wastes, this was the group to travel with.

It was a struggle to get up onto the horse. He had not mounted one of the beasts in years. Soon, he hoisted himself up onto his precarious perch, wobbling uncertainly, and following the rest of the little posse out the big barn doors and into the alleyway outside.

*****

One of Maddox's guards led the way down from the high trail into one of the many ravines that scarred the land between Tolchico and the Coconino Forest. Dusty red runnels showed the scouring effects of the winter rains, but the desert had been dry now for weeks. Nothing marred the tracks they followed down from the trail.

The mayor had told Soza that two of his men, out on a regular patrol, had found something he thought the railway man needed to see. They had ridden hard, having to swing back around and collect the lagging old man every hour or so, until midday. There was little hope of anyone leaving tracks on the hard pack, but the guard had known just where to look to find the scuffs and scrapes of a group leaving the trail about five hours out.

"They didn't have enough horses for everyone, as you know." The mayor's voice was calm, but there was a hardness there that sent a shiver down Soza's back. Maddox spoke no names, but an uncomfortable suspicion had begun to nestle in Soza's mind.

There were hoofmarks amidst the footprints they were following, but only a few. The guards had drawn their pistols and warily followed the carved trails of the winter rains down into the ravine. Soza had never felt the need to travel heeled, even when working the roughest railheads in the country. For the first time, in that little gully, he wished for a comfortable weight on his hip.

"Way we figure it, moving slower due to their lack of horseflesh, this here's where they decided to make camp their first night out." There was still some essential element missing from the mayor's voice. Compassion?Concern?Fear? He sounded like a man stating a mundane fact, as if he were addressing the weather, or the crops.

Soza started to do some figuring in his head. He had given little thought to Floyd Brant and his group after seeing them provisioned. It had taken them a few more days to get out of town, and he had lost track of them before they left.

He remembered someone saying no one would sell them horses, and so they had to leave on foot.

A cold flash down his spine challenged the desert heat as another memory rose into his mind. Someone had said what a pity it was, that such a big group, with a child in tow, had had to head out over the wastes with only a single riding horse and a pack mule to do their carrying for them.

A single horse and a mule.

The guard leading the posse sidestepped down the dusty scree into the bottom of the ravine. He swept the area with his drawn pistol, but Soza could see nothing himself, with the valley hidden behind an outcropping of dusty red earth. The other men moved down into the gulch, fanning out, and the mayor took the slope in three leaping bounds, coming down gracefully in the dust of the bottom; the giant, Euans, following close behind.

The smell struck Soza before he stumbled down to join the other men. Something in his mind screamed for him not to turn to where the guards were staring. He made a great show of looking everywhere but down along that high wall, but he soon found there was no safe place to rest his eyes.

The canyon wall opposite him was splashed with a great deal of black liquid. It seemed to have attracted an entire menagerie's worth of insect life. As realization donned, his head turned to the left against his will. He knew, in a heartbeat, that this moment would haunt him for the rest of his life.

The entire party from Tolchico was scattered across the dusty floor in an obscene mockery of sleep. Clearly, they had stopped here for the night, planning on forming a defensive camp. There was a fire pit carefully dug out from beneath an overhang, and piles of gear showed that they had unloaded their animals for the night.

Whatever had happened, it had struck later in the evening. He wished he could pretend it had happened in their sleep. Except that the expressions on the faces made it plain that they had been terribly aware before the end had claimed them.

Each body was laid out in its own torturous scene. In their last moments, even the companionship of their fellows had been stripped from them. It appeared that the bodies were naked. Their flesh, however, was so thoroughly slashed, ripped, and gouged that it was impossible to tell for sure.

Only the flesh of their faces had been left intact, allowing any fool to read the despair and anguish that had marked their last moments. The torture and indignities visited upon their bodies was nothing to Soza compared to the naked terror that glared from each pair of flat, fly-specked eyes. He staggered from one horrific scene to the next, aware with a strange, silent corner of his mind that Maddox and his men had drifted off to the edges of the ravine. They were not inspecting the scene at all, but watching him instead.

There was little to distinguish one person from the next. Limbs had been removed in some instances; wood, metal, and other substances gleamed within the wet wounds, everyday items of camp gear perverted into the most horrendous tools of torture and cruelty. With each step, he felt as if he were submerging deeper and deeper into a nightmare. He had hardly known these people, but to see this done to anyone . . .

He stumbled to his knees beside a sodden pile of meat that was barely recognizable as a human being. Each of the limbs ended in a shredded tatter with splintered bone stabbing from the mess. The middle of the huddled form was a crater, with glistening gobbets and viscous strings scattered like a profane spider web all around. The head was bald, the hair and flesh of the scalp scraped away as one raw wound. The ears seem to have been pulled out by the roots. As was true of the rest of the bodies, the only area that was not entirely flayed was the face; the face of Floyd Brant, his blue eyes staring sightlessly into the sky overhead.

The horror in those eyes would stay with Soza forever.

A smaller pile of flesh was arrayed not far away, and he looked quickly enough to identify the pile of burnished, red-gold hair, matted and darkened with blood and other matter. There were still tears in Reba Preston's eyes.

A single tear peeked over the lip of her eyelid and coursed down a track already carved through the blood and filth on her face. It took Soza a moment before he realized why there were no flies on the body. The movement was nearly imperceptible, but against all hope or pity, the woman was still breathing.

He lunged across the foul mud between the two bodies and fell down on his splayed hands by her head. The eyes flared wide as he moved into her field of vision. They darted from side to side, working through the gummed film, they alighted upon the railway man's face hovering above her, and flared again in fear. There was no understanding there, no plea for rescue or deliverance; just mindless horror.

The ruins of her arms and legs twitched weakly. Maybe she was trying to stand, or crawl away, or throw her arms around him. Arms that she no longer possessed. All she could do was jerk weakly.

He had no idea what to do. He sat there on his haunches, staring at the woman's face. She was still looking directly at him. Her jaw worked with small, spasmodic movements. Her lips quivered. She was trying to speak.

He leaned in closer, nodding desperately. There was nothing he could do for her. He knew that with a desperate hopelessness he had never felt before. He could at least bear witness to her last words.

"Eewee." It was a sound, not a word, and almost all breath, with no power or force behind it.

He shook his head again, tears leaking out beneath his begrimed spectacles. "I can't understand, miss. Please, try again."

Her lids slid down over her hazel eyes and flicked opened again. The muscles beneath the pale skin of her face was jumping as if she was trying to express something, but there was no meaningful movement there. Her jaw worked again, and again she breathed out the strange sound.

"Eewee . . ."

He shook his head again, tears blurring her desecrated form. He could not even do this for her.

Soza had not heard anyone coming up from behind him. When Maddox spoke, he jumped as if someone had stabbed him in the back.

"Wasn't that sister of hers named Ellie?" He stared down at the body without the slightest shade of emotion. "Maybe she's trying to say Ellie."

Soza looked from him back down to the girl. The tears were flowing steadily now, and her head was jerking up and down with tiny movements. She was nodding. But why . . . He looked more closely at her mouth. Blood, mostly dried, was caked all around her lips and chin. There was nothing he wanted to do less in the entire world, but he forced himself to peer between the twitching lips.

They had taken her tongue.

Soza wanted to be able to offer her something, anything, that might ease her suffering as she faded into death. He knew she was dying. The only miracle here was that she had survived this long. He stood stiffly, looking around. None of the bodies had appeared small enough to be the little girl. Maybe she was not here. Maybe she had gotten away. He staggered away as if drunk on the merest shred of hope. If he could give the woman even this much before she passed, he could feel like he had done *something*, at least.

"There's no comfort here." Maddox gestured toward the deeper wall of the canyon. Soza did not look at first. He did not want to look. But he lacked the strength of will to walk away.

Sure enough, a tiny body was fastened somehow to the wall, placed there with almost ritual precision. He looked away before he could register any details.

He did not know what to do, but he knew that he could not leave Reba Preston alive but alone for even a moment more. He fell back to his knees before her, shaking his head, tears coursing down his cheeks. She watched him for a moment as somehow, through her pain-wracked eyes, he saw that she understood. Tears flowed down into the bloody mud around her head.

Another shadow slid across the ruin of the girl's body as Euans moved up to warn the mayor that it was time to think about heading back soon.

At the sound of the big man's voice, the girl's eyes flicked from Soza's tortured face up behind him, past the mayor, and up and up and up. And then they widened. A guttural, formless sound of animal terror escaped her raw throat. Something seemed to click within her chest, her eyes widened again, and then all the tension drained away as what life had been left to her fled. Her body sank in upon itself with her last, tortured breath. Euans shrugged and moved away.

Soza eased himself back until he was sitting in the blood. His stained hands were clasped in front of him. He found himself trying to remember any of the prayers from his childhood. His head moved back and forth without conscious thought, as if his body were trying to deny everything he had just seen or experienced.

"Now, you see why I wanted you to be here with us, Tucker?" The mayor's voice was gentle as he squatted down beside him. He reached out and patted the railway man on the back. "No one back in Tolchico is going to believe this. They've heard stories, sure. But these people were our own. These deaths are going to cut deep. And they needed to be seen by someone who everyone trusts."

Soza's mind was a swirling mess of sounds, mostly breathy screams; and colors, mostly red. He heard the mayor, and he understood him. He even agreed, to a certain extent; but it was all just too much. There was no way that pile of wet meat was young Brant. Just no way. The railroad was a violent way to make a living. Men died nearly every day on the railhead when things were going full speed. But this scene of deliberate slaughter, torture, and vileness was something that should not exist in the waking world.

"The people of Tolchico need you to tell them what's out here, Tucker." The words were soft, almost hypnotic. "There are terrors beyond our walls that none of us are equal to meeting alone. You need to tell them what waits for anyone who wants to leave."

With a sudden, lurching dive, Soza pushed himself away, staggered through the red-stained ravine, and fetched up against the far wall, resting his forehead on his forearm against the warm rock as the contents of his stomach came surging up in a sour wave to splash into the thirsty dust of the desert.

Mayor Maddox was behind him again in a heartbeat, patting him gently on the back. "It'll be alright, Tucker. It'll pass."

Soza stared into the off-color puddle. His voice was harsh as he pushed it through his burning throat. "How did you know . . ."

There was a pause, and then Maddox spoke again. "I knew, from the ranger's reports, that it would be bad, Tucker. I'm sorry I couldn't warn you. I needed you to see things with fresh eyes, so you'd believe." He gently forced Soza to straighten up so he could look into his face. "I needed someone who would see how bad it is out here. It's the only way we'll be able to stop this from happening again."

Soza shook his head. He would not look down the gulch to where the mayor's guards were busy digging holes. "Who . . ." He shook his head again. "Who could possibly . . ."

Maddox slapped him on the back. "They're animals, Tucker, and no mistake. Who knows? Savages, deserters, marauders of one stripe or another; they're no civilized men, is all I can tell you." The man shook his head sadly. He pressed Soza's shoulder, moving back up the ravine and toward the trail above. "C'mon, Tucker. There's no more we can do here. The boys'll see that these folks are covered up. We need to be getting back toward town."

Soza allowed himself to be led back up the treacherous slope. His mind stuttered between flashing, gory images and the sickening torture of Reba Preston's last moments. No matter how he tried to school his mind to quiet, he kept seeing her eyes, round with fear and horror, the moment before she had breathed her last. Nothing in the valley behind him had shaken him worse than the last moment of that girl's life.

Chapter 13

The remaining initiateswere led down a long and silent corridor, their clothing fresh and clean. There had been no explanations, of course. There almost never were. But there was less urgency than usual, and so Varro's mind relaxed just a bit. Rather than allow his thoughts to drift, however, he focused on his surroundings, his fellow trainees, and *Mimreg* Zain at the front of the line. He had taken to this constant observation in an attempt to school his unquiet mind in moments of stillness. He thought it was working quite well.

The walls of the corridor, as was true of most of the Acropolis, were sculpted in intricate detail. They were not merely carved from the living rock of the mountain, but were augmented with many other types of stone including marble, basalt, and various colored granites. How all of this stone had been brought so far from civilization, he could not imagine. The work must have taken decades. Of course, if what Jomei had said was true, it would have been even more difficult back when the Acropolis had first been built.

He turned his mind to his fellow initiates. They walked with the strong, easy grace of men and women who had their own measure after countless hours of training and drill. Each was infinitely faster and stronger than when they first began. There were holes in their ranks, of course. There had been several more deaths during training, each one eliciting slight reaction from Zain and the other trainers. Three others who had survived to this point had been gone that morning. Both of the remaining older candidates had been among the missing.

There had been something different in the air that morning. Breakfast had been filling but bland, as always. They had finished their gruel in silence, and when they were done, *Mimreg* Zain had come to collect them, leading them down into the mountain. Varro was unsurprised to see that the other initiates' faceswere as impassive and enigmatic as he knew his own to be.

They were brought at last to a wide door set into an intricate, multicolored frame of stone. The design seemed to hint at desperate battle and noble sacrifice in some abstract way he could not describe. There were no recognizable images; no warriors or foes clearly in evidence, and yet the impression was undeniable.

The doors opened into a large chamber that could have comfortably held four times their number. Hard stone stairs in tiers faced a low dais at the front. The initiates were led to the front rows, where they filed in and sat without hesitation

A large disk of marble sat upon the dais with a series of varicolored stone plates arrayed around its outer edge, each polished to a glossy sheen. The object faced them on its edge, held in a huge stone framework with small wheels cradling it. Varro took in the apparatus, schooling his thoughts to calm, quiet analysis.

Clearly, the disk was designed to spin within the frame. He could see that each multicolored plate along the disk's rim had a symbol etched into it in a contrasting color. He was a little alarmed to realize that, although the symbols were alien to him, he could almost understand them. Throughout his training, he had been exposed to this strange language time and time again. Even more unnerving, they swam at him out of his memory as if he had been dreaming them all his life.

Mimreg Zain mounted the dais and turned to them. He managed to look at each in turn in a clear yet silent admonition as to the importance of the coming events. Without a word, the *mimreg* stepped off the edge of the platform and the great doors boomed shut behind him.

The echoing report was still repeating into silence when the reliquary lighting in the room dimmed, except for those domes around the dais itself. The wheel, seemingly of its own volition, began to move. There was no grinding sound, no feeling of weight or friction. The disk seemed to spin without touching anything at all.

As he watched the stone machine, he noticed an elaborately framed window at the top of the carved framework. The symbols fit perfectly into that window as they spun past, faster than the human eye could register.

A cold wind seemed to rise within the dark chamber, blowing across Varro's shaved scalp. The hairs on the back of his neck began to rise as if a thunderstorm were approaching. The disk came to a smooth, abrupt stop, revealing a symbol within the frame. Before he could register which symbol it had been, the wheel spun off in the opposite direction, pausing again to reveal a new symbol. He felt like a red-hot needle was suddenly thrust through the pupil of each eye.

He tried to read the symbols as they flashed past, but it was impossible. However, as the flickering continued, it was as if a message was somehow being shot directly into his mind. Words and phrases formed themselves whole, traveling along the burning needles. His body was shocked into rigidity as the energy of the message pulsed through him.

The words warned him that he was about to experience something entirely alien. They told him that he would be transported to remote times and places. They told him everything he knew about the world, even what he had surmised while at the Acropolis, was a thin veil of lies.

Then the words detonated in the forefront of his mind. Fragments of symbol and meaning flashed before his eyes, their colors shifting wildly, and a vivid image burned there in his thoughts, as alien as the voice that had plagued him throughout training. There was a moment's fear as the comparison occurred to him, then the images began to register, and all conscious thought ended.

*****

The room around him went dark. Slowly, over the course of what seemed like forever, tiny pin points of light began to fill the shadows. It took a while for him to see the darkness in a new context. He was looking at the night sky; a rich, velvety black, spangled with stars. His perspective shifted drastically when a large blue and green circle, swirled with white, swept out of the darkness and hung suspended before him.

Varro had not paid much attention in the charity schools of his youth, but his mind was sharp and his memory excellent. He knew he was looking at a planet, although the pattern of greens and blues seemed all wrong. He had once seen a globe in a classroom; aside from the basic elements of shape and color, the sphere before him did not match his memory at all.

His view seemed to swoop again, and a second sphere soared into his field of vision. It was almost lost in the distant shadows, its colors much less hospitable. There was an aggression that flared from the dark greens, a hostility that emanated from the pale blues. He was overcome with impressions of burgeoning youth and vigor. Behind the two orbs an enormous ball of fire flashed into being. He knew, somehow, that it was infinitely farther away than either of the two planets, and yet dwarfed both in size and majesty: the sun.

Without conscious direction, his attention returned to the original planet. Shadow swallowed the sphere as what he realized must be night swept across the planet. Lights began to sparkle as the darkness moved across the surface, and with a mild shock he knew he was looking at enormous cities coming to life. He remembered the darkness of the Five Points at night and the faint light from Manhattan. He knew that the planet below must be far more crowded than Earth, and far brighter.

Although there was no visible sign, he felt a benevolent presence cradling the planet. A similar presence blanketed the younger planet in the distance, but somehow he sensed a darkness eating at the fabric of that farther presence. He was reminded of a hurt animal, nursing a wound as its mind curdled, turning inward. A chill flashed through his thoughts. He was glad when he was turned back to the nearer planet. That comfort, however, was short lived.

The darkness growing within the far planet reached out to touch the guardian presence here as well. The stars around him began to flicker in a way that told him time was accelerating. Areas of the surface below were blotted out as angry red and black clouds rose above them. As a succession of nights flickered past, he saw that the city lights dim and die, those that remained pushed into smaller and smaller areas. The greens and blues began to shift and change. Deep, angry red wounds opened up across the planet, spreading out to engulf more and more of the surface. The invisible presence of the ghostly custodian, the cancerous darkness now dominating its ephemeral body, convulsed around the planet, strangling it.

In a moment, the winking lights were all but extinguished. Black clouds and red deserts engulfed nearly the entire planet. Something deep within one of the remnant cities flashed. An object shot upward, arced past Varro's perspective, and soared back down to strike the further planet like a shooting star. On the nearer planet, the surface roiled with movement, as if a blanket of vermin writhed across it, devouring everything in their path. The last light was swallowed by the darkness.

The sun in the distance flared. The devastated planet below lurched in its orbit, wrenched out of true by powers he could not even begin to comprehend. The sun's light died back, and the planet below him spun on, red and empty and dead.

Varro's viewpoint swung around again, without conscious direction. The far planet swept into focus. The sun, burning with less energy, caressed this planet more gently now. The greens moderated, becoming somehow more welcoming. The blues deepened, seeming cooler and more encouraging. Again, the stars began to flicker with flowing time. The region where the shooting star had fallen became tame, the greens tempering further into gentle hills and golden fields as marble cities grew up all across the region. Other cities sprang up around the globe, and he realized that, as alien as the patterns of greens and blues had been with the first planet, the pattern beneath him now was more familiar. He was looking at Earth.

The marble cities spread across the globe, but the alien awareness, the presence that had infected the distant guardian with its own rot and destroyed all life on the first planet, rose again. The glowing white cities were shattered. First, the far-flung colonies were crushed, and then the outskirts of the original city, the home of the artifact that had fallen from the sky in its shooting star, itself felt the hammer blow of the guardian's hatred.

The vast metropolis convulsed with violence visible even from his distant vantage point. The malicious vermin that had devoured the sister planet erupted again, engulfing the city. The defenders were pushed back, deeper and deeper, until there was a moment of hushed silence and stillness. With a roar, an enormous cloud surged into the sky from the center of the city. The cloud rose, blue-white bolts of lightning exploding from its expanding flanks and crawling across its domed summit. The cloud dissipated quickly within the accelerated time of the image, and the city was gone. The land it had sat upon was gone. Only a vast expanse of shimmering water remained. Atlantis, first and greatest city of Man, was gone.

Again, the stars pulsed. Mankind spread across the globe once more, scattering from the vanished city. Civilizations rose and fell. Like tiny, shining stars, gleams of light flashed now and then, visible and then gone. Each time they appeared, great nations rose up out of the ruins. Under the guidance of the shattered Relic, fallen to Earth in lost millennia and broken to banish the tide of ravenous creatures sent to destroy them, mankind strove to recreate the fallen greatness of the past.

The entities that had destroyed an entire world, changed the course of planets and altered the power of the sun, had been thwarted by the defenders of the glowing white city. They had sacrificed themselves, and the terrible, nightmare end that had seen the destruction of the sister planet had been postponed.

But those powerful beings, once set to guide and protect the younger races, had been twisted and shattered by eons of disappointment and despair. They hovered over the world. Smaller aspects of their vast power stalked the surface below, sowing discord and hatred. Empires of evil rose and plunged the world into blood and fire. Every great culture to arise was their prey, and even the constant vigilance of those descended from the last great defenders was not enough. The ancient evil, the Enemy of all life on Earth, stalked through the shadows, waiting for their chance.

For, as mankind scattered from hisearliest roots, it had been impossible for the Enemy to pull him down with one concerted effort. As humans dispersed across the planet, it took more and more effort to track down the strong and the just, to destroy them before they could build. The Enemy divided themselves time and time again, hunting down the greatest champions of humanity. Splinters of hate shed from a consciousness so vast, no human could ever fully grasp its dark majesty. And yet, with each division, these shards became more and more petty. As creatures of spirit and thought, they could not cause damage themselves. Although able to spin illusions so complete that they appeared as real as any other man or woman, concrete to all five senses, they could not directly harm anyone or anything. They needed to corrupt humans for that task.

And there was never a shortage of humans willing to take up the evil work. Generations of ambitious, selfish men rose from history to do the bidding of the Enemy. Knowledge was lost. Cultures were drowned in blood. Each time mankind clawed his way out of the mud, the Enemy was there, surrounded by willing lieutenants, to push him back down.

Except that it never completely succeeded. The common run of mankind was not alone and defenseless in its struggle against the great Enemy. The descendants of those ancient, selfless guardians of the white city stood ready to hold the line wherever the Enemy reared its head. No matter how devious and cunning the Enemy became, there was that last line of defense, born and bred to protect mankind from the predators that had hunted it through the mists of prehistory: The Holy Order of Man.

And yet, even as Varro watched lasting civilizations rise, spreading enlightenment and illumination across the globe, he sensed a rising fear and dread in the defenders. Records had been lost, memory had failed. The Holy Order was a pale shadow of the great army that had once defended that first city, now claimed by the sea, and met the Enemy face to face. There was a growing concern.

The hordes that had swept down the avenues and boulevards of that lost city, that had submerged the surface of the sister planet in their inexhaustible numbers, had not been corrupted humans, or Tainted members of that brother species now lost in time. They had been horrible, nightmare creatures more terrible than any legend. A single word flashed into his mind – Watchers –these monsters had erupted from the very air, called forth through some arcane ritual by minions of the Enemy. They had devoured everything in their path.

Ignorance paralyzed the Holy Order with fear. With the cold certainty of newfound knowledge, Varro understood that no one knew why, how, or when the Enemy might summon the Watchers again. Although ever-vigilant against the machinations of the Enemy, struggling to keep mankind safe and progressing forward, the true mission of the Order was to prepare for the coming of the Watchers, when the Earth would need to stand as one against the evil beings that had hounded intelligent life through time and space.

Varro knew a cold shock of realization. The Holy Order of Man did not believe it could defeat the Watchers when the fated day arrived.

But who *was* the Enemy? Of the many mysteries not revealed in this rolling barrage of images and information, *that* haunted him the most. How could you fight something that could appear as anything, or anyone, it pleased? And if the Enemy wasone creature, or countless creatures, of energy and thought . . . was it the Enemy who had spoken to him in his mind? Was that why Zain had warned him? *How*could Zain have known what was happening in the silence of his heart?

The images began to flicker again. This time, however, the trembling light did not convey the passage of time. A crimson glow infiltrated his field of vision. It leached in from the edges like a sunset bathing a sky in blood, but continued to run inward until everything was a uniform, sullen red.

From out of the pool of glowing red emerged two objects, rushing at him with a terrifying speed. Eyes; enormous, hooded orbs. They carried all the contempt and hatred in the world within their swirling red irises. The eyes fixed upon Varro, and the ruby light vanished. He was back in the Acropolis, seated on the hard stone chair and surrounded by his training wave. The huge stone machine was spinning wildly, fat sparks flying in all directions.

And still, the eyes hovered there, bearing down upon him.

The massive door boomed open. *Mimreg* Zain rushed in, followed by half a dozen other members of the Order. They ushered the initiates out of their seats and toward the hall outside. Each of them seemed oblivious to the eyes, and the eyes showed interest in no one but Varro.

Zain rushed at the machine, a large ivory staff in his hands. He jammed the length of it into the mechanism's spinning wheels. There was a horrific, jarring pop. Splinters of marble, rock dust, and white fire flared out in all directions, showering the *mimreg*, Varro, and the fleeing initiates.

Overhead, the eyes began to fade, unseen brows drawn down in frustration or annoyance. Zain turned around and saw Varro standing, still transfixed, by the shallow stairway.

"Go! Go now!" the trainer's voice sounded strange, but the note of command was unmistakable. Varro pulled his eyes from the disappearing image, and trotted after the other initiates and warriors, his gait steady and even.

*****

Mimreg Antum sat in the dark cellar, hunched over the spinning marble disk. The controls were cold in his hands, his tense face flickering with the actinic glare of energy flashing from the disk's granite mount. The light flashing over his eyes obscured any hint as to what he might be thinking.

"What are they saying?" *Spica* Luys knelt beside the commander, his head seesawing back and forth between Antum's face and the communications disk. "What's happening?"

Tensions in Washington D.C. had been ratcheting up for weeks. The dark and hostile atmosphere of a capital city, stalked by the very Enemy they were sworn to face, had pushed the mission team to the breaking point. Any contact they made seemed to be discovered at once, removed with horrible speed and finality. Those few willing to even meet with them had dried up completely as word of the killings spread.

Optimism had been harder and harder to maintain, and even *Spica* Fener's ready smile was a thing of the past as the men tried to gather what intelligence they could, hoping to avoid discovery. The usually jovial *spica* was currently away, sent to investigate a great commotion just south of the city the night before. A chaotic scene at Armory Square Hospital had followed just hours later, and the *mimreg* believed the two might be connected.

Antum could not have said why he was so concerned by the sudden disturbance, but Fener had been dispatched with sharp words and an urgent command that he return as soon as possible. Moments after the *spica* had left, the reliquary disk had spun up of its own volition and began to flash an urgent message into the house.

"Something's happened back in the Acropolis. Something the *Etta* believes may be tied to Washington." Antum's head jerked back as his eyes flashed, catching each symbol as it burst forth in bright sparks before giving way to the next. "That new initiate that came in through Sacred Lake is preparing for his final trial, and something's gone wrong."

Luys sat back, his dark eyebrows lowering. "Something's gone wrong? In the Acropolis? What could go wrong in the *citadel*?"

The *mimreg* shook his head. "There's been a great deal of speculation about the boy." His eyes flicked over to the other warrior for a moment before returning to the device. "They say he wears a serpent tattoo."

The younger man's eyes widened, but he said nothing.

The flashing dulled, the spinning slowed, and the reliquary light faded away. Antum sat back, took a deep breath, and looked over to Luys. "They believe what's happening over at Armory Square might be involved. The Enemy is on the move." His eyes darkened. "This could be it, Luys."

The young *spica* shook his head. "Not a chance, *Mimreg*." A ghost of a smile settled in the corners of his mouth. "I won't be facing the end of the world as a lowly *spica*."

Before Antum could respond, Fener came crashing through the front door above them. The other two warriors rushed up the stairs, their eyes wide at their companion's disheveled state.

"It was Grant." The man was winded, which said a lot for how far and fast he had run. "There was some kind of attack."

Antum shook his head. "The Confederates?"

The mission team kept a close watch on all the most important people in the capital. General Grant had taken a large house just south of the city from which to oversee the preparations for what everyone in the Union assumed would be the final campaign of the war. In fact, it was such a nice house, the general's family had been invited to join him . . .

The *mimreg*'s face paled. "His family?"

Fener shook his head weakly, his blonde hair bobbing with the motion. "Dead.All dead."

Antum reached back for one of the rickety, cast off chairs and sat without looking back. All of their plans for the general had revolved around the man's wife, Julia. She was a religious woman, active in several churches. Earlier mission teams, including the much-missed Uri's, had cultivated rich ties with many churches in Washington, and often they worked in concert with the Holy Order's will without even knowing. The woman had always been a calming influence on her warrior-souled husband, and as the dark shadows of the Enemy stretched over the capital, the Order had been counting on Julia Grant to keep the general on the right side of history.

With her dead . . .

"What happened?" Antum's voice was dull. "The Confederacy has been pushed back to Petersburg. How could they have mounted an attack so deep into Union territory?"

Fener shook his head again. "It wasn't the Confederacy, *Mimreg*." The man's eyes were haunted. "Witnesses said the house was attacked by three men bearing some strange new type of weapon." His eyes flicked away. "They said the weapons shot bolts of red fire. The entire house burned down."

Antum's mouth hung open in shock: weapons that fired bolts of red fire. Throughout the history of the Order, only the weapons of those touched by the Enemy were known to fire bolts of crimson flame.

The great Enemy had placed horrible technologies in the hands of its puppets since the dawn of man's time on Earth. In every age the weaponry was different. It always looked different and was powered by different arcane or mystical forces. But no matter what form the weapons took, from where they drew their power, or what violence they inflicted upon their targets, they always had one thing in common: they shone with red flame.

The *mimreg* shook his head. "That can't be. Witnesses?"

Luys looked between the two older men. "They don't leave witnesses." His voice was small. "They don't ever leave witnesses."

Antum looked up. "Unless they want to. If they've decided they no longer have to hide their presence, they would very much want someone to carry word. Terror only works if the terrorized know what is happening." He looked back up at Fener with a sudden, wary suspicion. "The General?"

Fener looked sick. "Horribly burned over most of his body."

Antum nodded. "But . . .?"

"He survived. They've rushed him to Armory Square Hospital." A slow-dawning horror swept over his face, and his commander nodded in response.

"He survived the savage destruction of his family by assassins sent against him on the eve of battle, wielding strange weapons out of some dark romance story." The commander's voice was dull and heavy.

Luys let his frustration leak into his voice. "So what? Isn't it better that he survived?"

Mimreg Antum turned his head in a slow arc toward the young warrior. "The man who commands the Union Armies, *all* of the Union Armies, has always been a cold-blooded strategist driven by his own understanding of honor and obligation. He has never allowed any compunctions of conscience or principle to come between him and his duty." He stood and began to pace nervously.

"This man now lies near death. His family has been slaughtered, most likely before his very eyes. When he awakens, and I have no doubt that he will, his soul will bear even more horrible scars than his body. And with nothing left to live for, he will turn to vengeance."

"The Confederacy." Fener spoke the words without inflection, but looked puzzled when Antum shook his head.

"Not just the Confederacy. The Enemy would not have revealed themselves without deeper reason. In this one, burning moment they have created a new weapon." He nodded once to Fener. "It will consume the Confederacy, I have no doubt. But even a reasonable commander acting prudently will have ended the war in the next few months. How much more quickly will a tortured madman with no regard for human life crush the enemy under heel? And where will he be aimed next?"

Fener's eyes widened. "The tribes."

Antum spun around quickly. "The tribes? Why do you say that?"

"One of the orderlies that carried the general into the hospital." Fener shook his head, his eyes lost in the memory. "He said Grant was muttering, screaming really, about man-beasts."

It was Luys' turn to shake his head. "No. The nations would never stoop to wielding the red fire."

Antum nodded. "And any war leader powerful enough to have forged such a close bond with his spirit guide would never lead such a craven attack. It was an illusion. Nevertheless, that changes nothing. Grant will recover his wits enough to launch an attack on the Confederacy, and then he will immediately turn his eyes to the west."

"It *is* the end." Fener's eyes focused on a distant sight far beyond the rundown little house. "They have been planning this since—"

"Long before Uri's team was stationed here." A new energy infused Antum's motions as he turned back toward his men. "Whatever is going to happen, the Enemy intends for it to happen in the western territories, clearly. And they intend to destroy the tribes in the process."

"And if they're aiming for the tribes, they will be aiming for the Order as well." Fener said, his eyes tightening.

Luys' eyes widened. "The initiate!" He nearly shouted the word at Antum, and the commander nodded.

"Whatever is happening at the Acropolis must be related." He turned back to Fener. "If they intend to strike west as soon as they crush the Confederate remnants at Petersburg, we can't waste any time. There's only one person left who can stop Grant from heading west with blood in his eyes."

"But we haven't got a hope—"

"We have the plan you and Luys put together in case things took a sour turn." There was almost a smile in Antum's round face. "I can't imagine things much more sour than this."

"But . . . kidnapping?" Luys' face was pale beneath his Spanish complexion.

"We know his every move. There will be an opportunity in the next couple of days, and we will be able to minimize the danger to everyone involved."

Fener nodded. "It's not ideal, but we have it all planned out. I think we can do it."

The young *spica* shook his head. "Kidnapping the President of the United States."

The ghost of a smile returned to Antum's lips. "Well, it will be a tale worthy of a song, anyway."

Chapter 14

Agony shot up through the soles of his feet, up his shaking legs, and into his core, setting his heart pounding harder and harder. Pain-sweat beaded on his forehead and ran into his eyes. The tall, narrow chamber was brightly lit from above. It appeared to be sunlight, but it burned with unnatural heat. He knew he was deep beneath the mountain. Perhaps it was yet more of the blue-white energy granted to the Holy Order through the ancient Relic.

From his sessions in front of the great wheel, Varro knew that the Relic had once been a powerful weapon constructed by desperate warriors of another planet in ancient days now lost in time. In its full glory, the Relic had been capable of stripping away the lies and illusions of the great Enemy, rendering them vulnerable to attack and perhaps even destruction. In its current, shattered state, the Relic granted the Holy Order untold power through the countless reliquary items bonded to its energy matrix.

Everything he did within the Acropolis had taken on a whole new meaning since the lessons of the spinning stone wheel. He understood more about the Holy Order of Man than he had ever grasped before. Their mission, and its importance, had been slammed home to him by both the soul-searing images of the machine and those burning eyes, alight with baleful hellfire.

Knowing how real it all was, and how far back the lineage of the Order stretched, had made his inner doubts more cutting, rather than alleviating them. He had glimpsed what was at stake, and he knew what would be lost if he faltered. It was a crushing weight that pushed down upon his every step since that harrowing lesson.

His feet began to shift and he had to rein them back under his control. He was standing upon a tall, thin pole, slick with his own sweat and blood. His feet would not entirely fit on the cap of the pole, but he managed to steady himself with each foot partially resting on the wood. The edges had gouged into his flesh more than once, but he refused to allow himself a single flinching grimace. Instead, he stared at a slightly off-color stone set in the wall close before his eyes and schooled his thoughts to stillness.

Varro had redoubled his efforts since the lesson in the wheel room. He had mastered the gauntlet room to the point where he could defeat the spinning staves with any weapon on the rack, although he had settled upon the massive two-handed broadsword when given an option. His focus and concentration had improved to the point that he was now the fastest in his training wave, the strongest, and could endure the torturous stamina drills the longest.

But still, in these quiet moments of endurance, he feared the return of the alien voice. Even more than the voice, now, he feared those strange, unnatural eyes. He had not felt that remote, powerful presence again, but those eyes, and that voice, returned to haunt his dreams almost every night. He lived in constant dread that they would return to his waking world.

He felt his feet shift beneath him and snarled a curse that echoed closely back from the confining walls. He knew it happened every time he allowed his thoughts to wander down these dark paths. He had lost track of how many cuts, scrapes, and burns he had suffered due to these lapses. And here he was, his balance tilting within him, his eyes sliding wildly away from his point of focus, and the grinding pain of his feet shooting up into his chest.

His arms flew out from his sides in a futile attempt to steady himself. All worry over the Enemy fled, replaced by the very human fear of falling. The rough-hewn floor far below reflected the glaring light, and his head began to spin as he made the mistake of looking down. He felt his center of balance shift fatally out past the log and knew that he was done.

Varro felt himself falling before his feet left the pole. He pushed off with both screaming feet and hit the wall behind him hard, barely shifting enough to push off again with his hands as he slid, trying to grab at the solid pole as it sailed past. His grip failed him and he continued to fall, but he slapped the rough wood with one hand, sending him spinning back against another wall. This time, he twisted his body through a full turn and took the front wall with his pain-wracked feet, pushing off with a few running strides and then reaching out again for the pole. His hands grasped around the rough bark and he spun in a tight coil as he spiraled toward the floor.

By the time he hit the bottom, he had partially wrested control of his descent from uncaring gravity. Anyone outside the Acropolis would have seen this feat as nearly miraculous. That did not, however, mean he had defeated gravity entirely. He hit hard, the air exploding out of his lungs as he dropped into a shoulder roll across the irregular stone floor and fetched up against the far wall.

He lay there, breathing in slow, shallow gasps for a few silent moments. He took a quick inventory of his body and decided that he had suffered no lasting damage. He was dizzy, however, and his head swam from the impact and the pain.

A hidden door in the wall behind him opened without a sound. From his back, Varro watched as *Mimreg* Zain entered with no expression gracing his bearded face. He merely looked down at the initiate with blank eyes.

Varro felt guilt boil up within him. He knew how important success was now. He wanted nothing more in life than to be worthy of standing by these men and women, of washing away the callow offenses of his youth with the energy and commitment of what life remained to him. He did not want to fail this man.

He scrambled to his knees and bowed his head. "I apologize, *Mimreg*. I—"

Stars exploded in his mind as the *mimreg* backhanded him roughly, sending him tumbling back down to the stones.

Varro pushed himself back up onto his knees. He stood, gave the trainer a single, strong nod, and waited for what would happen next.

Zain looked into his eyes for a long moment, and then turned, without signal or word, and left the chamber. After a moment, Varro followed.

*****

Mimreg Zain led Varro through the ornate hallways in total silence, of course. He had never considered it before, but the initiate was suddenly struck by the fact that the intricate decorations and carvings of every hall made navigating within the Acropolis almost impossible unless one was intimately familiar with the carvings. In fact, hidden within the designs might well be a wealth of information for a person who could read it.

Zain stopped outside a door that seemed familiar but could have been miles away from anywhere he had been before. The training officer pushed the door open and gestured for Varro to enter.

The room *was* familiar. It looked exactly like the small chamber where Zain had given him the note, what seemed like a lifetime ago. There were only two chairs and a single table within.

Varro moved slowly around the room. There seemed to be nothing for him to do, so he turned back to the door to see if Zain would give him further instruction.

The door closed with a hollow boom, and the lock clicked ominously within the heavy air of the room.

*****

There was no way to know how long he sat in the hard, stiff-backed chair. He had sat down soon after he realized he had been locked in the chamber. If he had been placed here, it was because the Order had decided this was where he belonged. He had faith enough in the Order to feel confident in that.

Time had marched on outside the little room, and there had been no sign or message. He could tell nothing of the passage of time in the dim light, but his grumbling stomach told him he had missed several meals. His dry, gritty throat told him he needed water, as well, or his effectiveness was going to be compromised.

And yet still he forced himself to sit quietly in the chair, cultivating the stillness of his mind. He pushed down his fear and frustration, regarded his intertwined fingers, and focused on the steady pattern of his deep breathing.

It became more and more difficult with the insistent rumbling of his empty stomach.

*****

Varro's head was bowed over his hands. He kept his mind on a tight leash, allowing his body to relax into near-sleep even as he kept his thoughts focused but serene.

He was meant to be here.

He clung to that through the countless shadowed hours. The pain of hunger had passed into a numb emptiness. Thirst scratched at his raw throat, but he had mastered, long ago, his ability to deal with physical discomfort.

He was meant to be here, and he would be here until there was somewhere else he was meant to be, or until he died. And if he died, it was because the Holy Order of Man had decided, in its wisdom, that that was for the best. He focused on this fresh new faith, refusing to allow his mind to wander.

*****

When the door opened, he jerked up with a start. He would have sworn he had not fallen asleep, but newfound honesty forced him to a sheepish twinge of guilt.

Mimreg Zain stepped into the chamber, his expression grave. He was dressed in elaborate silver armor chased with slate-gray enamel. He gestured with one silent hand for the initiate to rise.

Varro pushed himself off the table and almost tumbled to the stone floor. He held one hand out to Zain, but palm out, denying the need for help rather than reaching for it. He gathered his legs beneath himself, braced one hand on the table, and slowly straightened his body against the tingling, numb pain. He looked at the *mimreg*, his face carefully impassive, and raised a single eyebrow in query.

For a moment it seemed that an emotion moved beneath the gleam of Zain's eyes. Then he nodded once, turned, and gestured for Varro to follow.

*****

The sun had set over an hour ago, more than enough time for even the phantom swirls of sunset to have seeped from the sky. The warmth of the spring day had fled as winter's chill reasserted itself with the darkness. A rutted dirt road twisted through the textured shadows of tall trees on either side as a bright half-moon slowly rose in the distance.

The sullen glow of Washington loomed over the horizon, illuminating the sky in that direction. In the other, unrelieved night swallowed the pathway as the trees rose up all around. Taken by itself, there was nothing to distinguish this lane from any other stretching out into the surrounding countryside around the capital. Hidden within the forests, however, was the refuge known as the Soldiers' Home, where, unbeknownst to most Americans, President Lincoln often retreated when he needed to be alone with the weighty issues of the day.

As the dark days of winter had settled down upon Washington, the president had taken to sneaking off to the Soldiers' Home on a more regular basis. There had been a time when Mrs. Lincoln had accompanied him, but as the bleak season progressed, she had become less interested in these sojourns in the countryside, and the president continued to take them alone.

The Holy Order mission team had noticed the change in the president's routine. The *Etta* had agreed that, should direct action be necessary, the road between the White House and the Soldiers' Home would be the most logical place. When he travelled to his distant retreat, President Lincoln always left Washington with a single guard and driver for his small carriage, but was met on the edge of the bordering forests by two wagons full of soldiers.

Mimreg Antum crouched by the side of the road behind a carefully-crafted blind and checked a pocket watch by the light of the rising moon. The president always passed into the deep forest within two hours of full sunset. Soon, the mission team would have either taken an important step toward securing the New World once and for all, or they would be dead at the Enemy's hands, all their scheming and maneuvering come to naught.

A sharp whistle caught Antum's attention and his head came up to peer into the night. Flickering lights approached through the trees. Although he could not differentiate the various targets from this distance, he could tell there was more than one wagon approaching: the president.

Antum took his reliquary necklace in hand and focused upon the stone, cupped in his palm to hide it from the approaching vehicles. He sent a brief flash up into the trees, waited for an answering gleam, then settled down deeper behind the blind. Luys, in a tree over the road, would have signaled Fener, farther down the road, and everything would be in place for their desperate plan.

The first wagon was a large, boxy vehicle pulled by two heavy draft horses. Both the driver and the man sitting beside him, cradling a massive shotgun, wore crisp Union uniforms, illuminated by shuttered lanterns hung from stands on the cab behind them. They had the alert bearing of professional soldiers, and the wagon would carry at least four more. The president's personal cabriolet came next, pulled by a single, spirited horse that managed to trot with energy and style despite the sedate pace forced upon it by the heavier wagons. Two figures sat in the cushioned seat of the carriage, one of them markedly taller than the other. Smaller lanterns were affixed to the vehicle's canopy frame, illuminating the road ahead while leaving the two men within in shadow.

Bringing up the rear of the little column was another heavy wagon, probably carrying at least six more soldiers and bearing another pair of strong lamps that spilled pools of light over the glistening mud of the road.

Antum always hated these last moments before an action, when there was nothing to do but wait. All of his orders had been given, and the initiating action would not be his. When the moment came, he needed to be near the president's vehicle.

Still, the waiting was hard.

His thoughts were shattered by a massive blast of flaring white light off to his left. The detonation was brutal. A thunderous concussion accompanied the blinding flash, and the light from the lamps and lanterns of the procession were blotted out entirely. Burning sparks soared high into the dark sky and fell among the wet grass and pine needles of the forest floor. The horses pulling the lead wagon reared back from the explosion, their eyes white with fear as their front hooves pawed the air. Their cries were pitiful as they pulled at the traces.

A giant maple, old when the first colonists had stepped onto the New World, began to sway in slow, ponderous arcs, bright spring leaves falling in a shower of vibrant green. The tree began to dip toward the road, the base of its trunk a splintered wreck. It crashed across the rutted mud, further startling the wagon horses. The crunching, discordant chorus of breaking wood, flailing branches, and crushing weight settled into a stillness punctuated by the sharp, disciplined cries of the president's guards as they jumped from their armored wagons, pistols and rifles at the ready. They fanned out to form a line between the cabriolet and any threat that might be approaching from the front or sides. The pools of light from their lanterns, now challenged by the smoldering flames of the fallen tree, cast wild shadows across the frantic scene.

Before the men were in position, however, another blinding bolt flashed out of the darkness. Another tall tree was struck, this time just behind the rearmost wagon. A sphere of cerulean energy billowed out from the base of the tree, scattering burning chunks of rock and bark in all directions. This second tree performed no graceful dance, however, but simply crashed into the road, nearly crushing the wagon.

The men in that last wagon had been in the process of deploying when the second tree fell. They crouched down beside the armored flanks and iron-rimmed wheels. Their faces, thrown into stark relief by the large lanterns, peered sternly into the dark forest all around. These men carried heavy naval pistols and shotguns, their weapons swinging from side to side.

Mimreg Antum gave this second group a closer look. They did not appear to be soldiers at all. Instead, he saw formal suits more appropriate to bankers or solicitors. Their clothing may have been civilian, he saw, but there was nothing slack or unprofessional about the way they handled their weapons. These new agents quickly established a professional cordon to defend the president from the rear or sides.

The mission team held their fire for a moment, allowing the cries of the horses and the stink of charred wood to work on the nerves of the guardians before making their next move. Antum hoped one set of defenders would oblige him. The *Etta* had been quite clear in their instructions: they were not to endanger the lives of the president's menif at all possible. Every opportunity to surrender peacefully was to be afforded them before the team used their weapons in earnest.

Antum's best interpretation of those instructions, given the very real threat of the professional killers around the man in the middle wagon, called for a spectacular display of firepower and destructive capability that would make clear to any objective observer that the president's guards were outmatched by a mile. Those men would still fight to the death if pressed, of course. They had been selected for just such dedication to duty. Antum hoped that such a show of force would convince the president himself that a moment's judicious parlay might be worth the chance to avoid the slaughter that would surely result in direct confrontation.

Unfortunately, felling the two trees that had trapped the convoy on the muddy road had clearly not done the trick. The men had now formed a ring around the central wagon, where the president now stood, one hand grasping the canopy frame and leaning out from the cabriolet, lending his own sharp eyes to the search for danger.

The soldiers from the lead wagon had fallen back to cover the president, leaving the protection of their own vehicle, as the horses, still shying from the fallen tree and its smell of burning and danger, had hauled it half into the woods to the right of the road. It was not ideal for the defenders, but it was just what Antum had been hoping for when they had concocted this ridiculous scheme in the first place. He only hoped that Fener had seen the opportunity as well.

The thought had only begun to form in his mind when the wagon disintegrated in a harrowing ball of lightning-tinged flame. One moment the heavy armored wagon had stood there, half-buried in shaking greenery, and the next it was outlined in flaring cerulean light that shattered the giant box in a heartbeat. Bits of armor and wood planking, trailing streamers of white fire, flashed out in all directions, setting smaller fires in the underbrush and in the trees overhead, while the men around the president crouched down further, shielding their faces from the light and heat of the explosion.

The sorry draft horses, now terrified beyond reason, screamed like wounded women and threw their broad chests against the traces, hauling the burning wreckage deeper into the trees. Their screams faded with the light of the bonfire dragging behind them. The guards, their weapons up and steady, spoke in calm, deliberate voices. The light from the remaining wagon lamps moved about them as the horses fidgeted in their leads. The soldiers backed toward the president's wagon now, with nowhere else to go.

One of the suited men walked up to the cabriolet and exchanged a quick, brief word with the president. The tall figure nodded and swung down out of the carriage, his driver working with several of the soldiers to try and turn the little vehicle around within the tight confines of the ambush box Antum's men had created.

The *mimreg* knew he needed to act now, before the resourceful men guarding President Lincoln managed to work their way free. He moved to the side of his blind, not presenting a target, and called out in a loud, clear voice.

"Mr. President, we only wish to talk."

The bodyguards immediately shifted their attention to the left hand span of forest, their weapons hunting for targets. Several moved to put themselves between the president and the trees, but he touched each reassuringly on the shoulder and moved forward. Peering through a chink in the blind, Antum could see the president's expression was bleak; clearly the man saw that his current situation was indefensible.

"Well, I won't lie, son." The voice was mild, but stern. "Blowing up my friends' wagon is a funny way of showing it."

Antum almost smiled. "We needed to get your attention, sir. No one was hurt."

The man in the dark suit moved beside the president and whispered urgently into his ear, gesturing back toward the last armored wagon. Lincoln shook his head, his lips pursed, and said, "I don't think that would do much good, Robert. You saw what they did to the last one." And he flipped a long hand over his shoulder toward the smoldering wreckage of the lead wagon and the fading cries of its team.

"We mean you no harm, sir." Antum knew this was going to be the delicate part of the conversation. "We only wish to speak with you."

Lincoln nodded. "You mean me no harm. But if I choose to turn around now and walk out of this forest? Will I be allowed to go?"

The *mimreg*'s face soured. He had been afraid the president might call his bluff. He also knew that the longer he was engaged in this discussion before he secured a moment's safety for himself and his men, the more likely it was that the president's defenders would locate his position and render the entire discussion moot with a shattering wave of lead.

"Sir, I've gone through quite a bit of trouble to speak with you away from the capital. If you're willing to walk away from that, then I don't think we could help each other anyway." He sighed. "So yes: if you chose to walk away now, I would let you."

The president nodded thoughtfully, waving away another objection from the man beside him. "You know, you have purchased yourself no good will with my keepers, here, by conducting your business in this way." He paused, his head cocked to one side. "In fact, you could have saved everyone a long haul of grief by coming directly to the White House."

"We tried that, sir." Antum did not try to hide the bitterness in his voice. "Your guard dogs were less than amenable."

The president paused again, his eyes tight as his mouth worked as if he had tasted something sour. Then he nodded. "They can be over-cautious. Very well. Let us speak, and see what we have to say to each other."

Antum was a trusting man, within the confines of his understanding of the world. He liked to deal with men and women whose word meant something to them. He had heard that said of the president, but he had no desire to end his service to the Order here in this cold little forest, back-shot by an over-eager night watchman.

"Sir, just to be clear: I am not alone. My men are armed with the weapons that felled the trees and destroyed the wagon. Please see that yours do not take any untoward actions while we talk." It took all of his Order training to keep his voice steady and reasoned. "I know you are a man of your word, Mr. President. A quick consultation with your people there will be all the assurance I need."

This time the president did smile. He turned to the irate, well-dressed man standing beside him, and muttered a few quick directions, jerking his head back toward the big wagon.

The man glowered up at the president, then out into the darkness. "If you are trying to abduct the president let me disabuse you of that notion. You would not leave this little stand of trees alive. If you think, after what was done to General Grant this morning, we are inclined to give you the slightest slack, you are sorely mistaken." Then he muttered something dark under his breath and turned, gesturing for the soldiers and civilian guards near him. They all moved back to the opposite side of the carriage or to stand near the big armored wagon.

When the area around the president was clear, Antum emerged from the shadows. He wore the customary cloak and hood of an Order missionary, tones of gray and light green blending into the shadows around him. His hood was trimmed in dark leather. He kept his hands wide, away from his empty holster, as he twisted toward the flickering lamp light to show that he was unarmed.

The president regarded him steadily as he approached. The man's face was heavily lined, but many of them seemed to lend themselves more to smiling than to expressions of concern or fear. There were streaks of white in his iconic beard and at his temples, sweeping out from beneath his customary stovepipe hat. Even backlit, with the fitful jerking of the lanterns, there was a gleam of intelligence in his eyes. Behind him, his guards, soldiers and agents alike, watched with suspicion. They kept their weapons oriented out into the surrounding woods. Again, Antum was reminded that he was dealing with consummate professionals. If he made a wrong move, he and his men would die here.

"Well, Robin of Loxley." The smile lines deepened. "What is it, exactly, you would like to say?"

Antum nodded to acknowledge the barb. He spoke quickly, words he had memorized days before. "Mr. President, I represent an organization that is very concerned over several developments currently at play within the Union. I am authorized to offer that organization's assistance in dealing with these developments, as well as other difficulties you may be experiencing." He was no orator, but he thought he had summed the situation up nicely.

President Lincoln nodded thoughtfully, the shadows shifting across his face as he tilted his head slightly. "An organization, hm?" He surveyed the woods around them with pursed lips, as if searching for a committee or board of directors hiding among the trees. "Am I to assume, then, that exactly *what* organization you represent is not going to be part of this evening's discussion? Can I assume this has nothing to do with what happened to General Grant? I'm not sure how much good will we can apply to this conversation under the circumstances . . ."

Antum shook his head within the hood. "Sir, we have reason to believe that many of the men closest to you are compromised. What happened this morning could well be involved, yes. I would be happy to tell you more, if we could step away a little further?"

The president's eyes narrowed. "And this is exactly the kind of thing I would expect a man to say who is trying to separate me from my chosen, trusted advisors, son. I'm going to need a bit more from you before I play any more of your cloak and dagger games."

Antum looked back at the guards, then to the tall man before him. "Sir, how many of the men currently advising you are the trusted men you chose yourself?"

Lincoln frowned. He began to speak, and then stopped himself, his tall frame shifting beneath his long coat. When he spoke, it was with a thoughtful undertone. "Interesting point." He gestured toward the downed maple tree before them. "Why don't we take a seat?" He called back over his shoulder to the young man who seemed to be the leader of the bodyguards. "Robert, don't get your knickers in a bunch. We'll be right over here."

The agent in charge muttered under his breath but stayed where he was, his arms crossed angrily over his chest.

Antum and the president moved toward the log and sat down. "Sir," the *mimreg* spoke slowly, marshaling his thoughts. "I represent an organization that has been active on this continent for a very long time. In fact, we were here before the first colonies from Europe sank their flags into the soil."

The president politely kept the skepticism from his voice. "Well, that certainly is a long time, son. What are we talking here? Masons? Illuminati?"The corner of his mouth quirked.

The names of conspiracies created by the Holy Order over the centuries to hide their own activities, used now in this context, were enough to cause the *mimreg* to curse the cleverness of those earlier generations. He shook his head. "No, sir. The people I represent have worked for the defense and betterment of mankind for longer than you can know. We serve mankind and the divine potential each man and woman carries within them."

President Lincoln smiled again. He took off his hat and made a great show of rotating it slowly in his long hands, inspecting the brim. "Those are some fine sounding words. But you have to understand how they sound to adult ears. Especially as we sit here in the middle of the woods, feet away from a cavalcade that you so skillfully brought to a sudden and abrupt halt with a well-planned ambush." The president worked his shoulders against the cold. "And that says nothing of the terrible subjectivity of the terms you've conjured with, as well."

Antum shook his head with a sigh, and leaned closer to the president. He ignored the guards tensing in the distance. "Mr. President, I represent powers you are not currently aware exist. Powers that have been fighting the battles you have since taken up as your own for longer than you can imagine. We wield forces that you can only dream of, and we can put these forces at your disposal if our goals continue to coincide. We believe that may well be the case."

The president's lower lip thrust forward as he seemed to chew over the words. "Forces such as those used most recently to fell these might trees, and lay low the chariot of my defenders?"

The *mimreg* nodded. "For a start, Mr. President."

The tall man shrugged. "I'm not sure we need such formidable firepower to confront the sad, stubborn remnants of the Confederacy. I have to assume, therefore, that you are referring to some future conflict with some more fearsome foe?"

Antum nodded again, and his shadowed eyes tightened. "Foes you are singularly unprepared to confront, sir. Foes armed with weaponry just as terrible as that which my men carry right now. A dark cabal of truly evil creatures that will stop at nothing to tear down everything you believe in. Foes you are, in fact, currently clasping to your bosom."

Lincoln settled back at that, the suspicious look settling once more across his features. "Son, that's the second time you've laid an accusation upon my best and brightest. I think, before we go any further, we need to hear a bit more about that."

Antum stood, again ignoring the men clutching their weapons behind him. He paced a few steps into the shadows and then spun on one heel, moving back toward the president. "Sir, we don't know who they are, but the very creatures we are sworn to confront, have somehow infiltrated your cabinet. They appear as normal men, they behave as if they have your best interests at heart, but they work only for your destruction and the destruction of all humanity." He took a breath before finishing, "We believe they are responsible for the recent attack on General Grant and his family."

Lincoln sat quietly on the fallen tree for several moments, his eyes haunted. When he spoke, he was not looking at Antum. His voice was spectral, as if he was speaking from a great distance away. "That would certainly explain some . . . difficulties, I've been having lately." Then he looked up at Antum. "But I'm sorry, son. This tale you're spinning is just too fantastical. You've got some mighty fancy shooting irons, and that's for certain. But these 'castle in the cloud' conspiracies, and ages of darkness, and whatnot? Well, it sounds like just so much poppycock to me." He shook his head, a look of pity touching his eyes. "I'm sorry."

Antum had known it would come to this. He reached into his shirt, holding his left hand out quickly to indicate he meant no harm, and pulled his medallion into the open air. It spun on its gold chain, winking slightly in the dim lantern light. The *mimreg* slipped the chain over his head and held it out to where the president could see it clearly.

The pure white stone shone dully in the light, winking slightly as the medallion twisted and turned at the end of its tether.

"This stone holds just the smallest part of the power that my Order wields, Mr. President." Antum looked closely at the medallion, focusing his mind and his spirit on the matrix within the mineral, and felt the connection build between himself and the Relic fragment far away within the Acropolis.

The medallion slowed in its gyrations and then stopped, hanging from the chain with an unnatural stillness. The stone began to glow from within, pulsing with a pure blue-white light that quickly suffused the entire gem and began to blaze out, throwing the faces of the two men into stark relief while their shadows plunged into the darkness around them.

The president's eyebrows arched as he watched. He reached out, holding his hand to the stone as if testing it for heat. "Well that *is* extraordinary." The light continued to pulse, brighter and brighter. Antum held it out nearer to the president, and this time the guards did not try to hide their alarm, and advanced, their weapons leveled at the *mimreg*'s back.

A bolt of searing white lightning flew up into the branches overhead from the forest off to their right. Several small fires burned sullenly up in the leaves overhead as starlight glittered down through a hole blown in the foliage.

The soldiers and guards crouched lower, stopped in their tracks. The president raised a hand without looking up. "There's no danger here, boys." The president's voice was awed as he leaned toward the medallion. "Stand down."

As the stone moved closer to the tall man's face, it glowed more and more brightly, the light shining out in pure cerulean glory that bathed the lined face. His eyes, glittering in the brilliance, were filled with awe.

"What is it?" His voice was almost a whisper.

"It is a small shadow of the power that I represent, Mr. President." Antum's voice was hushed also. Channeling this much energy through the medallion always made him feel like an initiate standing before the Relic fragment for the first time.
"I feel as if it is speaking, but I can't comprehend its meaning." Lincoln's face looked younger as he stared into the light.

Antum schooled his face to stillness and summoned all of his training to intone the official response. "It is passing judgment upon your soul, sir. And it has found you worthy."

The president shook his head as if clearing it of the cobwebs of some dream. He looked over the stone, its glow fading as Antum relaxed his concentration, and stared into the *mimreg*'s eyes. "Well, you certainly know how to turn a man's head, son. But I'm afraid I don't understand exactly what it is that you're offering."

Antum looked out into the woods. He was hesitant to make the offer he had been ordered to extend. He had not told his men, and he was not sure how they would react when they heard, crouching out in the black woods with their reliquary weapons clutched in their hands. What he was about to suggest had never been contemplated in the long history of the Order.

"You have now felt the power of what we call a Relic fragment. The might of my Order comes from these fragments, pieces of a far larger, far greater talisman that was shattered in the earliest days of man. A fragment such as the one you have just glimpsed is the only hope we have against creatures that would see all light on this planet extinguished. They cannot stand hidden when bathed in its light. They cannot warp the minds of men when it is near. Our weapons, the only weapons with any hope of facing the forces this foe will marshal, are all charged with the power of the Relic fragment."

A strange, deep hunger lit within the president's eyes. He leaned forward with a renewed eagerness. "Well, that does sound mighty impressive." The man looked suddenly tired. "If I can be honest with you in turn, son, this job is beginning to wear on me. The country's needs are so great, and so disparate, that I feel as if I'm being pulled in every direction at once. I feel as if I cannot focus on the true dangers to the Republic. Any assistance would be grateful, at this point."

Antum shot a quick look into the surrounding shadows, then said, conscious of the full weight of his voice, "I have been ordered to tell you that such a fragment can be put at your disposal if you choose to stand with the Order."

Two sharp gasps sounded from the night-shrouded wood as Luys and Fener heard the offer. Before they could do anything drastic, the *mimreg* rushed to continue. "It will not be under your control, you understand. It will be accompanied by an honor guard of the most powerful warriors of the Order. But its strength will be yours to direct, in the furtherance of your current goals and the goals of the Order."

The President of the United States straightened at this offer. His eyes were wide with disbelief. Antum knew what the man had felt through the link. He had experienced it himself once, long ago. There was no denying the might of the Ancients and the Creators, or the power of the Relic, once a person had looked into a bonded medallion. And the Relic, reaching through the stone, had touched the president, and thought him to be true. Still . . . the power he was being offered was unprecedented. There was no way to tell how a man not initiated into the mysteries of the Order might react.

Lincoln unfolded his ungainly length up to his full height, stretching his back with his hands on his hips. He looked down at Antum with a growing smile on his face. "Son, I believe I'm right glad you detonated my armored wagon after all."

Mimreg Antum settled back with relief. As he reached out to clasp the president's hand, however, he paused. A crawling feeling skittered down his back and he looked out into the impenetrable forest, suddenly overcome with the certain sense that something out there had its eyes fixed upon him with less than friendly intent.

He shook off the feeling of foreboding and took the president's hand. There were too many real dangers stalking the land now, for him to give credence to formless fears crouching in a dark and empty forest.

Chapter 15

*Mimreg*Zain walked with brisk, confident steps. He looked neither right nor left as he moved past the ornately-carved walls of many-colored stone. Passages loomed up on either side, their decorations declaring, for those who could read them, what lay beyond. Varro struggled to keep up with his trainer, hunger and thirst burning within him, his mind dull from deprivation and pain.

They moved down strange passageways and dimly-lit stairwells, heading deeper and deeper into the earth. The full weight of the mountain loomed above them like a silent threat, its weight pressing down on Varro's neck. And yet, his mind was calmand cold, far from the fiery distraction of just a few months ago. Whether it was the lack of food and water, the exhaustion, or a final epiphany brought on by his months of training, he could not tell. Finally, in this moment, his thoughts were as still as the water of a subterranean lake; deep and dark.

Varro counted out over five hundred echoing paces before they stood before a set of double doors whose elaborate carvings and layered stonework were more ornate and beautiful than anything he had ever seen. The scene depicted upon the two doors was of a shining white city surrounded by lush jungle and turquoise seas. He remembered the unmistakable skyline from his first session in the disk chamber: the city the Order called Atlantis.

Zain stood silently before the door with his head bowed. Varro sensed some deeper significance behind the pause and the gesture, and so stiffened in his own stance, bowing his head in the same manner. After a moment, the *mimreg* reached out with both hands and gently pushed the doors aside. They moved with a smooth silence. The room within was dark, but conveyed a sense of massive space.

Small reliquary lamps glowed upon a long table set deep within the room, barely revealing six figures seated on the other side. The lamp's illumination touched neither walls nor ceiling. As the *mimreg* and the initiate approached the table, their footsteps echoed with a hollow, distant sound that added to the impression of space and majesty. The table emerged from the shadows and dim light, and Varro forgot all about the chamber. The figures seated there demanded all his attention.

The three figures to his left were the oldest. A robust man of middle years wore elaborate cream and gold robes over an impressive suit of armor of the same shades and tones, a tall, archaic-looking headpiece settled low over his short brown hair. Several items built into the robes and cloak glowed with the distinct cobalt blue of reliquary power, and even his eyes shone with the light of his spirit's strength. A neatly trimmed full beard and mustache nearly hid stern, thin lips as he watched the initiate approach with an enigmatic expression.

Varro hid his shock as he realized that the next figure was a woman. She presented an imposing, warlike image. Her clothing was form-fitting, combined the flowing elements of a robe or gown with polished ivory and silver armor picked out with burnished gold. The woman's face had an ageless quality, her unblemished skin a marked contrast to the ancient, tired wisdom behind her eyes. Her own headgear was more helmet than hat. A wealth of silky chestnut hair fanned down from the crest of the helm, shimmering in the soft light. Again, various gems, runes, and other elements of her uniform glowed with cerulean energy. She also watched the initiate without expression or acknowledgement.

The third figure, sitting toward the middle of the table, was by far the oldest in the room. His beard was white, matching the fringe of hair that clung to the sides of his head. There was no armor in evidence here, although his robes, of similar cut and color to the man and woman sitting to his right, were by far the most elaborate, with the unmistakable winking of blue-white gems throughout. Aside from his lack of ironclad splendor, this man was set apart from the rest by the open, friendly smile he gave to Varro, accompanied by a nod of recognition. There was something about him that reminded the initiate of Jomei, a vague and distant memory of friendship and warmth from what seemed like a lifetime ago.

On the right hand side of the table, three men, each older than Varro by a decade or more, regarded him with a cold indifference. Two of the men were far darker than the initiate would have expected. One man was clearly African, his skin as dark as any of the freemen Varro had ever met. A drooping mustache gave him a brooding appearance. Beside him was a man whose skin was only slightly lighter, with the strong facial features of a desert prince from a dancehall show.

Both of these men wore full suits of plate armor similar to the suits he had seen on the marshaling field the day of his arrival. This armor, however, was far more ornate, plates of cold hard iron detailed with graceful, curving panels of polished gold. Reliquary gems glowed within recesses scattered across the hard metal surfaces. Heavy, crested helms sat beside each man's chair.

The last man, sitting at the end of the table and set apart from the others by some slight but noticeable distance, was not wearing armor. This man wore robes that matched the oldest man, albeit considerably less extravagant. He was pale, his brown hair close-cropped as almost all members of the Order he had met. Varro looked down at the helmets, then over to the headgear worn by the two figures sitting on the far left, and realized that the style must be to facilitate wearing the ancient-looking headgear.

There were fewer reliquary stones on the clothing of this last man. His eyes looked haunted and distant. Where the expressions of the other five had ranged from welcoming, in the case of the old man, to shades of cold indifference with the rest, this man seemed to be looking right through Varro, as if his mind was fixated upon far more weighty matters than the events taking place around him.

A chill ran down Varro's back as sudden realization dawned upon him. Their elaborate clothing, the stern expressions, and the grand ceremony of the six, all sitting together in judgment . . .

He was standing before the *Etta*.

It had only just hit him when a further realization froze his heart: they were sitting in judgment of him.

Mimreg Zain, his demeanor now formal and distant, strode around the left-hand side of the table to stand beside the older figures, the *sircans* of the *Etta*. Far behind him, Varro heard the double doors close with a hollow boom. His head turned despite himself, but the closed doors were lost in shadows. Looking back, he saw seven people, each radiating power and presence, staring at him without words.

He knew he could not speak; he still bore the bruises of his last sharp lesson. His hard-won fortitude, still foreign to his fiery, fighter's spirit, was beginning to fray as he stood, waiting for some direction. He closed his eyes for a moment, took a deep, cleansing breath, and settled back on his heels, unlocking his knees, and opened his eyes with a slow, deliberate thought.

Some imperceptible barrier was apparently crossed. Each of the older members of the *Etta* nodded once. The younger members seemed to relax by an almost undetectable degree, and Zain nodded in response. The *mimreg* took one step away from the table and raised a single, leather gauntleted finger before Varro's eyes. The finger curled back into his fist as he lowered his arm, and a door swung silently open in a distant wall to the left, barelydiscernible in the darkness. There was a weak light visible through the door, a slightly brighter shade of black. The soft light of the reliquary lamps outlined the open door, fixing the position in his eye.

Zain's gaze flicked toward the door, and then back again. Varro looked down at the men and woman at the table, but their faces offered him nothing. Varro looked again at the distant door, then to Zain. Without thought, he found himself turning sharply on one heel and striding toward the open door. As he reached the portalhe paused, but decided not to look back. There would be no assistance there. A slow, frustrated annoyance was building within him. He wanted to face whatever lay beyond the door without further delay.

*****

As Varro crossed the threshold, the door boomed shut behind him. The corridor beyond lacked any of the embellishments of the halls above. Small, low-set reliquary gems provided what little light there was, casting the floor in blunt relief. The walls pressed in upon him, almost as if the hallway was narrowing as he moved. He raised one hand to push before him just in case it was not an optical illusion.

He walked for several hundred paces. The walls appeared no closer together, but still he felt like he was being pressed by the weight of the mountain overhead. The hall stretched onward, unrelieved by door or alcove. He drew one hand along the rough, gritty texture of the unfinished wall. There was a sense of extreme age, and he remembered the ominous hints to the Order's antiquity. This coarse wall, more than all the talking and the visions of the reliquary disk, brought home how long the Acropolis must have sat within the high mountains.

The corridor widened into a black, shallow chamber. Backlit by the dim glow of the gems behind him, Varro eased his way into the space. He moved carefully on the balls of his feet, shifting to allow the little light behind him to leak into the distant corners.

He had moved into the chamber, his hands out, his legs bent, when something darted out of the shadows on the opposite side. He caught only a glimpse as his attacker moved through the faint light. It looked like a man, features hidden within the shadows of a dark hood. A long knife glinted in one hand; a very long knife. Varro shifted to meet his attacker, arms low, left shoulder forward. He put one hand behind himself to feel for the corner. It had looked like a very long knife, indeed.

His assailant was upon him before he could set himself. The blade, easily three feet long, probably more deserving of the title sword than knife, came whistling down at his head. Varro's training took over, his body moving faster than conscious thought. His left arm snaked around the descending blade, settling on the attacker's elbow as his right hand darted across his chest to grab the hand that held the sword. With a vicious twist, the weapon stopped short, and then began to shake, rising once more as the initiate strained against the surprising strength of his attacker.

He had the man, he knew. He felt completely in control of the situation, but he was at a loss as to what he should do next. Should he be satisfied with subduing his opponent, or did the Order expect more? He did not want to injure the man; at the same time, nothing was going to keep him from successfully completing what he realized now must be a rite of passage; a trial by fire under the watchful, unseen, eyes of the *Etta*.

Varro grunted as he threw his left elbow up and over his assailant's head, twisting around behind the flailing man. The attacker was now locked in a bear-hug, his sword arm pinioned to his chest.

"Yield and I let you go." He whispered into the man's ear. Speech sounded strange after so much silence, but he did not want to hurt this man any more than necessary. All of his training within the Acropolis had been vicious and painful, far more real than he would have ever anticipated, but no one had ever been purposely killed. When it became clear there was an obvious winner, the vanquished always conceded.

He was wondering if he should make the offer again when the man in his arms spasmed suddenly. Varro loosened his grip slightly, and immediately regretted it as the man, sensing his moment, lurched backward, driving the back of his skull into Varro's nose.

The sound of the sword clattering to the stones was the only comforting element to the wild, pain filled moments that followed the attack. Varro reeled back against the cold stone of the wall, his vision flaring with bright lights that sent the little room dancing around him. He could taste the salty tang of blood in his mouth. The attacker, crouched before him, was catching his own breath, but had drawn a pair of long knives from somewhere and was already sliding forward, the blades held out to either side.

Varro shook the remaining sparkles from his eyes and eased back down into a loose fighter's stance. The sword was a flat, dull line on the floor against the far wall, but his attacker stood between him and the weapon. He would have to face the knives with his bare hands until he could make it around.

The man came in with two wide swings, one after the other, and the blades whistled through the cool air. Varro punched low, beneath the first blade and into the man's elbow. The second attack bore in, sweeping low, and Varro spun up inside the man's reach to elbow him in the biceps, sending the second knife clattering. There was a rewarding grunt, and Varro drove both of his elbows back into the man's gut before swinging away again.

There was not a moment's reprieve, as the man drove back in, now tossing his remaining knife from hand to hand in a confusing and flashy pattern. It was almost impossible to track the threat in the dancing shadows. The point of the blade darted out toward Varro and back almost faster than he could see, feinting time and again to keep him off balance. He had a moment to wonder, again, how real this training was supposed to be.

Then the knife snapped out of the darkness and sank into his upper back, skittering over his shoulder blade.

Varro screamed with the pain and surprise of the wound. He clutched at his woundwith his right hand and felt the blood soaking into his tunic. He could see it gleaming wetly on the blade as it flashed back and forth, the hooded man's mouth just visible by the glint of teeth in a vicious smile.

The initiate backed up. There was no denying he was wounded; a deep, painful wound, not something that an expert might have visited upon him as a lesson. He could already feel his left arm weakening, as a sick, gut-wrenching sense of violation welled up in his throat.

The knife flashed in from his left, and he was barely able to slap the knife-wielding hand aside. Without pause or warning, the knife came in from the right, and again, he was barely able to stop it. What followed was a flurry of attacks that drove him back until he was pressed against the stone, his wound throbbing. He forced his mind to rise above the pain and the frustration, moderating his breathing and keeping his eyes on the darting blade in the shadows. He struggled to find his silence. He let his shoulders slump slightly, trying to give the impression that he was more wounded than he really was. Perhaps that might give the attacker pause. It did not.

The man eased into a series of slashing, diagonal blows that came nearer and nearer to Varro's face each time before he was able to dodge or punch them aside. Suddenly, the initiate sensed his moment, a lull in the movement as the knife arced up from one hand to the other. Varro ducked low, coming up hard, planting his wounded shoulder into the attacker's gut and lifting him up into the air.

The man grunted as the breath was forced from his lungs, but he continued to fight without pause, his wiry body writhing within Varro's grasp. The knife came up, dull in the low light, spinning around in the attacker's grip until the cruel tip pointed right at Varro's back. That blade rose into the air, banishing all doubt from his mind, when he finally drove his attacker into the far wall. The man slapped against the stone, his head making a gruesome hollow sound as blood and breath sprayed out over Varro's shoulder. The knife fell from lifeless fingers and clattered against the stone.

Varro lowered the still form of his attacker, kicking out with one foot to slide the sword out of reach should the man recover his wits. But he was not going to recover any time soon, the initiate saw, as the dull lights from the hall gleamed weakly from the man's open, empty eyes. Blood ran down his cheeks like tears, and a trickle ran like a mountain rill from one ear. The man's chest looked flattened and empty, and after a moment, Varro could see that no breath stirred there.

The initiate reached out with his uninjured hand and pulled the hood away. His attacker had been an old man. Face wrinkled with worry and care, laugh lines settled among the others showing a softer, more human side. His hair was shorn down in the Order fashion. He had clearly been a master of the blades and a warrior of great skill. Why had he attacked with such vicious finality, forcing Varro to do the same?

He stood, shaking his head. Even now, after months of living among them and training to become one of them, he felt that there would be things he never understood about the Order. He looked around and found the sword, picking it up with a hand slick with his own blood. He searched the body, finding a broad belt with a long scabbard for the sword as well as a matching dual scabbard for the fighting knives. With a muttered apology to the dead, he undid the man's belt and fastened it around his own waist. He sheathed the weapons, and then looked around the room. There was nothing more there. A single hall stretched off into darkness on one side, and continued on into a similar darkness on the other.

While he stood, trying to decide what to do next, the floor beneath him began to rumble and a distant, grumbling growl shook the air. He turned to watch down one hall and stumbled back as a series of metal poles, each tipped in sharp, gleaming silver, slid out of the ceiling and hit the floor with a sharp click. Another set, nearer to him, fell into place. Then another fell, and another. Each set snapped down closer to him, and he felt a sudden rush of energy as he realized he was being herded.

Another set of iron bars fell, and Varro decided that a wound to his pride was far better than stubbornly standing his ground only to be impaled on the glittering spears. He spun and moved down the hall at a loping run. The unfamiliar weight of the weapons around his waist threw him off his stride while his wound pulled painfully each time he moved his left arm, but he adjusted and continued trotting down the dark hall.

The rumbling continued beneath his feet, and the sharp, skittering click of spearheads hitting the floor grew louder and closer, faster and faster.

Varro put his head down and dug deep for more speed. His hunger and his thirst, forgotten in the novelty and tension of the trial, started to gnaw at him, but he pushed them aside. The impacts of the spears were closer despite his burst of speed, and he knew he needed to focus solely on his pumping legs if this latest menace was not going to claim him.

He ran down the dimly-lit corridor, the impacts of his booted feet sending dull echoes out into the shadows. He almost missed the pit opening up before him. He leapt up into the air, clearing the gaping chasm by inches, and came down hard on the other side. For a moment, he wondered if the falling spears would end at the gap, but with a clatter the next set crashed down, and so he continued to run. Chasms opened more and more frequently in front of him, until he was not running so much as leaping from one firm perch to the next, each pit between stretching down into darkness below.

He took another leap, his lungs burning, his vision flashing, his wound pulsing with dull pain, and his foot passed into open air. He fell, his arms flailing at the sudden loss of control, and slapped face-first into cold, hard water. He took in a desperate breath with the pain and shock, and choked as his mouth filled with brackish liquid. He lost his bearings as he tumbled in the darkness, his lungs demanding breath he could not give them. When his head finally broke out into the air again, he sucked in great whooping breaths. The rumbling was gone, as was the sharp clatter of spearheads on stone.

His feet thrashed beneath him in a constant battle to keep his head above water, and his hands flailed around, trying to find walls that he could not see. There were no reliquary lamps here, the only light from the flares of pain dancing across his eyes, illuminating nothing. His gasping breath echoed off distant stone as the sound of splashing water filled his ears. He pivoted around in a full circle, looking for anything that might give him a hint of what he should do now. All around him was nothing but unrelieved darkness.

The desire to curse rose strongly within him, but he thrust it away and focused on the moment. There was no way they were going to dump him into this dark cistern and leave him after all the time and effort they had spent to train him. Although . . . was he not supposed to kill the old man? Was this punishment for going too far in what was clearly a training exercise? The fear, the first he had felt in a while, had not even had time to put down roots before a low, chuffing sound erupted somewhere off to his right. In his fall and the flailing that had followed, he had completely lost any sense of direction in the darkness. He splashed around to face the sound. It came again, a gusting puff of stinging gas, as if from some tainted bellows. It happened a third time.

Without warning, the gas, whatever it was, ignited. The entire cavern burst into flames. The rolling wall of fire churned across the dark water, throwing the rough-hewn walls and ceiling into glaring prominence. There was no time for thought. Varro spun around, his limbs thrashing, and dove under just as the bright cloud swept over him and continued on down the cavern. He could see the churning fire, glittering above the water as if he was looking through a cloudy window into Hell.

He waited for the fire to dissipate, but it continued to roil there above the surface, and his lungs began to scream for air. He pushed off a rough wall with his good arm, his legs flailing behind him, and tried to get up some decent speed away from the original source of the fire. He kept looking over his shoulder, but the fire was still there, sending shafts of dancing light stabbing down into the water all around him. He forced himself to keep swimming, even as dark blotches began to crowd the edges of his vision and the pain in his chest threatened to overwhelm him.

His arms were leaden, his legs numb, when the light above him flickered and died out. He barely had the strength to claw his way to the surface. The air was hot with the passage of the flame, and the stone around him glowed a dull, sullen red. Ghostly wisps of steam lingered in the air, curling lazily over the dark water. Even so, he took in deep breaths and savored each one like a mountain breeze. He could just make out a series of iron rungs sunk into the carved wall before him. He drifted in that direction, his legs kicking feebly beneath him.

The rungs glowed as well, radiating a burning, acrid heat. He looked behind him, and then above him. The light was fading, but he knew where he had to go. After only a moment's hesitation, he reached out and grasped the lowest rung with his right hand. The metal was painfully hot to the touch, but it had cooled enough that it did not char his flesh. It was brutally uncomfortable, but he checked his hand for damage, and although it stung and throbbed, his skin was intact.

With a grim twist to his mouth, he began to haul himself up out of the water. His hands groped for each rung without sight. As the glow from below faded, the shadows once again moved in to swallow his world. He forced himself upward, pushing with exhausted legs, dragging his body up with drained arms, the pain of his wound in his back growing worse with each pull. He slapped the stone wall above him with his right hand, his body near collapse, and it took him a moment to realize that there were no more rungs. He slid his hand to either side, dragged it closer and then pushed it as high as he could reach. Nothing.

The shaft continued upward; there was no lip that he could feel. He knew a moment's despair as he realized that once again, he had no idea what to do. In his continued thrashing, however, his arm struck a thick, rough cord hanging down the center of the shaft and set it to swinging. Of course: rope. His mouth twisted into a bitter smile as he pushed his forehead against the cooling stone. He was going to have to climb. He was going to have to climb with a pounding knife wound in his back and at least the first layer of skin burned from his palms.

He reached out, grabbed the rope with his left hand, and with a last breath leapt up as far as he could and grasped the thick cord with his right hand. Hand over hand he moved upward, his mind focused with crystal clarity on the certainty that he would reach the top eventually. Except that he did not. The rope ended at a metal bar sunk into the shaft's walls on either side. Another rope dangled not far above it, found again with flailing hands, and he had to climb onto the cross bar with arms and legs shaking with exhaustion, reach up, and continue climbing.

He had to switch ropes three more times before he finally reached the lip of the shaft. He was in a round chamber with a single door leading out into further darkness. A ring of dim reliquary lamps were set around the room. His shoulder burned, his hands were numb, his legs ached, and his arms felt like lead weights. Despite the cool air of the caverns, sweat glistened on every surface of his body. He collapsed onto his hands and knees, his body trembling with fatigue.

A familiar sound broke into his semi-collapsed state; a whirring that he had heard countless times before. His sweat-slick scalp rose and he looked through the dim outline of the doorway and into a shadow-filled hallway beyond. He could see nothing, but the sound continued, soft but insistent: the sounds of the gauntlet chamber.

Varro pushed himself back up to his feet with a soft grunt and shuffled toward the doorway. He peered into the shadows but could not pierce the darkness. The sound was clear. He knew that somewhere down in the black, an array of obsidian cylinders awaited to pummel him into jelly. He had worked in the gauntlet room in all different states of readiness, from fully awake after a heavy meal and a day of rest, to the time he had been dragged out of bed just after a forced march through the winter mountains and thrust into the testing chamber with nothing but his pants. He had never faced those swift, blurring staves as tired as he was now.

The final ordeal had pushed him beyond his understanding of pain. He knew he must continue down the tunnel. There was no path back the way he had come, short of dropping back down, the Creators alone knew how far, into the cistern below. With a sigh that caught in his chest in a painful hitch, he stood up to his full height, threw his shoulders back, and walked confidently into the shadows.

The sound grew louder as he moved. There were no doors, and only the noise ahead drove him on. He continued to walk long after his ears told him he should have reached the chamber, and still there was nothing but the dark tunnel stretching away before him. His pace had slowed considerably by the time he came to a closed door. There were small carvings on this door, reminiscent of the doors and walls in the rest of the Acropolis. He could make no sense of them, as his sapped mind struggled to remember vague bits and pieces of his recent past. There was nothing.

He pushed the door open and entered a familiar-seeming room. It was an exact replica of the gauntlet chamber, with large stone cylinders standing out from the floor, holes along their flanks where the hard-edged staves would emerge to trip and slap and batter. The drums were spinning already, although no staves were yet in evidence.

This was not the same chamber, however: it was longer. As he watched, he realized that there were far more cylinders stretching on into the dimness. With another sigh, Varro hitched up his shoulders, ignoring the twinges of pain, and with a starting hop, he jogged toward the gauntlet.

The first cylinder pushed a staff out at ankle height and almost tripped him up. He leapt over it and continued moving. The next two each produced their iron-hard bars even with his head, and he had to duck into a tight shoulder roll to avoid another that came swinging in from his side. A grunt of pain was forced past gritted teeth as his wound was pushed into the stone of the floor. Soon, he was dodging and jumping, trying to move through the forest of brutal machines before they could dash him down to the floor.

He drew his knives and began to parry aside the blows he was too slow to escape. He whirled through the room with abandon, his exhaustion forgotten as he spun and twisted, the blades glittering. He mistimed one leap, however, and a staff came crashing down from the left. The dagger rose to meet it but was slapped aside, and he lost the knife as his hand was stunned by the heavy blow.

With no time to mourn the lost weapon, he flipped over another pair of staves, catching the flash of another threat approaching from the right. He brought his last dagger up to parry it aside and was shocked at the clashing ring of metal on metal that echoed around him. He came out of his combat trance for a moment to stare in horrible fascination as he saw that the staves were shedding their wooden sheaths to reveal glittering steel blades. He would be sliced into quivering chunks of bloody meat if he missed a single step or beat.

He leapt high into the air, moving toward a cylinder whose blades were deployed low, giving him a moment to draw the old man's sword. He came down into crouch, held it for just a second, and moved back into the eternal dance his body knew better than his mind.

A flaring heat burned across his back and he knew that a staff blade had grazed him below his earlier wound. He kept his eyes focused in the middle distance, his peripheral vision catching the gleaming threats before he could focus on them. He continued to leap, spin, dodge, and weave, the ringing of steel on steel echoing around him as he moved down the chamber. The lighting got more and more dim as the reliquary lamps became fewer and fewer. Eventually, he was spinning through the course in near-darkness, the whistling of blades more warning than the half-seen glimpse that was all the lighting allowed.

He spun out of a high shoulder roll on his good side, coming back up onto his feet, dagger and sword held ready, only to see that there were no more cylinders. Behind him, the rotating barrels slowed, clicked several times, and then stopped.

Struggling for an even breath, Varro crouched with his elbows on his knees for a moment, weapons dangling uselessly between his feet. He tried to control the crushing frustration and despair. This gauntlet chamber did not end in a doorway, but in a blank wall.

Slowly, Varro sank down until he was sitting with his legs crossed beneath him. He stared at the blank wall with disbelieving eyes. He looked down at his lap, took a deep breath, and found the calm stillness within his mind that was still so new to him. When he had brought his thoughts and his breathing back under his conscious control, he looked up at the wall again. It was not featureless, as he had first thought. Three small niches rose from the floor, and above each the wall was polished smooth, a noticeable contrast to the rough-hewn surfaces all around.

Rising, Varro moved toward the wall. Each smooth section contained a brief passage carved in a neat, clean script.

Over the first, the inscription read,

"GIVE ME FOOD AND I WILL LIVE. GIVE ME WATER AND I WILL DIE."

Over the next was,

"I RUN WITHOUT FEET. I ROAR WITH NO MOUTH."

And the last,

"I CAN MAKE ONE MAN BLIND, WHILE I MAKE ANOTHER MAN SEE. I CAN MAKE ONE BUILDING STRONG, WHILE ANOTHER I TEAR DOWN."

Varro slumped down to his knees before the three niches. Riddles. He had always hated riddles. These seemed fairly basic, but he could barely remember his own name, never mind think his way through a foolish puzzle!

His breathing came in deep, convulsive gasps, his shoulders heaving, and his limbs shaking, threatening to collapse. His chin fell against his chest as a throbbing pressure built behind his eyes. Food, life, water, death.Running without feet, roaring without a mouth.And as for the last? He could make no sense of what he was reading.

His headache grew worse while his breath failed to moderate, rushing louder and louder in his ears. Life.Death.Running.Roaring. Blind, sight, strong, destruction . . .

Something in his brain clicked through the pain. His head whipped up and he stared at the small alcoves. He stood, turning behind him, and moved toward one of the cylinders. Its blades glinted in the soft light, but they did not move. He put a hand on the smooth surface

Crouching down by a cold, still cylinder, Varro put a hand on the barrel. The glistening blade was fastened to a stout wooden staff with leather strapping. The wood was rough, with a pronounced grain. He brought out his remaining dagger and slid the blade along the staff. Shavings curled up around the metal and then fell away. He did this several more times until he had a small pile of wooden slivers at his feet. He made no attempt to hide the smile that tugged at one corner of his mouth.

Placing the shavings within the niche beneath the first riddle, Varro drew his sword with his left hand and laid the blade down, edge upward, so that it was above the pile. He braced the dagger in his right, silently asked for forgiveness, and sharply struck down with the dagger blade, slicing across the sword blade.

Nothing happened.

He bowed his head, took a deep, steadying breath, and then snapped his hand down again.

Again, nothing happened.

The initiate snarled. He understood these were less than ideal circumstances, with less than ideal materials. But honestly, if this was what they wanted him to do . . .

His brows lowered in concentration, Varro brought the dagger down once more . . . and sparks jumped from the blades down into the wood. He almost dropped the weapons in surprise.

It took several more tries before he could nurse one of those sparks into feeding on the curls of wood, but soon tendrils of gray smoke rose out of the pile, a glowing ember buried deep within. The walls around were suddenly illuminated in the warm orange glow of honest flame. A gentle gong sounded throughout the room, and the little niche lit with the cool glow of reliquary light.

Varro stood up, a smile on his face, and looked at the next riddle. He felt the sweat still cold on his body, but some irreverent impulse brought a sly cut to his smile and he went to one knee before the alcove, leaned in, and spit into the space there. Again the tone sounded, and this niche, too, lit up.

The last niche remained dark and cold.

Varro rested back on his haunches, staring at the last riddle. There was a theme forming, obviously. And no matter how bone-weary he was, his brain was not entirely useless. A distant memory stirred in his sluggish thoughts; a glint of light reflecting off of something. He was suddenly struck with the image of Tucker Soza, and lively eyes behind dusty panes of . . .

His head jerked back sharply. He looked around the room. The light was still soft, most of the chamber still lost in shadow as his tiny fire had all but died away. But he thought he saw something near the wall . . .

He rose as gracefully as his pain-wracked body would allow and moved toward the wall. Squatting down, he brushed a hand along the crevasse where the wall and the floor met. He smiled at the gritty, coarse feeling of sand. Digging his fingertips deep, he pinched up as much as he could, and carried it carefully back to the niches. He flicked the sand into the alcove, and laughed out loud as the light glowed to life, the gong sounding through the still air.

There was a quick grinding sound, and a small shelf slid out of the wall just below the riddles. A fitful, flickering light shined against the words, and he stood up to see the shelf was more of a lidless box. Within the box burned a small candle.

With a shrug, Varro leaned down and blew the candle out. It was a theme, after all.

Immediately, a much louder grinding sound shook the floor, and the entire wall split in half. Each half slid sideways, disappearing into the further walls. Before him, the chamber now continued on a few more feet to a proper door. The carving of the revealed walls, and the door behind, were as ornate as anything else in the Acropolis. Moving forward, Varro could hear nothing coming from the other side. Not so much as a glimmer of light escaped around the doorframe.

Varro looked back behind him. The cylinders were still and dead, their blades gleaming dully in the muted light. With a shrug, he placed his hands on the cool stone of the door, feeling the intricate carvings beneath his numb hands, and pushed.

A brilliant golden light spilled through the opening, casting his shadow back into the crop of machines behind. One of his arms came up, without thought, to shield his eyes from the light. He had no way of knowing how long he had been lost in the maze of shadows beneath the fortress, and the light was painfully bright. His other hand grasped the hilt of his sword. He moved through the door as if he was pushing against a steady wind. His wound pulled tightly as he hunched against the resistance.

The chamber beyond the door was eerily familiar, although his exhaustion-addled mind could not place why. The bright light illuminated the ornate decorations with a soft golden highlight. It was a large room. The light was emanating from the top of a small pillar the height of a child, standing in the center.

A long table sat on the far side of the radiance, and seated at the table were five figures, rendered to dim silhouettes by the hazy glow. A sixth chair, at the far right, was empty. He knew who they were without seeing their faces: The *Etta*. Something about their bearing, or the tilt of their heads, indicated a jagged tension he could almost taste. The empty chair seemed ominous, but he could not bring himself to care. His eyes slid back to the object upon the pillar, dismissing the warriors beyond.

As he took several steps closer, he saw that the object did not, in fact, rest upon the pillar, but was somehow suspended several inches above it. There was something wrong with the shape of the thing, something shattered and incomplete. As he neared, he could see that it was longer than his forearm, and about twice as thick. Along one smooth flank were carved familiar-looking runes that he could not read. A setting of glittering silver wrapped around glowing stone, sculpted into flowing, liquid designs that cradled the object in gilded shadow. He could see where a large portion had been somehow sheared away, and suddenly he knew what he was seeing.

A fragment of the Relic that granted the Holy Order its power and its purpose floated before him, not four feet away. The object that had, from all reports, fallen from Heaven to stand between mankind and its most venomous foes was nearly within arm's reach. The warmth of the glow took on a daunting weight. And as he hesitated in his approach, he felt as if the Relic somehow reached toward him, the light penetrating his mind through his dazzled eyes, warming his spirit with its radiance.

The golden glow began to change deep within the stone. A darkness swirled into being, churning as it sifted outward in a growing cloud. The cloud boiled within the stone, and the tension of the figures beyond intensified. Several of them shifted to share unseen glances whose importance he could not know. Even as the warmth of the Relic washed over his face, a cold fear rose in his heart as every weakness and lack he had every felt came rushing back into the forefront of his mind.

The darkness expanded throughout the artifact, thinning as it spread, its bluish color growing more pure and intense as it reached the surface of the Relic. Eventually, the hue suffused the entire stone, glowing now with a powerful cerulean radiance that shot out across the room, casting everything in soft, shifting tones. It was as if the chamber was suddenly submerged beneath an exotic sea.

As the color became apparent, strengthening and spreading, the tension of the *Etta* drained away, replaced with an eager energy he could sense through the dazzling glow.

The warm embrace of the cerulean light filled him with a power that washed away his doubt and exhaustion. The pain of the myriad scratches and bruises decorating his body faded into a dull, background ache that was easily ignored. Even the throbbing wound from his trialin his back cooled and eased. He shook his head in disbelief. He knew, in that moment, that he could undergo the entire ordeal again without a second thought.

The light dimmed, returning to its original, buttery-gold glow. Varro was surprised to see the figures on the far side standing. He had completely forgotten them, lost in the Relic's grasp. He shook his head, bracing himself for whatever must come next. His mind was clear and calm, filled with a confidence he had not felt in many years. He sheathed the sword and clasped his hands behind his back, content to let the *sircans* and *arcsens* of the council make the first move.

The three leftmost figures came around the table, moving past the Relic. Shadows slid across their faces as they came, the golden light softening their solemn expressions. The old man, remnants of wispy hair escaping from beneath his elaborate headdress, came forward while the younger man and the woman held back, looming, faceless figures in their heavy armor.

The serious expression on the old man's face softened into a kindly smile. One hand reached out from within the ivory robes, held forth in an unmistakable gesture. It was so unexpected, after months and months of cold indifference, that it reached him even within his unnatural calm. After a moment's hesitation, he took his hand from behind his back and clasped the old man's. He had meant to be gentle, the hand resembling nothing so much as a bundle of sticks wrapped in parchment. But there was a strength to the *sircan's* grip, and the man's smile broadened as he tightened his hold, ever-so-slightly, as if to prove a point.

"Congratulations, *Spica*." The voice was strong and deep despite the man's age, and all the more surprising considering it was the first friendly human voice he had heard in so long. His surprise was compounded when the two *sircans* standing behind the old man murmured their own compliments. To his right, the two dark-skinned men approached from the other side of the Relic's column. Both seemed even more excited than the old man, their solemn masks hardly concealing the animated gleam in their eyes.

Varro looked from the two younger men, to the trio of *sircans*, and back. He had no idea what he was expected to do next. His voice had been denied to him for so long, the thanks that he wished to convey stuck in his throat. He satisfied himself with a deep bow, first to the *sircans*, and then to the two *arcsens*.

The old man's eyes twinkled in the warm light of the Relic as he cocked his head with wry humor. "You have no idea what to do, eh?" He waved away the need for Varro to respond. "Don't fret. Everyone who passes through the ordeal feels the same."

"Actually, you have an advantage over most initiates, *Spica*." The woman's voice was lower than he would have expected, and it took him a moment to realize that she had not called him by his name, but by the rank of *spica*. As realization dawned, he remembered that the old man had called him the same. A wave of elation rose within him, quickly suppressed by habit and solemnity. He simply nodded, forcing himself to stillness.

"Most initiates spend a great deal more time in training than you have, son." The old man nodded. "Many, in fact, are never even allowed to attempt the ordeal, spending lifetimes of silence and training, hoping for an opportunity they can never earn."

Some small shadow of the doubt that had plagued him for years rose up in Varro's mind. "Sir, I—"

The old man held up his hand again. "Please, *Spica*, I am *Sircan* Ignatius. My esteemed colleagues are *Sircans* Nura and Abner." The two figures in their ornate armor nodded their heads. "And these two are *Arcsen* Siraj," the lighter skin man nodded. "And *Arcsen* Noor." The African nodded, his long mustaches giving him a frowning aspect despite the smile of vindication just visible beneath.

The old man, *Sircan* Ignatius, he reminded himself, let his smile slip just a little. "I'm afraid you will have to be introduced to *Arcsen* Ivar at some later date. He . . . became indisposed . . . during your ordeal."

Varro did not miss the exchange of shadowed looks between the two other *sircans*, nor the edge of what almost seemed like contempt or doubt that colored the look the *arcsens* shared. He remembered the pale, dark haired man that had sat to the far right of the table before his ordeal; the man who, even at that point, seemed to have distanced himself from the rest of the *Etta*. Something was pushing at the back of his mind, but too many thoughts demanded his attention, too many impressions, hopes, and fears clamored for acknowledgement.

"Thank you." He turned and bowed again to the *Etta*. "Thank all of you. I am—"

"Not who you think you are." *Sircan* Ignatius held up a hand. "You have passed through a trial few men and women could ever even comprehend." He gestured toward the Relic, the long sleeve of his robe flowing behind. "A power more ancient than any you can imagine has looked into your soul. You have been judged by celestial powers, and been found worthy." The smile peeked through the solemnity. "You are no longer the man you were when *Spica* Jomei first brought you to us."

The old man looked at the four other members of the *Etta*, his hands rising in what seemed to Varro to be a ritualistic posture. "This man has crossed the desert, he has moved through fire and ice and steel. This man has stood before a holy Relic of the Old Ones, and he has been found to be true. Does the *Etta* accept this brave, proven warrior into the Holy Order of Man?"

Sircan Nura and *Sircan* Abner nodded gravely, their eyes aflame with excited vindication. In a quiet voice *Arcsen* Noor said, "We do." *Arcsen* Siraj nodded his regal head once in agreement.

Sircan Ignatius nodded himself, and then turned back to Varro. "And do you, Giovanni Varro, accept this offered place amongst us?"

Varro's brow knit, alarmed. The weight of the ceremony, coming as it did without warning or preparation, seemed to bear down upon him. The exhaustion of his spent body came rushing back to fill the void left by the Relic's nurturing light. He tried to speak, to say yes, but his voice caught in his dry throat. After a second attempt, he closed his mouth and simply nodded.

"Welcome, my son!" Sircan Ignatius came forward to embrace him, and then turned to the others, as if introducing him for the first time. "My friends, allow me to introduce you . . ." He paused, and Varro thought, for a moment that the old man had forgotten his name. His heart dropped in his chest at this seeming sign of insignificance. But when Ignatius continued, he realized that the ritual was not yet over.

"Allow me to introduce you," he resumed, "to *Spica* Lucien, newest warrior of the Holy Order of Man in the Sunset Lands."

Varro's smile faltered, his heart falling further. He looked at the man in confusion while the others smiled at his reaction.

Ignatius's smile shifted into a grin and he patted Varro on the back. "You are no longer the same man, my friend, and thus the same name will no longer do."

"Every warrior who passes through the ordeal is granted a new name to commemorate their transformation in the eyes of the Creators." Nura's voice was full of emotion as she explained. "Each of us is renamed in the light of the Creators, and in the light of the Relic of the Old Ones. Our new names signify that we now walk in the light of true sight."

"We are the last defenders against the darkness." Abner's gravelly voice took up the chant-like refrain. "We alone, among all of mankind, see with the true light of the Creators."

"And we shall stand together," Noor continued, "so long as the darkness looms."

"And we shall hold aloft the light," Siraj's voice was grave, "with all the strength of Man."

"And we shall not fail," Ignatius took up the thread with an apologetic shrug of his shoulders, "so long as the light of the Creators shines within us."

"Welcome, Brother Lucien, to the Holy Order of Man." The five voices rang off the ornate stonework all around, and Varro felt something wrench deep within his chest. Behind them, the Relic flared with a brilliant blue-white radiance that washed every shadow from the room and left spots of aquamarine dancing across his vision.

Chapter 16

A door hidden in the intricate scrollwork of the wall behind the gathered *Etta* opened, and *Mimreg* Zain stepped through. The man's characteristically stern face had broken into a bright, honest smile. There was still an edge there, but the hard, almost tangible wall that had separated trainer from initiates was gone. He approached Varro with an open hand.

"Congratulations, *Spica* Lucien." His grip was hard and firm. With a slight twist, Zain trapped his arm in a wrestler's grip and gave it a quick warning shake, his brows drawing down. "Had you failed to rise to the occasion within the next few days I stood to lose a great deal of silver." The smile returned. "I'm glad you came to your senses and validated my opinion."

Varro's confusion was clear as he turned to the *Etta*. It was Nura who spoke, her voice burred with amusement. "*Mimreg* Zain has been agitating for your right to undertake the ordeal for almost a week."

"Ever since your encounter in the Chamber of Memory." *Sircan* Abner continued. Images of red eyes swooping toward him in the disk room jumped sharply to mind, but lacked the power to shake him.

"Anyone who could look the Enemy in the eye and calmly turn their back was not going to have any problems with the ordeal." Zain folded his thick arms with finality.

The newly-minted *spica* could only give a confused grin and look from one warrior to the next. Facing the congratulations of the *Etta* was unreal. But having the man who had tormented his days and nights for more months than he could even recount approach him now with an open hand, a warm smile, and a kind word was almost as disturbing as that first time he had beheld the Acropolis.

"*Mimreg*, I believe you had intended to orient our young *spica* with the rest of the stronghold?" Old Ignatius clapped Varro on the back, careful to avoid the wound there, and gestured toward the door. His voice was still light, but his smile was gone, his eyes grave. "I believe a field bandage would suffice for your wound until afterward? Time does not stand still for our little celebrations, ceremonies, or weaknesses, I'm afraid."

Zain nodded. "Absolutely, *Sircan*." He reached out and took Varro by his bulging biceps, leading him toward the door, arching an eyebrow silently at the deep wound in the young man's back. "We'll see to that first, then start with the training halls, I think, before we head deeper into the vaults."

All three *sircans* nodded, while the two *arcsens* grinned coldly. "Make sure you give him a cloak or a blanket before heading into the deep vaults." Siraj tilted his chin toward Varro. "He might not feel it at the moment, but his body is near collapse, and he will soon remember the chill of the deep water."

At the words, a shiver ran up Varro's spine as those memories, indeed, rushed in, conjured by the *arcsen's* amusement.

"Certainly, *Arcsen* Siraj." Zain called over his shoulder. "I know my duties."

Outside in the hallway, Varro tried to shake off the chill while the *mimreg* closed the door behind them. "I'll be fine, *Mimreg*." He forced his shoulders straight against the dull pain, standing tall. The touch of the Relic had seemed to soothe the wound, pushing the sharp discomfort into a flat, background ache. "I feel fine."

Zain gave him a look he recognized from training, the jovial smile gone. "You are useless to the Order if you do not acknowledge your human weaknesses and limitations. The stress and dangers of the ordeal are not to be held lightly. You are still warm with the memory of the Relic's embrace, so you cannot judge the price you have paid. We will take a quick journey through portions of the Acropolis you will need to familiarize yourself with, including the medics' hall, and then I will take you to the *spicas'* mess, where you will eat more than you currently believe possible, and then I will show you to your new quarters where, if history is any judge, you will sleep for more than a full day."

Varro wanted to deny the *mimreg's* words, but with every step, he could feel the aches and pains of his shattered body returning, the throb of his wound demanding attention, and the bone-deep chill of the subterranean water coming back into the foreground of his mind.

Instead of wasting breath on arguing, he decided to ask other questions that had been niggling at the back of his mind since his emergence into the Relic chamber.

"*Mimreg*, may I speak frankly?" He did not know how to broach the subject, and the enforced silence of his training still weighed heavily upon him.

Zain looked sideways at him, a grim smile on his craggy, bearded face. "It won't be easy to continue your training if you won't."

Varro nodded. "The man from the ordeal," he patted the scabbarded sword at his hip. "The man I . . . The man I killed . . . Who was he?"

Zain walked several paces without responding. When the *mimreg* spoke, his voice was slow and thoughtful. "That was Dryte. An *arcsen*, actually, who had served with the Order all his life."

The answer made no sense. The *arcsens* were among the highest ranked within the Order, second only to the three *sircans* themselves. "And he allowed me to kill him? For the sake of a trial?" He made no attempt to keep the horror from his voice.

Rather than being angry, however, Zain chuckled. "Not if I knew Dryte." He gave Varro a strong look. "And I did know Dryte. No, you defeated him in fair combat."

"But . . . why did he have to die?" The waste, allowing one of the highest ranking warriors of the Order to die in order to bring a new member into the fold made no sense; not on any level. The very idea seemed foul.

Zain, perhaps sensing the younger man's pain, or perhaps in defense of his old friend, stopped and grasped Varro's good shoulder. "He died because he felt it was necessary. Not every initiate is forced to kill during the ordeal. But with some, especially to whom the Enemy has taken a particular interest, the *Etta* find a deeper test is necessary. When that comes to pass, those among the Order who are reaching the end of their Creators-allotted span will volunteer to test the initiate to the mortal boundary and beyond."

Varro shook his head. "So, this man volunteered to fight me? Knowing that he might die?"

Zain nodded. "Dryte volunteered to fight you, knowing he would most likely die. He spoke with me for a long while before going to the *Etta*. He knew how good you were."

Varro's eyes passed over the serious face of his trainer and focused on a carved wall beyond. "But, why?"

Zain shrugged. "He had fallen ill. There was a darkness eating him from within. Our doctors believed he would continue to fade away, withering before us, for weeks or months or years. But ultimately he was trapped within a body that could not sustain his drive, his commitment, and his fire. Rather than face that certain doom, he decided to put his faith to the test and sacrifice himself for something he believed in with all his being."

"Sacrifice himself for what?" The horror was creeping back into his voice. "For *me*?"

It was Zain's turn to shake his head. "Not for you, *Spica*, no.*Arcsen* Dryte believed in a prophecy that many within the Order carry within their hearts. And like many of those devotees, he felt that you were touched by that prophecy." The *mimreg*'s eyes were steady, but there was a weight to them that bore into Varro's mind.

Varro freed himself from the trainer's grip, shaking his head. "That doesn't make any sense. What prophecy? What does it have to do with me?"

Again, Zain shook his head. "That is not for me to say. But you deserve to know what others are thinking, whatever the *Etta* feels might be appropriate. There is, within the prophecy, the belief that the End Times will be heralded by a great conflict between two figures, known only by typically cryptic, mysterious titles." His eye flicked to the tattoo on Varro's arm, and then he shrugged. "It could mean almost anything, though."

Varro was horrified to think that anyone might believe him so important. It was too much, too soon after everything that had just happened. One more question rose in his mind that he could not leave for another time.

He looked into Zain's eyes, watching for the slightest flicker or dodge. "Do you believe in this prophecy?"

Zain smiled. His eyes were steady, but revealed nothing. "Come on, young *spica*. Time grows short. Let's see that wound mended before you collapse."

In silence he turned cleanly on one heel and strode away down the hall, leaving Varro the choice of being left behind or chasing after.

*****

From their brief stop with the medics,*Mimreg* Zain led Varro upward through several grand staircases with elaborately carved rails and newel posts. He saw more members of the Order than he had since his first day on the fields of the Acropolis. Each time he had seen the inhabitants of the great fortress during his training, they had fallen silent as he marched past, staring as he averted his eyes. Now, warriors and servants alike were approaching him, bowing their heads with desperate smiles, shaking his hand with a diffidence he found unnerving.

After the latest in a long line of such greetings, he grabbed at Zain's elbow and pulled him into an ornate alcove. He gave a quick look down the long hallway before leaning in close.

"You can't tell me every initiate is treated this way. They're acting like I'm the new mayor or something!" A strange, burning shame was smoldering in his chest. He knew he did not deserve such treatment. He was a strong man and had been honed into a worthy weapon for the Order. He was confident in that now, but this level of deference made no sense to him at all. He was sure in his worth, and he knew it did not reach this high.

Zain shrugged, the half-smile pulling at the corner of his mouth. "It's the prophecy, as I told you. Many within the Order believe that your presence among us signals great events in the offing."

Varro wanted to punch the delicately carved stone. "I'm no warrior of legend, *Mimreg*! Hell, you could crush me anytime you cared to try!"

"Could I?" The question seemed honest, and there was a wistful undertone that Varro could make no sense of. But the *mimreg* continued. "Nevertheless, *Spica* Lucien, the prophecy actually says nothing of the prowess or abilities of the combatants; if, indeed, it refers to you at all. The heights to which many of these have raised you says more of their own desperation than it does of the prophecy itself."

Varro let that sink in, and then stated, "And you won't tell me what you believe."

Zain moved back into the hall. "It is a private matter, held within the heart of each member for him to share or keep close as he deems appropriate. I merely warn you that there is a dark undercurrent running through many of your new brothers and sisters that will affect their perceptions of you."

Hurrying to catch up, the young warrior muttered. "And I don't know about this nonsense of giving me a new name. I've had mine for a long time now; nearly all my life, in fact. I'm quite fond of it."

This time the smile and laugh was more genuine and light-hearted. "Oh, never fear for your name, Lucien. You have given up your life beyond the walls of the Acropolis. The rest will be spent with those who understand the significance of being named in the Light of the Creators. They will give proper weight and deference to your true name. Given time, you will come to accept it as your own." He looked sideways with a wide grin. "When I'm out with a mission team now, I hardly even jerk when I hear the name Joe."

Varro barked a laugh before he could stop himself. "Joe?"

Zain nodded. "Not very intimidating, is it? And yet, I could have trussed you up as neatly then as I did throughout your training." He shrugged. "So, I leave it to you to decide what is in a name. Within the silence of your head I have no doubt you will be Gio, or Varro, or whatever you call yourself, for some time to come. But to those of us within the Order, you are Lucien now, and that name carries more meaning and weight than any other."

They came to a large set of double doors. Again, the carvings were impressively ornate and suggestive. He seemed to see sweeping plains filled with swirling battle, menacing clouds hanging overhead. There were things soaring through the sky that intrigued him. Far too large to be birds, they were dropping fire down upon the combatants on the ground. He glanced at Zain with raised brows, and the *mimreg* just nodded with another of his newfound grins and pushed the doors open.

A long, narrow room stretched before them, brightly lit with reliquary lamps. Now that he had been in the presence of the true Relic, whose power was somehow granted to all the varied technologies of the Order, he could see the echo of its great strength in their color and intensity. He realized that he found comfort and reassurance in their soft glow.

The left-hand wall of the chamber stretched away from them in subtle, wave-shaped carvings, meeting a similarly-decorated wall at the far end. The right-hand wall, however, appeared to be the largest single pane of glass he had ever seen. It stretched from about a foot off the floor all the way up to the stone ceiling, and threw back reflections of the lamps opposite in smooth, flawless sweeps of light.

Scattered throughout the room were benches, chairs, and low tables. It appeared to be some sort of observation room, with all the furniture oriented toward the long window. It was empty now, and Zain swept in and took up a relaxed stance by the glass. With a studied nonchalance, he leaned against it as if it were solid stone. He jerked one thumb over his shoulder into the space beyond.

Varro moved up beside the *mimreg* and looked out into a cavern so vast that he was stunned into silence for several long minutes. The walls of the enormous cavern were carved to resemble mighty trees. The trunks rose to a ceiling far above him, itself carved like a roof of leaves and intertwined branches. The size of the carvings gave a false sense of scale, he saw, as he realized that the tiny figures far below were warriors going through various exercises and maneuvers. It reminded him of the distant, blurred memories of his first day. He saw lines of riflemen moving through what he realized was a model of a town, blasting away with their weapons in flashes of blue-white light that he remembered from a tiny alley in a distant shantytown. The memories were vague and strange, buried beneath countless surprises and wonders piled up within his mind.

In other areas he saw groups of men meeting in mock battle. Colored kerchiefs tied around an upper arm seemed to designate the allegiance of each warrior. Clothed in shades of gray and black with flowing cloaks and deep hoods, these men fought with over-sized pistols and glinting knives and swords. They charged through a variety of terrain, from open desert, to forests of carved trunks, to small towns. As they came crashing together he watched them fight with a swirling, tireless grace that he suddenly recognized from his own practice sessions in the gauntlet chamber.

When Varro turned to look a silent question at Zain, the man's bearded face was serious, his eyes dark. "That, *Spica* Lucien, is the reality of the Holy Order of Man." He waved a hand at the glass and the men and women struggling far below. "Our lives are spent preparing for battle, and fighting battle. Ours is a war without end. There is no leave, there is no rest or surcease from our struggle. Our foe is tireless, inhuman in his dedication and commitment to our destruction, and so we must be as well, or all will be lost."

Varro nodded and looked back down. "It's amazing. Forests, plains, villages . . . Is that a city back there?"

Zain had turned around to look down, himself. "Yes." Buildings of three and even four stories thrust up above the shadows of an entire false forest. "A model of the center of Boston, I believe. That steeple there? That would be the Old North Church." He smiled through the glass. "Our version of it, anyway."

Varro shook his head. "All of this . . . just for training?" The *mimreg* turned and eased himself into one of the chairs scattered through the observation room. "Lucien," he smiled briefly. "And you're going to have to get used to people calling you Lucien, by the way." He shook his head. "Anyway, the Enemy is insidious. They are everywhere. We must be prepared to meet them on any terrain, at any time. And when we strike, we must strike swiftly, without doubt or hesitation, and within the silence of a shadow."

Turning from the window, Varro took a seat beside the trainer and rested his elbows on his knees, keeping his sore back away from the chair. "But who are they? I saw everything in the . . . visions . . . of the disk training sessions. I know they are powerful, and appear to be ghosts or spirits." He shook his head, still not entirely comfortable with a reality that he would have dismissed as hokum less than a year ago. "But who are they? *What* are they?"

Zain took a breath, pursed his lips, and leaned back in his chair. "Not an easy question to answer, *Spica* Lucien. We don't even rightly know. Not for certain. We have lost more knowledge through our eons of war than we can even remember. We know even our own past only incompletely. They are not of this world, of this we are certain. They are powerful beyond measure, capable of weaving illusion and deceit to turn even the most virtuous man down the path of darkness and damnation. However, they are incapable of directly harming a human being. Whether some force greater than themselves denies them this; if it is a self-imposed constraint, or some natural law, we do not know. But they are more than capable of turning others to their work."

Varro rested back, his elbows now thrown over the arms of his chair. "So the preacher in the alley . . ."

"Was not the Enemy, but one of their creatures." Zain nodded. "We call them the Tainted, or Possessed, depending on how far they have fallen. From the reports I have seen of your encounter at the railhead, I would assume your reverend was very nearly Possessed, without much of his humanity remaining to him at all."

"His eyes . . . and his skin . . ." It had been so long since Varro had spoken at all, never mind of such dark topics, the memories were long in coming. He was surprised to feel how strongly those memories still affected him.

"Those with a strong connection to the Creators, or with the Earth, are often sensitive to the signs of Taint and Possession within others. It is one of the first indicators that a man may be called to the Order." He gave the younger man a kind smile. "Young Jomei felt very strongly that you had been called, after hearing your stories of this reverend and the railhead."

Varro's eyes were distant and his brow furrowed as he worked through this new information, piecing together all of the hints, clues, and guesses he had harbored for so long. "And so the Holy Order exists to battle these Tainted and Possessed."

"And to ferret out the plans of the Enemy, thwarting them wherever we can, yes."

Varro's eyes sought out the *mimreg*'s. "And things are not going well."

Zain paused before answering, and then gave a single jerky shake of his head. "No, they are not going well."

"And that is why you are here, giving me a grand tour, and why so many of your folks seem to be wrapping their heads in this prophecy business." He heard the note of judgment in his own voice.

"These are dark times," Zain's words were conciliatory and admonishing at the same time. "We are still human. And humans will take what comfort they can in dark times. The Dark Council, our ancient Enemy, has been planning for centuries. Everything we have been able to uncover indicates that their plans are nearing completion, and that the blow will fall here, in the New World."

"The Dark Council?The New World?"

Zain smiled, but there was a sadness in the expression. "The Dark Council is how we refer to the great Enemy. Whether they represent a single entity or countless shards of enmity and spite we do not know, but the Council takes the form of limitless individuals, and so we refer to them as such. And as for the New World," his smile warmed. "We have been here for longer than you can know." He gestured to the graceful carvings surrounding them and the massive window before them. "All of this was here, and ancient, before the first of the free tribes moved up into the mountains from the south, after all."

Varro nodded, processing such information much faster, and with more faith, than he ever would have even a month or so before. "And you keep referring to the Creators . . ."

Zain shook his head. "We have *altcaps* and *arcsens* that specialize in such things, Lucien. Such topics are not a strength of mine. But basically, what our records tell us, and what the Relic seems to confirm, is that everything we know, from our Earth, to the sun and stars in the sky, was created by beings of power so vast we cannot even perceive them. They spread seeds of life throughout the stars, and then, for reasons not even our most ancient scholars can tell, they retreated from us. But they are still out there, we believe, and so we must carry within us the faith that they have not abandoned us, and will return someday. It is truly our only hope."

"Only hope?" That seemed ominous, even in the light of everything else the *mimreg* had said.

Zain turned to look into Varro's eyes and held his attention with a daunting, leaden weight. "There is no way we can vanquish the Dark Council, Lucien. Their power, and the number of men and women around the world willing to stand with them, are beyond our ability to defeat. The best we can hope to do is hold off their victory long enough for the Creators to hear our prayers."

"Do they know we fight them?"

A bitter smile pulled at the *mimreg*'s reluctant face. "Oh, they know. It is a game to them. They are not all-knowing. They can sense our minds, and the weakness of our humanity, but they do not know where we reside unless they can find us in the physical world. They would like nothing more than to find the Acropolis and destroy us, but we have, so far, been able to hide our whereabouts from them."

"But surely, with the weapons we have . . . ?"

The smile faded. "Our weapons are as nothing compared to the weapons *they* can bring to bear. They have all of the knowledge of two worlds, or more, and more ages than we can imagine at their disposal. They lead their puppets to discoveries and technologies that more than match anything we can create. And, whenever it appears that we might prevail and that they stand in real jeopardy of defeat, they will call their darkest allies from the shadows. Then we will be washed away in a tide of blood. Humanity will then stand alone, defenseless against them."

A cold chill gripped Varro's spine. "You don't provide much hope, *Mimreg*."

Zain looked up, his eyes bleak. "Providing hope is not my responsibility, *Spica*. Providing reality is. The Dark Council has twice before called forth demons from the shadows. On our distant sister planet our brothers in arms were defeated, their entire world lost. Only a single message, the Relic that gives us our power and our purpose, survived. They sent it down to us, before we even first drew breath, to help us in the inevitable battles to come. As we rose out of the mud, the Relic guided us and granted us the light and understanding of the Creators. Without it, we might still be living in huts, cringing in fear at the shadow and the lightning. But, at the height of our first burst of life, the Dark Council tried to batter us down. The earliest men were strong, however, having developed in the comfort and glory of the Relic's light. They could not be swayed.

"And so the Dark Council called forth their allies from the shadows. From other worlds or realms or times, the great devourers came; the slayers of worlds, servants of a darkness that even we, living in constant battle with the Enemy, could not imagine. And it was only through the sacrifice of the greatest of that first generation, and of the Relic itself, that we were able to fend off the monsters. The Holy City was destroyed, our leaders and defenders gone, and the Relic was shattered into many pieces."

Zain stopped in his story, his eyes coming back into focus to look at Varro. "You have seen the Relic. You have felt its warmth and its power. But that is only a part of our inheritance. Can you even imagine what it must have once felt like, to be in the presence of the Relic before its sundering? And if that Relic, in the fullness of its power, was barely able to stem the tide of darkness unleashed by the Council, what hope do we have, who only possess fragments?"

Bits and pieces of the tale Varro had absorbed during training floated back into his mind. "But there are other fragments, right? Held by the other citadels of the Holy Order? Couldn't we try to reassemble the Relic? Surely something—"

"And where would we deploy the Relic, if we could?" The tone was of a teacher dealing with a student whose promise was falling into doubt. "The Enemy could attack us anywhere on the planet. Further, the Enemy covets the fragments for themselves. They cannot use it, of course, its very presence is painful to them. But every piece they can deny us weakens our defenses and brings us closer to the end. We have lost several fragments through the ages, and could not assemble the complete Relic even if we wished to."

"How many pieces are left?" Zain's story was filled with shadow and death, without hope. Varro felt his newfound faith and confidence pushed to the edge of despair. It was a most uncomfortable sensation.

Zain shrugged. "I doubt if even the *Etta* know the exact number. Each citadel has one, I know. There may be others secreted around the world, secured for future need. We have the fragment you were just introduced to. There is a rumor that another fragment was brought to the Acropolis a few years ago, when the various *Ettas* decided among themselves that the Sunset Lands was the most likely target for the Dark Council's next major effort."

A restless energy pushed Varro up from his chair and back to the wide window. Down below, hundreds of men and women went through the motions of war. Knowing that they prepared to sacrifice themselves in battles with only a single, hopeless outcome caused a painful tightness in his chest. He rested one forearm upon the glass and settled his forehead against it, following the ebb and flow of one of the mock battles on the floor of the vast chamber.

"If there's no hope, then why all this?"

A rough hand patted him on the shoulder, drawing a hiss of breath as it came down near his wound. "Buck up, *Spica*." The gruff voice was lighter than Varro's lowered spirits expected. "I didn't say there was no hope, remember? We must have faith that the Creators have not abandoned us. They *will* return one day, and bring the Dark Council to heel."

Varro shook his head and did not turn from the dance of violence spinning across the floor beneath him.

"I think maybe we should visit the vaults next." Zain pushed warmth and energy into his voice, taking Varro by the shoulder. "You need to see what we've got down below. It might make you feel a little better about the realities of our situation." A smile brightened his voice further. "We're not so close to defeated yet, *Spica*. There are great battles to be fought yet before the final decisions are to be made."

*****

Varro's legs were weak from countless stairs by the time they stood before the enormous doors of what Zain called a vault. They were deeper than he had ever gone before; deeper even than the longest forced marches through natural caverns and rough-hewn passages of his training. This deep, the walls were smooth and finished, polished to a mirror sheen, but lacked the elaborate decorations and multi-colored stone of the upper levels. A single plate of green stone stood out above the pair of doors, with what appeared to be a torso etched into it.

"I thought we should start small and work our way up." *Mimreg* Zain's smile was like that of a child with a surprise. He placed a hand on one door and quirked an eyebrow at Varro. "Ready?" Without waiting for a reply from the exhausted *spica*, he pushed the door open.

They walked into a room crowded with shadowy figures. On either side, like ranks of ready soldiers, suits of full armor stood at full attention. It was not the ornate plate armor of the elite warriors and commanders of the Order, but far more solid than the armored sections that adorned the uniforms of the mission teams. Cream and silver, they stood silently, stretching off into the shadows. The high, broad ceiling held small reliquary lamps every ten paces or so. The lights gleamed in the far off darkness, shining down on more armor, tiny in the distance.

It was a truly awe-inspiring sight. Varro could tell that similar ranks stretched off into the enormous room on both sides. There was enough armor in this chamber to equip an entire army.

"Impressive, is it not?" Zain's grin was wide. "And there are several more armories like this one on this level alone. And of course, there are many more with personal weapons, as well."

Varro looked over his shoulder at the smug commander. "Why aren't the mission teams wearing this?"

"The Watchers." Zain's smile faltered slightly. "If we reveal too much, the Dark Council will call them all the sooner. We must play our cards close to the vest for the time being. But when the final trump sounds, and we march off to total war," he gestured with a broad sweep of his arm. "We will be more ready for them than they know."

He tapped on Varro's bandaged shoulder, steering him gently back out the door. "But come. As I said, we have started small. There are plenty of other things you need to see before I release you to your rest."

*****

Varro stood with his mouth agape. Even if he had been aware, he would not have cared. They stood upon a graceful balcony overlooking a wide, low chamber that stretched into the darkness below. Down upon the floor of the hall stood row upon row of massive machines of war. They looked like a cross between armored wagons and the ironclad naval vessels he had seen pictures of in the broadsheets.

And yet, somehow, each of the machines below exuded far more menace than anything else he had ever seen. The barrels of what must have been cannons thrust out from their steel-clad hulls, larger than the artillery he had seen by the naval wharf. What he could not understand was how these beasts might be brought to battle. Were they pushed from behind? Pulled by teams of horses? He immediately dismissed that. It would take a herd of horses to pull just one of these monsters into battle, and the horses would be vulnerable to enemy fire the whole way in.

The lighting here was even more dim than in the armory, but each vehicle had several elements of their own, gems or lamps or warning lights, that shown with the dimmed power of the Relic. The lights, twinkling like countless stars as they vanished into the surrounding gloom, struck him with their importance just as he was about to ask how so many vehicles could be moved.

"They are powered by the Relic." The awe in his voice widened Zain's smile.

"Indeed. The Holy Order owes everything to the power of the Relic and the ingenuity of our ancestors." He nodded out at the sea of machines. "For thousands of years the Order has hidden such caches away for future need. The designs have changed little since the fall of Atlantis, thousands upon thousands of year ago. They represent nearly the entirety of our inheritance from the ancient Order, in fact."

"You have had such things for thousands of years?" Awe swept through his mind yet again despite the many wonders he had seen witnessed since he came to the Acropolis. "There's no way such a secret could have been kept for thousands of years. There has never been a corrupt member of the Order who decided, back when your most powerful opponents couldn't summon up better than swords, bows, and arrows, to ride out with a few of these and make himself a king?"

The *mimreg* nodded with pride. "Well-reasoned, Lucien. It is rare that a warrior tested by the Relic falls from grace. It has happened, but less than once in a thousand years. And when it has happened, it has given rise to some of the most enduring legends of all time." He smiled widely. "There has even been a time or two when the *Etta* of Europe or of Asia took it upon itself to more directly influence the outside world. You could trace our failures through the bloodiest moments of history, as the Dark Council, sensing our involvement, rose up itself to wrest control from our fledgling empires and drag our brief creations back into the mud."

Varro rested his arms upon the balustrade of the balcony, looking out over the silent rows of machines. Among the massive vehicles were many smaller creations. Single-man mounts with a lethal edge no armored horse had ever possessed. Rows of what appeared to be giant hollow wheels occupied an area to the far left, more weapons standing off their hulls and pointing up into the darkness. All of the contraptions were clearly children of the same design and technology, with sweeping, graceful ironwork and gilded detailing that would put the fanciest locomotive riding the rails of America to shame.

As he looked out over the impressive collection, an errant thought shook loose in Varro's mind. He turned to where *Mimreg* Zain stood against the railing, gazing with contentment down into the chamber. "What about the flying machines?"Zain looked a question at him, and he continued. "I saw images of flying machines on the decorations in the upper keep. Have you lost those over time?"

Zain's smile returned. "No, we have not lost them. We keep those at another facility, even more secure and well-guarded than the Acropolis. Back down in the desert, a remote place we named Groom Lake." His smile turned feral. "Those chariots are fast enough, they can reach any battlefield in the Sunset Lands at the first sign that their time has come."

"And even with all of this . . ." Varro's voice was wistful as he looked back down again.

"And even with all of this, the Dark Council will wear us away one day, yes." Zain shrugged. "But it will be a glorious battle." The blue-white lamplight glowed in his eyes as he turned back to look out over the sea of war machines. "It will be a glorious battle indeed."

Epilogue

Soza sat hunched at the battered bar, staring at his dry glass with hollow eyes. Despite the restless crowd, the stools on either side of him remained empty. This bubble would have made him self-conscious a month ago, but he had had plenty of time to get used to his new position in Tolchico. He spent every night in one of the low dives that had been thrown up along the river, just inside the palisade he had helped to build. He spent what little coin he could gather on the cheapest bottle of rotgut he could get his hands on, and ignored the other patrons as aggressively as they ignored him.

Things had turned dark for him from the moment they had entered the fly-blown arroyo out in the desert. Seeing Brant and the Preston girl laid out like that, butchered with the cold intent of some street magician, had broken something inside him. Maddox had brought them back to town directly, and Soza had dutifully told the men and women of Tolchico exactly what he had seen. The fear had spread like a foul stench.

The town had begun to die that day, it had just been too afraid to lie down.

The stories about the surrounding settlements had continued to trickle in with bloodied, bowed survivors. A few more parties of the brave or desperate had departed, claiming they would return with help. They had not returned, and Maddox's scouts claimed to have found no sign of them.

A small, thin voice in Soza's head had been shrieking at him, a little louder every day, about everything he had seen in the desert, and everything he had been told since they returned.

Maddox had waited until the palisade was complete before letting Soza know that there was no more work for him. Cut loose in the middle of the fear-laden camp, he muddled through as best he could, taking odd jobs, fixing things when they broke, and doing whatever other scut work folks would stoop to throw his way. He had given up his little room above the dance hall weeks ago and now dossed down wherever he could find a sheltered spot for his blanket and his pack.

He had been down on his luck in the past, but that had been a long time ago. He had been a well-respected employee of the Atlantic and Pacific Railroad for years, and it had been a long time since he had laid his head down on the cold, hard ground. But Maddox had gotten everything he needed out of the old railway man, and without his patronage, it was getting harder and harder to get by in the fear-haunted town.

Most of the younger men were now wearing the tin badges Maddox had produced one night during his many fiery speeches out in front of the trading post. Only his old hands carried those enormous, terrifying weapons, but all of his newly-minted deputies were holding iron of one kind or another. They were the only ones that walked the dusty streets with their shoulders back and their heads held high.

Everyone else in Tolchico walked around like prisoners with a heavy sentence hanging over their heads. No attempt had even been made to put down a crop in the meager soil, despite the rushing of the Little Colorado. The prospectors and the trappers were still going up into the hills, but always in large groups, and they always took a few of the mayor's boys with them.

Fear lay over the town like a cold blanket, despite the heat. During the day, people walked through the streets with their heads down and their shoulders hunched. Even ladies of the town, most of them working girls, were quiet. Maddox made sure, somehow, that the saloons and the dancehall were well-supplied with drink, but food was getting more and more expensive, and folks were getting less and less curious as to where it was coming from. Most assumed their meager provisions were being foraged from the surrounding failed towns, but no one knew for sure.

Someone broke into his dull thoughts by bumping into Soza from behind, causing him to jerk in his seat and grab onto the rough wood of the bar to stop from sliding underneath. He did not look back, though, and whoever it was mumbled a quick apology and disappeared back into the raucous mob. He could smell the fear coming off the manic crowd in waves. It had not been this bad, despite everything the scouts had found and despite what Soza had said about Brant's expedition, until a few weeks ago. When folks had started to disappear from Tolchico itself, the atmosphere had turned frigid mighty quick, and things had only gotten worse since.

The first to disappear had been old man Rusty, the aged, half-wit miner that had been helping, off and on, at the dancehall for as long as folks could remember. Most had assumed he had wandered off and fallen into a gulley or some such, and there had not been much a fuss about his loss. A week later, one of the ladies from the Pink Palace, toward the front gate, had disappeared in the night. None of the other girls could say where she had gone, and she had not mentioned any plans of leaving.

Since then, another denizen of Tolchico went missing every two or three nights, and the tension ratcheted up with every disappearance. No sign of them was ever found, and everyone knew, in the silence of their bones, that whatever was stalking the desert wastes had found its way into their little town despite the high walls and the strutting guards.

Soza hunched his shoulders tighter. He had an idea that whatever it was that had killed all those folks out there had not been bothered by the walls. The way he reckoned it, whatever it was that haunted the emptiness stretching around them, it had been behind the walls for some time.

*****

The mule's head swayed back and forth in a dismal pattern, it's dry, cracked muzzle nearly dragging in the dirt. The wheels of its cart screeched with the dirt and grit that had settled into the axle grease, and a broken spoke set the entire cart lurching wildly every few paces. With each wobble, one of the hands hanging limply from the back trembled as if waving for attention.

The cart was piled high with human bodies. Horrible wounds had been torn into their flesh, and the people of Tolchico, gathered around the main gate to watch the wagon shamble in, stood in silence as Euans led the mule in by its worn old harness.

Soza, standing at the back of the crowd, could not tear his eyes away from a fluttering bit of fabric, a bit of a flowered dress dragging in the dust. The poor woman wearing it must have been at the bottom of the pile. Dark red stains marred the delicate calico pattern, and that shred of cloth seemed to sum up the tragedy of the entire scene. He could feel his hand shaking by his side and wondered if he had enough for a bottle of popskull that he could curl up around in some shade down by the river. As the stench of the bodies reached the crowd, he felt the flesh of his scalp recoil in a chill ripple. Somehow, he knew these latest arrivals heralded a horrible new chapter in the history of the damned town.

Maddox came stomping down from the trading post to examine the cart. The crowd parted for him, a strange combination of relief and nerves coloring their movements. They mayor almost never emerged from his lair anymore. Soza averted his eyes, shrinking down behind the crowd, as if the mayor would have stooped to notice him at all. Maddox had not so much as glanced in his direction since he had been dismissed.

The mayor slowed as he broke through the crowd around the cart. Euans nodded silently, stepping aside to give the man a clear view. Maddox moved around the side of the wagon, his eyes taking in every detail of the ravaged, desiccated bodies piled there. Limbs thrust out in all directions, jouncing slightly with the mule's nervous pulling. The faces Soza glimpsed were stretched in expressions of horror and pain that brought images of a shadowed arroyo and Reba Preston rushing back through the alcohol-fueled haze he always tried his damnedest to maintain.

Standing by the cart, Maddox held a heated conversation with Euans, his arms snapping down as he made several strong points. The enormous man looked over his boss' head, eyes fixed on some distant point, the muscles of his face tight as he ground his teeth together. Hot sunlight glinted off the burnished copper of his bristly hair as the mayor's enforcer jerked his head once in a grudging nod.

Maddox turned back to the townsfolk as if seeing them for the first time. He dragged his Stetson off his head and rubbed his forearm across his brow. Despair and determination seemed to war across his face as he scanned the crowd with dark, earnest eyes.

As they passed, unseeing, over Soza's cringing form, the railway man froze in mid-flinch. Something about Maddox's face struck a false note. He looked sincere; he seemed to be concerned for his flock and regretful of the deaths stacked up behind him. But the shimmer in his eye was a shade off, the set of his jaw a touch too studied. A chill stabbed Soza between his hunched shoulder blades as he saw through the performance. He had no idea what might lay behind that face, but he was suddenly struck with the certain knowledge that it was a mask; perhaps it had been a mask all along.

A flash of amber eyes, widening in fear in a pale, ravaged face and then fading into death, struck him like a blow. A gasp escaped his chapped and cracking lips, and the men and women around him hushed him into silence. They stared expectantly at the mayor, standing in all his earnest glory by the cart of dead bodies.

Soza knew, with a certainty he had never felt before in his long, colored life, that he needed to get out of Tolchico as soon as he could.

Before he could even think to turn away, however, Maddox's voice rose up over the dusty street and the desperate crowd. "I ain't gonna lie!" His voice was stern but oddly comforting, like a father speaking to children whose behavior has not been the best, but who would be spared the worst of a feared punishment. "These were good folks, and they been slaughtered like all the others hereabouts."

Euans jerked his head toward a couple of the mayor's rangers. The men started, and then came forward, grabbing the poor mule's lead and pulling it through the crowd and up the hill.

"Good folks, dead, just like we've been seeing for months and months now, everywhere except right here in Tolchico." Maddox waved a hand with a reassuring nod and the crowd parted to let the cart move past, the hand swaying hypnotically with each jolt of the broken wheel.

"Folks been dying around here too long, my friends." His face dropped with a sorrow that swept through the people of Tolchico. There was not a single person in the crowd who doubted the mayor's sincerity, or his desire to keep them safe.

There would have been one man who doubted, newly come to a terrifying realization, but Tucker Soza was making his slow, determined way back behind the line of buildings that fronted onto the main street, moving doggedly toward the little garret where Old Andy let him store his few possessions during the slowly dragging days.

Maddox's voice echoed off the buildings around him, hardly muted by distance and the maze of slapdash construction from the earliest days of the settlement, back before even a hint of the fear and horror that had settled down upon Tolchico had reared its head.

"I've done my best to keep ya'll safe." The sincerity dripping from the voice spurred Soza to stumble forward even faster. "Haven't I done my best to keep ya'll safe?" The rumble of agreement from the crowd sent a sudden spill of ice water through the older man's veins. Maddox was working up to something, playing the crowd like a well-tuned fiddle with his usual skill.

"And we've done what we could for all the other settlements hereabouts." Soza's head came up with a sharp jerk at that. He turned in place, craning his neck over to bring his ear more directly to bear. The voice was sad, heavy with regret. But something lurking beneath it made the railway man's stomach churn. When the mayor continued, it was much harder to hear his words over the rustling of the crowd.

"We've spent more time and effort than we could afford on trying to protect those other folks, and we've lost good men doin' it." A muttering rose up from the mob and drowned out his soft words for a moment. When Soza could understand again, the man was saying, "and we'll need to make some changes." Again the muttering, but this time, Maddox raised his voice and spoke over them. "Let me think it through, and everyone come on up to the trading post on toward sundown. We'll see what we can come up with."

Much of Soza's life had been spent working the rail lines connecting the northern states with the plains and the west coast. He had spent more than his fair share of time drenched in cold rain, ankle deep in freezing mud, and wishing for just ten minutes with a fire under a dry tarp. Standing in the baking shadows of that alley in Tolchico, fear-sweat mingling on his brow with the moisture wrung from him by the blazing sun, he was struck with a sudden memory of that cold, frozen misery.

Nothing from those bad old days, not the freezing rain, not the howling wind, not even the gelid mud sucking at his sodden boots, had been a match for the cold fear that gripped his heart as he stood there, listening to the future take shape just one street away.

*****

He should have left. He knew he should have left. Soza set his shoulder against the rough-hewn support of the brothel's upper walkway, pulling a battered hat he had grabbed off a rack inside, down over his face.

If he had left as soon as the crowd around the gate had dispersed, he would be out in the middle of the wastes already, well on his way to the Coconino Forest. His fear of the unknown killers of the deserts all around was no match for the fear that even now clutched his heart with its cold talons. He knew that he would never again know fear the equal of that which he now felt for Maddox and Euans.

Yet there he was, waiting for the mayor to emerge onto his porch and address the growing throng. Somehow, he knew he would have been safe out in the wastes, with the so-called mayor and his men back here in Tolchico, plotting whatever it was they had planned for the doomed town.

Soza could not have said why he stayed, or what he hoped to do about the events he saw unfolding around him. Something in his heart would not let him leave. Something whispered that to go now would be the worst act of cowardice in a life not overburdened with heroism. He knew if he turned his back on Tolchico now, he would never be able to look at himself in a mirror again. But what good he thought he might do by staying, he could not have said.

The crowd up the hill, already quiet and somber, fell into a cold, worried silence as light poured through the heavy doors of the trading post and fell down among them. The light flickered for a moment as first Maddox, then Euans, and then several others came out to take up positions along the stone balustrade. Soza pushed the rumpled hat brim up just a tad, and watched as Maddox looked out over the crowd, hands on hips, massive pistol glowing an ominous red in its heavy rig.

The crowd was gathered less than a railroad car away from where Soza crouched against the boardwalk post. Their restless, nervous muttering faded into an expectant silence as they stared up at the mayor.

Maddox surveyed the crowd with a cold blank stare before speaking. When he began, his voice was even and patient, but a hard edge lay beneath it that Soza heard plain as day. Whether the rest of the townsfolk of Tolchico heard it, however, he could not have said.

"I won't lie to you. Things are bleak." The people in the crowd shot worried looks at each other from the corners of their eyes, but kept silent, waiting to see where their mayor was heading. "But you know that. Things've been bleak round hereabouts for a long time now."

The mayor's shoulders slumped slightly beneath his long duster, his head fell forward and his face was hidden by the low brim of his Stetson. "When I first came to Tolchico there was nothing much here but an old lean-to and some scrub brush. But the land was alive with potential. The people were alive with the energy and excitement of the new frontier. I knew this place, on the very edge of the unexplored, could be something truly special, if someone would just give it a chance."

His voice had a low, sing-song quality to it that seemed to settle into the people, calming them while touching them with an undefined sadness. Up on the red stone porch the mayor leaned forward, his hands falling to the dusty balustrade.

"Folks came here from all over the territories to make a go of it. Trappers and traders knew they could get a fair deal here. Prospectors knew that, no matter how cold it might get up in the hills, there would be a warm bed waiting for them down in Tolchico. Pretty soon, we had cattle hands coming in, we had tradesmen and merchants throwing up their shops, and things were looking pretty bright for us here on the edge of nowhere."

His voice had gotten stronger as he listed the accomplishments and milestones of the town's founding. The energy transferred itself into a sort of civic pride that Soza found fascinating, given the more recent history that had drowned them all in fear and misery for months now.

Maddox looked up again, and there was a fire in his eyes that set the crowd back on their heels. "But someone, or something, didn't see Tolchico as a decent place to live, or as an oasis of civilization on the edge of the borderlands. Something out there saw us as nothing more than prey. They stalked our folks and our animals, pushed us back to the very edges of our own town worse than a pack of rabid wolves." His lips twisted in anger, snarling the words out as if he were half wolf himself. "And we didn't even get the worst of it! Settlements up and down this side of the big forest've felt this evil hand upon their necks. There've been dead bodies and missing folks from all over."

The mayor shook his head. "We've done our best." He gestured with one thumb at the line of men behind him. They were the old hands, the men carrying the massive, strange-looking steel weapons. Their eyes were hard and dark as they surveyed the crowd from the shadows of the portico's overhang. "We've done our best to keep you all safe, and done what we could for the other towns as well." His hand now flung out into the darkness beyond the palisade with an angry, dismissive gesture.

Thoughts of the palisade sent a quick, rippling pain through Soza's guts. Back when he'd built the wall, he had truly believed he was working for the good of the town. Building something that would help keep folks safe; keep the monsters away. He looked back up at the men clustered around the mayor, and the wall transformed in his mind, turning the town from a safe fortress to a bleak prison.

"We did everything we could, but no one wanted to believe us." Maddox pounded one angry fist on the stone, raising another small cloud of dust. "All those chiselers out there wanted to go their own way. They smiled at my boys, and then did nothing to keep themselves safe. Some of them wouldn't even let my rangers into their damned towns!"

An angry rumble rose from the crowd, but quickly subsided as the mayor continued. "They stood there and did *nothing*, and their folks died!" Maddox threw his hand back in the direction of the low hills behind Tolchico. "It's happened again and again, and tonight we got a whole new crop of innocents cooling in the holding crypt up on the hill, because the blamed fools who proposed to lead them couldn't keep them safe!"

Now the rumble from the crowd was more pronounced. Soza had seen it before on countless work gangs up and down the rail lines. Fear was the doorway, but anger was what came through. And these folks, steeped in terror for months on end, were ripe for that kind of conversion.

"Every day they refused to keep their own people safe, they made the whole region more dangerous for the rest of us!" Maddox threw his arms wide now, and his face, within the shadows of his hat brim, seemed wild. "Their laziness and foolishness didn't just kill their own people, it killed ours as well!"

Several men in the crowd threw their fists into the air, shouting their indignant support of the mayor. One enthusiast fired a heavy revolver into the night sky, which set the entire crowd cringing, then rising back up more passionate than before.

Fading back into the shadows, Soza's brow crinkled as he tried to make sense of the tune Maddox was playing on the ill-tuned emotions of the crowd. Why ignite their fear into anger and then aim it at the hapless settlements who had suffered even worse than Tolchico?

"They didn't listen when the winter cold swept down from the mountains and food started to grow scarce."

The crowd muttered, "No."

His voice gained strength. "They didn't listen when the first folks went missing, and fear stalked the dark desert."

Again the crowd responded, "No, they didn't!"

"They didn't listen when the dead began to pile up in the night, when innocent folks were torn from their beds, or struck down on the trail, and entire towns were scoured away in the blink of an eye!"

The crowd's response this time was wordless, caught between the horror of the remembered pain and the new-forged anger toward the other settlements.

"Well, they're gonna listen now!" The mayor's balled fist struck the overhang with a resounding crash that sent dust cascading down in front of him. "We aren't none of us going to be safe until we're all working together, pointing in the same direction, and hunting down these monsters, whatever they are, as one!"

The crowd roared its approval as several more sharp cracks announced men resorting to their hoarded ammunition to convey their enthusiasm.

"And if they won't stand up like men, then we'll have to show them how it's done, and drag them kicking and screaming to the right way of thinking, if that's what it takes!" He leaned back out over the balustrade again, his forearms stiff, his hands on the railing.

"We'll bring them all in line, and we'll make the territories safe for the men and women who came out here to make something great of this dust-swept, god-forsaken wilderness! The law ain't been no help, the Union and the Confederacy are too busy gnawing at each other's corpses to be of any help, and if we aren't going to lay down and die, or scamper back east and admit defeat, we're going to have to make a go of it together. And the way I see it, there's only one way that's going to happen."

Maddox drew the heavy pistol and laid it gently on the stone before him like a sacrifice on an ancient altar. "These folks hereabouts are going to have to understand, we either stand together, or we get dragged down into the dust alone."
Soza had heard enough. Something in his mind clicked as he saw his vague, unformed fears snap into reality before him. Suddenly, he knew that this was why he could not have left. This was why he had needed to stay. He needed to see Truman Maddox's plan laid bare before he left. But where could he go? Who could he warn?

The old railway man reached down without looking and picked his satchel up, throwing the carry strap over his shoulder. It was light; too light for a journey across the wastes alone, but he was fairly confident that he would be able to scavenge up a little something up along the way. But Maddox was right when he spat on the lawmen and the governments that might have claimed the territories for their own. The people west of the Coconino were alone. Where should he be headed?

Soza moved quietly along the boardwalk, head down, staying to the shadows, when a tall shape stepped out of an alleyway and into his path.

The old man looked up, and then up, and then up some more. Bruce Euans stood there, massive fists resting easily on his narrow hips, an evil grin twisting his slab-like face.

Soza had not noticed Eauns leave the mayor's side, but clearly he had. The old man's heart began to race. He saw, again, a girl's pretty, pain-filled eyes widen in terror. He saw the torn and ravaged bodies of the winter, of Brant's party, of the cart that had gone up this street just a few hours before. He fell back a couple paces, but his brain was frozen and he could think of nothing to do.

"Hey there, Mr. Soza." Eauns's flat, Ohioan accent did nothing to hide the anticipation beneath it. "Goin' somewhere?"

The End

About the Author

Craig Gallant spends his hours teaching, gaming, podasting, being a family man and father. In his spare time he writes outlandish fiction to entertain and amaze people .

In addition to his position as co-host of the internationally not too shabby podcast – The D6 Generation, he has written for several gaming companies including Fantasy Flight, Spartan Games and of course Outlaw Minatures.

You can follow Craig's writing experience and other fun things at:

www.Mcnerdiganspub.com

Zmok Books – Action, Adventure and Imagination

Zmok Books offers science fiction and fantasy books in the classic tradition as well as the new and different takes on the genre.

Winged Hussar Publishing, LLC is the parent company of Zmok Publishing, focused on military history from ancient times to the modern day.

Follow all the latest news on Winged Hussar and Zmok Books at

www.wingedhussarpublishing.com

Look for the other books in this series

Other Books by Craig Gallant

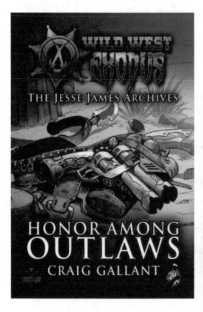

For all your fantasy, science fiction or history needs look at the latest from Winged Hussar Publishing